Dedicated to a Grandfather and Grandmother I never knew.

THE LAST PENNINE.

CHAPTER ONE.

Arthur Townsley is forty six years of age. He is swigging from his brandy flask as he surveys the cricket field covered in icy snow that glints in the winter's morning light. His breaths form clouds as does his full strength Capstan when he lights it up.

It is January 1938.

He imagines a red hot cricket ball leaving a meteor trail across the frozen ground followed by an echo of people clapping.

Behind him a Jubilee train pulls red carriages, almost the same colour as the cricket ball. Smoke gushes from its chimney as it gets up steam in preparation for the long drag. Arthur in his time has copped all the trains. He loves their sense of power and the smell of hot steam and the noise of their wheels thrashing along the lines.

The cricket field sparkles in the faint sun. It is Sunday and this is one of his days away from everything and everybody. He is thankful for these moments. His mood is steady today.

The woman is a surprise. She is pushing a large wheeled pram across the field leaving parallel tracks in the snow. Arthur watches her. Does she see him with his trilby, overcoat open to show his suit and waistcoat, a middle aged man sat in front of the pavilion smoking?

Is the woman aware of this odd situation?

She is young, unsteady in her high heels, a blue coat, gloves and a small hat tilted over her forehead. Her hair is auburn and shoulder length. She tilts forwards with the effort of pushing the pram over the crusted snow.

Arthur finds her immediately attractive. He warms slightly to the woman's presence wondering what lies beneath her Sunday best coat. She is pale with high cheek bones. He wants to smell her hair, touch her face. There are fantasies blossoming in the winter air. He allows them.

In his imagination he goes over to talk to her.

A relationship is formed. It could lead to everything he wants.

Arthur is too imaginative. He desires too much of what he sees. He is greedy and has been ever since the war. He is friendly, caring, helpful, talkative, knowledgeable, interesting, well liked, but intense, driven, passionate, unpredictable, sometimes vain and too fond of the drink.

The woman is trudging erratically through the glistening snow in her high heels. Suddenly he gets up, walks down the snow crusted slope towards her asking whether he can help push the pram up the ground's steep embankment leading to the exit. There is no surprise in her response. She thanks him before they both grip the handle and push the pram with a young baby aboard, its tiny head appearing out of layer soft white blankets, a knitted hat tied under its chin and is fast asleep.

At the top of the slope the woman smiles and thanks him again.

Arthur is smitten by her wide mouth and hazel eyes before watching as she disappears through the main doors.

He wonders if he will ever see her again. So many strangers he thinks to himself are like ships in the night, never to meet again. Only chance governs these moments. Everything has meaning one way or another. Coincidences are part of one's destiny. They can blossom or quickly fade.

Would he ever lose his hunger for a good looking woman? He hopes not.

Alice with her clever mind and beautiful body had at the time seemed like a step up for him. The mistake had been considering his mind more than his body when he had married her. Returning to the bench in front of the pavilion he takes another swig of brandy from his flask, lights a cigarette and ponders on what went wrong after he returned from the war back to Skipton and a job at Slater's.

Their daughter Mary had been four years old. He had been lucky that Slaters had taken him back on, but in 1919 he did not care what job he did. Slaters was the biggest building firm in Skipton, big enough to require an office manager and two secretaries and an accountant. Paul Slater who had interviewed him before the war had obviously been impressed and as the years had gone on had chosen him to become more involved in all sides of the business. This left the boss to concentrate on his real passion which was farming. Slater had over a thousand acres in the Vale of York and only rarely visited the company yards on the outskirts of Skipton.

But it is the effect of the pervious night's dream, the often repeated nightmare that he is trying to supress. An orange Pennine bus that is usually a dull orange colour has been painted black including its windows. He is standing at some night time bus stop as it approaches, its headlights so bright he has to look away. He is filled with dread. He knows he has to get on the bus. He cannot refuse. As he mounts the steps there is no driver to greet him. By now he feels sick with fear as he starts walking to the back of the bus noticing each passenger sitting straight backs, eyes closed, theirs faces white masks of death. This is the Black Pennine haunting too many nights, too many dreams of the dead waiting for him to sit down and join them on their journey to nowhere. He knows inevitably one day the bus will in reality be there ready to pick him up and take him away from life and all that he cherishes, that he needs.

Thankfully there is the sound of another train approaching, a Black Five, its huge wheels turning fast along the down line on its way to Leeds, its noise thundering through the Sunday quietness. Settle is settling down. Lunchtime approaches, the one big spread of the week if you can afford it. Arthur is looking forward to a few pints in the Golden Lion. That is his idea of Sunday best.

In the years before the war he had started taking reading seriously. It became an obsession visiting the library and taking out as many books he thought he could manage, fiction, biographies, history, poetry, books of romance, tragedy, thrillers, anything he could get his hands on.

How naive and nonsensical it all seemed now. The war had smashed him into shapes he had never expected. Life was a serious matter when you saw so much death. Everything is a serious business now. At least being a Yorkshireman Arthur still has a sense of humour both perceptive and ironic. The 1930s are the times for sarcasm. The world is beginning to lose its sanity again and those in power need to be ridiculed for the mess they are making.

But this morning is too fine and glorious to have such thoughts. Coming to Settle has been a good idea. He got off the usual Pennine bus in front of the town hall and walked straight down to the cricket ground that is still covered in myriad jewels sparkling in the sun's pale shafts of light. He feels content and free of the usual trawl of worries. Moments like this have to be taken and absorbed. For him they are rare, a combination of self consciousness and acceptance, to just look and breath and enjoy what there is because at that moment that is all there is, nothing more, no past or future.

Only the Talbot can compete with the Golden Lion except on Sundays when it us full of the rowdy lunchtime crowd, dominoes players shouting out the odds while others concentrate on the darts. So today it will be the Lion.

Diagonally across from the pavilion where he is sitting is the scoreboard and the groundsman's shed. Beside it the big roller has its handles resting in the snow. There are trees in the corner, their dark trunks stained with lines of snowy ice, their branches cutting complicated pieces out of the winter sky.

Arthur lights a final cigarette as the town hall clock strikes twelve. He does not want to appear too keen to down the first pint. By the time he has walked up to the Lion he could predict who the first customers would be and what they would be talking about. Familiarity and repetition are becoming increasingly important to everyone. Hitler is making sure of that.

He waits for the next goods train to appear, its engine blasting steam as it approaches. Arthur imagines himself there with the guard in his long fogging coat and hat with earflaps. They will stand at the back of the guard's van as the train powers its way along the top of the high Pennines drinking from his flask and sharing a cigarette. The snow covered Dales will spread beneath them with their isolated farms and patchwork of walls. It is the best train journey in the country, Settle to Carlisle on a glittering winter's day.

When he finally gets off the ice crusted seat and has wiped down the back of his coat, he looks beyond the high railway embankment to the hills stacked up behind the town. Their sparkling whiteness is ridged against a pale blue sky. They are like huge waves ready to crash down over the valley, ominous, silent, glistening.

'Does the price of sheep matter in the scale of things?'

'Of course it bloody does. We have to feed the nation.'

The first conversational pieces he hears as he enters the Golden Lion.

George Tinsdale laughs and says his cheery hello, the owner behind the bar pulling Arthur's pint before he has said a word in reply.

If he has time George will want to talk about Yorkshire's chances of winning another championship and Arthur hopes to have the opportunity to remind George what he promised for his son Harry.

It is his first question, asking how the eleven year George's eleven year old son is getting on.

'He's doing not so bad all things considering,' the boy's father answers.

'And what about those new callipers they were fitting him for the last time I was here?'

George at that looks a little strained, saying, 'The polio makes everything difficult for the poor lad. He tries his best, tries not to complain too much but I know it's hard for him, really hard.'

'Well just remind him I'll be taking him this summer to Headingley for Yorkshire's first match. I promised him I would and I know he's keen on cricket.'

'He is that. I take him down to the ground whenever I can when Settle are playing.'

'You just remind him George.'

'I will Arthur, I will.'

After that he goes over and sits by the windows that look out onto the main road. There is a blazing coal fire at the end of the lounge. The brass work on the walls reflect golden glinting through the faintly smoke filled air.

Arthur loves the Lion's atmosphere. He is wrapped in the colour of his beer that glows from the light coming through the windows. He can smell the smoke. Time slows. Breathing slows. He has taken off his trilby and coat and sits there turning his glass listening to the men at the bar.

For some reason he starts thinking of his daughter Mary. Nowadays she is always ready to challenge him, to ask too many questions, to push him further and further. It is because they are too alike. He is proud of her and how smart she looks on her way to work, so slim, almost petite with sharp features and dark bobbed hair. She is even prettier than she realises although he would never tell her that. Now he is wary of her, unsure of how she is going to respond to him.

Their other daughter Sylvie is much more like her mother creating two sides to the family with two contrasting views on life. It is an equation he knows will never be solved. There is nothing easy when four people share the same house.

'We're not prepared,' he hears someone exclaim.

'Neither are the Germans.'

'It's the same old bloody muddle. There's no plan. It's just shifting from one thing to another. Chamberlain and his cabinet have no idea. Some of them want one thing and the rest want the opposite. That's no way to run a country.'

It used to be just sport and the price of a pint. Now it is always politics.

Arthur finds it tedious. Talking does nothing and everyone is scared. The country is becoming obsessed by the chances of there being another war.

Twenty years ago the last one ended and already the world is shifting towards the next.

Arthur is just relieved that he is too old to be involved.

Mary always looks smart. He likes the way she dresses. She is confident, sharp, amusing, a talker and has so much energy. She is a small bird constantly pecking at life. That is how he sees her. Alice is a heron. Sylvia unfortunately is a pigeon whereas he must be a crow, four birds trying to feed from the same dish of breadcrumbs left out each day in winter, one of Sylvie's jobs.

CHAPTER TWO

Mary's appearance is always fashionable. Her customers expect her to look professional. She likes such an image. It is why she takes such care of the clothes she wears. They give her customers reassurance that she knows what she is talking about.

She prides herself on her fashion sense. She has an eye for colour and design. She can put a whole picture together in her mind and sell it.

She wants every woman who walks into her department to leave it feeling better about herself. That is why being so friendly and helpful she has so many regulars. Instead of travelling all the way to Bradford or Leeds Mary wants the ladies of Skipton to be confident that Dawsons is just as up to date and just as cheap as the big city stores.

Today it being so cold and the snow still falling she predicts it is going to be a slow day. She is standing near one of the large ground floor windows, hands clasped in front of her, straight backed looking out onto the High Street. Mr Norris is at the cash desk dealing with one of the first customers of the morning. He has been floor manager since anyone can remember but depends so much now on Mary's flair. He is small, slightly built, in his late fifties. The rumour is that he dyes his thinning black hair that is brushed back off his glistening forehead.

On the floor in Dawsons only surnames are ever used. Mary likes Mr Norris. He smiles a lot, is genuine in his concern for his staff and likes everything to be neat and well displayed. He makes her only a little nervous. Not like Mr Twistleton who likes to pat backsides and squeeze arms as he is passing. The girls do a tally every Saturday to whose backside has been fondled the most that week.

Doris Naseby is a recent addition to the department, straight from school, eager, loves clothes, giggles too much but is a girl who Mary thinks has potential. At that moment Doris is pulling out a rack of coats from the store room.

June Allbright is the real challenge, newly married, two years younger than Mary and full of herself, overconfident, often pretends to be bored, thinks herself more fashionable than anyone else and is too much of an influence on Doris who listens to June's every word. June is replacing hats on dummies heads, carefully taking her time over each one.

Mary walks over to check on the coats Doris is bringing in. With one last look at the snow drifting down onto a quiet High Street she steps between racks of woollen skirts.

'Did you go last night?' is Doris's first eager question.

'Me and Shirley, yes.'

'So what did you think?'

'You don't have to think Doris.'

'But you know what I mean.'

'You just have to watch Fred Astaire and imagine he's singing and dancing in your own front room.'

'And is he?'

Mary smiles and quickly looks around the shop floor, 'Well to be honest our front room is getting overcrowded.'

'All for sixpence a time.'

'But you like the stars as well Doris.'

'Oh yes, give me Cary Grant and Clark Gable and I'd….'

'It's Humphrey Bogart for me.'

'He's too mean looking.'

'That's what I like about him.'

'In 'Dead End,' he was scary.'

'And what about the way he smokes a cigarette?'

Doris looks uncertain, her eyes bulging with interest, 'What… what about it?'

'It's provocative.'

'Is it?'

'He hides the cigarette in his fingers and takes a smoke and you don't see him do it.'

'You're teasing Mary.'

'I'm deadly serious.'

Doris forces a smile, 'I love the cinema.'

'Except for a few town hall dances it's the only thing that keeps me going in this place.'

With each at either end they pull and push the rack of coats closer to the front of the shop.

'Now I've got….' Mary starts only to stop when the glass front door is pushed open and new customers arrive, three women all covered in snow.

The store is never the same two days in a row. Its mood is constantly changing. Mary thinks it must be Mr Frobisher who sets the tone. Whether he spends all day in his office or is walking about chatting to the staff he seems to make such a difference. Mary knows he affects her and wishes it was otherwise. She does not like to be so flustered whenever he appears. Unfortunately her reaction is inevitable.

Other than Mr Frobisher, Twistleton and Norris there are two other men on the staff. Mr Fuller is in the home department. Mr Bentley is the accountant and has his office next to Frobisher's on the top floor. Overall there are twenty two women who work at Dawsons, the only department store in Skipton. Not one of them is in any post except as a shop assistant. This to Mary is a disgrace and something she is working hard to change. At least if she, when Mr Norris finally retires, becomes floor manager it might inspire some of the others to try for their own promotion.

The rest of the morning is busier than expected. The weather has been so bad that no one is thinking yet about spring fashion. It is still winter coats, skirts and high necked jumpers. At least there will be less winter stock to get rid off when warmer days finally arrive.

When she has time Mary helps Doris at the cash desk. She looks to see everything is neatly folded and packaged in brown paper before being placed into Dawson's branded shopping bags. Ladies still like to be seen carrying them down the High Street. Mary knows so long as that continues Dawson's will maintain its reputation. This is important to her. Now more than ever the department store is an essential part of her life. She is committed to its success and always worries if things slacken off for a few days and figures are down.

By lunchtime she is looking forward to her tea and sandwich with Shirley at Bell's café that is behind the town hall. It is where they meet twice a week.

'They're getting to be such a morbid lot. All they can talk about is the chance of there being another war and who wants to hear about that from first thing in the morning until I can escape at five o clock? There's too many who see themselves as some sort of heroes. I don't think they have a clue what they're talking about.'

'At least we don't have that problem,' says Mary as the waitress brings over their order, 'They're all too old.'

'And it is a problem, well I think it is. We're going to talk our way into it if we carry on like this. Who cares what Hitler's doing so long as it's in his own country?'

Mary has noticed how over the last weeks Shirley has begun to sound increasingly exasperated. Even her facial expressions have become more exaggerated. She has short blond hair, full cheeks and a wide mouth and even though the café is warm with so many people crowded into it, Shirley is still wearing her coat and matching hat.

'You should write to the Craven Herald or the Yorkshire Post.'

Shirley scoffs at the suggestion, 'Oh there's too much being written about it all as it is. The last thing I want to do is contribute any more rubbishy comments. I'll leave that to the men I work with.'

'Who want to be heroes.'

'Such things don't exist anymore. Heroes I mean'

'What, not even Humphrey Bogart?'

'He's different.'

'Of course he is,' Mary agrees before pouring the tea.

'Well you wouldn't say no to a night out with……'

'Alan Ladd,' is Mary's interruption, 'I'd ride off with him into the sunset any day.'

'Not a bad choice Miss Townsley.'

'Glad you agree Miss Watson.'

The café's windows are steamed over. People come in and take off their snow smeared coats and hats. The place is busy as the waitresses in their black dresses, white aprons and hats move between them.

Shirley has been engaged for over two years and is to be married this coming May to Roger Allbright who works with her in the Building Society. Mary knows how worried she is that everything is ready on the day and that nothing goes wrong.

'Your wedding will be a grand affair Shirley.'

'That is if Roger hasn't been called up by then.'

Her friend gives her a meaningful look.

'What?' Mary asks.

'I'm not sure whether you take it that seriously.'

'Of course I do.'

'I wonder if it's Roger you have a problem with.'

'Shirley, I don't have a problem.'

Again her friend gives her a quizzical look.

'Alright,' Mary finally starts after a strained pause, 'I must admit I think spending so much time and money on just one day is....is.'

'Is what?'

'Well it's not for me. That's all. I personally wouldn't want it that way.'

'That's because you don't want to get married.'

Mary forces a smile, 'That might be true, so what? That shouldn't affect you.'

'Of course it does. If my best friend doesn't believe in how I want things to go then it makes the whole thing....'

'What?'

'Oh I don't know,' Shirley miserably sighs, 'Just undermines it.'

'I don't want to do that.'

'But you don't exactly sound encouraging Mary.'

'I am. I'm happy for you Shirley. You know that.'

'I hope that's true.'

'I wouldn't say if it wasn't.'

It is when Shirley finishes her last cup of tea that the mood between them suddenly changes.

Mary is on full alert when she is asked how she is getting on with Mr Frobisher. It is a question that accelerates her thoughts into a confusion of answers.

What can she say? It is her own private business and yet one she is desperate to share. She has already told Shirley that James Frobisher is married with two children and lives outside Gargrave, that he has own business in Leeds but is helping out at Dawsons until a new general manager is found. The Frobishers have been friendly with the Dawson family for generations. Shirley is curious about why Mary and Frobisher work together in the evening when the store is closed.

Mary watches her friend's doubtful expression as the café door is opened letting in another flow of cold air. Should she say that some questions are harder to answer or that she just does not want to talk about it?

She has to say something. She smiles to herself, while turning her saucer round slowly. Too much openness and honesty will only create confusion.

In the past when they were teenagers they shared everything. They even used to read out of their diaries to each other, confess to any misdemeanour, any new feeling or thought. But when Shirley became engaged all that changed and for over two years now Mary has been trying to understand why. They pretend that nothing has altered. Luckily Roger Allbright does not like going to the cinema which means they still go to see a film at least once a week as well as meeting for lunch and having their hair done together at the same salon. So much has remained unchanged and yet beneath the surface Mary is now uncertain how much she wants to share with her friend.

James Frobisher is handsome, tall, has greying hair, wears tailored suits. His voice is soft with a only a tinge of a Yorkshire accent. His eyes are greeny blue and as far as Mary is concerned he could star in any film he wanted. It is all this that makes him such a threat to her, such an awful challenge, someone she has no idea how to manage. If only she could stop thinking about him.

'We're getting on alright,' is her hopeless answer.

Shirley pulls a doubtful expression as though preparing to be unconvinced by anything her friend might say.

'You don't have to tell me,' she responds defiantly, deftly stroking at the side of her mouth for any crumbs.

'I know I don't,' says Mary just as strongly.

'You like him?'

'Yes.'

'Like him a lot?'

'Yes.'

'I know that much. You've told me that much, but recently you've gone all quiet about it.'

'There's nothing else to say.'

'Oh come on Mary, of course there is!' Shirley exclaims a little too loudly.

A few heads turn. One of the waitresses stops what she is doing for a moment.

In a quieter voice Shirley continues, bending forward over the table, 'He's a married man and therefore should be out of bounds.'

Mary feels the tension squeeze tighter. She is hot and bothered and wants to leave.

'It's alright for you,' she says going on the defensive, 'You're engaged. Your future is already mapped out.'

'No, it isn't. Just because I'm getting married doesn't mean everything is planned out. We have no idea where we're going to live for a start. You're only saying that to avoid....'

'You're right,' Mary interrupts, 'I'm only saying that because……because I'm not sure what to say.'

Her hands are nervously on the move, rubbing along the edge of the table. The pressure is pushing her towards another edge. Her heart is beating faster and she is beginning to feel sick.

Shirley's voice softens and asks, 'Is it that bad?'

'I think it probably is.'

'Mary, you've got to be careful.'

'That's the trouble, I don't know what that means.'

'And does he like you?'

The question is one Mary thinks about all the time. She has no doubt that James Frobisher is interested in her, the way he looks at her, the way he speaks and thanks her for everything she does. But there has been nothing else, just looks and smiles. How much lies behind his good manners and film star features? Has she to wait to discover if he really does like her? Is it always the woman who has to wait for something to happen?

Should she try and describe his office to Shirley, the place she finds so intimidating, the intimacy it creates, a soft, low lit atmosphere with colours of brown and grey dominating? It is large with Frobisher's desk at the far end. There is enough space for two armchairs, a long sofa and a beautiful Persian carpet. Three windows look down along the High Street and up towards the castle. When they are working she sits on a hard back chair with him at his desk looking through this year's catalogues. He wants her to choose the best lines for the spring/summer season. He is making her responsible for all the new stock, something she knows she can manage. He gives her the kind of confidence she has never experienced before, but she does not want it to just depend on her good looks. She wants it because he sees in her someone who has the talent and vision to run a whole department. And yet she still hopes for more.

Mary drinks the last of her tea feeling constrained by her nervousness.

'He wants me to choose this year's summer clothes for the store and that's what we do some evenings. We look through catalogues from here and America and try and work out what would be best.'

'And he let's you choose?' Shirley asks, sitting back into more of a relaxed position, 'Why doesn't Mr Norris do all that? I thought you told me he was in charge of the women's department.'

'He is, but he's going to be retiring next year and would rather leave it to me. He said that last autumn, said he was getting too long in the tooth to know what the ladies wanted nowadays.'

'Lucky for you.'

'I suppose so.'

'But you're not sure what else might be going on between you and your boss. Come on Mary, you must have some idea.'

'We'll just have to wait and see,' says Mary tentatively, already regretting the way the conversation has gone.

'This isn't waiting for a bus, it's serious Mary.'

'Only if I want it to be.'

'And what about Frobisher with his wife and two children? He'll know exactly what he's doing and if you're not careful you'll be having an affair that'll go nowhere. How can it?'

'You're right. It can't.'

'Well, there you are then. You should forget about the whole thing.'

'But I'm not going to stop working with him. He said I could be the first woman to run the department when Mr Norris retires.'

'Promises Mary, that's all that is.'

'I believe him.'

'Of course you do.'

'And what's that supposed to mean?'

Shirley notices the café quickly emptying, looks at her watch and tells Mary she has to get back to work.

'I'll call round for you on Thursday,' she adds.

It is Mary's turn to pay the bill. She goes over to the counter feeling more on edge than ever.

In the street it is still snowing. Mary fumbles with the buttons of her coat. Her fingers are stiff and she feels dizzy with the sudden rush of cold air.

Watching Shirley walk away she wonders if she will ever be able to express what she wants. If she cannot manage it with her closest friend then everything will always remain locked up. The worries are growing. Over the other side of the road the windows of Dawsons are rimmed with a strange golden light.

CHAPTER THREE

Alice seems to live in her mind. There is little else out there except the sound of the milkman clattering his bottles down on the front step, not even a tinge of light behind the bedroom curtain, only the winter darkness. Her face is cold. Her eyelids are heavy as she listens to the sounds of the house, a place she used to be so much a part of of before her first heart attack.

In her mind is the summer garden when she was seventeen. She is often there now in her memory. That is all there is left. Images help. She feels thankfully a little happiness, yes, the joy lived in that summer garden.

Sylvie will be first up. In the kitchen she will light the gas to heat up the kettle, rake the fire and pull open the curtains. Arthur soon follows. However much he has been drinking the night before makes no difference. Mary is always last, spending so much time on getting herself washed, dressed, makeup on, no breakfast and out of the door in just a few minutes. She used to pop in every morning but not anymore. Alice knows Mary well enough to understand why.

Now she hears Arthur stirring. He coughs, sighs loudly and creaks across his bedroom floor to get his dressing gown.

The house is a ship moving slowly through the murky darkness. She is in her own cabin, all the crew avoiding her.

Back in her memory Molly and Esme are playing hide and seek in that garden full of flowers and warmth. Alice is searching for them. Paul and Julia are sat on deck chairs sipping gin and tonics. They are from a generation that thought such summers would never end.

Where are they now, the Jamesons, the family she loved, cherished, wanted?

Years after they had left Skipton Molly and Esme had sent a letter via the chapel knowing that Alice never missed a Sunday service. It had been such a charming, caring letter, something that Alice found too difficult to answer, something she has regretted ever since. At the time she had still felt embarrassed and ashamed at what had happened. The last thing she wanted was for their father to discover she was writing to his daughters.

But her busy mind cannot let them go. The longer her illness has lasted the more she needs them.

What would they say if they saw her now? Would they be shocked, but also a little sad, appalled but sympathetic as well?

Arthur comes in smiling as usual to ask her if she wants a cup of tea. The night before he had come in to apologise. His pride never stops him from saying he is sorry. But it happens so frequently it has become meaningless and exaggerated, a performance of guilt and remorse that he plays so well or he thinks he does.

She can hear Sylvie and Mary muttering to each other in the kitchen. Her daughters are starting days that are such a contrast from each other, Mary off to Dawsons, Sylvie to stay and look after mother. She too is imprisoned. There is no escape for her except Chapel and Sunday school, the two highlights of her week.

The pain tightens across Alice's back and down her legs when she tries to move. Once doctor Donnolly started to describe her condition, but she panicked and told him she did not want to hear anymore. The whole thing is grotesque. This is not her. This is not the Alice Townsley she once was.

After the game of hide and seek, when the girls are found, they rush over for lemonade on the table between Paul and Julia seated under their large summer umbrella. Paul would smile and tell the girls not to gulp it down too quickly. Julia would look away across the lawn to the house towering above them.

Julia was like that, quiet, whimsical, always on the edge of one illness or another. For the wife of a doctor it was ironical that she was often so poorly and her husband could do so little about it. Summer was Julia's best season when her face took on a little colour and she could spend more time with her daughters. Being their governess Alice found Julia's temporary interest in her daughters' education an intrusion into the world that she with Molly and Esme had created for themselves. It was a place for their young imaginations to prosper and she had loved to share it with them. But when Julia showed some interest everything had to become a little more formal, a little more organised which the girls found difficult. Esme the youngest rebelled against any limits put on her adventures whereas Molly was more considerate to her mother, as though she understood that it would not be long before she would once again be ill and would have to take to her bed. Then they would only see her for a quick visit before their bedtime.

Where were they? The Jamesons never grow old. It will always be the early years of the century in Alice's memory and they are there unchanging, there in the golden light of a summer evening.

Alice has thought about it enough. It is her other life now. Then she was clever, sympathetic, careful, happy, enjoying life and yet in her was always that deeply entrenched romantic streak, that enhancement of everything she craved. It had caused her downfall and the end of the dream, another fantasy like the ones she shared back then with Molly and Esme.

She knew having such romantic notions could be destructive. And now she was doing it again, allowing her mind to wander into such dangerous territory. If she was not careful the day's mood would be dominated by that sense of longing and guilt. She was being stupid and immature. This was her escape, anything was better than lying here wallowing in self pity. God had given her this time to overcome the challenges and accept what had happened to her.

Was that really possible? Was this God of hers not asking too much? How could she accept what she had become, the bloated whale washed up on some miserable shore?

The front door slams shut after Mary calls goodbye to her from the hallway. Outside comes the noise of the milkman's horse and cart going along the street and the hooter from one of the mills down by the canal. Skipton is coming alive this winter morning, grey light illuminating the bedroom curtains and Alice swallows hard and feels her skin tightening with every small move she makes.

Her bedsores are bothering her more than usual. Everything aches. Everything is heavy and stretched and painful. God is with her. Faith is her only hope. Without it she knows all of this would be impossible.

'Mother I've brought your tea,' says Sylvie when she appears at the open door, 'And some toast.'

Alice forces a smile and thanks her.

'And how did you sleep last night?'

As always Sylvie's expression shows care, interest and concern.

'Not very well last night. I couldn't get settled and I kept hearing those cats from down the street fighting again.'

'Mary's already gone, and father will be up in a minute to see you before he goes.'

'And you,' Alice says, 'How are you my pet this morning?'

'I'm alright mother. I'm wearing that new pinny I bought at the market.'

Her round face is always in earnest. Behind her thin rimmed glasses her eyes are slightly enlarged.

'Come and sit down for a minute,' adds Alice patting the bed, 'And let's have a look at you,' she adds, taking hold of her hand.

'I have to clear up the ashes.'

Well, do that later and then come back up. I've that jigsaw and I want to try and finish it today.'

'Do you want any more breakfast?'

Alice shakes her head and reluctantly lets go of her hand before Sylvie goes off down the stairs.

It was the most dreadful decision, to ask Sylvie at the age of fourteen to give up school to look after her. First it had been the heart attack and then the swelling disease. Alice and Arthur had argued for days as to what they should do. Both of them knew that Mary would never manage looking after the house and be a nurse to her mother at the same time. Arthur said they needed Mary's weekly wage to help out. That was out of the question, so the only thing left was for Sylvie to give up school and stay at home. For Alice it had been a terrible time. She and Arthur had argued day after day. She had hated him then, hated the way he was only thinking about himself and all the money he could spend. It was always about money, about his smart suits and car and his weekly evenings out on the town. Nothing she had said had made any difference. She had felt guilty, disgusted and angry at something she could not control. That had never changed. Often she looked at Sylvie and felt ashamed.

There had been no complaints. Sylvie had just got on with it.

'So how are we this damned cold morning?' is Arthur's question as he enters the bedroom already in his overcoat.

'Is it still snowing?' Alice inquires after he has come forward and kissed her on the forehead.

'No, but it's lying thick so it must have been snowing through the night.'

'You never hear it, not like the rain.'

'Sylvie will lay the fire I expect. She seems in a rush this morning.'

'And what have you got on today Arthur?'

'Depends what can get through. We're expecting a load of bricks this afternoon,' Arthur answers as he stands at the foot of the bed, his brylcreemed hair shining in the light.

She often wonders whether there is any love left between them, whether their marriage vows had ever meant anything to him like they had for her.

'So, doctor Donnolly on Friday, what time is he coming?'

'In the afternoon. He wants to check my blood pressure again.'

'And I'll have to try and see him sometime.'

Alice feels suddenly troubled. There are stages to her illness, symbolic milestones to pass and Arthur talking again to the doctor is one of them.

'What have you got to say to him?' she wants to know.

'Oh, just ask how he thinks things are going.'

'You know how things are going Arthur. You know what his answer to that will be.'

'No, I don't or wouldn't be wanting to ask him. It's alright Alice. I can leave it. I'm sure if there's anything new doctor Donnolly will tell me about it.'

'Our Sylvie would have him visiting everyday if she could. I think she likes the doctor.'

Arthur laughs, 'He's twice her age and losing his hair.'

'No he isn't.'

'Our Sylvie will have time enough for that sort of thing.'

Alice does not want to respond to such a comment. It is too painful, too demanding. Instead, she sips from the teacup she is carefully holding in both hands not wanting to spill any and give Sylvie more unnecessary washing. Her daughter is her friend, her companion, her strength, the daily presence in the house which alleviates some of her loneliness.

Her illness has created a barrier between herself and everyone else even Sylvie. She is no longer a wife or mother. She is an invalid, a problem. At least Arthur tries whereas Mary avoids coming up and only then comes under sufferance.

She likes to see him in his dark blue three piece suit with his shirt and tie. Even though he has put on a few pounds over the years he still looks smart. Alice considers this has always been part of the problem. However much he has drunk the night before he is up next morning sharp, focused and ready for the day. His looks have always given him confidence, that and his deep Yorkshire voice, the one she heard long ago from the crowd watching the first recruits from Skipton going off to war.

But this morning he is lingering beside her bed with a concerned expression on his freshly washed face. At least Alice has the energy to ask him tentatively if everything is alright.

'It should be me asking you that question.'

'You would tell me if there was anything wrong?' she asks, feeling her meagre strength quickly draining away as always. 'We're not in trouble again?' she manages to add.

Arthur is bothered. She can hear it in his voice when he answers a little too loudly, 'For God's sake Alice we're not in any trouble and it saddens me that you even have to ask. You worry too much.'

'I've got plenty of time to worry,' she says breathlessly, 'I've got one daughter who doesn't want to come and see me and a husband who's hardly ever in the house.'

'Mary does come and see you.

'Only when it suits her.'

'And I'm here, here now.'

The morning has started badly. She wants to retrieve the situation but is not sure she has the energy. Not wanting Arthur to leave on such a note she stupidly tries to lift herself, tries to shift her huge body.

Arthur watches her. After all this time you would think she no longer cared about what he saw.

He avoids looking as he comes along beside the bed, kisses her again on the forehead and then tells her he will come in this evening to tell her about his day when the cricket committee meeting is over.

'Imagine,' he says before he leaves, 'Snow outside and the committee already looking at this summer's fixtures.'

By the time Sylvie comes up with the warm ashes from the kitchen fire Alice is already fading back into a state of semi consciousness.

'Do you want your jigsaw mother now?'

Her daughter's question rouses her as she swallows hard and licks her lips to get rid of some of the dryness.

'It's cold,' she manages, 'Sylvie, I'm cold.'

'Starting to snow again. I'll get the fire going to warm you up.'

'You used to love the snow, and Mary did too.'

She watches Sylvie light the bedroom fire before she goes down to the back shed for more coal and returning quickly to put the full scuttle near the hearth.

Beside Alice's bed sits the large radio up on its table.

She just wishes the BBC would start its programmes a lot earlier.

There is already one radio in the kitchen. Sylvie listens to some foreign stations in the daytime. To Alice's liking there is far too much music on the Home service so she will wait until teatime and hope to be entertained by something different.

Sylvie next props the jigsaw tray against her mother's huge stomach.

'I don't know if I like this one.'

'Bamburgh Castle,' says Sylvie.

'There's too much blue sky and sand and stonework.'

'You'll manage. I've never seen you beaten yet.'

'There's always a first time.'

The fire spits and crackles. Sylvie has opened the curtains so Alice can look up from her jigsaw and watch huge flakes of snow drifting down.

500 pieces it says on the box. There seems a lot more. She feels the town around her, Skipton with its dark rooftops and winter streets. She does not have a watch. It was one of the first things she had discarded after she had returned home from the hospital. Time is the enemy. There is too much of it and yet never enough. She wants each day to go on and on however empty and bored she can become. That only happens when she is tired, when thoughts and memories are covered under a blanket of exhaustion.

BAMBURGH CASTLE ON THE NORTHUMBRIAN COAST.

She visited it several times as a child, had seen men on horseback galloping along its endless beach. On the way back the chapel coach trip would stop at Seahouses for fish and chips.

By lunchtime the jigsaw is nearly complete. She waits for Sylvie to come and set the tray carefully on the dresser before she brings up her mother's lunch consisting of a cheese sandwich and a cup of tea and a biscuit.

A few minutes later Alice hears the front doorknocker and then Sylvie talking to someone in the hallway.

'It's Mr Elgin mother. Do you want to see him?' asks Sylvie out of breath from running up the stairs.

'Yes, tell him to come up, and put the kettle on.'

'He's just taking off his coat.'

Alice waits expectantly quickly brushing her hair while Sylvie waits on the landing for Mr Elgin to come up and pass her into the bedroom.

'And how are you Alice? It must have been before Christmas I was last here. I don't have to ask about Sylvie,' are the minister's first words.

'You can if you like,' Sylvie jokes having only seen him last Sunday and then inquires whether he wants a cup of tea.

'My wife tells me I drink far too much tea and coffee. She wants me to cut down but I'm not sure if I can.'

'A cup of tea never harmed anyone,' Sylvie replies.

'You should know,' her mother put in, 'You drink enough.'

'Oh listen who's talking mother.'

'This time Sylvie,' the minister says, 'I'll let you get on while I have a chat with your mother. You've probably already told her about the Christmas show and the bazaar we held.'

'I'm sure she'd rather hear it from you Mr Elgin.'

'Yes,' Alice agrees while pulling her bedclothes straighter, 'I would.'

She has known Mr Elgin for over twenty years, ever since he became the chapel's minister near the end of the war. He is a small, precise man with dark hair brushed back from his forehead and has finely boned features. Sometimes he comes on a mission to save her from her darker moods. Then his voice has the ring of a sermon. But today is different. She enjoys his descriptions of the Christmas bazaar and show especially Harry Hawksley, who she remembers from Sunday School, singing Jingle Bells dressed as a court jester which caused such a reaction from the audience he had to repeat the song again.

'He was marvellous and very funny,' Mr Elgin adds.

'I wished I could have been there,' Alice says before he goes on to tell her about plans for a new youth discussion group, the Chapel choir singing at Earby church and the retirement of Mr Drew from being the Chapel's treasurer.

'And I've brought you a copy of this month's chapel magazine,' he adds then.

By the time he eventually leaves it is growing dark outside and Alice is exhausted.

Shadows from the fire are already quivering and dancing along the ceiling while she listens to a truck rattling along the Keighley Road.

'Mr Elgin said that jumper you knitted and the two dresses Mary made were sold straightaway at the bazaar,' she says as Sylvie puts more coal on the fire.

'Well at least that's something done that was worthwhile.'

'Everything you do is worthwhile Sylvie.'

Her daughter stops at the end of the bed and looks at her, a serious expression on her chubby features, her glasses reflecting some of the firelight.

'I know that Doctor Donnolly says so. He tells me.'

'And so do we all,' Alice insists.

'Mr Elgin seemed in a chipper mood.'

'Yes, he did.'

'And smelling of his mints.'

'His favourite mints.'

'Do you think he smokes?'

'Oh Sylvie.'

'And he's trying to cover up the smell.'

'No, he doesn't smoke or drink, not like your father.'

'And Mary.'

'Yes, her as well.'

'Do you want the light on?'

'Just leave it for a bit. I like this time of day,' Alice says.

After Sylvie has gone downstairs Alice tries to imagine the Chapel hall full of the stalls for the bazaar. She once had worked part time in the town library so she was always put in charge of the second hand books. She can still smell them, that fusty, damp smell of old paper, old words, millions of words, crime and cowboy stories mainly.

She can see so many faces, hear voices, the hall crowded with everyone looking for a bargain. They would have been queuing up outside since it got light, women with their shopping bags, children desperate to get inside and the men trying to look disinterested.

They had all been there a few weeks ago and now in her imagination the hall is empty. Right at this moment its space is being filled with grey light before the further winter darkness extinguishes all its features, the stage, the stacked seats, the creaking floorboards, the high curtained windows. Alice is there in her mind. Nowadays it is the only journey she can take as she closes her eyes listening to the crackling fire and one of the mill hooters sounding off.

CHAPTER FOUR

Sheets are blowing in the wind on this bright but cold February morning. Sylvie is pegging them out in the back yard with the breeze in her face and the sun in her eyes. She enjoys washing days when it is like this.

'Fine day for it,' Daisy from down the street says as she appears wheeling her pushbike along the back lane.

Sylvie has the yard door open and stops what she is doing, shielding her eyes against the low sunlight.

'First for I don't how long,' is her easy answer, 'By the way, have you seen Mr Smeaton recently?'

Daisy in her long winter coat and black beret pulls a doubtful expression, 'I saw him, must have been last week out the front of his house, didn't look so good. He was using both his walking sticks to get about and that was only to go down the front path to close his gate.'

'He doesn't like it left open. He's always going on about our new postman leaving it open.'

'He's a dear soul Mr Smeaton, but he's never got over losing his Evylin. They were always close, always out and about together.'

'And how's your Michael?' Sylvie asks leaning against the frame of the back yard with her arms folded, wisps of hair blowing across her face.

'He's giving a talk at the Institute next week about his photography.'

'He must be good then.'

Daisy purses her lips, 'Suppose he is. Mind you he's never out of his dark room as he calls it down in the cellar. How he manages the winter down there. The place is like an ice box. Don't need any of these new fangled American fridges. It's cold enough in our cellar to keep anything fresh. Anyway I hear there's lamb chops on sale at Hodstons so I'm off. I hope you mother is alright. Tell her I'll pop on to see her later in the week!' Daisy calls as she toddles off down the lane.

It is only a few minutes later when she is hanging out the last of the washing that Sylvie hears the familiar thump thump against the back wall. She pegs up the last T towel and goes back to the yard door.

'Archie, you're supposed to be at school,' she says to the gangly teenager.

Wellingtons, long shorts and a torn jacket and hair that flops about as he kicks his football, that is Archie.

'Don't have to Sylvie, don't have to!' Archie shouts.

'You're not fourteen yet.'

'Nearly Sylvie, nearly fourteen.'

'And what has your mother got to say about it?'

'Nothing.'

'I don't believe that Archie. You're fibbing.'

'I don't listen and I'm not fibbing.'

'Well you should,' Sylvie insists as a dog starts barking further along the lane.

'I listen to you,' Archie says while still concentrating on kicking his football.

'I'm not your mother Archie, more like....more like a big sister.'

'Are you my friend Sylvie?'

'You know I am, a very friendly big sister.'

'Well that's alright then.'

'I've always been your friend Archie, ever since you started Sunday School.'

'Don't go anymore.'

'I know and that's a shame.'

'Daft carry on there, me crayoning in pictures of Jesus.'

'And listening to stories and singing songs.'

'Didn't want to. Daft carry on there,' Archie repeats himself before his next kick is so hard and the ball goes over her wall.

By the time Sylvie has retrieved it Archie is running away along the lane.

'Your ball Archie!' she shouts after him only to see him disappear round the back of the last house on the row.

'Archie Andrews,' are her first words as she enters her mother's room.

Alice is reading yesterday's Yorkshire Post. She rests the paper on her stomach, 'What's he been up to now?'

'Ran off without his precious football.'

'You said he's never without it.'

'Well he is this morning.'

'You've got a soft spot for him.'

Sylvie smiles ruefully, 'I have. He's balmy but funny and always well mannered, no swearing or anything like that.'

'I should hope not.'

'But you know what I mean.'

'Poor Archie,' Alice sighs before returning to her newspaper.

By evening the kitchen is full of the day's washing that did not dry out in the weak February sun. Mary is sat near the fire sewing. Sylvie is having a sandwich reading the Radio Times while listening to Jack Hylton and his orchestra on the wireless.

'Joie de Vivre,' Sylvie reads out loud.

'The joy of life,' says Mary without looking up from her sewing.

'I know. I did French as well as you.'

'Well what about Joie do Vivre?'

'Says here it's a matter of nerves.'

'No it doesn't.'

'It does Mary, it does. Says you should be enjoying life to the full but that you are not doing so if you are irritable, sleeping badly or feel depressed. Listen to this bit, it's sheer nervous overstrain when you bang the telephone or kick the cat. In such case you are certainly in need of Phosphorine and you will find yourself immediately the better for it.'

'We haven't got a telephone and we haven't thank goodness got a cat,' is Mary's curt response, 'Why are you reading out such nonsense?'

'I thought it might remind you of someone.'

'Oh very funny I don't think.'

'Anyway it wouldn't surprise me if a telephone is on father's next shopping list.'

'He was talking about a radiogram for the front room last night.'

'Room to room music!' Sylvie exclaims.

'We don't need another radio.'

'But playing records Mary.'

'That would be alright, I suppose, but if we got a telephone father would be the only one to use it.'

'You could ring Shirley.'

'I see her enough in the week as it is.'

'But you could, and I think having one would be a good idea with mother as she is.'

'I don't like using a telephone. And anyway what if my nerves are bad?' Mary unexpectedly asks.

Sylvie swallows the last of her sandwich and wipes her hands on her serviette feeling the usual tension, saying, 'I never know what that means, nerves are bad.'

'Yes you do,' Mary persists, lowering her sewing onto her lap, her face reddened from the heat from the fire.

'If anything it means what, that you'rer worried all the time?'

'Something like that.'

'Worried about what?'

'Everything.'

'But that's impossible.'

'I worry, if you want to know, that everything's going to go wrong and with mother like she is and all this talk about a coming war I have every right to be worried. It's not something I make up. I'm not looking for sympathy. I'm.......I'm just anxious.'

'You've never liked anyone being ill,' Sylvie says remembering the awful state her sister used to get into whenever she had to be off school because of flu or tonsilitis.

'Things can't be always right,' she adds.

The music plays on the radio. Upstairs Sylvie knows her mother will be listening to the same programme while working on her new jigsaw. The washing hangs down from the pulley above the fire while there is the sound of another dog barking outside.

She feels so tired. The kitchen is bathed in orange light with shadows flickering from the fire over its pale yellow walls. The table where Sylvie is sitting is covered in a heavy damask table cloth the colour of dull russet. The two sisters are seated only a few feet away from each other and yet to Sylvie it always feels a huge distance to cross. When she had been at junior school she had so looked up to Mary being able to make her own clothes, put on makeup, being given money for a new pair of shoes. She sat and watched her get ready to go to her first proper dance. She had stood at the door with her mother waving Mary off on her first day at Dawsons even feeling all hot and embarrassed at her sister bringing home a boyfriend to Sunday tea.

All of that felt so long ago. So much was different now especially the strain there is between them.

'I don't expect everything to go well, of course I don't,' Mary continues, 'I know that's not possible. All you can do is try and have some sort of control over your own life and hope for the best.'

'That's what I used to think, fat lot of good it did me. It would have been better if I just thought everything was up to chance and nothing else.'

'But you believe everything is fated, in the lap of the Gods.'

'No I don't,' Sylvie says heatedly.

'That you're the victim.'

At that Sylvie angrily gets up, 'Not that again Mary. I don't think I'm being martyred for the sake of this family, especially not for you.'

'Calm down.'

'No I won't.'

'I only meant that.....'

'I know exactly what you meant. I'm going up to.....'

'Check on mother,' Mary interrupts sarcastically.

'Yes, see how she is. It's more than you ever do,' Sylvie says back sharply before leaving the kitchen.

In bed that night she lies there listening to Mary turning from side to side in her attempt to get to sleep. It is past eleven o clock and father is still not home. Out on the front street comes the sound of mens' voices and a late horse and cart clopping along the Keighley Road.

She loves her sister but finds her difficult, moody and unpredictable. Now she lies here wanting her mind to go in another direction away from family problems. They dominate. They touch on everything until she is exhausted with it all.

'How could they ask you to do that, to just leave school?' her friend Margaret had once asked.

Now Margaret had started her first year at Edinburgh university and Sylvie could only wonder what the life of a student must be like. She was happy for her best friend, the only one who had kept their friendship going after Sylvie had to leave school. She could only dream of being at college and training to be a teacher. It had been her one ambition, her one plan for the future for herself.

'We need Mary to keep working and we can't afford a full time nurse. The doctor's bills are bad enough. I don't want to be asking you to do this but it's our only option. You understand that Sylvie? You do understand that?'

Her father had persisted and she had finally agreed. What else could she have done?

She remembered crying night after night. Her life had been blighted, had been taken away from her. She remembered being angry and miserable, of feeling a victim of her mother's illness. Day after day she would sit in the kitchen when her mother was asleep and cry about the whole awful situation. Initially she found everything confusing, difficult and exhausting. It was too much for anyone her age. For a time she became depressed and resentful. She was angry at her father and sister. In comparison with her they had to sacrifice so little. It was so unfair, so frustrating. Those first months had been a nightmare that somehow she had managed while having no idea how she had done it still feeling as raw sometimes.

Now she lies listening to the men out on the street while wondering as she does most nights where her father is.

It is another of her unanswered questions. There are so many. Once she believed that her faith in God would create a way forward. Sometimes she feels so much is possible while on other days in other moods there seems nothing but the endless drudgery and worry about her mother.

'You have to be strong Sylvie,' Mr Elgin had tried when she had just left school, 'And see this as an opportunity not only to help your mother but also to help yourself. This will be a different kind of education, but one that is worth more than any other. You won't be feeling that right now but I'm sure that over the next months you will begin to realise what the chance you have been given to learn from the school of life, the hardest but best school there is Sylvie.'

She can hear his voice echoing through the cold, still night. He had tried but had failed to convince her that he was right. It was though illness had become the new religion, the one she had to follow at all costs, the one which demanded so much of her.

She closes her eyes holding back the tears. Mary is breathing slowly, regularly. There is the sound at last of her father opening the front door as an owl sounds out from the wood up near the park. She is so tired she knows it will be hours before she falls asleep to leave only a few hours before the daily grind starts again.

Tomorrow she will write a letter to Margaret and tell her about the books she has been reading.

CHAPTER FIVE

'The government will take over whatever is needed to defend the country. What I'm saying is that's how it always should be. It's the only way that people will be on the same level instead of a few rich and the rest poor. After this bloody war is over we should take the bull by the horns and ensure we never go back to the old ways. Folk have had enough of them. If everyone finishes up having to do their bit against the Germans, then when it's all over they should reap the benefits of their efforts. They shouldn't have to accept going back to how things were.'

'Of course the government will have to take charge.'

'All I'm saying is you can't have freedom and equality at the same time.'

'And I'm saying Hitler wants neither for the Germans.'

Arthur smokes his cigarette. The coal fire is burning in the upper room above the entrance to the Black Bull. Their discussion group meets at seven thirty on the first Thursday of the month. The room flickers with shadows from the fire on this cold February evening. There are old rugs on the floor and even older paintings on the walls. The oddity of an ornate chandelier from the low ceiling has often been remarked upon.

'Chamberlain appears weak, but I reckon when push comes to shove he'll not back down from Herr Hitler. He knows what he's doing. He should do, he's experienced enough. But he has to be careful at the same time. If he's the diplomat I think he is then he should run rings round the bloody Fuhrer who I hear loses his rag at any disagreement. He likes things his own way. If you're not nodding at his every word then sparks will fly.'

John Metcalf is more optimistic. Arthur has heard his version of events, one that adds a positive gloss onto everything. John hopes for the best and yet is only preparing himself for the worst. It is a trick of survival. He is worried like everyone else.

But this is part of their world, beer and chat, Annie the landlady bringing up sandwiches spot on nine o clock. They have been meeting like this for years. Opinions are supposed to be expressed with no interruptions. No agreement needs to be reached. There is hardly ever a conclusion to their arguments.

Tonight Arthur listens, drinks his glass of brandy followed by mouthfuls of bitter and becomes increasingly bothered.

'And I'd like to know,' George Thornton starts up, 'what we're doing getting all hot and bothered about some place in central Europe that has nothing to do with us. It's not our concern what happens to the Czechs. That sounds a bit harsh I know but we can't go around defending every country that finds itself in trouble. Czechlosovakia is in Hitler's back yard. Let him get on with it. Half the country is full of Germans as it is, so they have some claim on it already. We should concentrate on our own problems. That's what I think anyhow.'

Arthur knows that if he gets started sparks will fly.

Sam Fuller, the town's chemist, in his broad accent, says 'The country's not ready. We're miles behind the Germans.'

'When have we ever been ready?' asks Tommy Johnston sounding frustrated, 'Look what we're doing for those poor buggers in Spain, not a thing.'

'I'm saying we need more guns and planes, bombs and ships. All of it takes time. We should have started rearming years ago. That could have solved unemployment a few years back. But our government never plans ahead. It's always playing catch up. If we're not careful we'll finish up last.'

'We've done it once and we can do it again,' George puts in before he takes a mouthful of beer.

As usual this Thursday night is filled with the sound of voices and the fire crackling and the mood thickening as Annie brings up more drink. The air is fuggy with cigarette and pipe smoke.

Momentarily Arthur wonders why he finds most men intimidating, something he has never admitted to anyone. Tonight his mind is in dangerous territory. He is dissatisfied with everything, sick of hearing about another war. Tommy Johnston is on his high horse again. They are seated at a long table with the surface shining from Annie's daily polish. There is dark wooden panelling along the lower part of the walls with a pale yellow wallpaper above.

Arthur is thinking another war would be the greatest outrage and obscenity. It is ridiculous that people are considering more death and destruction after only twenty years since the last war.

'What do you reckon Arthur?' Paul Arkwright, the one teacher in the group, is asking him.

Arthur looks up, forces a smile and says strongly, 'Get ready lads. I'd be getting ready if I were you.'

They react to this in different ways. Tommy frowns. Paul who asked Arthur the question smiles back at him as if impressed by this unexpected reaction.

'You think it's sooner than later?'

'How many times have we said it?' Arthur asks strongly, 'That politics is a dirty and sometimes dangerous game because it's playing with other peoples' lives. Like Tommy says it's always the powerful and the rich who are pulling the strings, our bloody strings and we're all puppets. The British are the best in the world at playing Punch and Judy. But this time we personally won't be in the firing line so we can talk as long as we like it won't be affecting us as much as the young uns. They're the ones who'll be marched off to God knows what bloody nightmare. And I'd be surprised if the Luftwaffe has Skipton in its sites. Even though Dewhursts are apparently already making uniforms I don't think this town will see any bombs. Business won't stop. We're all doing something essential, keeping people going. That'll be our role. At least we already know what that'll be. Young fellas have no idea what's coming their way.'

'Arthur's right,' George agrees, 'Skipton has got nothing to worry about.'

At the end of the night Arthur and John walk along the High Street together, the others shouting their goodnights walking away in the opposite direction, voices echoing in the darkness, the quietness. To Arthur they make a sad sound, an end to something, a meeting with his friends that for all he knows might never happen again.

'If you were in Manchester or Liverpool,' his friend starts and then stops as a group of women click clack their way home in their high heels laughing as they pass.

'I should have a dog,' Arthur states out of the blue.

John makes no response.

They are walking slowly from one dim street light to the next.

'The docks will get it I bet,' John finally mentions, 'A lot of Irish Catholics there, especially in Liverpool. Mind you I'm not saying there's owt wrong with them.'

'A dog keeps you going,' Arthur persists

'We have cats.'

Arthur looks at his friend with his trilby tilted back on his head. John never expresses what there is beneath the surface, the burden of being a man, this secrecy, avoiding any display of emotion, stiff upper lip, never showing weakness, never being your true self.

'My bad chest rules me out,' John says looking straight ahead, his face tilted slightly backwards like his hat.

Arthur's belligerence gets the better of him, a wave of sudden anger heating up his confused mood.

'Only a bloody fool wants another war,' he says strongly, his shadowed features pulled tight.

'Trouble is Arthur, there are plenty of them around here.'

This statement changes whatever Arthur is feeling. Now he wants to put his arm round his friend's shoulder and tell him he is alright being who he is, not to change, not to do anything but arrive safely home.

'Are you going to the match?' Arthur asks abruptly, 'If your missus will let you.'.

That is another thing they share, their love of sport.

'They were on form tonight alright, talking, talking,' John says before he wipes his mouth with the back of his hand.

'This is me then,' he adds, 'And yes, I will be at the match.'

He turns, holds out his hand and as they shake he continues with, 'You look after yourself Arthur.'

'Oh don't worry about me. I'm champion,' Arthur replies easily, 'And say hello to Sheila for us.'

'I will and give my regards to Alice and hope things get better for her.'

'Goodnight then.'

'Goodnight Arthur.'

He watches the back of his friend's tall figure disappear round the corner.

He stands there and lights one of his full strength Capstan.

At the house after he has found his key and just managed to put it in the lock, he takes off his coat and trilby in the hallway and finds Sylvie still in the kitchen.

'How is your mother?' is his first awkward question.

Sylvie is sat beside the dim embers of the fire sewing. She is still wearing her pinny and looks up at her father, her glasses reflecting the light in the room so he cannot see her eyes. He can only try and interpretate her mood.

'She's asleep,' is all she says.

Arthur stands with his back to the fire warming himself.

He is sober enough to try a conversation and not stumble over his words. It takes more than a few brandies and pints of bitter to affect his speech or that is what he thinks. Consciously he tries to soften his tone.

'And what about you, what have you been doing tonight?'

He looks down on the top of her head before she eventually looks up at him, her round face showing a quizzical expression as though she is trying to guess the mood he is in.

'I read to mother earlier on. Since then I've been down here listening to the radio and doing a bit of sewing.'

'Fire's nearly out.'

'I didn't know what time you were coming in, so I just let it burn down.'

'You should be in bed Sylvie by now. You shouldn't have waited up for me'

She sighs but makes no move to get up from her fireside chair.

'And what about your sister, is she still out?'

'Mary came in about an hour ago.'

'Pictures again I suppose. My hell she must have seen every film made in the last ten years. You should go with her and Shirley sometime. It'd do you good to get out once in a while. I could stay here and look after your mother.'

Sylvie looks doubtful. He wonders if he has said something wrong.'

'Mary would never ask me father.'

'I'll have a word with her if you like.'

Immediately he knows he has made a mistake.

Sylvie's tone changes, 'No father, just leave it.'

He sits in his armchair, lights another cigarette and stares into the deep red embers, 'You two never do anything together, not since you were little and Mary was trying to show you how to ride that old bicycle. You fell off, scraped both your knees and made a right racket coming up the street with all the neighbours out wondering what had happened. It was a right carry on. It took weeks before you tried on that bike again and this time it was me trying to keep you steady.'

'I remember,' Sylvie says, 'And I eventually managed.'

This is said with a dull defiance that Arthur immediately senses.

'It something you'll always be able to do. People never forget how to ride a bike.'

'I haven't forgotten.'

'I never said you had,' he answers a little too harshly.

Sylvie gets up and puts her sewing on the table.

'Are you off then?' he asks in a more conciliatory tone.

She leans forward and kisses him on the forehead. He lifts up his hand to touch her arm, a small gesture that he hopes she will understand and accept.

She makes towards the door saying, 'Goodnight father. Don't forget to put the guard up.'

'I won't. Goodnight Sylvie. I'll see you in the morning.'

'Yes,' she answers before setting off down the dark hallway.

He sits there for a while watching the dull embers of the fire. He takes another drink and closes his eyes before smiling to himself thinking at least there is Kitty.

For a moment he thinks about getting up and turning the radio back on but changes his mind and lights another cigarette instead.

CHAPTER SIX

'Oh, in my day it was all very proper. There was plenty of time. There was no rush. Edward's family was very formal in the way they did things. I was so embarrassed and nervous on the first occasion he took me to meet his mother and father. They had a house on White House Road. I knew then on that first visit that I had to watch my Ps and Qs. Not that I hadn't been brought up properly. We'd always been chapel goers.'

Aunt Rose stops to take a sip of sherry while Mary sits opposite listening to her every word.

'But nowadays.......nowadays. There'll be a war they say. People act strangely when there's a lot of uncertainty. That's why I'm not sure dear how Edward and I went about things is any good to you. That was a long time ago. I think the first war knocked so much back. People changed after that and no wonder. This country was in a mess. There was hardship and anger. Folk became cynical and critical of everything. I suppose there was no respect for those trying their best to get things going again. At least Edward never got to experience what a mess our country became. He would have been turning in his grave seeing how things turned out. We'd won the war but lost everything else.'

Mary listens and waits. Aunt Rose, Arthur's sister, is stout with her greying hair pinned away from her warm, caring features.

'Nowadays Mary I suppose things are a lot less simple than they used to be.'

'Nothing seems simple. I wished it was, but it isn't.'

Rose takes another sip of sherry, one ankle crossed over the other, just visible below her long Edwardian dress.

'Well tell me then.'

Mary gives one of her nervous laughs, 'Tell you what?'

'Is there somebody? Have you started courting yet?'

It is evening. The heavy velvet curtains are closed. The room has gas lighting. Aunt Rose has never wanted anything to change. The house is a memorial to the few weeks she spent with her Edward killed at the Somme like so many others.

'No aunt, there isn't,' Mary lies, making her more anxious.

There is nothing clear anymore. It is all a mess of worries.

'I've got biscuits. Do you want one? You won't get fat, not you.'

'I'll get them if you want some too.'

'I wouldn't mind. They're in the back kitchen in a round tin with the King on it on the second shelf.'

Every step Mary takes is into another era, the time before the last war, the time where her aunt's life still remains. It suggests poverty but according to her father aunt Rose is comfortably off. Even though she takes such a lively interest in the present she has left the house as it is to remind her of the past.

Mary knows her father has made many suggestions how he could modernise the place but Rose has refused them all except for the installation of an upstairs toilet. Arthur has stopped trying, accepting the house is how she wants it to stay.

The kitchen is at the back of the house down the end of a long, dark hallway. Its floor is slabbed in polished slate. It has a stone sink and smells damp. This room is always cold even at the height of summer. The window above the sink looks out onto a long stretch of grass leading to the abandoned privvy.

The whitewashed walls of the kitchen contrast with the dark slate shelves. Behind a low door is a sloping pantry where Rose keeps her cheese, meat and milk to keep cool.

When Mary steps into the kitchen she always has the same sensations, always expecting to see children playing out on the back green but all there is are two metal poles that holds up aunt Rose's washing line.

This kitchen to Mary is cold and haunted by other times. It makes her rush to find the biscuit tin and escape back to the front room and the well stacked fire.

Rose opens the tin saying, 'I should have had these properly ready on a plate for you.'

Mary picks out a piece of shortbread.

'Are you warm enough? You can put more coal on if you want.'

'No, I'm fine,' Mary answers still feeling the effects from her visit to the kitchen.

She remembers Dorothy Watkins, Dotty as she called her, who lived two doors down from her aunt's house. When they were children and Mary came with her mother on a visit she would be straight down the hill knocking on the Watkins' door to see if Dotty was coming out to play.

Memories in this gas lit room. The children she had seen from her aunt's kitchen window playing on the back grass were her and Dotty, the two of them in summer dresses running around, singing.

She had been free back then, happy and enjoying herself. Dotty with her freckles and light brown hair and who spoke in a posh accent. Mary has no idea what happened to her after the Watkins moved away.

'Here have another biscuit,' her aunt is saying, her voice echoing in Mary's chamber of memories.

She is remembering the time they took a shopping basket and went up the hill to start picking flowers from peoples' front gardens. It had been Dotty's idea, a lovely idea, summer flowers, stalks in first so the heads of the flowers flopped over the rim of the basket. They had marched back down the hill, across the Gargrave Road and then onto the bridge that looked down over the Leeds - Liverpool canal.

Every time a barge appeared they would take a few of the flowers and toss them down towards the person at the tiller end. They would wave or smile or shout up some comment.

She can see the two of them leaning over the side of the bridge dropping red, scarlet and orange flowers onto each filthy barge. Slowly chugging along the barges stank of coal dust and diesel. She could see a dirty faced woman look up at them shouting her thanks in an unfamiliar accent.

A childhood shared with Dotty who lived two doors down from her aunt's and disappeared so suddenly, no explanations, no warnings. Even aunt Rose who picked up all the street gossip was flummoxed by the Watkins leaving so abruptly.

Mary had been upset for weeks. She waited for a letter that never came.

Memories of her and Dotty sledging down Elliot Street turning right onto Gargrave Road in an arc of frozen snow. The gaslit street silvered and gleaming as they both sat on the sledge screaming their heads off. It had been made by Arthur and slid so fast down the steep descent they had to stick out their feet to steer round the corner hoping no horse and cart was coming along the main road.

She looks across at her aunt who is staring into the fire.

'Are you alright?' she asks.

Rose takes off her glasses to clean them with her handkerchief. Her eyes appear surprised without the glasses.

'My legs ache sometimes, can't get around like I want to,' she says but not as a complaint, 'Like I used to, up hill and down dale, miles and miles we used to walk. Didn't matter what the weather was like, a group of us out on a weekend hike.'

Mary visits at least once a week and has done ever since starting school. Aunt Rose is funny, generous, chatty, full of the past and the present. She reads the Yorkshire Post and the Times every day and her front room has shelves full of books. Being well off she can even afford a woman called Mabel who comes twice a week to help with the cleaning and shopping.

Like her brother she has a strong personality and likes to express herself with the same intensity. But after that they are very different. Unlike Arthur aunt Rose is funny, sympathetic, interested in everyone and what they are doing. Every Sunday she attends the Spiritualist church on the Keighley Road and on Thursdays holds her weekly seances here in the house. She is generous, accepting and easy to be with. Her aunt has always been interested in her neice. More than anyone it is her advice that Mary listens to.

'I've got something to show you,' Rose says as she gets out of her armchair by the fire, 'Mabel found it in a box under the stairs.'

She goes over to a dark rosewood cabinet in the corner of the room. When she turns she is holding something Mary has not seen in years, a music box.

Her aunt places it on the table set between them and opens the lid and twists the key for the tune to start and a ballerina to turn slowly round. As though from a sad circus the music plays. Mary stands there fascinated by the ballerina in her white costume, up on her toes, arms raised straight above her head, hands curved outwards. Mary used to often dream as a child of being this beautiful dancer.

'It's lovely,' she comments.

'I thought you'd remember. I'd forgotten all about it until Mabel found it. You can have it Mary if you want to take it home.'

Mary smiles, 'No auntie, I couldn't. It's yours.'

'I want you to have it Mary.'

The music and the ballerina together slow down and then stop and it feels as though a whole world stops with them.

It is past eight o clock by the time she leaves. Mary wonders if it is her aunt's gas lighting that gives her a headache. There is always something wrong, her nervous flushes, her heart suddenly pumping faster. Her anxious body makes her suffer and yet she is supposed to be a young, healthy woman. She is terrified of finishing up like her mother, always ill, always suffering.

When she reaches the Woolworth's corner she remembers what Shirley had asked her the day before.

'Don't you want to have children Mary?'

It had made her uncomfortable and angry. Her answer had been too harsh but inevitable.

'I'm not sure I do. Just because I'm a woman then everyone expects me to have children and it's nonsense. Why is that always expected? No, at the moment I can't think of anything worse than having a baby. Just because you're getting married and then soon after you'll be pregnant it doesn't mean I want the same Shirley. I don't and I'm not sure if I ever will.'

She had meant every word at that time but she could tell her response had really upset Shirley. As they had walked back from the Plaza her friend said nothing else, not even a goodnight.

Mary knows she needs to be more honest with herself. It is the only way she is going to get through the next weeks and months. There is a crisis coming and she has to be certain she is being true to herself. She is not sure whether it is the talk of war or her mother's illness or Frobisher's increasing attention to her. Everything is making her more nervous, more frightened that she is not in control anymore.

By the time she reaches the house she is tense and confused again. She stops, takes a deep breath and tries to clear her mind, but in that moment comes a dreadful sense of the war everyone is talking about. It is in the papers, magazines, on the radio. Is that all there is for her future, endless years of destruction and death? She is just left feeling helpless again.

'Is Sylvie already in bed father?' is her first question.

Arthur looks up from his paper, 'I told her I'd lock up and sort the fire.'

His jacket is slung over the back of his chair and his waistcoat unbuttoned, his face reddened from the night's drinking and the heat from the fire.

Mary is surprised at seeing him home so early.

'And how's Rose?' he asks.

'Aunt Rose is fine,' Mary answers.

'Was she asking of me?'

'No.'

Arthur laughs, 'Not likely.'

'That's because you never visit. She comes here to see mother but you never....'

'You're right,' he interrupts.

Mary feels a sudden anger.

'I'll leave you to it then,' she says strongly.

'Bed so early?' Arthur asks in an unconcerned tone.

She turns at the door, 'I've a terrible headache if you must know.'

'Take an aspirin. There's some in the cupboard above the sink.'

'I know that.'

'It's only a suggestion, no need to bite my head off.'

'Goodnight father,' she says abruptly.

There is the smell of the disinfected commode as she reaches the landing, that pungent stench of illness that is always there. It makes her feel sick.

Sylvie with a blanket wrapped round her shoulders is sat up in bed reading.

'Father's home for a change,' is the first thing she says.

Mary starts quickly getting undressed.

Sylvie returns to her book.

Mary finally says, 'Why's he home so early?'

'Mother's asleep by the way.'

'I know that.'

Sylvie looks at her, 'No you don't. How do you know? Did you……'

'Alright, you've made your point,' Mary interrupts.

'It's not a point sister, it's a fact.'

Mary pulls her nightie over her head and gets hurriedly under her bedclothes, turning away to face the wall.

'You see more of Aunt Rose than you do your own mother,' Sylvie persists.

'I have a headache and I want to go to sleep Sylvie, so leave it be.'

'I'm reading.'

'Good for you.'

There is a few minutes silence before Sylvie says, 'I don't mean Mary to criticise.'

'Yes you do.'

'She misses you, mother I mean.'

'I know.'

'And that doesn't help.'

'I know that.'

'You could try a little harder.'

'I will,' Mary sighs, 'Just please leave it for tonight.'

It seems a long time before Sylvie finally turns off her bedside light.

Mary listens to her settling under the bedclothes and the sounds of a dog barking further down the street. Someone bangs a dustbin lid before she hears voices coming from the back lane.

She curls up as tight she can, pulling her knees up to her chest to try and find some warmth.

She cannot sleep. Her mind is too bothered. Life has to have its constant shape. Its routine is its meaning. Ever since being a child she has been scared of anything that destroys that pattern of life, her family's and the town's. There has to be school, holidays and then school. There are the four seasons. There is the summer gala, the horse fair, the weekly cattle mart on the High Street, the Salvation Army band at Christmas. Everything is regular, repeated and secure. It is illness more than anything that can break that enduring shape of life into pieces. Her mother's heart attack has changed everything now. Nothing is safe.

She listens to Sylvie's regular breaths and then hears her father poking at the fire, locking the back door before he comes along the hallway to do the same at the front. His footsteps up the stairs are slow. He stops outside mother's bedroom before coming along to his own room where he can be heard opening the wardrobe to hang up his suit.

Mary listens, squeezing her hands together, pushing her head against the cold wall to try and ease the pain. She wants to sleep. She wants to relax away from the strain of her thoughts. She waits, the coldness creeping over her face and arms.

CHAPTER SEVEN

'Sylvie goes twice a week to the library for the two of us.'

'Where you used to work?'

'Part time, yes.'

'Arthur used to be a great reader, but in the end it was always sport with him, rugby and cricket daft.'

'He has never told me why he stopped playing.'

Rose with her black hat perched on her grey hair looks away as Alice takes a sip of water.

'When he left school he hated going to away games and what they got up to afterwords. It disgusted him the way they carried on.'

'He never said.'

'I think at the time it embarrassed him the way he couldn't accept what his playing friends got up to.'

'Young men. Most of them would have never survived the war.'

Alice immediately regrets her mistake, but Rose ignores it and says, 'Arthur was one of those who was different, just different, keen on school work and yet good at sport. Usually you had to be one or the other, but he wasn't. His grandmother Agnes was the clever one in our family and a great talker.'

'He must have inherited that as well.'

Rose is sat near the bed in her long black dress with a thin purple scarf tied loosely around her neck. It is her first visit in several weeks. Arthur is always a topic of conversation, the source of the conflict between the two women. Alice is tired of it, tired of the way Rose always makes her brother sound almost unrecognisable.

'Yes, he's a great talker,' Rose agreed.

There is a momentary strained silence before Alice eventually says, 'I used to believe what he said.'

Rose's features tighten as she lifts her chin slightly, a mannerism that Alice knows well.

'Well I suppose Alice, that's up to you,' she replies brusquely, her tone deepening.

'No Rose, I think it's more up to Arthur.'

'There has to be trust in any marriage.'

'The ideal marriage if there is such a thing.'

'And discretion.'

'I'm tired of all that,' Alice sighed, nervously fingering her bedclothes.

'Arthur is certainly not perfect.'

'Edward was good to me.'

'You should never compare.'

'But everyone does. It's second nature. Isn't life, social life, all about comparing one person, one family with another?

'If there were any we weren't married long enough for me to discover faults in my Edward. He had his way of doing things that was different to mine but that hardly mattered.'

'I'm sorry Rose, I didn't….'

'It's alright Alice. I don't mind talking about him. If I don't he'll be forgotten.'

'Not by this family.'

'That's kind of you to say so.'

'No, not kind Rose, just a fact.'

'Like you not believing what your husband says.'

The retort comes back so quickly Alice is unprepared for it. She stifles her irritation by taking another drink of water.

'Arthur comes around to the house so rarely these days. I think it's because I won't make all the changes to the house that he thinks I should. It rankles him to know I have the money to afford all he suggests yet won't do any of it except the toilet he had installed. He was adamant about that. It was his mission at the time to stop me having to cross the back green to the privy. He thought it was demeaning for his sister to have to do such a thing.'

'Demeaning,' Alice repeats suddenly regretting the way the conversation has gone.

She has always tried to like Rose especially as Mary has such a soft spot for her and goes to see her at least once a week. She often wonders how much the two of them discuss her illness and what the future holds for the Townsleys.

'I always like a fire in a bedroom. It's something that people don't have as much as they used to,' Rose says as though sensing Alice's need to soften the strain between them.

'Sylvie keeps it going.'

'She's a grand lass,' Rose says warmly.

'Yes, I depend on her for everything.'

'Things will improve Alice.'

'I'm not sure anymore.'

'Of course they will. You'll be up and about before you know it.'

'It's been over three years now.'

'I know. It must feel forever, but these things take time.'

'You mean my heart.'

Rose looks a little flustered, 'Yes, that, your heart, yes.'

When she has gone Alice closes her eyes and tries to slow her breathing. Rose has left her exhausted and confused as she usually does. Between them Arthur is two people, one from the Townsley's past, the other from the doubtful present. They can never be the same which means she and Rose can never agree on any of it. It is impossible.

Later in the evening the voices of Mary and Sylvie downstairs grow louder. For once their tones sound less harsh. They sound like they are provoking each other but in a humorous way. Mary can be sarcastic and her sister can be just as bad. She learnt from her elder sister. Even when a young child Mary had a sharp tongue. She refused to back down. She would even talk back to her father, something Arthur rather enjoyed. He never took either Mary or Sylvie too seriously. When they were younger most of the time he ignored them. They were in the way. Alice had often thought that he had never wanted children in the first place. It was obvious his children were on the edge of his concerns, something that had made her miserable and bitter towards him. It was only when he was half drunk that he showed any affection for them as though he had to remind himself that they were part of his life.

Listening to Mary down in the kitchen Alice thought how much she was like her father, sharp, self centred, liking her social life and yet as far as Alice knew she had never had a steady boyfriend, coming in at all hours, losing her faith, leaving school as early as she could to start at Dawsons, money being the main consideration and like her father smartly turned out. She seemed always in control, careful with her weekly wage, careful in how she organised her days. At twenty four her daughter was already approaching the time when most people were married. Alice was beginning to wonder if it would ever happen. Mary was very much her own person, always very private. Things had to be how she wanted them. If anyone disagreed she would just ignore them. Alice wonders how many young men she might have rejected the moment they went against Mary wishes.

Now Sylvie is raising her voice in an accent that is much broader than her sister's. Mary has spent years trying to alter how she speaks. She says her customers expect her to sound professional, to sound like someone on the radio, but she has never quite managed that BBC tone of voice leaving her accent posh with a bit of Yorkshire thrown in.

Alice feels a sudden pressure across her chest which starts her on her evening inventory of all that she is suffering. It is what she does every day. Her body holds the memory of all she has been through. Initially after the first heart attack there was anger and frustration eventually followed by a morbid acceptance of what had happened to her. Now there was fear as well as an increasing immobility. She could no longer wash herself or reach the commode without Sylvie's help. What had once been embarrassing and degrading was now part of the day's accepted routine. There had to be acceptance or despair would take over.

The fire in the corner has burnt low to leave only a few tiny flames. Her bedside lamp sends orange light over the ceiling. Drifting into the room come the sounds of men in the back lane shouting and joking with each other. But it is the light on the ceiling that absorbs Alice, the colour of sunlight, afternoon sunlight that she remembers reflected off the smooth river, faint orange divided into patterns from the reflection of summer tree branches, quivering jigsaw shapes. Her father further along the grassy embankment is fishing. Lucy her sister has found smooth stones that she is collecting in her bucket. A horse and cart are crossing the high stone bridge over the river and she is reading, always reading. On this occasion it is Wordsworth. What was once so natural has become such good fortune, her love of books, her constant need for her brain to be working, absorbing, connecting. It could have been Keats or Shelley. It could have been Tolstoy or Hugo or Jane Austen. But she remembers it was the Prelude opening new Lakeland vistas for her imagination to feed itself.

The moment is there in her memory, no sounds, only light, her father, her sister, the horse and cart as she looked from her page to capture it all in one vision, one moment in time. That is when she had felt such an urge for that moment to continue. Nothing must change. But the horse pulled the cart down off the bridge. Her sister accidentally dropped her bucket as her father looked up. In an instant the moment had disappeared, gone forever. She wanted it back, wanted time reversed or if not that then every moment to last as long as she desired, one moment stretched to infinity, lasting as long as she liked.

Such romantic notions. That was how things were back then, a young woman lost to poetry, fantasy, dreams and the life of her imagination, all based on the books she read and the education she had received. Thanks to the determination of her mother and father she like the rest of her sisters were encouraged to learn and study, to expand their minds in which ever direction they wanted. Only later did she realise how lucky they had been.

The romantic notions she had back then made life deeper, more exciting, ideas that only later did she come to understand had created such unrealistic innocence. Her mind is back in the chapel and one of the small meeting rooms that are between the main building and the hall and stage behind where Sunday school is held. On the wall above the mantelpiece in that room is a large photograph of a chapel outing to Heysham, a bus trip to the seaside. There must be over fifty people standing on the chapel front steps from toddlers to pensioners, all in their summer best, all with smiling, happy, expectant faces. Were they all innocent? Were they all like children in their exuberant naivete? Romance seemed to have fluttered in the air for a few years after the war, after the General Strike and the millions out of work. Was she just the same? But for her it had been before the war. She had trusted what she read. She had believed in the worlds created by all those great writers. They were her mentors and had created in her as strong a faith as her belief in God. She had been caught up in such Edwardian optimism, in the sense that her young years glowed in that summer light, warm, golden, reassuring.

CHAPTER EIGHT

Sylvie rakes out the ashes and shovels them onto newspaper spread out on the rag rug in front of the hearth. She then folds the paper up into a neat package that she takes out to the bin in the back yard. Next more paper is twisted into firelighters and a few pieces of coal added on top. After the fire is set she takes up a cup of tea for her mother who is sat up in bed waiting.

'You sure you don't want anything else?' Sylvie asks in her concerned voice.

Nearly four years of such concern have been exhausting but worry has become a familiar response.

'I'm not hungry,' Alice sighs.

'You should eat something. What about a piece of toast?'

'Later. I'll have something to eat later.'

Next the kitchen fire is lit. This is followed by some of the ironing she has to do. She turns on the radio to hear music coming from a foreign station.

It makes so much difference to use the electric iron her father bought for her the month before. She wonders how much his purchases for the house are to assuage some of the guilt he feels.

But before she can answer such a question there is a knock on the front door.

Sylvie switches off the iron and walks down the hall rubbing her hands automatically on her pinny.

'Good morning,' says Mrs Belmont in her sharp, precise voice, 'I'm going to the fishmongers and I wondered if you wanted anything.'

Mrs Belmont is a neighbour from three doors along the street, a large, fussy, curious woman who is always offering her help.

'No, I don't think so Mrs Belmont.'

'I just thought I'd ask.'

'That's kind of you.'

'Not at all. It's the best I can do.'

Sylvie wipes her forehead with the back of her hand before blowing a strand of hair from the front of her face, 'And how's Mr Belmont?'

'Oh George is his usual self. Where he got his humour from I have no idea. There's nobody else in his family with an ounce of anything resembling humour.'

'There's one or two good comedy programmes on the radio nowadays.'

'Well the BBC have to keep up our spirits somehow.'

'Yes, I suppose so.'

'It's just one depressing thing after another,' Mrs Belmont complains before she starts down the front path.

'If there's anything you or your mother need you know where we are,' she calls as she closes the gate behind her.

Sylvie returns to the kitchen feeling she has been patronised again, that sense that without the support of others she would not be able to cope.

As she switches the iron back on there is a sudden rush of anticipation. In less than two hours Doctor Donnolly will arrive on his weekly visit.

After a few minutes she hears shouting from the back lane and goes to see what all the commotion is about.

It is Archie Andrews crouching up against the opposite wall.

'Archie, what happened, what's the matter?'

He mumbles something that she cannot understand.

'Come on Archie,' she says as she goes over to him, 'I heard shouting. Who was shouting?'

He has his head between his knees, his hair flopping forward screening his face.

'Archie,' Sylvie tries again, bending towards him.

'Nothing,' he mutters.

'What does that mean? Who was shouting?'

'Nothing,' he repeats.

'It must have been somebody and it wasn't you. I know your voice and it wasn't you so.....'

'Them men,' comes Archie's interruption as he lifts his head and looks up at her with tears dribbling down his filthy cheeks.

She crouches closer so her face is opposite his, 'What men?'

'Them men.'

'What were they doing Archie? Tell me, please."

'Me....Me... they were....'

'What?'

'Shouting, laughing, laughing, pushing.'

As he starts sobbing she takes him by the shoulders and tries to get him to stand,' It's alright Archie, it's alright.'

'Them men.'

'They've gone now Archie.'

He is leaning against the wall wiping his face with the sleeve of his baggy jumper while gasping for breath trying to stop crying.

'Where were you going?' Sylvie asks as she keeps glancing down the now empty back lane, 'I gave you your football back, remember, remember Archie?'

With his glistening eyes he finally looks at her, 'Didn't bring it.'

'You always have your football with you.'

'Didn't want it, didn't bring it.'

'You should be....'

'Came to see you!' he suddenly exclaims, 'Came to see you Sylvie!'

'Don't shout Archie. There's no need to shout.'

At that he suddenly wipes his nose, rubs his face with both hands before turning and running off.

'Archie! Archie!' Sylvie calls to him, 'Come back!'

She stands there before a woman pushing a pram comes round the corner at the end of the lane.

Back in the kitchen she finishes her ironing, goes up to give her mother her morning wash before emptying the commode bucket down the toilet and washing it out under the bathroom tap, the whole operation leaving her feeling nauseous.

'What was all that commotion?' Alice asks in a weary voice.

'Oh, it's Archie. He says some men were bothering him,' Sylvie answers as she brings over a flannel to let her mother wash her own face.

'What men?'

'He wouldn't tell me or he didn't know them.'

'And why was he here again?'

'Likes my company. That's what he told me last week. I like your company Sylvie Townsley.'

'Well at least he knows your name.'

'Bless him. I feel sorry for Archie. Outside it's really cold. He was only wearing his long shorts, socks round his ankles, old shirt and a sleeveless jumper that had holes in it. Oh and Mrs Belmont came round to see if we needed anything from the fishmonger.'

'We don't, do we?'

Sylvie takes back the flannel and moves Alice forward so she can puff up her pillows.

'Do you want yesterday's Post?' she asks.

Alice gives her a strained look before inquiring what time the doctor is due.

'Around lunchtime,' he said.

'Coming every week. He must be worried.'

'He's just checking you're alright mother. It's his job.'

'And I'm not, am I? I'm not alright. I've forgotten what the word means.'

Sylvie senses the growing struggle her mother is experiencing. Whatever she does for her seems to have little effect.

'I'm sorry Sylvie, sorry. Had a bad night and my head aches as well as my chest.'

'Doctor Donnolly will be able to give you something.'

'How about a new heart? Can he give me one of them?'

'I wish he could mother.'

'Wish and wish,' Alice repeats in a dull, empty tone.

Back in the kitchen Sylvie keeps herself busy, practising in her mind what she will say when the doctor arrives. Time has to pass as quickly as possible until at last there is the familiar knock on the door.

'Doctor,' is all she can say when she opens it.

'Sylvie,' he replies before she lets him into the hall where he puts down his bag, takes off his trilby and overcoat and hangs them on the pegs at the back of the door.

'And how is your mother? How is she today?' is his first question as he starts up the stairs with Sylvie following.

'She told me she had another bad night.'

'And you Sylvie, how are you?'

'Oh I'm fine doctor,' she answers nervously before opening the bedroom door to announce his arrival.

Alice forces a smile as they enter and says, 'I thought I heard your voice doctor.'

He comes over and places his hand on her forehead, 'Sylvie tells me you've had a bad night.'

'Nothing different I'm sorry to say.'

Sylvie leaves them and goes back down stairs hoping that this is one of the visits where the doctor does not have to rush out to his next call.

She boils the kettle, puts some biscuits on a plate, flicks the tea towel over the table top and chair seats, tilts more coal from the scuttle onto the fire before standing at the back window to wait.

Expectancy creates a tension in her. She sees herself again opening the door and him standing there with his bag and his quick smile. His pale, thin face looks tired, but his brown eyes still glisten with interest as he looks at her.

Her mouth feels dry and she can hardly swallow.

A coal lorry goes bouncing along the back lane, its bulging sacks stacked in two rows. Momentarily she notices the men on the front seat with their dirty faces and caps stuck up on the back of their heads.

She is waiting. She can hear his voice talking to her mother, his patient. And that is the dilemma, the awful paradox of her mother's illness being the reason she can see him at all. If her mother had never had a heart attack the doctor would be a stranger to her. The feeling of guilt grows deeper as his visits become more frequent.

She is waiting as she turns to the fire hoping that he will come down the stairs and into the kitchen and not have to leave the house straightaway.

She tries to calm herself, tries to focus on something else but constantly keeps seeing his smile. She knows it is genuine. She is sure the doctor likes her.

Is the kitchen too hot? Should she mash the tea? Does he eat Rich Tea biscuits? Should she have lit the fire in the parlour?

And then at last she hears him on the landing before coming down the stairs.

She is pouring water from the kettle into the teapot when he comes into the kitchen.

'I'm making some tea if you'd like some.'

He stands uncertainly in the doorway before accepting her offer.

'Sit down doctor,' she suggests before putting on the tea cosy and carrying the pot to the table and adds 'There's Rich Tea biscuits if you'd like one.'

He sits at the table. It being lunchtime she anxiously wonders if there is anything else she should have thought of.

It feels unreal him being there sat opposite as she pours the tea and he takes a bite from his biscuit.

'I was just wondering how much your mother eats each day. Every time I visit she seems to have lost weight, too much I'm afraid.'

'Now it's only toast and sometimes a bowl of soup. I try and persuade her to have more but she won't. She just won't.'

'I know you do all you can Sylvie.'

It is his voice, that soft, concerned tone and the way he looks at her so intently. She knows it is wrong to feel what she does for a married man, but she cannot stop herself. Over and over she has tried to resist such emotions and always failed.

'And you, what about you? I hope you took on board what I suggested some weeks ago.'

'I do try to get out more. I meet my friend Sally Jones as often as I can. If it's not raining we take a walk in the woods sometimes. And there's always chapel and Sunday school. The rest of the time I'm too busy.'

'That's what concerns me Sylvie, you're doing too much, far too much for someone your age.'

She enjoys the fact that he worries about her, enjoys the way she absorbs his voice and makes it into a feeling.

'I'm alright,' she says.

'The last thing we want is you making yourself ill. Are you getting enough support from your father and sister?'

'I'm used to doing everything. I wasn't to begin with, but I am now.'

He takes another biscuit and asks her what she would have done if she had stayed on at school?'

'I wanted to be a teacher, to train and become a teacher of junior age children.'

'There's still time to do that, you know.'

'I don't know doctor. The way things are going it won't depend on what people can manage. It's what will be decided for us.'

'You mean the threat of war?'

'Is it just a threat? Do you think that's all it is?'

'I wished I could answer that question. I know your mother is as worried as well.'

'She listens to the news, reads the paper.'

'She likes to be well informed.'

'She has all the time there is, hasn't she?.'

'And you haven't.'

She glances across at him. Everything about the doctor feels settled and secure. The atmosphere in the room is changed by his presence. She wants it to always be like this.

'Will mother get worse doctor?'

It is the first time she feels confident enough with him to ask such a question.

'I've told you about her water retention. Sometimes she will swell in her arms or legs. At others it could be her stomach or her face. When or how that happens I can't predict. I wished I could.'

'And the pains in her chest?'

'Those I'm afraid are inevitable with her condition.'

'Poor mother.'

'Yes, but she has a strong will and is well looked after.'

'I hope so. I try my best.'

'You're doing a grand job Sylvie,' he says before taking a mouthful of tea.

As he gets up he smiles at her, 'And now I'll have to go. This afternoon is looking as busy as usual.'

As she follows him down the hallway he tells her that he will visit next week.

'Around the same time if I can,' he adds as he puts on his overcoat and trilby.

'And you make sure you dig out as much time for yourself as you can, alright?'

'Yes, doctor,' she replies as she opens the door for him.

'I've left your mother's medication on the bedside table,' he informs her as he turns round before opening the front gate.

'I'll see you next week. Goodbye Sylvie.'

She stands there until he has disappeared round the corner, greeting two women with bulging shopping bags as they pass going in the other direction.

She waits to settle herself before going up to see her mother, but it is impossible. She is too hot and bothered, too self critical and anxious. All of it is a worry of her own making and nothing she tries has any affect on what she feels for him. She knows the next hours and days will be another strain of waiting for him to visit again, waiting to see his face, hear his voice, be absorbed in his presence.

After an afternoon of the usual, dusting the parlour, several trips to check on her mother, sweeping the back yard and finally getting the tea ready she hears Mary's key turning in the door.

She comes into the large kitchen with its pale yellow walls, lino on the floor with one small rag rug in front of the hearth and a much larger one between the table and the dresser where all the plates, cups, saucers and cutlery are displayed.

Sylvie knows that the next few sentences will set the tone for the rest of the evening. She can never be certain of her sister's moods.

But Mary says nothing as she stands at the fire turning her hands to warm them up.

'Tea is sausages, potatoes and carrots with rice pudding for afters. Do you want to eat?' is the only thing she can say that is safe enough.

Mary is in her neat matching top and skirt, her dark hair sheened in the light and her pale features tightly set.

'I don't know why I bother sometimes. That awful Mathews woman was in again this afternoon. It took me all my time to stop myself from slapping her. The cheek she has. That woman is a liability. I hate it when she appears, always complaining about something or other. This time she said there was a stain on the blouse she bought last week. I wouldn't put it past her to have stained the blouse herself, anything for a little drama. That woman's life must be so empty, so hopeless. And yes,' she finally adds, 'I will have tea. I didn't have time for lunch today. A delivery was two hours late as usual.'

'You haven't asked about mother.'

'Give me time, I was just about to. Well, how is she?'

'Doctor Donnolly came on his weekly visit at lunchtime.'

'And what did he have to say?'

'That she needed to eat more.'

'And what did you say Sylvie?'

'I said I was trying my best to get her to....'

'And did he come in here for a chat afterwards?' Mary interrupted, 'I bet he did. Go on tell me what happened.'

Sylvie could feel herself reddening as she tried to control her response.

'Nothing happened.'

'Except you sat there ready to swoon on him at any moment,' Mary said lightly.

'Don't be so stupid,' Sylvie replied.

'Go on, admit it, you have a crush on our doctor.'

'That's just silly.'

'I know you do. It's obvious. The way you talk about him, all soppy and far too eager.'

'If you want to know he said I should get out more and enjoy myself.'

Mary pursed her lips, seated herself primly at the table and set her hands carefully down on the table top.

Sylvie was unsure how much her sister really understood what she felt.

'You just want to argue,' she finally said.

'I think you should do what the doctor suggests. They always know what's best.'

'And what is best according to you?'

'That we should go out somewhere. I'm sure I can persuade father to stay in for one night.'

Sylvie is unprepared for this. She goes over to the stove and serves Mary's food and then her own.

'Well, what do you say?' Mary persists as Sylvie sets the plates on the table and continues with, 'We should go out dancing.'

'You always go with Shirley.'

'The three of us could go.'

'Go where?'

'Next Saturday there's a dance at the town hall. It'll be full of the usual crowd. They're alright and there's usually a good band playing. There's no drink so I'll get something from Cunninghams. Come on sister. What do you say? I could make you a new dress. Yes, I can do that. It's about time you had a good night out. You need to try something different. Shirley could do your hair and I could do your makeup if you like and then you'll be a right bobby dazzler.'

Sylvie forces out a laugh and looks away to the window at the rattle of a horse and cart going down the back lane.

'I......'I'm not sure,' she eventually manages, not knowing how serious her sister's idea is.

'I bet if I said doctor Donnolly would be there next Saturday you wouldn't think twice about it.'

'I do like him,' she says strongly without any sense that this is what she was going to admit.

'It's more than like,' Mary immediately replies.

'What if it is? There's nothing anyone can do about it, especially me. It's stupid and childish and just plain wrong.'

'Meet a fella who....'

'Stop it Mary.'

'It's only a suggestion.'

'No, it isn't. I just want us to have our tea in peace.'

'Peace,' Mary scoffs, 'In this house?'

'Well, when did you have a proper boyfriend, not since that Robert?' Sylvie found herself retaliating, 'I thought he was nice. At least he asked questions and just didn't talk about himself all the time.'

'Is that what the doctor does, ask you lots of questions?'

'No, he doesn't if you must know.'

Mary starts to eat, stops and goes out for her cigarettes that she has left in her coat packet.

'Have a cigarette.'

'What was wrong with him?' Sylvie asks, ignoring her offer.

'Robert? He was alright, a bit boring. But you're not wrong,' she adds as she pushes her plate away and lights a cigarette, 'I'm twenty four and should be married by now.'

'I wasn't saying that.'

'Yes you were. Maybe I'll never get married,' Mary says in an unconcerned voice, 'Why should I? Just because I'm a woman I'm automatically supposed to get married, have children and settle down.'

'Most women do.'

'Some don't.'

'I want to get married and have children.'

'Good for you. That's your choice. It isn't mine.'

Sylvie suddenly gets up to put more coal on the fire before filling the kettle and putting it on the gas hub.

She turns round feeling hopelessly unsure and then says, 'Alright, I'll go.'

A surprised Mary takes a puff of her cigarette and blows smoke up towards the kitchen's ceiling and then says, 'If you do, if you really mean it then I'll go with you to chapel this Sunday morning. Is that a deal?'

'You always sleep in on Sundays.'

'Not this Sunday.'

'And you'll come with me to chapel?'

'Promise.'

'Good,' says Sylvie warmly.

Even though trust in still in short supply for once she believes her sister.

'You'll have a great time dancing.'

'I.....I hope so.'

'And Shirley's good fun.'

'I like Shirley.'

'She's the best friend I have.'

'Like Margaret.'

'The one at university?'

'Yes.'

'We're both lucky to have such friends.'

To this Sylvie makes no reply. There is this sudden change in her sister that leaves her lost to what is happening.

CHAPTER NINE

Arthur is in his bare feet. His jacket is off, his waistcoat open and his tie loose as he lounges in front of Kitty's country fire. He often wonders if someone asked him to describe her where he would start. Is there a beginning to who someone is, a hierarchical list of attributes? Or does one start with the personality? Can one be honest even to oneself?

His cigar is beginning to taste a little sour. That is one thing, every sensation feels different when he is with her, the wine they are drinking, the taste of Kitty's food that she prepares for him, the sound of Beethoven's sonata on her gramophone. Does she change as much as he does when they are together?

She works as a secretary at Charlesworths, a top Leeds law firm. She lives in a cottage outside Burley where she also stables two horses. She drives a smart 1935 MG Coupe. Her wealthy parents live in Somerset and she is thirty four years old.

That is the simple part, the factual description, a box into which everything else is placed. But no one could ever do that with Kitty, try and set a coral around who she is. After nearly a year she is still a mystery. She fascinates him. There is always more to know. Most of what he has learnt about her he appreciates, some of it he does not. The equilibrium often swings one way or the other especially after one of their arguments. They have a constant theme, that he has to come and live with her and make a new life for themselves.

But a completely new life when you're forty six is impossible. Too much of the past will be brought along and he realises that eventually that is what will have to happen, that a decision will have to be made.

All the rooms of her cottage are on one level. They have low ceilings, thick walls and small windows. In the past one room would have been the barn for the beasts, another for their feed and the last where the shepherd and his family lived. Now they have been converted into a bedroom, kitchen and finally the largest room where Arthur and Kitty spend their evenings together.

Everything is colourful, modern, functional and yet comfortable. Kitty has the money and the ideas to change the cottage into a place that they both enjoy. It is a part of her. That is how he sees it. He loves staying over when he can and this weekend he has told Alice and the girls he will be covering the cricket match at Headingley, Yorkshire against Sussex and has booked a room in a hotel near the ground.

Once the deceptions begin there can be no reversal. One lie necessitates the next. He accepts that. There is now nothing else he can do. The barriers have successfully been created between one life and the other. Still the recriminations are never ending. Everyone is deceived. Everyone is failed. There are no explanations except that he is full of need and regret.

He will never stop needing. He will never stop hating himself. Kitty is not the cause. There have been many women before he met her, women who he desired and tried to manipulate.

He sips his wine and listens to the music on the gramophone. Kitty is curled up on the sofa and has her head resting against his shoulder. Even though it is a warm summer's evening the curtains are closed and the fire burning. Because of its thick stone walls the cottage is always at least ten degrees cooler than outside. It means within each room the season never changes. They live within a constant autumn, the most intimate of days.

Alice would never curl up beside him like Kitty is doing. He can smell her freshly washed hair. It is bobbed and blonde. It feels silky and tickles his cheek when she raises her head to give him one of her inquiring looks. Alice's love was always from a distance. Her love was always more practical. This meant she did everything she could do for him, survive the war with a young child, set up house before Sylvie was born and then accepted his late nights and his weekends away. She was the strength behind his weakness. Alice had trusted him for the first years. Only gradually had she begun to understand how his life was built on a complicated construction of lies, begun to understand what a manipulator he was.

He pours them more wine. Kitty mentions the music. He agrees that no composer can produce such a complexity of sound and meaning as Beethoven. It is loud, quiet, straining, lifting, dancing, mournful, jovial and romantic. It is not about thoughts but emotions, the heart with all its confusions and sublime moments.

The first classical music he heard had been at a concert in Skipton town hall when a quartet had played some pieces by Haydn. From then on he has tried to listen to as much music as possible. Kitty has a big collection of records. They are stacked on shelves along the back wall. When he comes here they spend time listening to one piece or another. She will leave him on the sofa while she makes their supper and he lets himself be taken as deep into the sounds as possible.

'You hardly mention it,' Kitty states.

He looks at her, the wine hazing his focus a little.

'It's getting worse, isn't it? Most at work think Chamberlain and the French will back off. They know their people are not in favour of doing anything else. Anyway Arthur, aren't you too old to be called up? Goodness what will Charelsworths do, carry on when at least half of the staff are of an age to go fighting? No one is saying anything at the moment. There's certainly been plenty of meetings of the senior partners over the last weeks. We only hear snippets about what's going on.'

'Did you ask me a question?'

Kitty smiles and shakes her head, 'Oh no Arthur, I'm sure you'd tell me if you had anything to say on the subject.'

They have moved to the dining table. Rain is rattling against the cottage's small windows, the fire hissing from water coming down the chimney.

'We should have a dog, at least one.'

'If I didn't work every day I would.'

'A dog should be curled up in front of the fire.'

'And not bothering the horses.'

One was named Dare Devil, the other Careful. It is Kitty's sense of humour Dare Devil being the more passive of the two. Kitty always rides on Careful if Arthur accompanies her which is rarely. His attempts at riding end with bruised buttocks and a sick stomach. He can manage Dare Devil walking, but the moment Kitty suggests they break into a trot he loses all sense of balance and rhythm. The idea, the image of crossing the moors on horseback appeals to him and yet the reality is too painful.

He has always envied her confidence which he is sure comes from her wealthy background. Their interests are shared and yet Kitty is always more relaxed about them. Life for her has so many certainties except for their future, the one subject on which they still disagree. She wants to talk about it much more than he does. How can he tell her what she wants to hear?

'People are greedy,' she is saying.

He makes no response, momentarily wondering what they are talking about.

'The law is there to create ways for people to become richer.'

First he thought he was the lucky one. Some months later he changed his mind and decided she was the one who was lucky. Now he knows they are both fortunate to enjoy what they have together, something that cannot last, not as it is with such indecision.

The unknown is part of the intensity. But Kitty has become tired of the evasions, frustrated by his promises. He lies to her just as much as he does to Alice.

He can never leave his wife. He can never give up Kitty and the future she represents.

'I don't think old George Slater has many days to go,' he finds himself saying.

'Arthur, you said that last week,' Kitty reminds him, 'And you said you thought Harry might sell the business.'

'Yes, he might. I hope he doesn't. He's a bit of a waff but at least he knows enough about the trade to keep it going.'

'A waff?'

'A bit all over the place.'

'Not like you.'

'Of course not.'

Her remark is another implication. He almost enjoys the fact she is sounding sarcastic. It means she has not abandoned their uncertain future.

She has a finely structured face with high cheek bones that emphasise her large eyes. As usual she is picking at her food, moving it around with her fork.

'Eventually you'll tell me what you did in the war.'

Sometimes it is too much, too perfect and then he doubts all of it. None of his past affairs in any way compare with what he feels about Kitty. She is smart, fourteen years younger with a long, well shaped body that he constantly dreams about on rare nights when he is sober.

'You know what I did,' he finds himself saying.

Kitty pulls a quizzical expression before sighing.

'Learnt how to drink and smoke,' he continues.

'Learnt more than that.'

The sound of her horses in the stables across the yard come over the noise of the rain.

'They don't like it when it's as bad as this,' Kitty says.

It can seem unreal when he is conscious of what he experiences with her. It is what he does not want to lose. Another war threatens all of it.

'You don't ask about my past,' Kitty continues.

'That's because I'm more interested in you now.'

'You should want to know what I was like as a child, in my teens, as a young woman.'

'You still are a young woman. Anyway, I don't want to know everything I missed out on.'

'You didn't miss that much.'

'I find that hard to believe.'

'But you tell me so little, I have to imagine what you used to be like. You've never shown me a photograph of you when you were younger.'

He makes no response to this. He leaves the rest of his food and refills their glasses. On nights like this he tries to balance drinking and making love. The last thing he wants is to end up lying unconscious across Kitty's bed.

'At least thank God I was educated enough to keep up with you.'

Kitty laughs at his remark and raises her glass to him.

He wonders what she really thinks about him. There is no doubt she is eager that they live together although she has never mentioned him divorcing Alice, as though marriage is not a requirement.

Her dining table has a cluster of flickering candles in the centre.

Kitty gets up and comes over to bend down and kiss him on the lips. Her tightened mouth softens into this long kiss as she runs her fingers through his thick hair.

When she stops and stands away he looks up at her saying, 'I like it when you do that.'

'Yes,' Kitty answers.

The rain rattles against the cottage's small windows. Arthur feels content and roused at the same time. His emotions with her are never straightforward. They create a bubble of unreality from which he never escapes.

'Was the war that awful?'

She has sat back down across from him, her face illuminated in the candles' shifting light.

'I don't think about it.'

Her tone is suddenly serious and he knows he has to defend himself. She can be like a surgeon cutting through the tissue of his past, probing areas into which he does not want to go. And she cannot leave it. Kitty is determined to know all there is to know about him. It is as if she too suspects his lies, understanding what deceptions he has to construct for his family so they can spend a night together.

Does she trust him? How can she knowing what she knows? Except moving in with her there is nothing else he can do and that at the moment is impossible.

'Soldiers never forget,' she says, 'Or so they say.'

'I was never a soldier.'

'You were in the war.'

'But not fighting.'

'I know that. I know you were a messenger and then a stretcher bearer which was supposed to be the most dangerous job there was.'

'I finished up driving.'

'An ambulance.'

'Do we have to talk about this?'

Kitty smiles and asks him if he wants any cheese. He gets up to stand in front of the fire and light a cigarette.

'You look handsome standing there.'

'And you look wonderful.'

'I'm glad you think so.'

'I most certainly do.'

The music stops. From the stables comes the noise of the unsettled horses.

Arthur waits for Kitty's reaction. When she does not move he relaxes thinking about how easy it is to be with her when they share this sort of mood. He knows her social level is a lot higher than his. He knows how wealthy her parents are. She is a challenge and yet is surprisingly needy at the same time. She can threaten him, tease him, draw him into areas of his life he does not want to go. But he knows this is the best chance of a new future he has ever had and is not about to lose it, not if he can help it.

He can see imagine in her Leeds office, so professional, dignified, smart, efficient, sitting and walking straight backed with her hair perfectly in place, her high heels emphasising the shape of her calves, her business jacket and skirt discreet but fashionable. It is a fantasy image, one he wants to take to pieces by physically, lovingly attacking her with his mouth and hands.

Soon she will come to him. He is only slightly drunk, full of that warmth of expectancy. This is the best of times when everything intimate is possible between them.

He finishes his cigarette, tosses what was left into the fire and watches as she pushes back her chair and asks him whether he is ready for bed, the daftest question imaginable.

'Of course,' he answers.

'Good.'

'Yes, it is.'

'Will you put up the fire guard? I don't want the place burning down in the middle of the night.'

So long as they are in bed together the cottage can burn down around them. He will not care. How could he? Nothing is better than what is to come.

CHAPTER TEN

Mary is waiting. She hears him in the hallway shaking out his mac before he comes into the kitchen. He looks surprised.

'Had a good evening father?' she asks before he has time to sit down.

His reddened eyes narrow as he sighs, wipes his mouth with the back of his hand and then answers, 'Don't start Mary.'

'I'm just asking.'

'No. you're not.'

'Well go on then father, what am I doing?'

She feels love and contempt for this man in a confusion of response to the life he leads. She admires and is disgusted by him and has never had any idea how to solve such an equation.

'You should be in bed,' he tries.

At that she takes a packet of cigarettes from the kitchen table and watches him as she lights one.

Clumsily he goes into the larder to bring out half a loaf of bread, a dish of butter and some wrapped up cheese.

Ignoring her he sits at the table and starts on his supper.

'Drink makes you hungry, doesn't it?' she asks.

She feels nervous and angry. Two hours ago Sylvie went to bed and since then she has been sitting here waiting by a meagre fire listening to the rain lashing down in the back yard.

The smoke from her cigarette trails towards the hearth. She watches him tear off chunks of bread and cut thick slices of cheese. He eats quickly, greedily.

'So what are you standing there for?' he finally asks.

'Waiting for you to tell me what sort of night you've had.'

'None of your business.'

'Of course it isn't. That's what you think about everything, that none of it is our business.'

'And you're going to tell me I'm wrong.'

'I hear the rumours, the gossip. You can't live in Skipton and get away with anything.'

'How's your mother? And how about making me a pot of tea?'

She refuses to be bullied by him, to back down as he expects.

'Mother's asleep I think and yes I'll make you some tea if you tell me where…..'

'Mary!' he cuts in, 'Stop all this nonsense, stop it now.'

But she cannot. She feels too bitter towards him, too confused and threatened.

'At least you're home for once at a reasonable time,' she persists.

He stops eating, takes a handkerchief out of his jacket pocket to wipe his mouth with and says back strongly, 'Stop sounding so bloody sarcastic. It doesn't work, not on me anyway. I thought you would have known that by now.'

'I know you're hardly ever here.'

'And I suppose you are.'

'More than you, which isn't hard seeing there's hardly an evening when you're not out somewhere or other. You must have so many friends, so many committee meetings to attend and games to watch.'

'And don't forget the debating society.'

'Yes, that as well. You're a busy man father, a busy man.'

Then suddenly she cannot persist. Her mood is unsustainable. Her resistance to him fails as it so often does when she begins to regret, begins to need him more than hate him.

She tosses her cigarette into the fire feeling angrily disappointed at herself.

As she passes he takes her hand, 'We're on the same side Mary. You never forget that.'

'Goodnight,' she says as he releases her and lets her go along the hallway.

On the landing she stops, pushes open her mother's door a little wider to see her asleep, her face more swollen than it was the day before.

In her bedroom she quickly undresses as the rain rattles against the window. Sylvie is turned to the wall away from her. Mary puts on her nightgown and slips under the covers. She pulls them up to her chin, turns off the bedside light and lies there in the semi darkness listening to the rain and the wind.

She is angry at herself. It is always the same. With her father she can go so far but no further. She is terrified that everything she suspects about him is true, scared that for once Skipton gossip might not be wrong. Her need to love him and have his love in return is still too strong in her. He is the only man she is desperate to trust, to believe in, to feel he is not a threat. She knows he is too deviously strong to admit to anything even the betrayal of his very sick wife.

She understands it. She has always hated illness, the body's failure, being incapacitated in anyway. And yet for him to have his sordid affairs while his wife lies so ill upstairs is beyond anything acceptable. It disgusts her. He is her father. As a child she yearned for him to show her affection, yearned for the love in return for what she felt for him. Even then it was never there. It was the war aunt Rose has told her many times. He came back a different person, but she has no memories of him before he left. How is she to know what he was like and how much he changed?

She turns over, closes her eyes and listens to the rain. She feels the darkness outside, Skipton locked into the last of winter and then hears a vehicle going along the Keighley Road. Where is it going? She has never been further than Leeds so has to imagine anywhere different.

London, New York, Paris are places full of the most wonderful department stores. She would love to work in Harrods or Macey's, to be part of such amazing establishments and dream of becoming a floor manager.

Fantasies live like memories, secret, changing from one thing into another, transformed by the imagination. She wants to be released from the dread she has of her father's lies and her mother's illness and allow herself to dream of such Hollywood futures.

But as she tries to block out any more thoughts she suddenly has an image of herself with Shirley, Doris and Maggie on that train to Morecambe all those years ago, four teenagers on a summer's day out. It is a journey that has haunted ever since.

She pushes the memory back to be replaced by a conversation she and Aunt Rose once had.

'Your father is a complicated man Mary. I've never felt I understood him, and I certainly don't understand him now. I only see him once every few months which doesn't leave me much to go on. Mind you with Alice like she is no wonder he doesn't get round a lot. Maybe it's my fault. I should make an effort to come round to your house when he's finished work.'

Mary can find no excuse for anything her father does or does not do. She hoped her aunt could help her understand more about him, but the more she talked about when they were children the less any of it made any sense.

'He was ever so fat when nobody was fat. It was our mother who thought the answer to everything was food, was to eat all you could.'

'I can't imagine him fat,' Mary remembers saying as she sipped at her glass of sherry and nibbled on a biscuit.

'The other children on the street were always calling him names.'

'And what did he do?'

'Sometimes he went fighting and at other times he just got upset and ran home crying. It depended on who it was calling him names.'

'He was different.'

'He looked different and he thought differently, but more than that he got so worked up about everything. He was too emotional. Everything was at an extreme. He used to really worry my mother and father. They had no idea what he was going to come out with next. They never understood him and to be honest neither did I.'

'Does anyone really understand somebody else?'

Aunt Rose smiled but her expression was one of puzzlement, 'Or if you look at it the other way does anyone understand themselves?'

'I think more than other people do.'

'You might be right Mary. I hope you're right.'

When she finally left Aunt Rose came with her to the front door.

'You take care Mary and give your mother my love.'

'And father?' Mary asked as she stepped out onto the pavement.

'Oh yes, him as well.'

'I'll see you on Wednesday.'

'Yes, see you Wednesday.'

At the bottom of the hill Mary turned to see her aunt still standing in the doorway before she waved and went back into the house.

The next morning the rain has stopped leaving a cold wind to blow down the High Street as Mary makes her way to work.

'If you love someone there's nothing to be afraid of, but if you don't love them then there's everything to be afraid of.'

Ever since her aunt said those words she has been haunted by them. They keep being repeated in her mind over and over again as she crosses the road and approaches Dawsons with some of the other staff.

She knows today given the opportunity is the day she will confront June Allbright.

Mr Norris says good morning as Mary steels herself for what is to come.

It is after lunch when she sees June come out of the staffroom heading towards the floor counter.

Mary moves quickly between the racks of clothes to block her path.

'Can I have a word June, just for a minute?'

June's face tightens slightly, 'I'm supposed to be on the till this afternoon.'

'Yes I know.'

'What is it then?'

'It's about Doris.'

'And what's wrong with Doris?'

'It's you that's wrong with Doris.'

'I don't understand.'

'Yes you do.'

'Mary,' June sighs angrily, 'I have no idea what you're going on about so if you.....'

'Don't play the innocent June, it doesn't suit you.'

'Mary, I know we have our differences, but I don't see where you're going with this.,' June says sharply.

By now there are more customers looking through the last of the winter clothes. Mr Frobisher is coming down the stairs from an upper floor and Mr Norris is going towards him as Mary continues, 'You won't leave Doris alone. You're always at her, always criticising even though she's only been working here for such a few months.'

'That's ridiculous!' June responds in a louder voice.

'So just stop it June, just let Doris find her own way and if she needs any help or advice then I'll give it to her, alright?'

'I've never heard such nonsense,' June says strongly as Mary walks away aware of Mr Frobisher watching her from his position on the steps as he talks with Mr Norris.

It has been going on for weeks now, ever since she agreed to help the store manager to stay back one evening to help with the new stock. It had been an unexpected request. Uptil then it had always been Mr Norris who ordered whatever was needed for the women's department.

'George, Mr Norris, is fine about it, in fact he thinks it's a good idea, fresh face, fresh ideas and all that sort of thing,' Mr Frobisher told her.

It was too good a chance to miss. Even though it meant working after hours it was far as she knew an opportunity no one else had been offered.

'When there's just the two of us Mary let's have a little informality, so from now on you call me James, alright?'

Of course it had been alright. It felt special. Everything about her time with James Frobisher felt special and yet as always she had her doubts.

To begin with it was only preparing for the winter sale but then he wanted her opinion about what spring and summer stock to buy, which meant they started to meet one evening a week up in his office, which had its drinks cabinet, its record player and sandwiches to eat.

It seemed too good to be true and yet she wanted to quash her suspicions and for once relax and see how things developed.

'You're a smart young woman Mary and Dawsons is lucky to have you on the staff,' was one of his compliments.

Next came the promises.

'Bill Norris will be retiring soon and when he does I want you to think about becoming floor manager. It's about time we had a woman running the women's department. I mean Bill has kept the thing going, but I'm sure he'd be the first to admit that he's not the most fashionable or up to date sort of person. Don't get me wrong. Bill has been a true trooper for Dawsons. He's served the company well. I just think we need a change and I think Mary you'd be perfect for the job.'

She listened and wanted to believe. James sounded sincere enough. It was said in such a quietly smooth, almost secretive tone.

Promises she knew were the currency of any relationship. Trust was the bank in which they were cashed. She might understand that but needs and dreams tended to undermine such rational considerations.

Mary was balancing doubts against desire and hope. She was being pulled not away but more and more towards the James Frobisher she desperately wanted, the sense of a man who liked her and believed in what he said to her.

'I would have thought by now you'd have moved onto one of the bigger stores in Bradford or Leeds,' he once said as he handed her a gin and tonic.

Dance band music was playing in the background while the corner standing lamps shone orange triangles of light over the Indian carpet.

'I like Skipton,' was her reply as she sat beside him on one of the office's two sofas with fashion magazines on the coffee table by their knees, magazines that came from America as well as Britain and France.

It was as though James wanted to prove he meant business with the new summer stock, that he wanted Dawsons as fashionable as possible, something that Mary wanted as well.

'Skipton's alright but it's....it's....'

James started to smile.

'It's what?' Mary asked.

'Well, a bit provincial, a bit on the rough side, don't you think?'

'I suppose you're comparing it with London and seeing as I've never been there I couldn't compare the two, and anyway Skipton is only a small town not the capital city.'

'We'll have to arrange for you to go down there, see the sights, pop into Harrods and Liberty's.'

'I would like that,' she said too eagerly.

'That's the idea Mary. What you like. That's why we're here, for you to decide what you like.'

The implication was obvious, but she ignored it, sipping at her drink and accepting a cigarette from him.

He stood up to change the record, his expression more thoughtful when he sat back beside her.

'I was too young for the first war, but I could be damn well in the next. Here we are trying to predict what women will be wearing in the summer while our damn politicians can't predict a thing. They just dance to Herr Hitler's tune like a monkey on a wind up piano.'

'My father was in the last one.'

'At least he survived.'

Mary was unsure whether to continue. She felt more at ease with James Frobisher than she had with any other man but their conversation was still all on the surface, still carefully considered by her before she spoke.

'He had a bad time of it.'

'They all did Mary, they all did. You must admire him.'

'I suppose so.'

'You don't sound that convinced.'

She took another sip of her gin and tonic and then a puff of her cigarette suddenly aware of herself sitting there beside a married man and father of two children who when not temporarily taking over Dawsons as a family favour ran his own successful cloth business. Being so aware of the situation only increased the tension.

'I hardly saw him when I was a child until he returned when I was five years old. It was my mother who had to remind me that it was my father standing there in the kitchen. I remember I started crying and wouldn't go near him.'

'Poor father.'

'Yes.'

'But on your part an understandable reaction.'

The colour of his eyes deepened in the subdued lighting. They seem to sink back further into his head as though closer to his brain and the thoughts he was having. It was these thoughts she wanted to know more about. Was this just seduction and therefore so embarrassingly obvious? Did he think with her it could be that simple, that tawdry? Or was he just playing a game, the married man looking for a little diversion, having a Skipton woman on the side? Was he really interested in her ideas, her opinions or just going through the smooth, clever, cultured motion towards what he wanted?

Doubt created the excitement. Vanity made her feel he was honest and caring. Nothing was going to happen unless she wanted it.

She started to look forward to what he called their planning meetings.

'Nineteen Thirty Eight Mary,' he said one night, 'And it feels like a year that's in the balance.'

He was wearing a different suit, dark blue with matching waistcoat, a light blue shirt and green patterned tie. His brogues were highly polished as his face appeared in the light from the two corner lamps, his skin shining and smooth except for his carefully trimmed moustache.

'If you love someone there's everything to be afraid of,' Mary now thought contradicting her aunt. Fear could go deeper than any other emotion. It was the bedrock of her feelings.

It was only when she was with him that Mary was not nervous about James Frobisher.

'My father thinks it's all nonsense. He's blames people like you,' she said while James turned to look at her.

'Oh us lot, us business types, is that what he's saying? I don't think Hitler or Stalin or Franco see themselves as mere business men.'

'It's all to make profits out of different industries.'

'Well, he's right about that especially if you have anything to do with the arms industry. But never mind that, what about you Mary?'

'What about me?'

'I'd like to know more about you, that's all. We've been working together like this for weeks now and yet I feel I hardly know you.'

'There's far too much to know. It would take far too long,' she found herself confident enough to joke.

'Oh I see, if that's the case a brief outline will have to do,' he joked back.

'Can you draw a person so all is revealed?'

'Depends on what pose they take.'

In her Hollywood version she wants it to all to end happily, one kiss as the music plays and the sun sets on a glorious romance. It is the version she has been brought up on, years and years of the cinema's magical formula. She knows it is not possible and resents the fact. She needs something different if this relationship is to survive. Is that what this is, a relationship? Her friend Shirley is constantly telling her it is the complete opposite, only another married man wanting a quick affair. James is at Dawsons on a temporary basis which according to Shirley will be the perfect getaway after he has got what he wants.

He has patted her on the shoulder, touched her hand when they were turning magazine pages and offered her a growing number of gin and tonics as the weeks go by. The longer it can go on like this the more comfortable she will be. She wants to avoid any decision about him. She wants to stop being over anxious about the future. Her nervousness can destroy everything. She has to keep it in check and yet the more she sees of him the more uncertain she becomes. The dilemma is growing and she hates having such doubts opposing the need she has.

But in the end nothing can happen beyond kissing and patting. She knows that. It is the only certainty. Memories of that day out at Morecambe resonate through every moment she shares with James Frobisher and that will never change.

'I met Edward at a summer tea party held in the Castle courtyard. It was all very smart. All the town's dignitaries were there. People in those days were very careful about what they said in a social setting like that. I was seventeen at the time and knew very little about anything really. I'd lived up till then a very sheltered life. My mother and father had made sure of that.'

Mary is walking along the High Street to work and is thinking about the last visit to her aunt's. It was still not what she had wanted, but what she wanted she now realised was an impossible question to ask or even infer. How could she inquire about such a delicate, private subject? No one talked about it. Sex was a taboo subject, as though people had to pretend it never happened. Time in bed with her husband was something aunt Rose naturally would never discuss. Why should she? It was nobody else's business, especially not her niece's.

Mary knew about all the physical mechanics but nothing about what it was like, what it felt like. More than anything else it terrified her. To be so ignorant was an increasing pressure. It was ridiculous at her age not to know, and yet how could one find out without trying it, without going all the way and that Mary knew she could never do. It was a blight on her life, an ultimate frustration, but one she accepted as unavoidable.

At least Sylvie had enjoyed herself at the dance. Instead of being a perennial wallflower she had straightaway got on the dance floor first with Shirley and then with anyone else who asked her. Even though her sister had drunk nothing but lemonade she had never stopped laughing, dancing, talking. Mary had never seen her like that, the dedicated chapel goer swinging away to the loud band playing that night.

And even more surprising Mary had managed the next morning to drag herself out of bed and go off with Sylvie to the morning service. She had kept her promise instigating a flood of memories especially of her mother up there in the chapel gallery with the rest of the small choir. Services otherwise had been so boring. By the time she had left junior school none of it had meant anything except it had taken another two years to tell her mother that, to admit to her lack of faith.

Alice had looked at her with that fixed stare she had when she was upset by something.

'I'm sure you'll find it again,' was all she had said.

After that not once had there been any pressure to attend a service. All she had done was help out sometimes on one of the Sunday School trips to the Lakes or Heysham where the chapel hired a bus to go every year.

For a few moments Mary was aware of the morning High Street. She looked up as sunbeams shone through a knife slit in the clouds, straight shafts of silver light. The air was warm on her face and hands. It was early enough for there to be less noise than usual. It would have been a lovely morning if it was not for her muddled thoughts that roamed from one temporary subject to another.

She had understood ever since being a young girl that so much of life was lived in the mind. Thousands of thoughts a day bubbled beneath the surface of anything done or said. Feelings, images, fantasies and reactions were pushing for mental space all of the time. She was desperate for some sort of clarity, a way through the confusion and her dread of the future. There were the worries about her mother, her doubts about her father, constant arguments with Sylvie and always what to do about Alec Frobisher. As she approached Dawsons he was more on her mind these days than anyone else, a concern, a threat and more, a need that she did not know how to manage or even whether she wanted to.

'Can't understand Mary what a girl like you is doing in a place like Skipton,' he said the night before in his soft, careful voice.

The sun going behind the rooftops had shone its last beams through his office window.

'Call me Alec,' he insisted, When there's just the two of us there's no need for the usual formalities.'

The large room was so warm he had taken off his jacket, unbuttoned his waistcoat and loosened his tie.

It was his voice as much as his tanned features. There was no accent Mary could recognise. He spoke as he moved in a leisurely, confident way.

'And what's wrong with Skipton?' she asked, 'You're here working as well as the rest of us.'

They were standing over his desk looking through winter catalogues.

'Alec,' he reminded her.

'Alec,' she dutifully repeated.

He smiled, 'Yes, I'm here. I told old Dawson that's I'd manage the shop for a couple of months and yet here I still am after God knows how long.'

'So, there must be some things you like.'

'Oh yes, and I'm looking at her right now.'

Mary felt herself blushing. This was awkward but what she wanted to hear. It was the edge she was walking along, right before the long drop into......into what?

And then she has to react as Mr Bowes comes out of his grocer's shop to say good morning.

She likes Mr Bowes. When she was a child he used to give her an apple on her way to school.

But now there is Sylvie to consider. Until the town hall dance she has never imagined her sister getting married. She knows she will never leave their mother so long as her illness continues. But after that? At the dance with Sylvie being so chatty and alive it had made Mary wonder what her sister's future was going to be.

With all this talk of war was there going to be a future? Such questions only fuelled her constant anxieties. As a child Mary had been always nervous, always bothered and that had never changed.

'I just thought that a smart, good looking girl like you would have left Skipton by now, got a city job or got married or both.'

Frobisher never changed his tone of voice. It was relaxed, friendly like some smooth talking actor who was pretending he did not want to impress.

How to define such pretence Mary is thinking as she walks past the chemist. Does it matter if she knows its purpose? Isn't it just another tease, another part of the game? Society makes the rules that Frobisher is keen to break.

'I like living in Skipton. Everyone I know lives here,' she said back as lightly as she could.

'I run a business in Leeds.'

'I know that.'

'And I suppose I'm taking a break by working here.'

She did not know why he was telling her this except trying to create a little more intimacy between them.

And how should she respond? Does the woman always have to defer to the man? She hates such nonsense and yet finds herself waiting to be pulled by him further into something deeper, closer.

What would aunt Rose say? What would be her advice? How could she live so much in the past? Her house with its gas lighting, stone sink and lino floors was a memorial to her dead husband. At least Arthur her brother had persuaded to have an upstairs toilet installed, but the rest of the house was a damp smelling shrine to her dead soldier.

Would her aunt ever discuss what love and its consequences had meant to her? Mary guessed her friend Shirley was keen to tell her all about it but knew that would only make it all sound sordid and cheap. Was that in the end all it was?

Why the worry? That was part of her character and always had been. Ever since she could remember there had always been the sense that everything was constantly threatened, that everything was about to go wrong. She dreaded such feelings, dreaded change and illness and especially the sense that everything was failing. Life was failing.

'If you love someone and they love you back there is nothing to be afraid of, but if you don't love them then there is everything to be afraid of.'

That had been one of her aunt's pieces of advice, wise words gained from her love, marriage and loss of Edward, the man whose memory she lives within, their Elliot Street house ready for a future that never happened.

'What do you do when you finish up here Mary, how do you pass your time?'

It was another probe, another careful way of estimating who she was.

'I go to the cinema twice a week. I listen to the radio, argue with my sister, just the usual stuff,' she answered.

'There's nothing usual about you Mary Townsley, nothing at all, not in a place like Skipton.'

'I'm no different to anyone else.'

'Just let me, if you will, disagree, definitely disagree.'

'Go on then,' she challenged him, 'How am I any different?'

But his advances suddenly shifted in an unexpected direction.

'I have a suite of rooms in the Dawson's palatial house and most evenings after dinner I sit in my lounge, drink a couple of whiskies and read about the great men of the nineteenth century. That's who I'm interested in, Darwin, Napoleon, Marx, Gladstone, Disraeli and so many others, so many that it makes you wonder about this century we're in. Where are the great men of history? I wonder. Maybe Roosevelt, certainly not the mad Hitler and the pompous Mussolini, what a pair.'

'Always men,' she said with a little spite in her tone.

'Unfortunately, yes. I say unfortunately because it makes you wonder where we'd be if the other half of humanity had been given the same chances.'

Wise words, she thought, clever, ingratiating.

And what about her? What is she doing? Is it only pride that keeps her going or does she need answers to why Frobisher has picked her out of all the girls in the store? Maybe there are others. Has he a track record? Is that why he is here in Skipton and not in Leeds? And where is his wife and children?

Mary trusts none of it and yet she likes and is fascinated by him. Is this more about her than anything she feels about Frobisher, Alec as he wants to be called when there is only the two of them, and more about trying to find a different estimation of herself?

For the time they are together he makes her feel better about everything, but when such a night as last night is over all the worries start again.

She is approaching the shop and stops at place on the pavement to take a deep breath.

Why should everything fail? There is life and there is death and therefore nothing in the end can succeed. It passes into oblivion like everything else. She feels such terrible conclusions and always has.

'Morning Mary,' is Mr Mitchell's greeting, 'Nice morning, too nice to have many customers I should think, but you never know. They might be pouring in by lunchtime,' the floor manager jokes before he opens the main glass door for her.

'Do you like Chinese food?' Frobisher asked.

She is checking herself in the changing room mirror.

'I've never had any,' she confessed.

'Well, I know a smart one in Bradford. It's just opened. Maybe I could take you there sometime.'

When he said this he was leaning across the desk to get something, his hand lightly brushing across her breasts. He smiled, apologised and then said the material of her dress felt smooth and silky and that he hoped she had bought it from Dawsons.

'And if you like there's a production of Hamlet next month at.....'

'I'm not sure,' she interrupted.

'Not sure about what Mary?'

He kept repeating her name as though that brought him closer.

'Not sure I want to....'

'No rush,' he cut in.

'No,' was her weak response.

Just at that moment she felt stupid and immature and hopeless.

Why could she not believe in him? Where is her usual confidence in front of people? Frobisher is charming, very good looking, cultured for a temporary store manager and obviously experienced.

And in comparison, how would she describe herself, naïve, anxious, even morbid sometimes.

But the work day is starting. The changing room quickly fills with other members of staff who all seem to be talking at once about boyfriends and what happened the night before, what they heard on the radio or saw at the cinema, the usual chat, the usual change of atmosphere created so quickly drowning out Mary's thoughts until as she says hello to some of the girls and is about to leave she remembers her father and mother walking her in the park.

She is four or five. Sylvie has not been born. They each are holding one of her hands on a sunshine day with the trees blown by a warm breeze. She is happy but nervous at the same time. Her tummy feels sore and her coat is too thick for the day's temperature. She looks from one to the other trying to smile. She must not complain, must not ruin this Sunday afternoon walk. But something is wrong and she has no idea what it is.

In the sh

CHAPTER ELEVEN

The light outside has gone. Arthur closes the curtains and turns to her.

'Would you like me to put more coal on the fire?'

Alice is trying to control her sadness. The sense of time transforms feelings in that way. What is good becomes a longing for it never to end. And just now these moments are precious and so become almost overpowering.

'I want you to sit here,' she says, patting the bed.

Arthur does as she asks.

'You've heard the news then?'

Alice nods before saying, 'The BBC said the Austrians welcomed the Germans with open arms.'

'That doesn't surprise me.'

'It only makes things worse. It makes Hitler think he can do anything he likes. He's not going to stop there. Why should he when he can get away with just taking over other countries?''

'Which at the moment is exactly what's happening.'

'At some point we're going to have to stand up to him. We can't just let him carry on thinking he can do what he likes.'

'It must be the worse for the French. At least we have the channel. At least we have that.'

'It won't stop German planes.'

'No, you're right Alice, the channel can't do that. It's saved us in the past but it won't any longer, not unless Hitler tries to invade with ground troops. That would be a different story all together.'

She watches his expression changing as he speaks. His face can look so grave and then quickly soften into sympathy and concern.

'Would you like me to go and get the paper?' he adds then, 'So you can read the latest on what's happening.'

Alice shakes her head, 'No, I just want you here.'

He takes her swollen hand and smiles, 'Well that's what I'll do, I'll stay right here.'

Downstairs the radio is playing. Someone is calling from the back lane, a strangely distant sound echoing between the two rows of houses.

'I hear our Sylvie had a good time at the dancing,' Arthur comments.

'Her and Mary both looked lovely. Sylvie was wearing the dress that Mary made for her. She looked really smart in it. And yes, she did have a good time. That's all she's been talking about for the last days.'

'It takes something to keep up with Mary and Shirley.'

'I'm glad she enjoyed herself. You must give her more time Arthur when you can so she can get out more.'

'I suggest it, but she says she'd rather be here. I can't force her. But I'll mention it again and see what she says. I'm all in favour of Sylvie enjoying herself, but I'm not sure she's that bothered. I reckon she'd rather be here, at home looking after you.'

'And I don't think that's a good thing. She should want to be with her friends.'

The call from outside grows louder and then stops. Such a sudden silence emphasises the quietness of yet another cold night. Alice wants to be outside in the streets of the town walking arm and arm with her husband, up the wide High Street with its cobbles either side of the road. She sees herself walking around the busy market and then down past the cattle mart with its cows, sheep, pigs, hens, geese, all in their separate fenced off areas with the auctioneer shouting the odds and groups of farmers gathered round trying to appear uninterested.

But tonight she wants him near her. It is reassurance she needs.

'I enjoyed Christmas,' she unexpectedly remarks, I thought I wouldn't this year with me not being able to be downstairs, but I did.

Arthur laughs and grips her hand tighter, 'That was months ago, what brought that on?'

'I just did, the way you all came up with your presents and we all had sherry and….'

'Sat with trays on out knees, Sylvie on one side of the bed, Mary on the other and me on the chair all having our Christmas dinner.'

'It was nice, especially Mary joining in,' Alice says as she looks at him intently.

'And why shouldn't she? She enjoyed it as much as anyone. I could tell. Mary might be difficult to read sometimes but you can always tell when she's enjoying herself.''

'I'm glad you think she was alright. Nowadays whenever I see her, which is rare, I can never tell what sort of a mood she's in.'

'Anyway, tomorrow I have to go and see old Mr Slater,' Arthur announces, 'I suppose it's about the new warehouse they're thinking of building, expanding the business. It'll make a big difference and help get the yard better organised.'

With her free hand Alice pushes back stands of hair from her face, 'I thought you now only dealt with Paul.'

'I do until something important crops up and then his father wants my input as well as his son's. It's good he gets me involved. Most bosses wouldn't do that. Old Mr Slater has always been like that with me. I've been lucky.'

Downstairs the radio is playing the usual big band music. They both listen before she carefully traces the contours of her swollen face with her stubby fingers that are twice the size they were. She knows she must look hideous with everything swelling up including her legs and arms. She dare not ask Arthur what he thinks. It would all too awkward, too embarrassing.'

The room and the light of the fire seem to wrap around them to create a warm, subdued atmosphere that makes her feel close to him. She wants this more than anything. She wants to stop thinking and just for once accept how she feels.

'Do you know?' she starts.

'No, I don't,' he humorously replies.

'That I once believed in angels, real angels who were responsible for every part of the world. As a child I used to wonder about all those angels who had to care for remote parts of the world and the oceans. Imagine being an angel having to watch an area of the Atlantic or Pacific where there was nothing but endless seas, wind, waves, rain, snow and then the odd whale, so many empty stretches of the sea. I used to hope that God made sure that every now and then the angels had to change their areas of responsibility.'

'Angels?' Arthur queries, 'Where's all this coming from? You've never spoken about angels before, and anyway I never though you being a Congregationalist believed in such things.'

'Of course we do. Don't you think it's such a beautiful word, such a beautiful idea?'

'Yes well, I suppose it is.'

'I used to look in the library for any picture I could of an angel. The best were those of children wrapped in angels' wings made of such white, white feathers, beautiful long feathers like those of a swan. What would you do Arthur if an angel knocked on the door?'

'I'd ask him what he was selling.'

'No, I mean seriously, what would you say or do?'

'That is something I must admit Alice I haven't really thought about recently.'

Downstairs the music is sounding out while she thinks of herself before her illness, light, tall, straight and as light as an angel's feather.

Arthur lets go of her hand and leans forward to kiss her on the forehead.

Her voice changes tone as she tries to stretch a little 'I feel like a beached whale.'

'You're fine Alice.'

'I'm gross Arthur. I'm horrible.'

'No, you're not.'

'Well, what am I then?'

'To me you're still the person you were,' he says fondly.

'I wish that was true.'

She can smell the drink on his breath and cigarette smoke on his clothes, the usual mixture of odours.

'I remember the first thing you said to me,' she suddenly remarks, enjoying this feeling of closeness.

'Is this a quiz? Am I I supposed to remember? Your memory's always been better than mine.'

'You said, "This is a rum do, isn't it"? Those were your very words. To begin with I didn't know what you were talking about.'

He makes no response, looking at her with a puzzled smile before finally saying, 'You're in a good mood tonight Alice.'

She smiles back and then asks, 'And why shouldn't I be?'

'I do remember that the volunteers were marching past and you were nearest to me in the crowd.'

'And there was me thinking you'd picked me out.'

'And you I thought you were being very forward asking me why I wasn't marching with them.'

'And you answered that you wouldn't fight a war for a load of rich businessmen.'

'That's right, I did, and I meant it.'

'But you went further, telling a complete stranger that you did not believe that Britain should have a royal family, that it should be a republic.'

'That was me trying to impress you.'

'I'd never heard anyone say such a thing before or since.'

'And then I asked what your name was and before you know it…'

'You were asking to see me again. What a cheek I thought you had.'

Arthur nods, 'But whatever you thought you still agreed to meet me.'

'More fool me.'

'You don't mean that.'

'Cannon fodder you called those young men marching down the High Street and even went on to give your version of what the war would be like, machine guns, artillery, planes, poisonous gas. All that and then you asked if I would meet you on the town hall steps at seven o clock the next evening.'

'And you did.'

'I did.'

'How did we get onto cricket?'

'You predicted that the weather would be fine for our meeting seeing as Yorkshire were playing at Scarborough and it never rained when they played there. You were surprised when I said I liked cricket and that my father used to be a fast bowler.'

Suddenly she feels breathless, a pain firing through her chest.

'Alice?' Arthur says in a worried, concerned voice.

She gulps a mouthful of air and tries to speak but cannot.

'Have a sip of water,' he tries.

'It'll pass,' she manages to say.

'We should stop talking.'

'I like.....I want to....'

'You need some rest.'

'That's....that's what I'm always doing.'

He stands up and puts his hand on her forehead.

'You're burning up Alice.'

'I'm alright.'

'Now you rest. I'll pop back up to see how you are later on.'

'Arthur,' she gasps.

'You rest.'

He goes to the door, 'I'll be up again in a bit, alright?'

'Don't go, please, stay for a bit longer.'

'It's for the best Alice. You need to rest.'

She watches as he leaves and then sinks back against her pillows.

The pain is throbbing in her chest and down the sides of her head. Her stomach is so stretched it feels that if she moves it will spilt open. But more than anything is the sense of Arthur leaving as though he could not wait to be away from her.

A brass band played in front of the volunteers of Skipton. The High Street had been packed with people. It had been a hot, muggy day. There had been flags hanging from windows and tied around lampposts. The crowd too had been waving their union jacks and cheering while she and Arthur had been standing next to each other. They had spoken. Arthur had introduced himself and shaken hands and she had felt a blush starting up her neck as she had told him her name. She had turned to walk away when Arthur had shouted over the noise of the crowd and the brass band that they should meet again.

Can I?'

'What did you say?' she had asked hardly able to hear him above the noise of the band and the crowd.

'See you again.'

Why? Why do you want to do that?'

'Because I think it would be a fine idea, the best I've had in a long time if you don't mind me saying so.'

'I don't mind,' had been her response.

'Well, that's alright then,' Arthur had added happily.

Those few words of exchange had tilted her in a direction she had never anticipated.

She listens at his footsteps coming back up the stairs surprised at Arthur returning so quickly.

'I thought you weren't coming back,' she says as he sets the cup down on the bedside table.

'I said I'd pop back up. How are you feeling now?'

'I feel a bit better, just the usual aches and pains.'

She feels weak but relieved that he has unexpectedly returned.

'You and your angels,' he adds as he sits on the bed and takes her hand again.

In that crowd he had looked so fresh and handsome, eager, clever, sharp with eyes that were so focused on her it made her feel embarrassed and awkward.

'I told Sylvie to keep herself down there and listen to the radio while I took charge.'

'You like being in charge.'

'That's not fair.'

'But you do Arthur.'

He purses his lips and squeezes her hand, 'What you need is a tot of brandy.'

She sighs, 'Oh yes, your answer to everything. That's the last thing I want, thank you.'

'It'll help you sleep.'

He goes over to put a few more pieces of coal on the fire. She watches him stoop down, his back broadening as he reaches for the tongs.

'Is Mary still out?'

'At the cinema as usual. She must have seen every film released in the last....'

'Fifteen years or more,' Alice interrupts.

They talk about some of the films they have seen together and the plays and concerts they have attended. As the minutes quickly pass there is only this sense of sharing some time together. Alice feels drowsy and relieved.

'So you don't want any brandy?' Arthur asks as he finally makes his way to the door.

Her eyes feel heavy. She is tired now from all their talking.

'I'll sleep I think,' she says drowsily.

'Good night then.'

'Good night Arthur.'

'Do you want the light off?' he asks.

'No, just leave it, I'm fine.'

'Good night then, he repeats.

After he has gone she closes her eyes but sleep will not come. She sees Mrs Burrow in her pinny, tied back hair and constant smile. She is handing baby Mary over to her for the day, something she hates having to do and which she does every day except on Sundays. Mrs Burrows, a large woman with three of her own as well as looking after four more always has a worried smile and an inquisitive expression. All the mothers including Alice are working at the mill, the only work she could find, such a tiring, backbreaking job. There had been no time to look for anything else. She had to start earning some money.

Such difficult years followed by times that were even worse when Arthur was finally conscripted and shipped off to France. Years that are now lost under the shadow of other memories. To remember is to recreate and alter the past adding different colours, atmospheres, feelings. Alice is aware of this, but it makes no difference.

The fire in the corner is spitting from it being wet coal. She hears Mary's key in the latch and the front door opening. There will be the three of them in the kitchen, her family. She likes the word FAMILY. It is warm, round, bathed in autumn browns. Has she been lucky? Her painful heart pumps out a different experience, one of strain and lies and defeat. She is helpless. Only memories are the real food for her mind, those images haunting her after all this time, the Jamesons after all this time, Paul and Louise, Molly and Esme. Where are they? Do they ever think of her?

'Good night,' she murmurs as she struggles onto her side, pulls up the eiderdown before switching off the bedroom light.

Shadows flicker around the room. The three of them are talking together downstairs and the radio is still on. She feels lonely and lost to her illness. Heart disease the doctor calls it, a consequence of her first heart attack that had almost been the end.

CHAPTER TWELVE

To be walking along the street with Archie Andrews towering beside her makes Sylvie self conscious especially as she has to hold onto his arm to ensure he does not walk off in the other direction.

'Where we going? Where we going?' he constantly keeps asking.

'I'm taking you to help me at the Sunday school. Your mother said it was alright.'

'Mother?'

'She said you could help me at Sunday school.'

'Don't like school.'

'I know you don't.'

The streets are busy with church and chapel goers all in their Sunday best. Church bells are ringing and for once the sun is shining. It feels as though the town has turned to a new page, a new chapter when spring begins.

'Like you though Sylvie. You're....you're my girlfriend.'

'And I like you Archie.'

They turn round the next corner to see people going up the chapel steps. Once inside Sylvie hopes and prays that Archie will not act up as they find a pew near the back and she ushers him along and takes his arm to get him to sit down before handing him a hymn book.

The chapel is almost full with all the Sunday school children seated on the first two pews.

Mr Elgin comes down the steps out of the vestry and the service begins.

As Archie cannot read he makes a strange moaning sound while the first hymn is sung. Thankfully the singing is loud enough to drown him out. Sylvie is on tenterhooks throughout the service especially when Archie says he needs the toilet.

'Can't it wait Archie?' she whispers.

'I need a pee pee,' he repeats in a louder more urgent voice.

Apologising as they go along their pew squeezing between some of the congregation and out to the entrance hall. The toilets are on either side. Sylvie waits for him as the last verse is being sung. She does not know whether to be amused or embarrassed or both.

'Done,' Archie announces as he comes out buttoning up the flies of his long, grey shorts.

His hair is plastered down and he is wearing a jacket for once without holes and even looks like he has had a wash this morning.

'What if?' he asks before they go back in.

Sylvie anxiously waits for the rest of the question. Archie stands there towering above her, rubbing his face and murmuring to himself.

'We have to go back in.'

'Don't like it.'

'I'm not leaving you here and I have to help take the children to the hall.'

'Don't like it,' he tells her again.

'It's nearly finished Archie. The service is nearly over.'

He walks to the main doors, stops, scratches his bottom, turns and comes to stand next to her.

'Alright?' she tries.

'I like you Sylvie.'

'Come on Archie then,' she adds before taking him back in.

Before the sermon begins there is a pause as over forty children from the first two pews file out led by Mrs Tabbish and her daughter Samantha with Sylvie and Archie at the back.

'Are we going…..going home now?'

'Not yet Archie,' Sylvie answers as the line of children goes round the side of the chapel, up a narrow path to the door that lead into the rooms and hall built behind the chapel. In the entranceway it smells of gas and damp. They go into the main hall with its stage that has wooden steps up either side, one line of children taking the left, the other the right. There is next a wide corridor with boxes full of sports equipment and stage props before they enter a back hall where the Sunday school is held.

Mrs Tabbish sits at the piano as the children sit cross legged on the wooden floor. Archie and Sylvie stand at the back with Samantha in smart coat and hat who shuffles gradually further and further away from the heavy breathing Archie. Mrs Tabbish pounds on the keys as she starts on "All Things Bright and Beautiful". Sylvie joins in leaving Archie to moan his way through the five verses. Some of the children turn round and start giggling until a sharp reprimand from Mrs Tabbish.

Soon there are four groups seated in circles with a grown up leading the lesson on Easter.

'Jesus dies Miss Townsley.'

'He's....he's crucified,' says another from Sylvie's group with eyes wide open in horror.

'That means on wood.'

'They put nails through him Miss.'

'And he bleeds.'

'It's horrible,' says one of the girls.

Archie has sat himself down cross legged as well. He leans his head to the side listening to these young voices, a smile on his face as he walks his fingers across the floor.

'And then what happens?' Sylvie asks eagerly.

There is a momentary silence before Archie exclaims, 'He kicks his football!'

The circle breaks into silly giggling as the other three groups all turn to see what is happening. Mrs Tabbish comes quickly over.

'Now boys and girls let's show our new member just how seriously we take the Easter message. I'm sure he wants to hear all about it.'

Sylvie forces a smile and gives Archie a serious look before she continues.

Later Sylvie feels exhausted with the strain of it all.

'Now please, can we go home?' Archie asks as they follow the rest of the children down the chapel steps and out onto the pavement.

She takes Archie's arm and says, 'Did you like Sunday school?'

"Can't read Sylvie.'

'That doesn't matter.'

'Can't write or read....can't do...can't.'

He takes long strides so it is an effort to keep up with him as she looks up at his shiny cheeks, slicked back hair and buttoned up jacket.

'None of that matters. But I could teach you if you like, help you to read.'

At this he suddenly stops, his face creased with worry, 'No Sylvie! No! Don't like....don't like school.'

'This wouldn't be like school. This would be just you and me,' she tries as they continue along the busy pavement.

'Me and you.....You and me?'

'Yes.'

'Not school?'

'No.'

His features break into a huge grin showing some of his missing front teeth.

'I like you Sylvie,' he says yet again.

'And how was Sunday school?' Alice asks when she returns home.

'I took Archie with me,' is her answer.

'That must have been difficult for you.'

'A bit of a strain, yes. Mrs Tabbitt wasn't best pleased when some of the children started giggling at Archie. I've promised to try and teach him to read.'

'Good for you Sylvie.'

'I hope….I just hope it's not a totally lost cause.'

'It won't be.'

'Mary's at Aunt Rose's, I don't expect her back until late.'

'Yes, she told me that's where she was going.'

'And your father's in the front room listening to his new gramophone.'

'I can hear it, sounds really clear.'

'He's pleased with it. Says it sounds like you were in a concert hall.'

She looks at her mother's milk white, swollen features. At least she has become used to the changes in how she looks from one week to the next. Her body is always altering shape as though she was shifting along an array of hideously distorting mirrors. She knows her condition is worsening and wishes there could be a miracle.

'I'm seeing Sally this afternoon,' Sylvie says as she goes to straighten the curtains.

'I need to go to the toilet, can you help me?'

The routine is for Sylvie to support Alice to the commode before she waits out on the landing until her mother is finished and then finally helps her back into bed.

Sylvie then goes to swill it all out down the bathroom toilet.

'There,' she says closing the lid on the commode before returning to sit on the bed and take hold of her mother's swollen hand.

'I have something to tell you,' Alice mentions in a strained voice which Sylvie picks up on straightaway.

'Tell me what?'

'I'm thinking of changing doctors, of getting someone else instead of doctor Donnolly. It's been nearly four years now and nothing is getting better only worse.'

'But you can't,' Sylvie interjects in a shocked voice.

'I've discussed it with your father and he agrees it might help.'

'No,' again she interrupts, 'It's…it's a silly idea.'

'Be sensible Sylvie.'

'I am being sensible.'

'I'm not saying doctor Donnolly hasn't been any good. I just think after all this time another doctor might see things in a different way.'

'Mother, you've got a serious heart condition, what other way is there to look at that?'

'You're overreacting Sylvie.'

'And I think….think…..'

'Think what?'

Sylvie is too upset to reply. She can feel herself in shock at what her mother is suggesting. Without another word she gets up and leaves the room hearing her mother's voice calling her back but refuses to respond.

That afternoon her and Sally take a walk through Skipton woods.

'You're very quiet,' Sally remarks as she they stroll along a path between high trees just coming into bud.

'I'm sorry,' Sylvie replies.

'Nothing to be sorry about. If you want to be quiet that's fine with me. It's just not like you, that's all.'

There are couples and families taking their Sunday walks in the spring sunshine, all in their best clothes enjoying the first warmth in months.

'Is something wrong?' Sally finally inquires, 'Whatever it is you can tell me you know.'

Sylvie looks up at the mesh of branches cutting shapes out of the sunlight.

'There is something wrong,' her friend persists as they walk along arm in arm.

Sylvie feels heavy and weak at the same time. She can never remember being so angry at her mother before.

'Yes,' she finally starts, 'There is something wrong. My mother wants to change doctors and I think it's a daft idea, a really daft idea.'

'Change doctor Donnolly?'

'Yes.'

'Which would mean what?'

'I'd never see him again or not like I do at the moment and have done for so long.'

'She's doing this for a reason. It won't be about you.'

'Yes, it is. She always telling me I should treat doctor Donnolly not as a friend but as just as a doctor. And I know she might be right, but I don't care. I just enjoy seeing him.'

Sally frowns and says, 'She won't do it Sylvie. Doctor Donnolly is the best there is in Skipton.'

'You tell her that. She won't listen to me.'

'But if she sees you upset like this then she might definitely change doctors.'

They stop to let a large family come past them. The woods are a popular walk especially on Sundays The path follows a stream that runs round the side of the castle and heads to the edge of town. When they reach the first open field Sylvie and Sally turn back.

'It's the only thing I have to look forward to,' Sylvie complains as they cross over a wooden bridge.

'What about me?' Sally tries to joke.

'Oh you're just you.'

'Thanks very much!'

'You know what I mean.'

'We'll just leave that one, shall we?'

Sylvie forces a smile. She is light headed and feels sick. She realises how much she cares for the doctor. Without him her days would be empty. Of course she would rather have her mother fit and well but seeing as that is not going to happen she needs things to remain as they are.

When she leaves Sally in front of the castle gates instead of going home she makes her way along Swadford street and then stops on the bridge over the canal to watch a barge passing by, its blackened chimney belching out dark smoke and its engine churning up the filthy water.

She has such heavy, desperate feelings. Things are difficult enough as it is without taking the one highlight of the week away from her. She knows the alternative will be old doctor Cobden. He shares the practise with doctor Donnolly. Why is this happening? Why is her mother punishing her like this? She is angry and defiant and yet she knows it is not her decision to make. In her own way she cannot imagine not seeing him, talking with him.

'What's wrong with you?' is Mary's first question when Sylvie finally returns home, 'You've missed your tea, ham and salad.'

Sylvie takes off her coat, 'I'm not hungry.'

'Father's out to the rugby club.'

'Good for him,' Sylvie says sarcastically.

Mary looks at her blushed cheeks and moist eyes, 'You've been crying.'

'No I haven't.'

'It's about the doctor isn't it? Father told me they were thinking of having a change if it can be arranged. For goodness sake Sylvie he's not worth it. How can any man be worth it who's already married? What on earth are you thinking about? You're only punishing yourself, only making things worse and you've got enough on your plate without this nonsense. How does this help you or mother?'

Sylvie takes a breath, unpins her hat and places it on the kitchen table.

'Are you listening?'

Defiantly she looks at her sister, 'I know what you think Mary.'

'Well what I think should be.....'

'What I should do I suppose, just forget about him.'

'Yes.'

'Oh stop it!' Sylvie angrily exclaims, 'What I feel about him has nothing to do with you.'

'I never said it did. All I'm saying if you'd just listen is that this is only making everything worse and harder for you. Nothing can come of it. You know that. He must be nearly twice your age.'

'That's my choice.'

'The trouble is it isn't in the end your choice at all. You have no choice in the matter and that's what you're all worked up about.'

'How do you think I feel when the only way I can see him is if mother is ill, is bedbound like she is, suffering like she is, swelling up like she is?'

'You must feel awful.'

'Well I do.'

'It's not worth it Sylvie, it really isn't.'

'You don't think any man is worth it.'

'No, you're probably right, I don't think I do.'

'So how can you know what I'm feeling?'

'You feel angry, resentful, confused, guilty and goodness knows what else. I've always said this family is too emotional and at the moment you're proving me right.'

'I don't want to prove anything.'

'I'm only trying to help.'

'No you're not. You're telling me to forget doctor Donnolly.'

'It's up to you. Either carry on suffering or look for a proper boyfriend, one your own age.'

'Just like you I suppose,' Sylvie says harshly.

'We're not talking about me,' Mary answers in an angry tone before she starts clearing the table.

Her mother calls her when Sylvie reaches the top of the stairs.

She forces herself to go into the bedroom that is smelling of the fire smoke mixed in with the usual sickly odour from her mother.

'Where've you been? You're late and you missed having your tea.'

'Do you want anything?' Sylvie asks in an empty voice.

'I want you to look a little brighter than you do, and are you not going to chapel this evening?'

'I have a headache.'

'You should take two of my aspirins if it's that bad.'

Sylvie ignores this suggestion as she goes around the end of the bed to close the curtains.

'I saw the sun through the window for the first time since last October,' Alice remarks.

'Why on earth are you thinking of changing doctors?' Sylvie suddenly asks.

'It's just an idea me and your father have discussed. There's no need to take it so much to heart. I've told you before Sylvie that your feelings for doctor Donnolly are not healthy and will only lead to upset. How many times have I said that?'

'It's a stupid idea.'

'That's being selfish Sylvie which is not like you.'

'I am selfish.'

'That's a silly thing to say after everything...'

'I've sacrificed. I know mother. I know what I've done.'

'And stop being so angry.'

'I am angry.'

There is nothing said for few strained moments. They can hear music sounding out from the parlour.

'That won't go down well with your father, Mary playing about with his new pride and joy.'

Sylvie ignores this and is about to leave when her mother continues with, 'I know.....I know what you're feeling.'

'How can you?' Sylvie asks in a miserable tone of voice.

'Because I felt something similar once.'

'Similar? What does that mean?'

'Will you listen to me, carefully listen otherwise there's no point in me telling you anything?'

This stops Sylvie from leaving. She stands near the bed looking down on her mother's painfully swollen features, 'I don't want you tiring yourself,' she says then.

Alice's face stiffens. She screws up her eyes as she tries to lift herself further up in the bed.

'It's just....just something that happens all the time....young women falling in love with vicars, with doctors. It must have something to do with....with authority I suppose....with the sense of certain men holding that kind of authority.'

Sylvie is listening intently now on every word her mother says.

'It was a doctor, a young doctor just like doctor Donnolly.'

'And you cared for him? What was his name?'

'Jameson, Paul Jameson.'

'And was he married?'

'Yes, married. His wife was called Louise and they had two daughters Esme and Molly and I was their governess. I was seventeen and well educated in one way, but totally innocent at the same time of anything to do with emotions, human emotions, my emotions. I had such a crush on Paul Jameson, such a total infatuation that I could never stop thinking about him, wanting to be always near him whenever I could so I know Sylvie, I know what it's like and I'm sorry, deeply sorry that you're having to go through anything like I did.'

Sylvie thinks carefully before asking her next question, 'What happened?'

'Nothing happened, not really. I...shall we say....shall we say I made a fool of myself, nothing that nowadays would seem at all serious, and that was the end of it. I don't want to say anymore about how it ended except to say that the Jamesons moved from Skipton down south to a new doctor's practise and the two girls started school which meant they no longer required a governess.'

'Mother,' is all Sylvie can manage.

Alice tries to force a smile, 'So I know, I do know how you feel and I don't want you repeating the same mistake I made. I've never told anyone else, not even your father so this is between you and me, alright?'

'It's sad.'

'Of course it's sad. Anything emotional like that can only finish up with terrible sadness and regret and I don't want you finishing up feeling exactly the same, feeling confused and miserable and desperate, not you Sylvie, please Lord not you. We have been given the strength to control our emotions. If we didn't have that we would never survive.'

Syvlie's face tightens. She takes off her glasses, puts them back on, her cheeks flushed and breaths quickening, 'So you're punishing me for what you did all those years ago.'

'I didn't do anything, that's the point.'

'Punishing me when all you're really doing is punishing yourself. Doctor Donnolly knows you better than anyone. He's been your doctor ever since your first heart attack and now you want to....'

'I said we were only thinking of a change.'

'Well if it makes any difference to you I just know that you getting better is....is more important than anything,' Sylvie says breathlessly, leaning forward to kiss her mother on the forehead before she hurriedly leaves the room.

That night she sits a long time by the kitchen fire. Mary is in bed and Arthur still out. She cannot believe that she is going through something her mother went through over thirty years ago. When she came down she said nothing to Mary about what had been discussed. Now her mind is confused and upset by her mother's confession. It makes her wonder what else she has not been told. She begins to think how naive she has been, how ignorant of life and emotions, how they can haunt life forever. Suddenly everything is serious. Her mother has kept such a secret for so long.

She sits there watching the fire go out. She sits there until finally she hears her father opening the front door.

CHAPTER THIRTEEN

It is a sunny April day which should raise the spirits but not this morning. Arthur has spoken to Elsie about unpaid accounts. She is in the office next door burying herself in more paper work. Out in the yard Jimmy is overseeing the loading of one of Bradshaw's lorries. At least they pay on time. Foster and Mike are lifting up planks from the shed while Jonesy is barrowing some bricks ready for another order coming within the hour.

Arthur watches the pieces of this day being enacted through the window, a mime, a silent performance except the men are talking non stop and the lorry has its engine running. The yard is his stage.

His flask is in his inside pocket but it is too early to start drinking, a rule he has always followed so he lights a cigarette instead. He would rather have his mind empty of everything but the taste of tobacco and the sound of the men's voices.

A blackness crept into him through the night, a mixture of dreams, bad thoughts, fragmented images from the past. In the day time he can control them. He knows how to resist, to blank them out before they get started. But this morning he woke up and it was there, this mood of anxiety and pressure.

His life is so full and yet can still feel like this. This morning there is nothing but grey soil and dank weeds. Even his cigarette tastes foul. He stubs it out and looks up at the truck revving its engine. The men in their shirt sleeves wave it off and return to the shed. Foster takes off his cap to wipe his forehead with a rag of a handkerchief while Mike stretches his arms and back.

It is a good feeling when a day of manual work is finished and your body is humming with exhaustion. He liked that side of the job. At least he can still get out and see how some of the building work is shaping up. At the moment there is a barn outside Grassington being built and a new house in Gargrave. The rest of his job is ensuring all the other suppliers in the area have all the stock they need. Elsie is good at book keeping. He relies on her to do that side of things. She is sharp, with a good sense of humour and has been at Slaters for over fifteen years. He likes her. She is efficient, takes no nonsense from the men, tells Arthur anything he needs to know and sometimes accompanies him when he meets Mr Slater at his house to talk through the year's business.

Now the sun is shining directly through his office window. Elsie has put the diary on his desk. He gives it a cursory glance before getting up, putting on his trilby off the hat stand and walking out into the yard.

In that moment everything changes as a dark saloon drives through the gates and comes to an abrupt halt right next to him. Then nothing happens for what seems a long time. Arthur stands there waiting for the two men to get out of the car feeling a sudden rush of anxiety and hopelessness. These men or others like them are a problem that will not go away. Over the years he has just managed to keep them at bay, but that is becoming increasingly difficult.

At last they both get out of the black saloon. They are in suits with hair slicked back. The one called Gordon is heavier built than the other. This is Billy Smiles. He will do all the talking.

They both shake his hand before he asks them into the office.

'No, we're alright here Arthur, nice day, shame to be indoors,' Billy replies.

'As you like,' says Arthur trying to sound confident.

The following silence is like a sharp knife cutting through the atmosphere.

Gordon shifts from one foot to the other while Billy scans the yard, smiling as he does so.

'I have a hundred,' Arthur finally tells them.

Neither seem impressed.

'I'll go and get it.'

'Shouldn't leave money unattended like that Arthur,' Billy advises him.

He has a Southern accent and emphasises every word he speaks by leaving a short gap between each one.

'Do you want me to get it or not?'

'Not fussed either way, are we Gordon?' Billy asks his friend.

Arthur is irritated and bothered. He wants these two out of the yard as quickly as possible. The last thing he wants is his men wondering what is going on before answering their own questions.

He leaves his visitors and returns to the office to take out an envelope from the inside pocket of his jacket hanging on the hat stand.

He comes back out and offers the envelope to Billy who looks down at it with a blank, uninterested expression.

'Come on Billy, take it,' Arthur insists.

'I don't think so Arthur.'

'Why not?'

'Fuck off!' is a sudden loud exclamation from Gordon whose face is flushed from the sun.

Billy gives him a disdainful look before turning back to Arthur.

'You're supposed to be an intelligent man and an intelligent man should be able to follow simple, very simple instructions. Doesn't that follow? Isn't that correct Mr Townsley?'

'Bloody hell Billy, for God's sake take the envelope. It's all I've.....'

'No,' Billy interrupts angrily, 'Don't fucking start that nonsense again. We've heard all that before and it's just a load of rubbish so give it up and stop wasting our time. You're not the only one we're visiting in Skipton today.'

'I didn't think I was.'

Billy walks a few steps away looking at the stacks of different lengths of wood in the nearest shed that has its doors open. Arthur is too aware of Gordon standing restlessly only a few feet away. His muscles bulge against the fabric of his suit.

'Mr Andrews has had enough. He's at the end of his tether, a patient man who is no longer patient.'

'I can't do anymore this month.'

'Can't, can't, can't. That's all we hear from you Arthur. The needle's stuck and it's beginning to get on my nerves.'

Jonesy appears from the furthest shed, looks across the yard at the three of them before entering the stone building where the sacks of cement and sand are kept.

'We can shout for your men and then Gordon can punch you in the mouth in front of them, how about that Mr Townsley? How would that look?'

'You've never scoffed at a hundred before,' Arthur tries feeling fear's acid beginning to burn through him.

Again Billy makes no response, his thin features tight and threatening.

Down the far end of the yard a barge goes by along the canal, its engine chugging over the noise of the men sorting out more wood under the corrugated roof of the largest shed.

Arthur's nerves are being stretched. He knows with these two anything is possible. Andrews' thugs are notorious throughout the whole district. They drive over from Leeds in their big cars as if they owned the place and they probably do when it comes to personal debt. Arthur has always felt this as deeply personal. He hates the whole business but is more disgusted at himself allowing this situation to arise in the first place.

'I have work to do,' he tries next.

'Fuck off!' shouts Gordon.

'That's what we're doing,' Billy adds, 'Our work, and it's hard when we have customers like you Arthur, very hard. You make things difficult and we haven't the time so keep your lousy hundred.'

'Take it,' Arthur insists.

'No Arthur. It would only embarrass Mr Andrews and we don't want to do that do we?'

'I can't do anything else.'

'But that's where you're wrong. You can do more. Everyone can do a little more or a lot more in your case. You see Mr Andrews is sure there's going to be a war and he wants his debts brought in before we start all that bloody nonsense. Mr Andrews wants everything in his business neat and tidy before Hitler's mob starts shooting and our boss sails safely away across the Atlantic.'

'And where does that leave you Billy?'

There is no answer as the two men return to their car. Just as Billy is about to shut his door he says,

'Next week. Five hundred or you're fucked Mr Townsley, well and truly fucked.'

In the office Arthur takes several slugs of brandy from his flask, puts the envelope back in his inside pocket before putting on his jacket and trilby.

'I'm just going out,' he tells Elsie.

She looks up through her glasses, 'Right you are Mr Townsley.'

'Everything alright?'

She smiles and nods, 'Yes, everything's fine.'

He pops into the Craven Herald's offices on the High Street to see about the last rugby game of the season for Skipton against Ilkley and whether he can do a ten shillings report on the match. When that is agreed he walks along to the chemists to talk to his friend John Metcalfe about a game that night of three card brag.

They play in the back room of the Black Bull. This night there are six players and Arthur knows them all except one young farmer who has never been at the game before.

The anger and disgust from the morning's confrontation is still burning brightly. To begin with he is so wound up he plays badly, losing too much too early. He is also drinking quickly hoping the brandy and pints of best bitter might slow him down and eventually help him concentrate. Now he desperately, too desperately seeks to remain calm. The young farmer to begin with is doing most of the winning which Arthur cannot stop himself resenting. Then halfway through the evening things begin to change. The smoke filled atmosphere in the large room seems to relax. They are playing round the large, round mahogany table, the prize possession of the Black Bull, and Arthur is beginning to find his form. Now the cards are on his side while the other players especially the young lad from Hawes way begins to lose concentration. The others are getting drunk while Arthur is feeling that warm, slow glow sending him smoothly towards the next winning hand.

'You were well in tonight,' John says to him as later they walk down the High Street with the town hall clock striking eleven.

The next day he is down at the rugby pitch early looking for Sam Twistleton the head groundsman who takes all the bets.

'Bloody hell Arthur, you must be desperate,' says Sam when he hears what Arthur is wanting, 'Fifty pounds on Skipton when they haven't beaten Ilkley in Christ knows how long. That's a hell of a lot of money. I'll have to check with Donny and Graham whether it's alright.'

'We'll win today. Gentlemen we are going to win!' Arthur announces to the rest of the club house where the women are busy getting pork pies and sandwiches ready for the end of the game.

Outside there is a muted roar from the larger than usual crowd as the players come onto the field.

Arthur tries to calm himself. Even if Skipton come through his winnings will be still only a fraction of what he owes Andrews. It is a never ending game of give and take with the threat of violence in the background, always that. It is a sound droning through his brain like a low alarm system.

He waits and drinks. The club house is filling up. The atmosphere is becoming like the old days, loud, crowded, arguments, pints being swilled, more pies and sandwiches consumed.

Finally he goes out to see what is happening. The scoreboard on the halfway line tells him everything he needs to know.

In a few minutes it is over. Arthur lights a cigarette as the mud splattered players pass him to loud clapping and some cheering from those who have gathered outside the club house. He has made more than expected. He has held back the likely fist in the face for another few weeks. It is a bitter sweet feeling, relief mixed in with anxiety. Debt to a thug like Andrews can never be resolved. Arthur has realised a long time ago that it will be an endless struggle. But there is nothing he can do about it except hope that like today lady luck stays with him and produces a miracle.

'Never thought it,' says Sam Twistleton, the club's groundsman as Arthur approaches.

'Had to happen sometime,' he replies.

'The lads did well.'

'They did.'

'Grand way to end the season,' Sam adds in his gravely voice.

For the next hour Arthur drinks in the club house before going on to the Black Bull. Later outside his house he fumbles with the keys desperate for a pee.

'Bloody hell,' he mutters to himself before eventually finding the keyhole and opening the door.

Quickly he mounts the stairs to the bathroom. He comes out onto the landing trying to make as little noise aspossible. There are no lights on in the girls' bedroom or Alice's so he quietly goes back down to the kitchen.

Mary is seated at the table framed by the light from the fire.

Arthur is about to say something but changes his mind. The last thing he needs is another row with his eldest daughter.

'You don't look well,' is the first thing he says before he notices the bottle of gin and half filled glass on the table.

'I had to leave work early,' Mary explains in a strained tone of voice.

Arthur is taking off his jacket when he asks, 'What's wrong with you?'

'I....I don't know.'

'You must have some idea.'

'I just don't feel well. My nerves are bad, that's all.'

'I never understand what that means.'

She sighs in exasperation, 'I've told you I don't know how many times, I suffer from my nerves, I feel nervous, anxious.'

'About what?'

'Everything.'

'If you talked about it, that might help,' he says in a more conciliatory tone before he sits by the fire and lights a cigarette.

'That's what you always say father.'

'Well it's true.'

'I think talking only makes things more confused. The more you talk the worse everything becomes. It's like at work. I can't believe what some of the other women working in that store talk about. They have no discretion, no sense of privacy. It's as though they want to become like an open book so everybody knows everything about every little intimate detail of their lives. I find that….well…….it's awful having to listen it which usually I don't. I just leave the staff room on any pretext I can find.'

'It was you who wanted to work there, leaving school as soon as you could when you could have stayed on and had a good education, gone to college even.'

'Oh come on father, you've never said no to the money I contribute.'

'That makes no difference. You could….'

'Of course it makes a difference,' Mary says sharply before taking a sip at her drink.

'And what good does drinking gin do?'

'The same as drinking brandy does for you.'

'Oh, I can see we're in one of those moods tonight.'

'Yes I am.'

'Well I'm not.'

'Good for you.'

He takes a drag of his cigarette and looks into the dying embers of the fire.

'We never used to be like this before your mother's illness,' he eventually remarks.

'Like what?'

'Always arguing.'

'I'm not arguing.'

'You know what I mean. Her illness is taking its toll on all of us.'

'What do you expect? The house is like a hospital. That's what it's become. What mother's suffering dominates over everything and everybody. It has to. It's inescapable, but that doesn't make it any easier. If you must know I hate it. I hate the smells, hate the dread her condition creates, dread of what might happen, dread of never knowing from one day to the next how she's going to be except she's never going to get better. We all understand that.'

'She has a weak heart for God's sake!' Arthur says loudly.

'I'm sorry, I didn't mean it to come out like that.'

'It's the gin talking.'

'Probably.

He tosses his cigarette into the fire aware of the tension, that and Mary's usual accusatory tone. She is strong minded and knows what she wants. He has always liked the way she stands up for Skipton and how dedicated she is to her work. She takes care of her appearance. She is curious, chatty with a sharp sense of humour as well as being sarcastic.

'What are you thinking?' she asks him then.

'About you if you must know.'

'I don't imagine that's a very good idea.'

'And your mother.'

'It'll always be like this, won't it?'

He hears the strain in her voice and senses more than ever how much she suffers her mother's illness.

'There nothing else we can do. I wish there was. Thank God for Sylvie, that's all I can say.'

'Our martyr.'

'I don't care what the hell she is, she's still doing bloody well.'

'Not like me you mean.'

He studies her pale, strained features as she sits there turning her empty glass around.

'Like you said, you contribute. That's what's important,' he tries.

But his words have no effect. Gradually a tight, cynical smile appears as she pushes the glass away.

'I don't mind father. The Townsleys are fated like every other family. Nothing will be as right as we want it to be. Does anyone want everything to run perfectly smoothly? Isn't that just boring? Being a family means a struggle. There'll be trouble whatever happens. For us it's mother's illness. It could be something else just as bad or nearly as bad.'

'So that's what you think, is it?'

He feels himself suddenly losing the last shreds of composure as he gets up, goes into the larder looking for something to eat, changes his mind and sits back down again.

'You think too much Mary, that's your problem, thinking, analysing too much. There's no answers so what's the point? People have been trying to work things out for thousands of years and we've got nowhere. Oh we might be smarter and living easier lives than in the past but when it comes to our emotions we're still in the caves. We're emotional cave men. Everyone has to start at the beginning and learn all they can. It's called a life long education in feelings. That's what it is.'

'I'm going to bed,' Mary suddenly states as she picks up the bottle of gin.

'You're not listening.'

'I'm tired.'

'That means you're not listening.'

'No, it means I want to go to bed.'

He says nothing more as she opens the door and goes along the dark hallway.

Everything eases the moment she is out of the room leaving him to find his flask from his jacket pocket and take the last mouthful. Its warmth courses through him, the fuel that keeps him going and helps slow things down, helps him relax and forget.

He picks up the poker and stabs at the pieces of congealed coal. He can hear Mary moving upstairs. He puts down the poker, rubs his face with both hands, closes his eyes for a moment hoping that when he opens them everything will be different.

CHAPTER FOURTEEN.

There are these recurring images persistently claiming her attention and she finds it difficult to push them away, to forget, to forget forever. That is what she would like to do, but that summer morning is still there, still warm, cloudy, sultry as the four of them made their way to the station.

They were supposed to be at school and all told the same story. In their gym bags was a change of clothing, in their purses money they hoped would be enough for four fourteen year olds having a secret day out to Morecambe.

He was called Andrew, blonde, well built, open face, grey slacks and white open necked shirt with a posh southern accent and tanned skin. His voice was what she remembered the most, soft, confident. Sounds of the fairground mixed in with colours under a leaden sky and so many people, crowds of holidaymakers and the four of them wandering around, laughing, joking, on the lookout. Boys they wanted to meet even for only a few hours. Boys were the aim of the day and Mary was leading the way.

Organ music playing, stallholders shouting, dodgems smashing into each other, roundabouts full of happy, screaming children and it is all there in a brain that does not want it, does not want any of it.

His father was head of the history department at Lancaster Grammar where Andrew attended school. He was going to university to become an architect, facts, lies, happy stories, how will she ever know?

The worst mistake was leaving the other three. She turned, smiled, waved to them as she followed Andrew through the crowded fairground, Andrew with his hair shining beneath a grey sky, taking her hand as they strolled off along the promenade.

How had they reached the shed in that building site? Did it matter? How could she have been so stupid. It was there the nightmare began.

Kissing was alright. She had no idea whether she should have even allowed that much, to touch, feel, squeeze her breasts beneath her blouse. He had such big hands and all the time he kissed, pulled away, smiled and kissed again.

It was when he started unbuttoning her blouse and trying to reach inside her shorts, long, linen shorts bought especially for this day that the panic began, a wave of revulsion like bile in her throat, like acid burning through each moment as this Andrew, this ever so polite Andrew became suddenly the beast on the hunt, his hands wanting to prowl everywhere.

She pulled his hand away from her shorts then pushed him back so she could get out of that stifling hut as quickly as possible.

She was so stupid to think she was in anyway in control.

'Touch it Mary. Go on. Go on touch it,' he began repeating while trying to grab her hand.

She felt it as he pushed against her. It was hard and stiff. She knew what it was, knew what was happening and yet at the same time could not believe that he was already going this far, too far, a long way beyond anything she wanted.

The struggle started. They were almost wrestling and she was first shouting, then begging him to desist. He was too strong, too absorbed in what he wanted. She was of no concern. She was just a girl, a body, a thing to grip, prod, push against.

He finally pulled her hand towards it.

'Go on Mary, go on Mary, feel it, touch it Mary.'

In that moment her disgust, her shock and fear took over. In an instant she screamed, kicked out, slapped him with her other hand and somehow found her way of that filthy shed, running then, running and crying and turning round in case he was coming after her, which thankfully he was not.

Eventually she found her friends at the station. They all wanted to know where she had been.

And had never told anyone, not even Shirley about that sordid afternoon.

She has not gone to work today and wonders if she ever will go again as she sits in the parlour trying to keep out of Sylvie's way. The fire is unlit. The room with its flowered wallpaper and three piece suite is just warm enough. She is still in her dressing gown but has a scarf round her neck and thick bed socks on.

All she can think about is the day before yesterday, such a stupid, terrible day.

'I hear Mr Frobisher depends on your expertise,' was one of June's comments that morning.

Most of the staff Mary realised were aware of her evenings up in the store manager's office. Gossip was a fire burning and spreading along every level of Dawsons. Everything was exaggerated or false or maliciously made up. It was like Skipton itself, a town small enough for a lot of people to know a lot of other people and big enough for plenty to be going on.

'I don't think that's any of your business,' was her reply to June.

'We all share in the life of the store Mary.'

'Miss Townsley, surnames when on the floor. I expect you to know that by now Mrs Allbright.'

'I just hope Mr Frobisher appreciates the sacrifice you are making, giving up your free time after work.,' was another attempt to get under her skin.

But nothing June Allbright said had any effect on Mary. She disliked the woman which meant she had no interest in anything she thought or felt. Her words were a mild irritant and nothing more.

But the sense that everyone else was talking about her made Mary very uncomfortable.

'So what are the staff saying about me?' she decided to ask Doris Naseby when they were on their way to the staff room for their lunchtime break.

Doris stopped, looking flushed and surprised, 'What do you mean?'

'I mean Doris what's the gossip?'

'I don't.....I don't listen to any.....'

'Oh come on Doris. I thought I could depend on you.'

'You can depend on me,' the young Doris said earnestly.

'Well tell me what people are......'

'They saying you're having an affair,' Doris nervously interjected.

Mary took hold of her arm and guided her between two racks of winter coats that were close to the staff room door.

'Who says that?' she asked strongly.

Doris looked upset and sounded a little desperate, 'Just, you know, just some of the women who work in cosmetics and a few from furniture and.....'

'And?'

'That's all Mary, that's all. But I know they're talking rubbish.'

'And do you tell them that Doris?'

Sheepishly Doris turns her head away, 'No I don't. I'm.....I'm the youngest here. I don't think......I don't think it's my place to...'

'No, you're right. I'm just glad you've told me what you have.'

'Can I go now?' Doris asked uncertainly.

'Of course you can, go and get your lunch,' Mary replied.

'And what about you, aren't you coming?'

'Not hungry Doris. I'll see you later.'

That afternoon the tension had begun to increase. She could feel a nervous spasm coming on when her hands would start shaking and she would become dizzy with the effort to control herself.

Luckily it was busy in the store. With the weather improving people were starting to think about new spring outfits. The sun and warmth always brought on a wave of eager trade which meant Mary was always on the move, serving customers, helping on the till, wrapping or bringing out new stock.

By the time the doors were finally closed at six o clock she felt drained and more anxious than ever especially when the rest of the staff had finally left and she found herself mounting the stairs to the top floor. With each step her nervousness worsened. She was on edge. At least there was still the hope that the rest of the staff did not know that the previous week Alec Frobisher had taken her to an expensive restaurant outside Keighley. She had agreed and then had regretted her decision. It was not that she did not have a pleasant evening, it was just that she wondered what he would think of such a development in their relationship. Working in his office was one thing. Going out somewhere was totally different.

On the wide staircase she took hold of the highly polished banister, her hand running along its smooth surface. She was angry at herself for being so tentative. This was the situation she had wanted.

Low jazz music was playing on the gramophone and there was a smell of cigar smoke. James Frobisher was in shirt sleeves and tie, his jacket hung on the chair behind his desk as she entered.

'Mary, come in,' he smiled, 'Forgive the cigar smoke, I've just been treating myself. Would you like a drink?'

'Just a small one,' she replied, already sensing something different about him, something in his movements, his tone of voice, a subtle shift in the atmosphere around him that she could not interpret.

'I hear we've had a good day especially in the women's department,' he said while pouring the drinks.

'Yes, very good, the best of the year so far.'

'All down to you Mary. Can't be bad to know our evenings together are already paying dividends,' he said, offering her glass and smiling before adding, 'Cheers, here's to more success.'

Mary sipped her drink and accepted his offer to sit on the sofa beside him.

'Where are the magazines and catalogues I thought we were going to look through for next autumn and winter's collections?'

'All in good time Mary. We don't want to get too far ahead of ourselves. I thought this evening we'd have a break and just have a drink and a chat if that's alright with you. I enjoyed our meal last week.'

His statement came across more of a question.

'Yes, it was nice.'

'Nice?'

'Yes.'

'Alright, nice will have to do,' he exaggeratedly sighed as though expecting more from her.

The gin and tonic had no effect. Already she was feeling on edge. It was his overconfident manner. Suspicions were beginning to accumulate. She tried to stop her hands shaking after she had put her glass down.

'I'd like a cigarette Alec,' she said then.

'Of course,' he happily responded before going over to collect his cigarette case off his desk.

They sat smoking for a few minutes, listening to the music as the last of the light began to fade outside.

'Is this nice as well?' he eventually asked.

She was aware of his arm laid on the top of the sofa and his hand gently stroking her shoulder.

'I like the music,' was her awkward answer.

'Like is like,' he added.

He pulled her closer towards him.

'And I like you Mary, but you already know that, don't you? You know that Mary?'

His voice was more forceful as she turned to him, 'What do you mean?'

'What do you think it means?'

'That we work well together.'

'Oh come on Mary. It's a damn sight more than that.'

'Is it?'

'Of course it is. Christ, how many evenings have we spent up here together?'

'A lot.'

'Exactly.'

'It's only work James.'

'Is it hell.'

'I thought that's what you were trying to discover, whether I was up to more responsibility. You told me Bill Norris will soon be retiring.'

'So this all it's about, you taking over the....?'

'It's only what you said James,' she interrupted.'

'There were no promises Mary.'

His face tightened and the smile disappeared.

'I'm not looking for promises.'

'Well, what then, what are you looking for Mary? No, don't answer that. Instead let me tell you what I want, for you to be a little more friendly, a little more giving. Surely that's not asking a lot, surely it isn't. In the great scheme of things, I don't think that's expecting too much.'

When he had finished his arm was around her pulling her face closer to his.

Her neck stiffened, her eyes widening as she stared at him, stared as coldly, as emptily as she could.

'Bloody hell Mary, I don't understand what game you're playing at the moment.'

At that she dragged herself off the sofa. She wanted to go no further. Already she felt sick with nervous anxiety. For once the music, the drinks, the atmosphere was not working at all.

'I think I'd better go.'

'And I think you should stay.'

'I'm sorry Alec I....'

'I think you should Mary.'

He got up, went to the door, locked it, walked the length of the office and tossed the key onto his desk.

Immediately she made a move in that direction only for him to grab her arm.

'Bloody hell Mary, you're just a tease. Is that what you are, just a tease?'

'I'm not anything Alec except a woman.'

'And a damn attractive one at that.'

'And how does that make you feel?'

'How do you think it makes me feel?'

'I'd like the key,' she insisted becoming more fearful as every moment passed.

'And I'll give it you,' he said, stretching back to put the key into his trouser pocket, 'But you'll have to delve deep and you don't know what else you might find down there.'

Again he forcefully pulled her towards him so he could put both his arms around her waist.

She stood there stiff and ungiving. She refused to bend, to let him kiss her or anything else. Whatever happened she would not allow this man to do what he wanted.

But he was the stronger, the more desperate.

'Come on Mary.'

'I want to leave Alec.'

'Yes, yes, but in time Mary. Give it time. Give us a....'

'Let go of me.'

'Why?'

'Because I don't like it. I don't like what....'

'Like is like Mary and it always leads to something. You know that. You must know that at your age. That's one thing I never asked you,' he said breathlessly as he struggled to keep his arms around her.

'Please Alec.'

'Please is better but not enough.'

His mouth was forcing towards hers, wet lips shining like two pink slugs, two pieces of flesh trying to press against hers. She hated it, hated his mouth and his strength and his forcing her like this, hated all of it.

'I want to leave!' she suddenly screamed.

He pushed her backwards onto the sofa, but as he tried to climb on top of her she wriggled sideways and got back to her feet.

It was as he tried to stand up that she slapped him hard across the face, hard enough for his head to jerk backwards.

'Give me the key!' she demanded.

He sat up on the edge of the sofa feeling his face. Now there was even more intent in the way he looked at her.

'The key Alec.'

He smiled and shook his head.'

'I want to leave.'

Still smiling he got to his feet and stood in front of her.

'Go on then, into my trousers and feel what's there. Go on,' he insisted, grabbing her hand and pulling it towards the front of his trousers, 'Feel it Mary. It's what you really want, isn't it? You don't want the key. You want to....'

Again she slapped him across the face stinging her hand with the force of it.

He started laughing before she slapped him again.

'You can see if it you like,' he went on as he started undoing his belt and unbuttoning his flies only for her to rush over to the door and try the handle.

When she turned round it was as though nothing had happened. He was over at the drinks cabinet pouring himself another whiskey before he lit a cigarette and took the key out of his pocket, stretched out his arm and let it hang there between his fingers.

Uncertainly she approached him.

'It's a shame you couldn't be more friendly Mary because like I said I want us to be as close as possible, really close. We've spent all these evenings together and what have they achieved, really achieved, nothing except a few silly women buying new silly outfits for the summer and making a few quid more for dear old Dawsons, the love of Mary Townsley's life, the dedicated worker, a shop assistant who'll always be a shop assistant. What a waste, an absolute waste.'

She took the key from him, unlocked the door and hurried down the stairs.

'What on earth is the matter Mary, you look in a right state?' aunt Rose asked, standing at her front door.

She did not want to go home so had left Dawsons, walked quickly up the rest of the High Street, round the corner, over the canal bridge that led to Aunt Rose's house.

'Let's go into the front room. I've just had two ladies round from the church. They've only been gone a few minutes. Now sit yourself down and I'll....what would you like Mary, tea or something stronger, sherry perhaps?'

She sipped at the sweet sherry and tried to calm her nerves. She felt angry, disgusted and overanxious as though Frobisher was about to barge in and start his performance all over again.

Aunt Rose sat across from her in a room that was always dark with its deep red wallpaper, purple carpet and thick crimson curtains. Here the weekly seances were held, a room that to Mary always had a strange atmosphere. Now she was just relieved to be where she was.

'Do....do you want to talk about it dear?' Rose asked tentatively.

More than at any time Mary needed her patience and understanding.

'I do and .....I do and I don't.'

'It must be difficult then.'

Mary tried to slow her breathing. Her head was throbbing and her body ached. Even her hand was sore from hitting him.

'Just try and settle a little if you can,' Rose tried.

Mary nodded and sat on the edge of her seat before drinking down the rest of the sherry.

'It's work auntie.'

'What about it?'

'My boss.'

'You mean Mr Frobisher. I thought you liked him.'

'I thought I did…..No I did…….I did like him…..I do……but not now….I can't…can't.'

She could feel the anger melting into a hopelessly lost, lonely feeling Could she say anything more? Did she want to?

She looked across at the concerned, sympathetic expression on her aunt's face.

'I'm sorry to just land up on your doorstep like this.'

'Don't be silly dear. You've done the right thing.'

'I didn't want to go home.'

'You came here,' said Rose before she poured Mary another sherry.

'I….I thought…..I thought….oh it doesn't matter,' was all she could manage.

'Of course it matters especially if something's upset you,' Rose replied.

She was wearing one of her dark old dresses that went down to her ankles and had a favourite string of pearls round her neck with her hair pinned up.

Mary tried to concentrate. Now she was frustrated by her own indecision.

'My boss…'

'Mr Frobisher?'

'Yes….he was… he behaved inappropriately….he behaved badly towards me and I don't know auntie whether it was my fault or not.'

Rose's features looked suddenly grave and serious.

'I mean,' Mary had to continue, 'I don't know whether……..whether I led him on…whether it was me you see who….me who created the situation.'

'You're an attractive young woman Mary and attractive young women should always be a little wary of how they act, careful, in control if you see what I mean.'

'So are you saying it could have been my fault.'

'I'm not saying that at all. We are all responsible for what we do and if Mr Frobisher acted badly then he is to blame. He's the one in the wrong, not you.

The table by the window was covered in a deep orange damask and had a small aspidistra in a pot in the middle of it. The room felt suffocatingly small and seemed to hold a shadow over everything as if the spirits aunt Rose and her group tried to conjure up were there in the room listening to every word.

'Do you want to tell me what happened?' Rose asked.

Mary appreciated her careful tone of voice but could not respond. She felt empty and abused. In her mind was Frobisher pulling her hand towards that thing in his trousers.

'I didn't want to go home,' she found herself repeating.

Her aunt smiled awkwardly and held her hands together and rested them in her lap.

'I don't know….don't know if I want to be there.'

'At Dawsons?'

'No Auntie, at home, I don't know if I can stand living there for much longer.'

She could tell immediately that this bothered Rose who shifted in her armchair and squeezed her hands tighter together.

'That's an awful thing to say Mary.'

'I know.'

'But you must have your reasons.'

'I always look to you for…..for guidance auntie.'

'I'm a lot older than you and whether that makes me any wiser I'm not so sure.'

'But you've been through so much yourself.'

'I had a husband who died in the war. That's all there is to it really.'

'You loved him.'

'More than anyone can know.'

'And…and do you think when you have a séance that….'

'Of course Mary. Why else would we meet up every Thursday, go to church every Sunday and pray everyday? Of course we believe. It's the only thing I have, the only thing any of us have. The dead are alive somewhere on a different but parallel time level. They are all there now, in this moment and Edward is watching, listening.'

'It feels a bit like that in this room.'

'It shouldn't matter where you are because the dead are always there with you.'

'And is…is your Edward…is he….?'

'He is as I remember him, want to remember him, not a mutilated soldier but there in the time we shared together, out time. However short it was Mary, it was our time.'

'I can't…can't look at my mother,' Mary suddenly starts, 'Can't manage her illness, can't be in the same room, her room, that smells so bad. It's dreadful auntie and I feel terrible that I can't….can't accept her…can't accept my own mother, can't accept how she is. The house is only about her. Everything centres on her and her heart condition. Sometimes….sometimes she swells up and it's awful, absolutely awful. Sometimes it can be her legs and arms, sometimes her stomach swells up like it is about to burst. The worse is when her face becomes almost unrecognisable. Mother was so slim, tall, elegant even graceful and there she is like a face covered in plasticene, like a child has moulded her face into something else. I can't….I just can't live with that auntie. I just can't.'

'It's been nearly four years no, hasn't it?'

Mary put her glass down on the small table between them. Now she did not care what was said. Now it did not matter because she trusted her aunt more than anyone.

'So what are you going to do?' Rose asked.

'About….?'

'About home, about work. You're a smart young woman Mary but maybe now is the time you have to think carefully about what you want.'

'I want to….I want to live here…..with you.'

At that Rose stood up, went over to the window to close the curtains. Her face was relaxed as she turned round.

'Since Edward's death I've thought a lot……..about everything…..about what we are doing here on this earth trying our best to live…..to live properly. The church tries to teach us how we should act, but it's the heart that knows more than anybody else, what we feel, what we know deep down is the right thing to do. Only you know what your heart is telling you. It doesn't matter about anything else. This is your life Mary and I know you will make the right decisions. So please don't bother about anything other than being sure what you want to do. Of course I would love you to come and live with me. Of course I would. It might even mean I'll have the house redecorated, modern kitchen, New bathroom and anything else we might require. It's up to you Mary. I love you, you know that.'

Mary did not know how to reply. She had no idea what she would say next.

'So don't you worry about that,' her Aunt continued, 'I'd be more than happy for you to share this house with me, and I do mean share. You wouldn't be a lodger. The house would be as much yours as mine.'

'You're very generous auntie.'

'No I'm not. All you have to consider is the effect this would have on your mother and father and your sister. It is important but it's something we both will have to face. I have no idea what my brother will think. I'm sure Arthur would not be happy.'

'Nobody will be happy, that's the problem.'

'That's why you have to think carefully Mary.'

'Yes.'

'And don't say anything to anyone until you are sure about what you want to do. But remember this, my house is yours. We get on well together. We learn from each other. The young have as much to teach the old and vice versa and ever since you were a baby I've always felt something special about you. It's the heart that knows Mary. The brain is just there to cope with everything the heart feels.'

When she finally left she felt mentally and emotionally bruised, felt weak, empty, disgusted, angry. Out in her front garden she stopped for a cigarette hoping that everyone including her father was already in bed. She walked to the garden gate and stepped back out onto the pavement. Two men passed the end of the street and by the time they had turned the corner three other men followed them, talking, laughing, arguing, their cigarette smoke clouding in front of them on this mild April night.

Later opening wider her mother's door she stands at the end of the bed. The street light coming through the closed curtains casts shadows across the stuffy room. Trying to slow her breaths she comes round to look down on her mother's sleeping face. It is slightly bloated. There are folds of skin under her closed eyes. But at least her face is recognisable. It is the rest that is grotesque as she looks at the mound under her bedclothes from her neck to her knees. She cannot manage any of it. It is repulsive and terrifying and more than anything it is this utter failure of life, her mother's and her family's.

In bed she curls up as tightly as she can, listening then to Sylvie's steady breathing. There is only anger now and a determination to carry on whatever that might mean. She feels herself suddenly risking everything. It does not matter what happens now so long as she remains in control.

CHAPTER FIFTEEN

It was good to see Gillian after such a long time, Gillian who never married and has worked at the library for nearly twenty years, meticulously fussy, kind hearted, proper in all she did and said. But more than that, Gillian was someone whom Alice trusted, with whom she shared much of what was going on in her life. And above everything was their love of books, the basis to their enduring friendship.

She has just left and Alice after so much talking is drowsy as she always is when someone has visited. Light is glazing the room in silver waves, early summer light and warmth and the sounds of a breeze amidst all the other noises from the town. The atmosphere around her is delicate, peaceful, cherished.

They talked of past customers, new books, other library assistants, the growing and terrible sense of another war. Gillian asked about the family and had commented on Sylvie growing up so quickly which surprised her when she opened the front door.

Gillian was petite and grey haired, dressed in a skirt and matching jacket with a small hat perched on her pinned back hair. She looked at her with such sharp, concerned eyes. They had worked well together. Alice always felt secure with her, which was unusual and gratifying that she could share so much with anyone.

Closing her eyes Alice found herself involuntarily smiling. It was the morning light and early summer warmth and having been with a friend who really cared about her. Gillian Tomkins had been the head librarian for many years. She always sympathised with those men who used the library for some winter heat, taking hours to scan the daily papers. Now she said there were more in the library because they were genuinely interested in what was happening in Europe, who wanted to be up to date with all that Hitler and Stalin were getting up to as well as news from Spain's Civil War.

'It's going to end badly I'm afraid,' was Gillian's opinion, 'And I know I'm not the only one who thinks that.'

Opening her eyes again Alice feels the mood shifting slightly as she starts reflecting on Arthur's reason for being so opposed to a war in which he was forced to take part, a conscientious objector but on political grounds and not religious, which meant him eventually being shipped over to France. Instead of prison he had become a stretcher bearer, messenger, ambulance driver.

'The only ones who gain from war are the businessmen, nobody else. They're the reason for it in the first place,' had been and still was his opinion.

'Milkman's been and the postman,' says Sylvie the next morning as she holds the bowl so her mother can wash her face.

'Mary came in this morning to see me.'

Sylvie looks incredulous, 'Never!'

'I could hardly believe it myself.'

'You wouldn't credit it. How long is it since that last happened?'

Alice takes the offered towel and dries herself.

Sylvia carefully takes the wash bowl along the landing to pour it down the sink in the bathroom.

The darkness is absurd, obscene, impossible and yet beyond is the light that she must follow to find Jesus. Is death coming? It feels raw and hard and terrifying.

Doctor Donnolly says she will be drained on next week's visit. He will bring the nurse.

Alice's chest hurts and she can feel her heart thudding quickly. The skin over her stomach is so tight it feels like it could split at any moment. She feels like a child buried in sand with more sand being piled on top between her head and her knees, more and more. She can see the hill rising, a huge curve beyond which are her feet. The mound is smoothed off and she is left there abandoned for year after year. No tide ever washes away the sand. The wind piles up more until it gradually approaches her head, her mouth, her nose.

How can life just stop? How can there be one breath and then not another, only blackness, the endless sleep? God is the answer to all her fears. Alice feels so blessed, so lucky that she has her faith, that she has Christ as her companion. She will be saved. She will be taken beyond death's dark chasm into the light, into that golden light of God's forgiveness.

There have been doubts, terrible uncertainties. Without the chapel and the support of that community it has been difficult to sustain her beliefs. Alice never realised how much her faith depended on sharing it with others. Only Sylvie has been there as her rock, her fellow traveller. They read from the Bible and John Wesley's sermons together. They pray and sing hymns together. They are the best moments, a balance against all the doubts.

Another day used to be a gift, a blessing. Alice hears the radio downstairs and the low sound of traffic out on the Keighley Road as a horse and cart pass the end of the street. Some of the neighbours are talking as they go by on their way to the market, voices echoing as though from the past, the place Alice does not want to visit. She has all day and night, another day and night to float between the present and the past and feel all of it so intensely it makes her heart begin to race and her head to ache.

In the haze of a summer's afternoon she remembers leaving Molly and Esme out in the garden to go through the French windows into the house for a tray of lemonade.

This is her. This is that young woman, straight backed, tall, dark hair with straw hat, bare foot in a long white summer dress. She enters the house feeling happy, tired, hot and thirsty. This is her confident, clever, thoughtful, ready for anything except for what happened, only a small gesture, nothing extreme but still a motion that upset the one person she wanted to like her, love her.

'Love me Paul Jameson,' she murmurs and then feels stupid.

She just wanted to love and be loved, nothing more. Other than that she had wanted nothing to change. Everything must continue as usual except her and Paul would have their secret.

'Love me Paul Jameson.'

He had been seated on the sofa reading the paper. She was about to pass him on her way to the kitchen when he had said hello and asked her to sit down. Nervously she had done as he had asked. There she was and there he was, both of them in shafts of bright sunlight. He started asking her about the girls and how she thought they were getting on. The question had been a simple one and yet she had hardly heard it. She was concentrating on his face, his voice, his breath smelling of cigars and coffee.

'I loved you Paul Jameson, still love you Paul Jameson.'

Sing to him, quietly, sing a hymn to Paul, let him hear you across the years and know that nothing has changed. That heart is still pumping more blood into the life of the past. Those images are still locked away like precious coins.

Instead of expecting an answer Paul had begun telling her what he thought about his daughters' progress. She had tried to listen but was immersed in the warmth and the closeness of him, so close she could almost feel the temperature of his skin, such smooth, golden skin, he with his short moustache and thick eyebrows, deep brown eyes looking at her in such a way that she read everything into it, far too much, disastrously too much.

She could not stop herself because she did not know what she was going to do. She was lost to the moment as though it was totally hers, as though the rest of the world was insignificant and she could do what she liked.

'Forgive me Paul Jameson. Forgive me because I have sinned.'

She had put one hand on his knee and had leant forward with the other to touch his face, simple gestures that had caused an explosion of grief and regret. Her hands had been out of her control. She had no idea what she was about to do and then did it.

'Alice! What do you think you are doing? You'd better go back out and see to the girls! I'll speak to you later! Now go!'

'Alice! What do you think you are doing?'

'I was so stupid, so utterly stupid.'

'Alice! What do you think you are doing?'

She had rushed upstairs to her room and had burst into hysterical tears, flinging herself on the bed then getting up and throwing herself around the room before collapsing back on the bed, moaning and weeping so intensely she began to feel dizzy and sick.

Alice looks at the scar across her wrist, a thin worm, still pink like a slash across her memory. It remains but nothing else.

She leant across and touched his knee and his face, only a motion of endearment, nothing bad, nothing vulgar.

But his reaction had been loud and shocked. He had stood up immediately before she had rushed out of the room, stood up as if he was going to hit her, slap her, shake her. That is what he should have done, punished her for being so stupid.

The radio has music playing downstairs. She listens feeling waves of regret washing across her mood.

It was Julia who a few days later had told her the family was leaving Skipton and going to a practice down south where they had enrolled Esme and Molly at a good school nearby so that Alice's services would no longer be required.

By the end of the week she had packed up her things, said a tearful goodbye to the girls and with her suitcase and bag had walked out of the house.

It was over, no longer required, all within less than a week. She could not go back to face her family in Guisborough. She would have been too ashamed.

The vicar back then had been Mr Cranson. It was he who had suggested Alice try Mrs Burrows, a regular chapel goer, who had a lodging house on Water street.

Within a week she had taken a room at Mrs Burrows and got herself a job at Dewhursts, the last thing she had imagined herself doing, from a governess to a mill worker in such a short space of time.

She had lost the Jamesons, lost their love and regard, lost Esme and Molly, lost Julia and worst of all losing Paul, gone south, gone forever. For months there had been nothing to replace them but such a mood of bitter depression and self anger, criticising herself, hating herself for losing everything she had cherished.

She thinks now how dramatic it all was, the tragedy of a silly girl's gesture and Paul Jameson's ridiculously shocked and angry reaction. He had been as foolish as her. Romantic ideas could be dangerous and distorted. She had fallen into the trap of her own imagination.

Does it matter anymore? Is it only more fuel for the fire of her self condemnation, the way she can persecute herself.

'Daisy Anderson popped in with the Craven Herald a few minutes ago, asked how you were' says Sylvie coming in with a cup of tea and the paper, 'You probably never heard her because I had had the radio on.'

Alice smiles, tilts her head sideways to watch Sylvie settle the cup of tea on the bedside table and then looks up.

'Shall I read out some of it?'

'I'd like that.'

'Hear about all the nonsense that goes on every Saturday night in the town.'

'I know,' says Alice easily, 'It never changes.'

'The fair is coming. It seems late this year. I'm sure it usually comes in August. I like the fair. Me and Margaret have a laugh, well we did until the last time it came and that lad was injured on the dodgems and they thought he might have broken his back.'

'One of the Smiths who live on the Gargrave road, was that him?''

Sylvie carefully sits on the bed, 'That's right, it was. I think he joined the merchant navy after that.'

'His father used to run horses.'

'With the gypsies?'

'I can see him in his shirtsleeves and braces running one down the High Street, sweat pouring off him. Your father joked he would buy me one.'

'You on a horse!' Sylvie laughs.

'I would have liked that, just to try it but your father was only joking. Where would we have kept a horse?'

'On one of the farms. You pay for its feed and stabling and they look after it.'

'I think we had other priorities with you and Mary.'

'Oh using us as an excuse again,' Sylvie jokes before reading more out of the paper. This is interrupted once in a while by helping her mother to sit up a little to drink some of her tea.

After an hour there is nothing left in the Herald except one of Arthur's columns on a Skipton cricket game that they lost.

'He still writes well your father,' is Alice's tired comment.

Sylvie eventually goes back downstairs to allow her mother to drift into the afternoon, the quieter time, the space between one part of the day and the next.

She finds in the files of her mind Tom, Mrs Burrows' nephew, there in his uniform seated in his auntie's parlour one evening talking about the war, words describing some of what went on. They knew he could not tell them everything. What he did say sounded awful, Alice there with Mary on her knee listening to a description of where Arthur was, somewhere near Amiens, the trenches, the guns constantly firing and Tom saying how men would never come back the same.

Alice thought she knew what to expect, but never realised how different Arthur was going to be on his return, back to a wife, a two year old daughter and thankfully a job held for him at Slaters, their only piece of good fortune.

Who had he been? Could she remember him before the war?

The light is already darkening, a shift of pale yellow into grey into light blue across the wallpaper where small birds have been flying forever it seems between stems of pink flowers.

She had made choices back then. Now there are none to make. Her body is in charge, her illness dictating how each day will be. She is free of any responsibility. It is always now about how things used to be, how Arthur was when he came back from the trenches, a blighted, bitter man who had lost his sense of humour and easy ways. And she naively thought she had been prepared for how he would be.

That easiness had become a dark intensity, his humour turned into a cruel cynicism, his strong, ample body thinned down to a shadow of his former self, her Arthur lost in two years, long enough for a young man to become much older, more tired, watchful, bothered.

'Don't ask me about it Alice, please, just leave it,' were one of the first things he had managed to say to her.

And she had left it, left it up to him whether he wanted to talk about it or not. But from him there had been nothing, except the start of his drinking and his coming home late from work.

That was when the lies had begun.

CHAPTER SIXTEEN

What would she like, really like?

Sylvie is in the front garden doing some weeding when she asks herself this question.

Other than mother getting better she would like her hair professionally styled, new summer dresses and sandals. She would like to buy her own books instead of borrowing from the library, lots of magazines, attending concerts, taking bike trips into the Dales, new hats, lipstick and a pearl necklace. She would like to argue less with her sister and try to understand her father more, have a holiday week at Morecambe, grow taller, lose weight, not have to wear glasses and be able to catch up on all the schooling she has missed and find a proper boyfriend who is not married with two children.

Mr Fisher, their next door neighbour, appears at his front door.

'You're doing a grand job there Sylvie, and how's your mother today?' is his first question.

Sylvie straightens up from her gardening, 'Good morning Mr Fisher, I didn't see you there. Mother is just the same, thank you for asking.'

Old Mr Fisher, who used to own a hardware shop. His shirt is in open at the neck. He has on grey trousers and is wearing slippers, his thin hair combed over the top of his otherwise bald head.

'Your father must be glad the cricket has started.'

Sylvie, wiping her hands on her apron, says, 'He is.'

The old man comes further down the front path, 'You must tell him I enjoyed last week's piece in the Herald with his predictions for the season. He makes it all sound jolly important.'

'To him it is important,' she says smiling.

'Like most of us Yorkshiremen. It's in the blood you know.'

Sylvie laughs. She likes Mr Fisher. This morning he looks frail and is using his stick to help him walk.

'Your roses are coming on my dear.'

'Not that I've helped them. I've hardly been out here this year.'

'You're a busy young woman.'

'I am that.'

'And I'm an old man with not enough to do, that's my problem.''

'You're not at all.'

'That's kind of you to say so. Right, that cat of mine has been out all night and he'll be wanting fed.' He carefully turns towards his front door, 'I'll see you later Sylvie. Give your mother my regards.'

'I will Mr Fisher.'

She is about to bend down to fork out the next weeds when she hears Archie running along the pavement shouting, 'I knocked. I knocked……at the back….I knocked and you weren't there!'

'And good morning to you Archie.'

He stops at the gate, rubs his hands down his shirt front, tries to flatten his hair and then with a broad smile shows some of his missing front teeth.

'You're early.'

'Reading,' he says.

'Yes, good. I'm glad you came. This will be your fourth lesson now.'

'Reading,' Archie repeats as he pushes open the gate.

Sylvie takes him along the hallway into the kitchen where Archie has his lessons. He fascinates her, the way his mood is constantly changing, words from his large mouth flying in all directions and his lanky body always on the move. He is a loveable challenge. Except for her friend Sally he is the only diversion she has from the daily routine. She can never predict him. He tries so hard for her.

She knows any understanding is difficult for him. His mind works in a different way. It is impulsive. He cannot concentrate for long and yet can unexpectedly come out with the most provocative idea or fact.

Archie sits at the table and guzzles down the glass of lemonade she offers him.

'Planes,' he says then after wiping his mouth with the back of his filthy hand.

Sylvie sits at the table with notebook and pencil.

'Spitfire is fastest.'

'Is that right Archie?'

'Spitfire, yes, yes.'

'Tell me about it Archie,' Sylvie tries as she sharpens the pencil.

He frowns, lays his arms over the table, squeezes his hands together but says nothing more as he searches with his large eyes around the kitchen.

'Should we look at some letters?'

'Reading,' Archie replies.

'That's what we're here for, yes, to help you to read.'

'Don't like school,' he interrupts while yawning as he speaks.

'I know you don't Archie, but this isn't school, this is just between you and me.'

Sylvie understands that patience is crucial. So far he has managed to remember A B and C.

'If I give you the notebook and pencil can you write a letter A for me.'

'Draw....draw.'

'Alright, draw the letter A.'

He loops his fingers round the pencil and then says, 'Archie loves Sylvie.'

'I know, you've told me that many times.'

'Archie going to get married.'

'You don't say.'

'Secret.'

'Of course.'

'Secret.'

'Yes.'

'Archie marrying Sylvie.'

'That Archie I didn't realise. Now what about this letter A?'

'Hungry.'

'You can have a sandwich when you've finished writing your letter.'

'Hungry.'

'In a bit Archie, not just now, later.'

Slowly over the next half hour she manages to get him to write the first three letters before introducing the next. But by this time Archie has lost all interest. She makes him a sandwich and pours out more lemonade. His face is now empty of all expression. He looks bored and unsettled. Sylvie knows that the lesson is at an end.

Quickly he wolfs down the sandwich, gulps down the lemonade, pushes his chair back and heads for the open back door.

'Are you not going to say goodbye Archie?'

He stops, his features suddenly screwed up in pain, 'Them men don't like Archie.'

'Which men?'

'They don't like him, kick him, spit.......spit at him.'

'You must tell me who they are.'

By the time she finishes saying this he is gone, slamming the yard door behind him.

She sits there for a few minutes wondering about the world his mind inhabits and how his emotions shift from one feeling to the next so abruptly. These men he mentions are obviously frightening him. She has asked his mother about them but she has no idea who they are. With so many other children to look after Mrs Andrews finds it hard to find time for her eldest son. The Andrews house is a chaos of noise, smells, clothes everywhere and never a sign of a Mr Andrews. The rumour is that he went off to Ireland some years ago and has never been heard of since. Sylvie has got the chapel involved to help the family in any way they can

Now instead of worrying about him all the time she feels only sorrow for Archie and his struggling family and the fact there is a group of youths or men constantly bothering him.

Her father's response when she has described the Andrews home was that no one should have to depend on charity. It is the government and only them who should be doing something about it.

Sylvie finds it depressing and frustrating. She sits over a cup of tea thinking again about the question she asked herself earlier.

What do you want, really want?

It opens an exhilarating flood of possibilities. The question is a key to all that she wants to experience and the person she wants to become, cultured, educated, generous, helping others, but also dancing, going to the cinema, having a meal in a restaurant, having a lot of friends.

Her dreams are interrupted by the thought of a coming war. It would be like her mother's illness and become a huge obstacle to any future she might want however selfish that might sound.

And then there is doctor Donnolly. She knows how wrong it is to weigh up her mother's awful condition with the chances it gives her of seeing the doctor. Somehow she has to stop this romantic nonsense, this need for someone. He is a doctor. She has to forget her feelings for him and concentrate on her mother and her own uncertain future.

'Would you leave Skipton if you had the chance?' Sally asks as they walk back from Sunday morning chapel.

The streets of the town are busy on this bright day. The trees around the castle and in Skipton wood are bright green with a few smaller blossom trees all in pink and deeper red.

Sally is wearing a pale summer dress with a matching hat.

'You like asking questions Sally,' is Sylvie's response as they follow other chapel and church goers who have to dodge around the groups of men waiting on the pavement for the pubs to open.

'I'm interested,' Sally says, 'I'm curious. It's a good thing to be curious.'

'I suppose I would at some point, would like to leave the town.'

'And go where?'

'One question with you Sally Jones always leads to another.'

'I'd like to go to America. I have cousins in Baltimore, wherever that is, who run a big garage selling tractors. I think it's tractors.'

'I can't see you doing that.'

'No, I mean at least I've got someone to go to.'

'Anyway,' Sylvie says in a serious tone of voice, 'I can't think about going anywhere until….'

'Your mother gets better,' Sally interrupts.

'Yes.'

'She will.'

'I wish doctor Donnolly thought so.'

'I thought he did.'

'He says encouraging things.'

'He'd tell you, wouldn't he, if things were bad?'

'They are bad.'

'I mean really bad.'

'I don't know Sally. He might say other things to my father. I just don't know.'

They cross the bottom of the High Street where the cattle sales on market day leave a pungent odour. However much the cobbles are washed off the smell of the cows and sheep remain.

A few hours later that afternoon they arrange to meet again in Airedale Park. It being a Sunday and warm and sunny the residents of the town are in their best clothes walking around the park with their children in tow.

Sally has now on a straw hat and is wearing sandals. Sylvie has on a flowers patterned dress Mary made for her. Whenever she is in Sally's house Sylvie is always intrigued by how she gets on with her father. They seem to dote on each other. Mr Jones has a small printing works in one of the town's narrow back streets near the canal. He is a short, stocky man, always wears collarless shirts in the house and has a great sense of humour. He and Sally are always joking together, something Sylvie envies.

'Your father has a good singing voice,' she says as they start up one of the steeper paths to the top end of the park.

Sally is looking up at a line of trees with their bright green leaves rustling in the warm breeze.

'He likes singing. You should hear him when there's a song he knows on the radio.'

'You two seem to get on so well.'

'We always have,' Sally replies, 'Ever since I remember we've been close.'

'I've never been like that with….never like that with mine,' Sylvie says hesitantly and then wishes she has not started this difficult topic.

The truth is that she feels intimidated by her father. Whenever he is in the house there is a tension around him which makes her uncomfortable. However hard she has tried she does not understand this strained effect he has on her. Even though they argue a lot she can tell he feels a lot easier with Mary.

'You Dad is alright,' is Sally's comment, 'A bit stand offish sometimes.'

'What do you mean, stand offish?'

'I'm not being critical.'

'I just want you to be honest,' Sylvie says too strongly.

Sally stops to let a family with two toddlers and baby in a pram pass by.

'What's wrong Sylvie?' she asks then.

'I just don't have the relationship you do with your father.'

'And why should you?'

'I'm jealous. Every time I see you two together it makes me envious. I just wish things could be like that between me and my father. You two obviously get on so well together.'

Boys are shouting at a game of football, their voices drifting along the breeze that brings smells of the canal and the mills that for this one day of the week are silent.

'It's always been difficult between him and me,' Sylvie adds.

'And what does Mary think?'

'Oh I've no idea.'

'You don't talk about him? You don't talk about your own father.'

'Hardly ever and if we do we disagree as usual.'

'No, I must admit I'm not like that with my sisters.'

Sylvie tries to concentrate on her friend as they reach the top end of the steep park and turn to look back over the roofs of the town and the hills banked up behind.

'You like the town more than me,' Sally says as they watch a kite diving and rising, its colours accentuated by the clear blue sky.

'I suppose I do,' Sylvie answers, trying to sound enthusiastic but failing.

'I wonder if that's got anything to do with a certain doctor living here.'

'Oh don't you start on that Miss Jones,' she smiles back.

'I think I'm right Miss Townsley.'

'You always think you're right,' Sylvie says as they start back down the path.

'I'd take off my sandals and walk barefoot on the grass except I don't know what I'd be walking on.'

'Grass,' is Sylvie trying to joke, trying to alleviate her mood.

'Very funny.'

'Of course.'

'What about lunch next week?' Sally asks then.

'I'll see.....'

'How mother is.'

'Yes.'

'Fair enough,' is Sally's response as they try and shield their eyes against the sun to watch the child's kite flicking side to side just above them.

CHAPTER SEVENTEEN

'It's bloody nonsense and you know it Tony. Stalin is not going to do a bloody thing.'

Arthur listens. The group makes the same arguments, takes the same sides. The only difference is that everyone is getting angrier. They are increasingly worried. They are all concerned men and think they know what they are talking about.

The fire in the top room of the Black Bull is spitting from wet coal. Their large round table is covered in empty glasses and full ashtrays. They have had their sandwiches made by Agnes Armstrong's loving hands and have resumed the debate that is now hotter than the fire.

There are still the appeasers, the ones who would go to war tomorrow and finally Tony Johnston who thinks Britain should make a deal with the Germans and wait for the Russians to commit themselves.

Arthur knows there will be a war whatever happens. The only question is when. Whatever Hitler and Chamberlain are planning Arthur has his own concerns.

He leaves the debate early. At home Sylvie is in the kitchen when he returns.

'The doctor was asking again about his fees.'

She has mentioned this several times already.

He knows it is not fair, her having to deal with Donnolly's insistence.

'I'll give you the money if I don't see him myself on Friday, alright?'

Sylvie pulls a doubtful expression before she puts the guard in front of the fire.

'And did your mother get off to sleep?'

'No, I think she's still awake.'

She takes off her glasses to wipe them on her pinny. Arthur notices her tired eyes.

'You should be in bed Sylvie.'

'Mary's there.'

'So she should be.'

He says goodnight and smiles as she says the same.

The smile is forced. There is nothing he can think of to smile about.

CHAPTER EIGHTEEN

It was in the Craven Herald, the news that the new store manager at Dawsons was to be a Mr Maudsley from Manchester who would be taking over the shop from Mr Frobisher who was returning to his successful business in Leeds.

Mary is in the parlour drinking gin and smoking one cigarette after another. It is two o clock in the morning and she is drunk but wide awake. There is the first chill of autumn in the air which means she is in her nightie, winter dressing gown and thick bed socks.

There is no one with whom she could share any of this.

Disgust, anger, being abused, used, a numbness, a deep revulsion are only the start of it. She does not want to feel. She wants to be emotionless, to be empty of any reaction.

The house is around her like a silent shell. She is smoking quickly, one mouthful after another. Between one cigarette and the next she drinks more of the gin, wincing each time she does from the bitter taste it has without tonic.

Is she to blame? Is it always the woman's fault?

How stupid she had been. She could never win.

The furniture is in shadow from the street light outside. She watches a faint trail of her cigarette smoke spiral slowly up towards the parlour ceiling.

Does anyone wish oneself into a real nightmare?

Is this what she had done?

All this pain just for some pathetic promotion.

But it had been more than that. She had challenged herself.

Her hands are shaking. The smoke starts to rise in different directions. Her heart is thumping under her bruised breasts, patches of purple and grey on her white skin, one nipple torn, one still hurting.

She feels so cold, shivering now as she gulps down more of the gin, waiting for the alcohol to have its effect.

She wants to sleep through the next months, sleep for a year.

What a hideous story it now seems, sleeping beauty raised from her torpor by the kiss of a man, another male fantasy, another sick dream.

Think of all those she used to revere, Bogart and Cagney and Gable and Cooper and so many more, her idols, the romantic heroes of a twenty four year old child.

Condemned by Hollywood. Life played out on the silver screen. Condemned by its pretence that every relationship culminates in a kiss, lips to lips, the conclusion, the beautiful ending.

Mary the child hoping for such nonsense.

She sits back in the armchair, tries to steady her hands, looks at the empty fireplace with its tall blue vases at either end of the mantelpiece, bought by her mother at Bradford market for a few pennies.

Flicking her half smoked cigarette onto the grate she gets up and goes into the kitchen returning with a bundle of newspapers that Sylvie uses to light the fire.

She puts them on the hearth, holds up the gin bottle to see it is half empty before getting down on her knees and bundling up some of the paper. Throwing it into the fireplace she concentrates on striking a match.

A small flame flickers and twists its way into the rest of the bundle that begins to burn brighter and brighter, the newsprint curling into black ash that settles on the grate until the small conflagration dies down and finally stops.

Again she twists up more paper and watches it burn, the flames reflecting in her moist eyes as she leans forward to feel the fire's meagre heat.

In a cinema moment she is walking up a dark, empty High Street. She sees herself in her dressing gown and slippers as a crescent moon appears from behind grey clouds. Its light silvers each of her steps along the pavement. In front of Dawsons she stops, lights her thick twists of paper until they are flaming strongly, pushes open the main doors, walks around the racks of dresses and coats, lighting up each garment as she passes. Finally she leaves, walks across the road and stands there to watch the whole store quickly begin to burn, windows exploding outwards, flames licking through the roof as the heat spreads.

She pours herself another drink. The last of the burnt paper has settled another layer of ash on top of the rest.

For a moment she thinks about putting a record on the new gramophone but decides against it. Her family sleeps upstairs but what use is a family if they know nothing about what she has been through? She knows Sylvie suspects something, but what? How could her innocent, religious sister ever imagine any of it? No, let her sleep upstairs in the bliss of ignorance.

Romance dies with experience. Dreams become only dreams. How pathetically sad.

Block out those voices. Smoke another cigarette, gulp down more gin. Block out all of it.

If only that was possible? Why does the mind act so independently?

Do I live in my mind or my heart?

She sits there shivering with tension.

There had been blood on her pants and down her stockings.

The gin begins to give a glowing sensation that only emphasises it all she is going through. There is no escape. From experience she knows if alcohol cannot help, then nothing can.

Fear is there that her mother is dying. She cannot trust her father and argues too much with her sister. There is only aunt Rose who understands and sympathises. She is the only one upon whom she can rely.

She gets up, walks unsteadily into the kitchen and back out to go down the corridor to the front door, turns again brushing her hand against the wall for support and returns to the parlour. The light from the street is outlining the furniture in the room. The walls are dark. There is the smell of polish. Outside is a row of similar houses with similar parlours. Drunkenly she considers all those lives, thoughts, needs of so many people, most of whom she knows.

But as she sits back in the armchair and lights another cigarette she hears the voices she is trying desperately to resist, hears herself, hears him, and she cannot stop it, wants to stop it, tries, tries again, fails, panics, voices, she hears them so clearly, remembers every sickening word after word, the chorus to the worst nightmare.

'Mr Frobisher, what are you doing here?'

'Hello Mary, just thought I'd come and check how things were going.'

'I presumed you'd gone. Mr Norris gave me the second set of keys to lock up.'

'Well, I've been here all the time.'

Silence, looking at each other, even then beginning to feel nervous. Something was wrong, terribly wrong. She sensed it in the way he looked at her, with the way his breathing sounded loud in the store room where she had been sorting out some new stock, the store room on the ground floor at the back of the store far away from the front doors, faraway from everything and everyone.

He makes the first step towards her.

'Now we're here I want to apologise for my behaviour when......'

'It' doesn't matter,' she blurts out far too quickly.

'Oh but it does.'

'I don't really want to talk about it.'

'Come on Mary, let's just forget what happened and start again.'

'I don't know what that means.'

'Of course you do.'

It takes the next step to leave only a few feet between them. From there she can smell the whiskey on his loud breaths.

The rest has to be only words please. There must be no other memories please.

But there are. They are inevitable.

'Come on Mary.'

'I think Mr Frobisher that….'

'Oh come on, Alec, remember, I'm sure you do.'

'I have to get on with this stock,' she tries.

'No you don't. What you have to be is nice to me.'

'Alec, what are you doing?'

'A reconciliation Mary. Show me. Go on show me you agree.'

'I don't want to have any……'

'Come on Mary.'

'I said get…..'

'There's no need to be like that, just…..'

'Stop it.'

'I'm your friend, remember, so show a little….'

'I want you to….'

'Just a kiss for old time's sake.'

'No! Alec no!'

'Come on Mary.'

'Alec, please, don't do this.'

'Stop……stop struggling…..stop it……you're wasting your time……Mary……stop it.'

'You're hurting me.'

'Stop being so damned stupid.'

'I….I….don't…..'

'There's no one else here, just me and you, me and you so…..'

'Get off me!'

'I want to touch you....I want to feel your breasts and everything else...'

'No!.....No!'

'You've got a lovely body...lovely.....tight....firm....just....'

'Oh my God......what.....what......are you doing......doing?'

'Let me.....let me....come on......just stop struggling.....stop it Mary! Stop!'

'That hurts.'

'I want....'

'You're hurting me.'

'You're just a damn tease Mary Townsley.....Mary.....you're just.......sweet Mary.....quite contrary....aren't you?......aren't you?'

'No...it...hurts.....you're hurting me.'

'Just lie still then.'

'No!'

'Stay down....'

'No!'

'Stop it Mary....Oh!........Oh!......Yes!....Yes!....that's.....that's.'

'No!'

'God I love your breasts...they're......My God your nipples....And up.....come on Mary......up.'

'No! No! No!'

'Up here....yes....yes.....right.....up....stop struggling.....stop it.........right up....up.....up....up...My hell....you're so tight....tight......Christ....up.....up.....Christ Mary....you're.....you've... I never.....never thought that......Now.....Up....Now.....Up.....Oh Yes! Yes!.....Just....just like that.....just like that......Yes Mary......Yes!'

Bruised, bleeding she had somehow got home, had somehow said something to Sylvie before going up to their bedroom where she had laid down, crying, sobbing, angry, disgusted, abused, guilty, hurting.

His thing, that hideous, bulging, stiffening thing, that obscene thing banging, pushing, throbbing into her. It had felt like he was penetrating so far that his thing would come out of her mouth. Revulsion, frustration, shame had all been part of her reaction.

She had done all she could have to defend herself, to stop his thing pushing between her legs. She had hit, spat, screamed. She had sunk her teeth through his shirt into the flesh of his shoulder. She had kicked and lashed out, tossing her head from side to side.

It had hurt so much, ripping his way inside her, tearing and bruising like a dog on heat, the grunting pushing animal with his stinking breath and face straining with the effort of trying to split her apart.

For over a week now she has stayed at home saying she has flu. Her whole body aches but especially between her legs and her breasts.

This time when she gets up from the armchair she takes the bottle of gin with her. She stops in the hallway trying to focus on what she is doing and what she will do next, which is carefully mount the stairs, pass her mother's and then father's bedrooms before quietly opening the door of her own.

It is as she is hiding the bottle of gin in her top drawer that Sylvie wakes up, 'Mary, what are you doing?' she asks in a dull voice.

'I'm not....not doing anything,' Mary answers with her back to her.

'What time is it?'

'I've no idea.'

'It must be....'

'I don't know Sylvie.....don't know,' she complains turning then to hold onto the bottom of her bed.

Sylvie sits up in bed, 'You're drunk.'

'So what if I am?'

'Mary, tell me what's wrong,' Sylvie demands in an earnest voice.

'Wrong...wrong.....you always think there's something....something wrong.'

'Well is there?'

'What....are you going to save me?' Mary asks as she struggles at pushing off her slippers.

'Yes,' her sister unexpectedly answers.

'Oh shut up...shut up Sylvie...please.'

'Something is badly wrong with you and stop trying to hide it when it's....'

'It's what?'

'So obvious.'

'Obvious.'

'I just want to....'

'Help. Help, yes I know.'

Mary manages to extricate herself from her dressing gown before she pulls at the eiderdown that also finishes up on the floor.

At that Sylvie sits up.

Mary staggers against her bed, 'No...I'm alright...alright. Just leave it...leave me alone.'

Instead of picking up her bedding she holds onto the side of the bed to lower herself down onto the bundle on the floor.

'Mary, what are you doing?' Sylvie tries.

'Want to sleep.'

'Why don't you just lie down?'

'I want to sleep.'

Sylvie watches her sister close her eyes before she opens them again, 'Nobody knows….nobody knows anything….they think they do…..but they don't…..they think they're so damn clever….so damn smart when they aren't…….nobody is……because……because there's nothing to know…..we're just animals….just animals…..that's all we are….nothing else…..nothing at all…..like all the other……the other animals…we're born….live….and die…..just die…..so there's no point….no point trying to know anything….trying to understand…..not there…..not at all…..not…….not……not.'

Again she closes her eyes. Sylvie can smell the gin and cigarette smoke as Mary's breath eventually slows into a rhythm of sleep.

For a few minutes Sylvie is sat up in bed looking down at Mary's curled up figure. It is only then she notices a patch of dried blood on her nightie. She starts crying then, silently looking and crying.

CHAPTER NINETEEN.

Alice had read an WH Auden quote: "Britain was a country where nobody was well."

She wonders how true that is as she listens to Arthur stirred up about Mary quitting Dawsons.

'You can't force her to work,' she tries.

'I wished I damn well could Alice, I really do. She mopes about the place.'

'Something's wrong.'

'There's always something wrong, but I can't see our Mary going without new clothes, makeup and all the rest of it for very long. She'll have to find a job.'

Alice hears his frustration, hears his usual anxiety about money matters.

But she can do nothing. Mary is avoiding her.

Now she lies here as the day grows colder. It will not be long before Sylvie will have to light the bedroom fire. The summer is ending, the light changing. She heard on the radio that the Germans have taken over the Sudetenland. The papers are saying this is another step towards all out war. Will this year end peacefully? Is there still time for something to stop what now seems inevitable?

Alice's bedsores are getting worse. She finds it hard to swallow. Every movement, however small, is becoming more difficult. Her muscles are wasting away. She is growing weaker and all of this is part of the daily inventory of all she is suffering and how things are gradually deteriorating.

Days are going by leaving her condition worsening. She knew this would happen. She tries to prepare herself. Is it prayer? Is it being constantly honest with herself? Is it to somehow confront the fact of her own death?

She takes a sip of water. She can hear Sylvie trying to help Archie with his reading, his loud voice reverberating up the stairs.

Mary stays in her room like a ghost in the house.

Is that all that is left, worrying about herself, her husband, her daughters? There is so little she can do about any of it.

She is tired and begins to drift to the sounds of Archie and Sylvie downstairs and the noise of people ending another working day.

The bedroom door is left open a few inches. She hears another voice in the hallway and then footsteps that are not Sylvie's coming up the stairs. There is a tap on the door before Janice Burrows pops her head round.

'Alice, I hope I'm not bothering you. Sylvie is with Archie so she said I should come up. Is that alright?'

Alice tries to lift herself higher against the pillow while saying 'Of course it is, Janice, come in and take a seat.'

'I thought I'd just pop in after work to see how you are and whether you're up to having a chat.'

Alice forces a smile.

'Sylvie says she's teaching that Archie lad to read.'

'Has been for weeks now.'

'He's a strange one, but a harmless lad.'

'He's never at school.'

'And his mother won't bother. She's got enough on her plate with all the rest of her brood to look after.'

Janice is the daughter of Annie Burrows who owned the house from which Alice had rented a room before meeting Arthur.

'I'm sorry…..sorry I couldn't make it to your mother's funeral,' Alice sighs.

'We knew how poorly you were,' says Janice, 'We knew you wouldn't be there.'

Janice is pudgy and small, wearing a faded brown coat and old fashioned lace up boots. When she takes off her hat her mousy coloured hair spreads out in all directions.

'It was busy,' she continues, 'Mother would have appreciated that.'

'And how is work? I hear you've got a new job.'

'Oh working at Woolworths is mad!' Janice exclaims, 'It's balmy, so busy especially on Saturdays. They try you out on different counters. We're being moved about all the time. I like the sweetie counter best, seeing all them young faces looking really serious, trying to decide what they should buy with their mother standing behind them making sure they don't go mad.'

'You like it?'

'Well at least you haven't got time to think. You're in and then out and the day's gone just like that.'

She pauses, frowns before smiling and says, 'But that's enough about me, how are you Alice? You were always one of mother's favourites.'

'No, I think you were Janice.'

'Some fat chance! I was just a nag. That's what I was. How my mother didn't do away with me I'll never know.'

'She loved you. She loved everyone.'

'The younger the better. After five years of age mother knew that was when the problems would start.'

'She looked after Mary better than I did.'

'That's not true.'

'If it hadn't been for Annie I don't know what would have happened.'

'Yes, she helped a lot of women. Always said we had to stick together.'

'And we did.'

'Yes, we certainly tried,' Janice sighs thoughtfully, her round face like an open book.

The longer they talk the further into the past Alice is drawn so that when Janice finally leaves she is locked into so many memories, most of them happy ones.

She had met him on the station. Mary had been holding her hand.

'About time Arthur Townsley,' she had said warmly before he had taken her by the waist and pulled her towards him, kissing her and then kneeling down to give his uncertain daughter a hug.

The station is ringed by the memory's diffused light when no dimension is exactly clear.

She likes Janice, a woman who manages whatever life puts in front of her, never married, moving from one job to another but always chatty, friendly, warm in her caring response.

'If it hadn't been for Annie I don't know what would have happened.'

Arthur's uniform was too big for him. He was the only soldier on the busy platform. People looked at him critically as though the last thing they wanted was to be reminded of the last four years.

'So you've missed me?'

'Oh no, me and Mary have been getting on just fine, haven't we Mary?' had been her sardonic answer.

But Mary had been too shy to answer, curled into a shell that clung to her coat.

He was there but he was not there. He was still somewhere else, in a place Alice would never understand.

Mary was a quiet baby, playing happily by herself, only bothered by other people except for her mother.

Arthur had been an intrusion into this quiet, self absorbed life. Mary has always found him difficult, and he had certainly never really made the effort to make things any easier.

And what about Annie Burrows, buried, dead for over a year?

Dear Annie with her big heart.

'You just get along woman. I've looked after enough children in my time so another one won't be a bother.'

Annie with her filthy pinnies and old slippers.

Where are you?

Where are you Annie?

'Did you believe enough, pray enough?'

Alice looks across the room to the dimming light from the window.

Arthur slung his kitbag over his shoulder, took her arm and with Mary still clutching hold of her coat they had walked along the platform disappearing in steam.

She could smell that steam, that coal filled smell that rose upwards like a new weather cloud.

'You didn't mind Janice popping up, did you?' is Sylvie's question as she come in with a fresh jug of water.

'Of course not. It was good to see her. And how was Archie today?'

'That lad is as daft as a...'

'Brush.'

'Yes.'

'But is he learning anything? Is he getting anywhere?'

'Not really.'

'But at least you're trying.'

'No, he is mother, very trying, but I do feel sorry for him. He's just left to roam the streets. There'll be other folk who'll think he's a right daftie and some of them can be cruel to him and he doesn't deserve that.'

'The main thing is that his family still love him and that means more than anything.'

Even though no one had any idea when he would be home Sylvie always made Arthur's tea on the off chance he may be home at a reasonable time.

Alice listens to her clattering about in the kitchen.

'You look bonnier than ever,' he had said.

'And you sound Scottish. Where's that accent come from?'

'That's because I've spent the last months listening to the boys from the north. Anyway, I never told you the Townsleys come from an ancient Highland clan, the most feared there was, robbers, cut throats, cattle rustlers. The clan motto was trust no one except your own kith and kin.'

Her love for him was never that romantic, not like her love for Paul Jameson, never like that.

Can there be such a thing as a deep practical love, the need to care and look after someone?

He came back so changed.

He loved but needed more, always looking for more.

She hears Mary in the bathroom, hears the toilet flush and then her quiet feet tip toeing across the landing.

She has not come to see her for weeks. It upsets her and yet there is nothing she can do about it.

Again she remembers Arthur getting off that busy Leeds train. She had been nervous, hopeful, worried. The letters he had written had been disappointing, as though right from the start he was hiding what he was being put through.

Her heart is thumping again, a beating pain, tight, stretched.

Eventually it would stop. She would be there and then not there.

To panic is only to increase the pressure.

A rough Northern town on the edge of the Dales, Skipton where fate had brought her and now fate meant she would never leave.

Just a touch of a cheek, a knee, Paul Jameson's tanned face so close on that warm, sensual afternoon. How terribly sad for it to end like that.

She sips more water, turns on the radio, turns it off, tries to read but fails.

Annie Burrows in a messy house full of love, Annie with her smiling face tending to one child then another like a small caring dance.

When he returned to his job at Slaters Arthur insisted they find a place to live, two rooms above Anderson the butchers and that she would leave the mill.

'I'm earning enough,' he had told her.

But she quickly found out it was never enough.

She gained a husband but lost her freedom especially when Sylvie was born. At least Mary had started school, shy, nervous Mary gripping her hand before they reached the school gates.

Had she been happy then? Does it matter now? She wants to believe she was happy, two daughters and a husband lucky to have returned from the war straight into a full time job.

The 1920s so much poverty and yet the Townsleys were managing better than most. Quickly she knew what to expect from Arthur. His intimate needs were greater than hers. She tried to satisfy him without ever considering herself. She did not want her body to define her. Not that Arthur ever thought of her like that. They spent a lot of their spare evenings attending concerts, the theatre and going to the cinema.

'Culture is more important than anything,' he used to say, and she had agreed at the time.

Except gradually there was the drinking, the socialising, the sports reporting and all the rest of it.

His daughters, the sense of family were never at the top of his list.

Greedy Arthur was fighting another war with himself, a war he could never win.

She had sensed that right from the start.

But those first years had been the best because he had still been trying then to play a role.

The older Sylvie became the more Mary withdrew into herself. The two of them were strangers. The gulf between a two year old and an eight year made things difficult.

And yet they managed, they were perhaps happy. There was a rhythm to each day, each week. They were all together. Arthur became manager and they could afford a mortgage. Their life was changing, improving, at least for a time.

She asked him to remove the clock. She did not want time in the bedroom. If she had to spend the rest of her life within these four walls she wanted the hours to pass as slowly as possible. She might be bored, depressed, empty. It did not matter so long as each day was stretched to its limit within her sense of time. She wanted it to be endless, wanted her life to expand forever.

Faith helped. Fear did not. Prayer helped. Despair did not.

'You never stop thinking, Alice,' he used to say, 'I'd love to know what goes on in that head of yours.'

Think about who I was back then.

Proud of her children, of her new house, of her part time job at the library when Sylvie started school.

'It's enough, isn't it? Why isn't it enough?' she asked him on several occasions.

A distance began to separate them, a dull space, fraught and constantly unsettling.

Love was not enough. That is what was wrong. Nothing was ever enough. She was never enough.

'Life fails. It's a failure whatever anyone does. Whatever you start it cannot last. Don't you see that? Why can't you see that?'

'Because it doesn't matter to me like it does to you. Life offers so much. It has to Arthur. It has to.'

'We're not here just to be happy or satisfied.'

How sad she had thought at the time, how terribly sad, life as a struggle without end, without conclusion. It was tragic to watch him disappear into his own desperate world.

And as for her back then, back in the 1920s, the early 1930s, the girls growing up in such different ways and she was there to keep them safe, to keep them secure, to compensate for their father's neglect.

At least he never missed a day at work. At least there was some balance there. Old Mr Slater seemed to dote on him. Even though his son had taken over the business Arthur was still the apple in the old man's eye, was still someone he trusted to keep Slaters on track while his son spent most of his time playing the lord of the manor farming and hunting.

'Ever since I was a young lad and did Mr Salters garden he's always looked out for me.'

Lucky Arthur. That was the one piece of luck that kept everything afloat.

And yet he had been punished more than anyone would ever know.

'Why Arthur?'

'Because I didn't believe in their bloody war, that's why, didn't fall for that King and Country rubbish.'

The light is fading. Autumn is coming. Sylvie will be up with the last cup of tea soon. Mary has still not stirred from her room.

Speak to me Mary. Come and see me.

Soon the fire will have to be lit and the thick curtains put up. Soon another season will be over and even without a clock time creeps into the air, the atmosphere, the light. It is inescapable.

I am kept within this prison of my body.

Emotions are the food of life. Without them we are nothing but things, clever, stupid things.

This evening Sylvie will ask me how I am, and I will lie and tell her I am not so bad when in truth my heart is breaking.

Mary come and see me, talk to me. What is wrong?

Sylvie is a treasure.

Arthur is out with…..with whoever he is with.

I have another jigsaw to finish.

When I listen to music on the radio I grow nostalgic. I see thousands of smartly dressed couples all dancing together making exactly the same moves, back, forwards, the man spins the lady, all together, thousands of couples on some massive ballroom making waves of replicated movement.

I only watch.

Where is Arthur?

Why isn't he there in one of his smart suits taking my hand and leading me through the waltz? Did I ever want to dance? Not really. Dancing seemed so conventional, a social mime.

Not like Fred Astaire.

Feet that moved over the ground as though the ground was not there, straight backed, arms stretched for balance and then spins, curves, shoes tapping out movement, ballet in a tuxedo waiting for Ginger to join the performance.

Watching them and admiring but never wanting to be like them.

Imagining Arthur as Skipton's version of Fred Astaire! I don't think so.

Poor Arthur, so lost, so blind to what is in front of him.

Tired now.

Thinking, thinking, thinking.

Where's my last cup of tea?

Sylvie will bring it soon.

Everything will be soon, too soon, far too soon.

CHAPTER TWENTY.

'What?' Mary wants to know, 'Go on, tell me.'

Sylvie tries to remain calm.

Rain is rattling against their bedroom window.

'Mother is worried.'

'I know she is, of course she is.'

'Well go and talk to her.'

'And say what?'

'I don't know, anything,' Sylvie tries, words that feel as though they are falling into a deep, empty well.

Mary is curled up in her dressing gown on top of her bed as Sylvie gets undressed.

'You're getting fat Sylvie.'

Sylvie pulls her nightie up against her breasts, 'It's the third of October!'

Mary looks at her with a dull, sarcastic expression.

'You've been off work for exactly three weeks,' Sylvie adds sharply upset by her sister's remark.

'I'm not going back.'

'But why?'

Mary sighs, sits up, takes off her dressing gown and climbs into bed.

'Well, if I'm getting fat it's your fault,' Sylvie persists, 'I eat when I'm worried.'

'Suit yourself.'

'I will.'

'Good for you.'

The next morning she is still asleep when Sylvie gets up. The milkman is early this morning, his bottles rattling on the back of his horse drawn cart. It is dark outside and there is a chill in the air as Sylvie goes to the bathroom before going downstairs to put on the kettle and light the fire.

By nine o clock she is walking along the High Street with her shopping bags looking in at the grocers and the bakers before stopping to buy some ham shanks at the butchers to make some soup.

The town is locked into autumn, grey, dull, sombre colours everywhere. The busy streets are muted by the misty atmosphere. People are already dressed for winter. Sylvie feels the weather closing around her until her own mood is as miserable as everyone else's. There is change but no change. Life moves forward and yet she is stuck in the usual routine. She will never be free of it. She is tired. For once she wants to concentrate on herself. But she is scared. Fate has moulded her into someone who is only a shadow of the woman she hoped to be. To be selfish only makes her feel empty and desperate.

Back in the house she puts her shopping bags on the kitchen table. After taking off her coat and unpinning her hat she throws more coal from the scuttle onto the fire.

'The shops are busy this morning,' she says to her mother when she pops up to see her.

Alice is working on another jigsaw.

'This one is hard,' she mentions.

'You like them hard.'

'But this is….'

'You'll do it,' her daughter interrupts.

Sylvie sets the tea cup and plate of Rich Tea biscuits on the bedside table.

'Is Mary up?' she asks.

'I haven't heard her,' Alice answers

'I'll go and see how she is.'

Sylvie checks the fire in the corner before emptying the bucket from the commode down the bathroom toilet and then goes to check on Mary.

She is sat up in bed reading a magazine and looks up when her sister enters.

'I've been out to the shops. Do you want anything?'

'No thank you, and if I do I can manage myself.'

'Do as you like then,' Sylvie says bitterly.

'I wish I could.'

'And what's that supposed to mean?'

Mary gives a sardonic smile, 'Don't worry Sylvie. It's not going to be like this forever.'

'But you're not going back to Dawsons?'

'Definitely not. I told you, I've handed in my notice. You posted the letter for me and promised not to tell mother or father.'

'What are you going to do?'

'I'm going to have a bath, get dressed and meet Shirley for lunch. That's what I'm going to do.'

'Mary you have to go and see mother.'

'And I will.

'When?'

'After I've had my bath and got dressed,' Mary answers moodily.

Back downstairs Sylvie tries to calm herself knowing that doctor Donnolly is about to arrive on his weekly visit. There is so much she is trying to control. Inside her is a whole avalanche of different emotions ready to crash down. She needs the doctor to trust her. She needs him to respect her.

'I thought Sylvie it would be only right that I tell you what we do when we drain your mother, now that is has become a regular process. We bring in a nurse, not that I don't think you could manage the process, we bring one in just in case something goes wrong, not seriously wrong, just something the nurse can deal with and make things more comfortable for your mother.'

He has already been up to check on Alice and is now in the kitchen drinking his tea and wanting to explain things in a voice Sylvie has never heard before, serious, slightly bothered and almost apologetic.

'I think I know some of it,' she says.

'Of course you do.'

'I just never thought having heart problems could make mother's body....'

'Yes, it's unexpected and not easy to deal with, either for you or your mother,' he intervenes.

She stops herself and waits for him to continue.

'Do you want to hear about it?' he asks.

'If you think it's important then yes.'

'I do Sylvie. I do think it's important.'

She listens. She tries to concentrate on his words and not just his voice. She tries to absorb what he is saying without admiring his face, his hands, his eyes. These moments are the most precious in the whole week and yet she must stop herself wanting them to be repeated over and over again, wanting him never to leave.

What she hears is of insertions and tubes and liquid drained into a receptacle, her mother deflated like a party balloon.

She imagines the nurse taking the container of stained liquid and pouring it down the toilet, pouring the weeks of pain that her mother has suffered only for the whole miserable process to start all over again.

Later in the afternoon she is out in the small front garden cutting roses for the chapel. She cuts the dark red flowers, the last of the year. They do not smell. There are enough to fill a vase that she will place on the altar. It is her turn, the last of the season.

It is four o clock when she enters the chapel. She takes the old flowers from their vase, goes back out and round the side of the building where there are two dustbins. She holds up the lid of one of them looking at the dried out stems she has just deposited, light, yellowing green with most of the petals scattered over yesterday's ash from the vestry fire.

Back inside she gets fresh water from the sink in the women's toilet and starts placing the roses in the vase being careful not to prick herself. It is at this point that the vicar appears from the vestry, coming down the steps.

'My, my Sylvie those roses look grand.'

She turns in surprise, 'I didn't think anyone was here.'

'I'm about not to be. I have two elderly members of the congregation who I promised I would visit. They're unfortunately too frail to manage to come to a service so I go to them instead.'

'The roses are from our garden, the last of the season,' she tells him.

'Yes, I'm afraid autumn is upon us,' Mr Elgin responds, his pale features shining from the light coming through one of the high windows.

'The chapel feels nice and warm.'

'That's because Willie Brewster has been giving the boiler a run today just to check everything is as it should be,' he says of the chapel's caretaker, 'And how is your mother today?'

'So..so. She has her good days and her bad ones. Today she seems as tired as usual.'

'You must tell her I'll pop in sometime later this week.'

'I will.'

'Right, I'm off before they think I'm not coming. The roses look just right Sylvie.'

'They'll do,' she says, placing the vase on the altar before turning to watch the vicar go down the aisle, through the swing doors and out into the main entrance.

She hears the heavy front door close behind him.

The chapel returns to its empty silence. She settles herself in the first pew and looks up at the high pulpit and the organ up in the gallery behind it. At the other end are three plain, tall windows. The place smells of polish and a vague odour of the dead lilies she has just thrown in the dustbin. It is a sombre, dark atmosphere which makes her acutely aware of herself alone in the building with only faint sounds coming from the street outside.

She tries to absorb the chapel's atmosphere but instead she thinks of London, of all the dreams she has of taking a train down to see St Pauls and the Thames, Buckingham Palace, Westminster Abbey, to just walk around the busy streets, watch the red buses hurrying by, hear the calls of the newspaper boys on every corner. It is the one place she wants to visit. It offers such a splendid alternative to her daily routine. There is nowhere else like it. Ever since being a young child she has dreamt about it, fantasised about it, longing for this city that shines in her imagination. Next come images of her at the town hall dance with Mary and Shirley which she enjoyed so much and wants more of such occasions, more dances in a new dress, meeting some young man who will finally propose to her and she will accept. Such thoughts race through her mind, London and dances and a boyfriend and marriage and children and on and on.

Without thinking she gets up and strides towards the altar, takes up the roses and takes them out to throw them in the dustbin on top of the dead lilies. Banging down the dustbin lid she notices the blood from where the roses have pricked her. She licks off the blood, takes out a handkerchief and dabs it on the tiny wounds before returning to the front of the chapel. Quickly descending the steps she walks away, tears in her eyes, her handkerchief grasped in the palm of her hand.

She hardly notices the people she passes or the Pennine bus turning into the bus station, the lorry full of turnips driving by as she turns over the bridge onto the canal path. Here she stops. Her handkerchief is covered in fresh blood but the bleeding has been staunched. She tosses the handkerchief into the filthy grey water watching it float towards a pool of multicoloured oil staining the surface.

A barge chugs towards her, its engine churning up the murky water. She pays no attention and continues along the canal path.

Her few special moments of the week with the doctor, his presence in the house, his quick chats, are her only compensation. And then there is Mary lolling about the house and her father never at home.

On a sudden impulse she returns quickly to the chapel, retrieves the roses from the dustbin, fills the vase with fresh water and arranges the roses, steps back to check on how they look before leaving as abruptly as she arrived.

Later that evening back in the kitchen she hears Archie shouting for her.

She ignores him.

For once she does not want to see or speak to anyone.

Her sister is in the parlour listening to the radio on the gramophone.

Her father is out.

Her mother is reading.

And she, where is she?

CHAPTER TWENTY ONE.

The scrum half sells a quick dummy and darts through the mud towards the line. It is the second time he has cut loose, small, wide bodied, with short cropped hair, his face and arms splattered in December clag. The small Skipton crowd shout him on as Arthur watches before jotting down the time and name of the try scorer.

'What the hell was Atkinson playing at?' Dave Thornton asks in a loud voice over the crowd in the rugby club bar.

'Go and ask him,' someone suggests.

'I damn well will,' Dave shouts back.

Arthur has a quick pint and walks over to the Craven Herald office to type out his match report later crossing over to the Black Bull to join others from the rugby club.

'Our Tommy Middleton, he gave it to them today alright,' says one supporter.

Arthur joins some of the others at one of the window tables.

He likes the chat, the game being analysed in detail and then onto the next match between Yorkshire and Lancashire before football is mentioned and the arguments between Leeds, Burnley and Blackburn supporters begin. This goes on for most of the night as they drink more and more and the arguments grow louder.

For Arthur a Saturday night should be like this. Sport dominates and why not? He loves the detail some of them go into about the merits of their team, the fired up predictions and good humoured condemnation of the opposition. Drink and sport are the best combination. The night is passing quickly. By nine o clock the Black Bull is busier than ever. He is supposed to have phoned Kitty by now but does not feel like moving. This is where he wants to be at least until last orders are called.

Outside a cold sleet is cutting across the road. He pulls up his coat collar, tilts his trilby to cover more of his face, shouts goodbye to some of the others coming out of the Black Bull and crosses the street, the brandy warming his brain as he concentrates putting one foot in front of the other.

In a few minutes he is banging the knocker of a door set between two shops on the Keighley Road.

'Well, well if it isn't Arthur Townsley? Go on, tell me you're lost, tell me you remember my name and that you've been missing me for weeks, make that months.'

'Oh, come on Gracie, no need to be like that,' he says to the woman who has opened the door.

'Come on, he says.'

'Are you going to invite me in?'

'And why the hell should I do that?'

'Thought we might have a drink together.'

'Too late Arthur.'

'No. It's fine Gracie, it'll be fine.'

She is wearing a silky dressing gown and is holding a cigarette as she lets him pass up the narrow stairway into her tiny flat.

At the top of the stairs on a short landing she watches him take off his soaking hat and coat.

'Still dressing smart I see,' is her amused comment.

She is short with blonde hair and heavily made up features.

'I've only got a drop of whisky,' she answers following him into her over heated from room.

Arthur politely asks her if he can sit down.

She smiles knowingly, 'And you've brought your manners with you.'

'As well as a flask of brandy.'

'Oh of course, Arthur and his brandy.'

'In case of emergencies.'

'And is this one?'

'No, it isn't.'

'So we're not that desperate?'

'I've come to see you Gracie.'

'I'm surprised you can even remember where I live it's been so long since you...'

'I hadn't forgotten. Why would I forget?'

She stands in front of the well stacked coal fire that sheens her dressing gown while he sits back in the room's only armchair and looks at her.

'Anyway, you're here,' she says before going into her tiny kitchen for two glasses and a half empty bottle of whisky.

He gets up and goes out onto the landing to retrieve his brandy flask from his coat pocket.

She hands him a glass then pours herself a drink.

'Cheers Gracie,' he says warmly.

There is an absorbed silence between them as though both are trying to work out what their next approach should be.

Finally Gracie asks, 'So why are you here Arthur as if I couldn't guess.'

'Is it that obvious?'

'Yes.'

'I don't like being predictable.'

'You're as predictable as any other man. Why the hell should you be so different?'

'Now don't get tetchy Gracie, it doesn't suit you.'

At that she opens her dressing gown, 'Was it for this? You came for this, didn't you?'

Her breasts are large with prominent purple nipples. She has broad hips and thighs but a tight, flat stomach.

Arthur admires what he sees, his body warming to her nakedness, thankful that he has not drunk himself over the edge but has kept himself balanced enough, ready, wanting, needing.

Two hours later he leans into the cold rain on his way home. On the bridge over the canal he stops.

'You're a fucking coward Townsley. Well, we know what to do with fucking cowards.'

In the mist is the voice. In the mist they are stood listening to the voice as one after another is cursed and bullied.

The rain slants across the nearest street light as he pulls his trilby further down.

'You're here because you're a fucking disgrace to the army and to the country. You're fucking going to stand here in the pissing rain. You stand and don't fucking move a muscle.'

From the past comes the voice and still he hears it. Over and over again he hears it.

'I bet you thought Townsley you were going back to Blighty with the rest of the lads. Well, you can fucking think again.'

Mist and rain presses over a sea of mud, waves and waves of dank, stinking earth.

'Dig you fuckers! Go on, fucking dig!'

The rest of the streets are deserted as he leaves the bridge and walks the rest of his way home.

Going up the stairs in his stockinged feet he hears Alice.

'You still awake?' he asks as he comes into her bedroom and then adds, 'Sorry, silly question.'

'I don't feel so good,' she answers in a quiet, dry voice.

'Can I get you anything? Do you want more water?'

He switches on the bedside lamp to see her pale, swollen features with grey bags of lined skin under her eyes.

'No, I don't…….I don't want anything.'

Carefully he sits on the edge of the bed and takes hold of her cold hand beneath the eiderdown.

'It's freezing out there,' he mentions.

Alice is silent.

The rain is rattling against the window. The room is full of the odour from the commode and old smoke from the fire. Arthur has to try but has no idea what to say to her.

Thankfully Alice helps him out. She asks about the match he has already forgotten about. It seems to have taken place days ago. He feels guilty at his lack of feeling. He is empty, scraped clean by stupid memories and Gracie's enthusiasm. It has been a long day, but he has to make an effort. He has to force a reaction.

'We won. We won easily, the best I've seen them play all season and I managed to get my report in on time so Vernon was happily surprised.'

'I think I slept for a while and then had a headache and……and then I heard you.'

'I went with Dave to Shuggy Andrews for a game of cards.'

'I never knew Dave played cards.'

'He doesn't usually.'

'His Eleanor won't be pleased when she hears her husband has been so badly influenced by mine.'

'He makes his own mind up.'

'You're a fucking lying piece of shit,' came the voice as someone put his arm round his shoulder and added, 'You lie all the time. You Townsley. Yes, fucking you.'

'Listen to it,' Alice says breathlessly of the ceaseless rain.

He needs a cigarette. He wants to lie down and yet he has to remain where he is.

'Mary's looking for another job,' he says without thinking. The last thing he wants to talk about is Mary.

'Sylvie says she's never going back to Dawsons.'

'No she isn't.'

'What's wrong with her Arthur?' Alice asks desperately.

'I don't know. I wished I did. She won't talk to me about it.'

'She won't talk to anyone.'

'Something's not right,' he agrees, worried and confused by anything to do with Mary.

He tries to focus. Mentioning either of their daughters produces a kind of emotional numbness, a lack of response.

They remain silent for a few minutes, Alice looking at the paler shape on the wallpaper left on top of the mantelpiece where the clock used to be while Arthur stares down at his free hand resting on top of the eiderdown.

'Things will.....' he starts only for Alice to stop him.

'No, Arthur, they won't.'

'How do you know what I was going to say?'

'It's what you always say. I know it's what you want but it isn't going to happen. Things with me are not going to improve. We have to stop thinking they will.'

'You can't be sure Alice.'

Her face stiffens before she says, 'Please Arthur. It....it doesn't help....it really doesn't.'

He remains with her for a while longer, eventually kissing her on the forehead, saying goodnight, leaving the door slightly ajar. Instead of going along to his room he turns back downstairs instead.

In the hallway he puts on his boots, his coat and hat, goes into the pantry where he has a fresh bottle of brandy. Over the sink he steadily refills his flask, screws the top on, returns the bottle onto the pantry shelf and goes back down the hallway.

Outside the rain has turned to snow. He stops on the pavement to watch the silver needles swirling and flashing through the light from the street lamps. He takes a mouthful of brandy, fastens the top button on his coat and start walking back towards the centre of town. He needs to be out, needs to be in the freezing air. The house is suffocating. He hates the stench from Alice's room and the sense of hopelessness he feels when he is with her. There is nothing he can do for her. Her illness has taken over. It is undermining everything, and it disgusts him to be so helpless.

He is marching now, one stride followed by the next as he hunches against the snow flying into his face. He does not care where he is going. He has to be out of the house. He will not sleep. His mind is too full of everything, all of it flashing at brandy fuelled speed into moments of consciousness and then gone.

'March you fuckers! Pretend you're real fucking soldiers!'

Where does it all come from? Where does he come from? Why is he the person he is? Questions start when his mood is like this.

He walks. He shivers. He stops and takes a drink. At the entrance to an alleyway he tries to light a cigarette.

'Dig you bastards! Dig! Use a fucking pickaxe! Try and put it a bit of effort into it Townsley! You're such a weak, pathetic shit Townsley! Has anyone ever told you that?'

Inside the womb, the thing, the slug, the fish, the something.

'They're all fucking heroes and you lot aren't! Just cos they're dead and you're fucking half alive means nothing except they're heroes and you lot aren't!'

He is walking along the the Keighley Road at two o clock in the morning trying to understand why Arthur Townlsey is Arthur Townsley.

Like the millions of snow needles flying out of the darkness his identity is made up of so many tiny fragments, moments, feelings, thoughts, other people, his surroundings at any given moment in time, what is happening in the rest of the world, what he reads, is told, what he imagines, what he desires, and all of it started right at the beginning and has been adding layer after layer, reaction after reaction ever since. It is school, his parents, his childhood friends, his dreams. It is a fraction of a second view, a pulse of an idea, a quiver of delight, the ultimate complexity that is forever developing, changing, which is Arthur Townsley.

'Me. Me,' he mutters to himself.

He passes unlit houses. There is nothing but snow and the growing sounds of the wind coming down off the moors.

'Beneath all this shit is an army, a fucking stew of bits and pieces and you bastards will find it all, every piece of equipment, every mouldy skull, shredded diary, bits of leg, teeth, badges, cigarette tins! Everything! We want it all, every last scrap! Do you hear you thick shits? DO YOU UNDERSTAND?'

He stops and turns to face the full force of the snow blasting wind. Holding onto his trilby with his coat flapping around his legs he stands there.

'The dead are alive! They're fucking waiting for you to fucking resurrect them!'

Gracie opens her dressing gown. Alice looks dried out. He has not phoned Kitty. None of it makes sense and yet all of it is perfectly understandable.

'I am understandable!' he shouts at the growing storm.

He gasps out more of the pain, the endless pain of who he is.

Without making any decision he turns and heads back. In the shelter of a disused shed he lights another cigarette. Walking in the middle of the snow covered road he takes two quick drags and then flicks the cigarette away.

He is cold in his body but warm in his brain. He is angry, sad, determined, forcing everything.

Finally he reaches his front gate and holds onto it. His wife, his daughters are inside the house. So much of his past is inside there. He does not want to enter but knows he has to, has to do what is expected.

In the hallway he pulls off his snow soaked hat and coat before supporting himself against the wall to take off his boots.

Quietly he mounts the stairs, passing Alice's room to reach the toilet and unbutton his flies, swaying from side to side as he tries to concentrate on what is leaving his body and reaching the toilet bowl.

Finally he unsteadily gets into his pyjamas, pulls back the eiderdown and blankets and collapses into bed.

There is a frozen landscape. Mist shifts like the hands of a ghostly conductor.

The voice has been silenced.

He does not want to hear any more.

He wants to…….

Not any more.

His lips are still cold.

His eyes are still stinging from the wind whipped snow.

He is waiting.

Waiting to sleep.

CHAPTER TWENTY TWO

Mary flicks through one of her scrapbooks looking at photographs of

Shirley Temple who has the baby voice.

Bette Davies with those strange old woman's eyes.

Jean Harlow, is her blond hair really natural?

Marlene Dietrich with the tight lips of a foreign mouth.

Greta Garbo so sad, so tragic.

Katherine Hepburn always showing her teeth.

Ann Sheridan and her devilish expression.

James Cagney, dapper, short, quick speaking.

Clark Gable with his slow, come on voice.

Cary Grant the tall, dapper American aristocrat.

Fred Astaire who dances with Ginger in the moonlight.

Gary Cooper always uncertain, unsure.

James Stewart on the side of all that is good.

So many black and white years when life was black and white, the bad and the good, the villain and the heroine. The cinema had made such stupid dreams possible right through her formative years, right through growing up.

She tosses the scrapbook into a bottom drawer.

Sitting on the edge of the bed she tries to slow her breathing. Regret is like an acid burning through her system. She wants to be alone and not bother with anybody. There is no one she can trust, not even herself so the last thing she wants to hear is Sylvie plodding up the stairs.

'Shirley's downstairs. She's come to see you,' she says.

'Tell her I'm not well.'

'She's brought her sister's boy George.'

'I don't want to see her.'

'I told her you'd be down in a minute.'

'Oh for God's sake Sylvie!'

'I'm sorry but she's downstairs in the parlour and I've lit a fire.'

'She could have....'

'I've lit a fire,' Sylvie repeats herself angrily before leaving the room.

George is about five years old in long trousers and a thick jumper for the cold, his chubby face red from the winter cold. Shirley has put on a lot of weight.

'I know you're not working at Dawsons anymore,' Shirley says as Mary enters the parlour.

'So this is George. Hello George,' she says automatically.

The boy hangs onto his aunt's coat.

'Auntie Mary, I'm nearly five.'

'He calls every woman he meets auntie,' Shirley explains.

'No one has ever called me that before George.'

'I told Sylvie we weren't stopping long but she insisted that we should have a fire,' Shirley puts in, 'She brought in hot coals on the shovel. It's freezing out there.'

Sylvie is standing at the door and asks Shirley if she wants a cup of tea and whether George would like a drink of lemonade.

Mary sits on the edge of the armchair, clasps her hands together and tries to force herself into the situation, tries to be the friend she once was. She has not seen Shirley in months and that was only in passing. Their friendship has never been the same since Shirley was married.

'I like the flames,' George announces as he sits in front of the fire warming his hands.

'Don't you get too close,' Shirley warns.

'How are you?' Mary tries only to be interrupted by Sylvie bringing in a tray with a plate of biscuits and George's lemonade.

'The tea is nearly brewed. Do you want a cup Mary?'

She looks at her sister and gives a forced smile while shaking her head.

Meanwhile Shirley has taken off her coat and hat and balanced them carefully on the back of the sofa.

'Fine Mary, I'm fine,' she eventually answers her friend's question, 'George's mother is expecting another baby soon so I'm looking after him for a few days. June is in hospital at the moment, nothing serious, just the doctors checking on things. My Roger is working as many hours as he can. He's always on the go.'

'What does that mean auntie Shirley? What…..what does on the go, what does that mean?'

'It means George that Uncle Roger is always busy.'

'I'm always busy.'

'Yes you are.'

'Where did that other lady go, the one who brought me my drink of lemonade?'

'That's your auntie Sylvie and she's making Shirley a cup of tea and then she's going out to the shops.'

'Is she going to buy me anything? Can I have a comic?"

'George!' Shirley exclaims.

Suddenly the boy gets up and jumps onto the sofa.

'You don't ask questions like that,' Shirley continues, 'And take off your shoes before you climb onto the furniture.'

'Why can't I ask a question?'

Sylvie appears in her coat, boots and hat appears with Shirley's cup of tea.

'I'm just going out to the shops. I shouldn't be long,' she informs everyone.

Mary is trying to relax, trying to accept what is happening as she concentrates on her sister standing there.

'You watch the pavements,' Shirley puts in, 'They're really slippy.'

'I will,' Sylvie answers before adding, 'Right, nice seeing you Shirley and you George.'

'Say goodbye,' Shirley tells her nephew.

George looks cross and flustered and says nothing.

'Goodbye then,' Shirley says watching Sylvie close the door behind her.

Mary offers the plate of biscuits to George.

'Have as many as you like,' she tells him.

'Don't say that Mary or he'll scoff the lot,' is Shirley's advice.

There is a pause as they watch the boy eating one biscuit after another.

What was there to say? What was there to talk about? Mary just hopes that Shirley will talk about herself.

Thankfully for a time George takes over with his demand for more lemonade and whether there is any cake.

'What's the funny smell in your house auntie Mary? Do you have pets here? We have a cat called Tiddles and two goldfish called Horace and Hector,' he asks seriously.

'I'm glad you came,' Mary remarks, trying to sound pleased.

Shirley's expression is uncertain, 'I thought it was about time. How long has it been?'

'Too long.'

'I popped into Dawsons a few weeks back and they said you'd handed in your notice. That your leaving was unexpected. That's what June Allbright said.'

'Oh she did she? I'm afraid Jane and I never saw eye to eye.'

'She was the first person I spoke to.'

'I always thought she was too clever for her own good.'

'But I never thought you of all people would leave Dawsons. You seemed to fit perfectly there.'

Mary looks thoughtfully towards the fire, 'Things change I suppose or I've changed.'

'So what are you going to do?'

'Find another job.'

'In Skipton?'

'No, I don't think so.'

'I'm sure you'll manage Mary whatever you set your mind to.'

There is a momentary silence.

Shirley watches George clamber off the sofa and lie down in front of the now blazing fire and then get up again.

'What's this auntie Mary?' he asks as he goes over to the long, highly polished gramophone cabinet.

'It's a wireless and a record player,' she answers going over to lift up the lid to let George peer in.

His eyes grow larger as he watches her take a record from the rack, pull it out of its paper sleeve and place it on the central rod before she repeats the process until there is a stack of records set one on top of the other.

'Now,' she says, 'If you watch, I'm going to turn it on and see what happens.'

George leans a little further over as the first record drops onto the turntable followed by the arm coming over and placing the needle in the first of the spinning grooves.

Loud, crackling big band music sounds out much to the boy's delight as he watches the record going round and round and then is more fascinated as the music ends only for another record to drop down from the stack and the music to continue.

'Why haven't we got one of them?' George demands to know laughing as he dances around the room.

Shirley shakes her head, 'You'll have to ask your mother.'

'I'll ask Dad, he'll know.'

'Have you heard enough George?' Mary asks patiently, smiling as he spins round.

'Thank you auntie Mary.'

'Here, do some colouring in,' Shirley suggests as the boy resettles himself in front of the fire and she hands him from her large handbag some crayons and a colouring book.

'It makes a lovely sound,' she says of the gramophone.

Mary sits down on the opposite armchair, 'It was father's idea. He's wanted one for a while.'

There is another strained silence before Shirley comments, 'Sylvie told me your mother is not so good.'

It is the last thing Mary wants to talk about. She is beginning to feel hot and anxious.

'She has a failing heart. There is no other way to describe it,' she answers quickly, 'She has better days and then worse. Sometimes she's almost back to who she used to be and then everything changes and she's really ill and sleeps a lot and it's been like that for months now. It's so unpredictable.'

'It must be hard on all of you.'

'It is, especially for Sylvie.'

'And what does the doctor say?'

'What he always says, what he's said for years, that her condition is serious, serious enough to mean she'll be bedbound and that there will be days of remission when she seems better, but there are less and less of days like that.'

She knows Shirley has heard the strain in her voice and hopes they can change the subject.

'And your sister?' Mary asks.

'Oh, she's fine, won't be long before she has her next baby. They're wanting a girl.'

'So they should.'

At that Shirley smiles, 'I thought you'd agree with that.'

'And why shouldn't I?'

'No reason except you've always had plenty of reasons' her friend says lightly as George stretches out becoming more absorbed in what he is doing, 'But I still can't get over you leaving Dawsons like that,' Shirley unexpectedly adds.

Flustered for a moment Mary answers 'I'd had enough.'

'You went there straight after leaving school.'

'It was the right thing for me at the time. I was promised things by the management that didn't happen or didn't happen fast enough. I've always been impatient, you know that.'

'Do you think, do you think all this talk of war is making people more unsettled or more likely to hang on to what they've got? It seems there's going to be big changes whatever happens. Roger thinks it's all going to start sooner than later. Mind you when it comes to politics, he's always been a pessimist.'

'And you Shirl? What about you?'

'Oh things will sort themselves out one way or another. That's what I think.'

Shirley's tone is empty. It alters Mary's response. She suddenly focuses on her friend in a way that is both sympathetic and sad. She remembers that all that Shirley ever wanted was to get married and raise a family just like her sister is doing. The idea of bringing a new life into today's world must be frightening even for someone as desperate as Shirley.

'I imagine a future where people are always wanting change,' she says, a thought coming from nowhere as she feels another headache coming on.

'I can't see myself like that.'

'Maybe we all worry too much about the future,' Mary adds.

'That's all folk want to talk about.'

'But we can't do anything about it. That's what my father thinks. People have no say on what happens. We're helpless. Chamberlain lets Hitler have Czechoslovakia and we all just sit back and read about it in the paper. Father thinks the one ally we need more than any other is Russia.'

It is the most Mary has said in weeks. Words create an endless staircase she is trying to climb. She knows she will fail and yet for the time being she wants to stop thinking about herself and concentrate on her friend.

Suddenly the boy sighs, tosses down his crayon, turns his head to look at Mary and asks, 'Have you auntie Mary seen Snow White and the Seven Dwarfs?'

'I will George when it comes to Skipton.'

'Dad has promised he'll take me.'

'Well, if for any reason he can't manage you let me know and I'll take you. I'm sure your auntie Shirley would like to come.'

'She told me you go to the pictures a lot.'

'Not as much as I used to.'

'I've never been,' the boy says in a sad voice.

'Don't worry, you will,' Shirley puts in.

'Of course you will. It's the best George. You'll really like it.'

'I could go to a…..a ma…a.'

'A matinee.'

'They're for children.'

'Yes they are.'

'And I'll drink Spanish water and have a bag of sweets.'

'It sounds marvellous,' is Mary's easier response.

'We'll have to be getting home,' Shirley sighs. 'Thank Sylvie for the tea and lemonade and the fire,' Shirley adds as they go out into the hallway.

'And the biscuits!' George exclaims.

Mary watches them go down the front path. She shuts the front door and steadies herself against the hallway wall. She feels light headed. The pain is just above her eyes, a throbbing, penetrating pain.

She manages to put the fireguard in front of the parlour fire before going upstairs.

'Sylvie, is that you?' her mother calls as Mary reaches the landing.

She forces herself to stop and push further open Alice's door.

'It's just me mother. I've just seen out Shirley and her nephew George.'

'I....I don't know any George,' Alice struggles to reply.

'He's never been here before. He was intrigued by our gramophone. He's big for a five year old.'

'And how is Shirley?'

'Big as well. She's put on a lot of weight since I last saw her.'

'You....you always think everyone is big.'

'No I don't.'

Alice sighs, her face showing the effort she is making, 'It doesn't.....it doesn't matter.'

'Sylvie is not back from shopping yet,' Mary says while trying to stifle the smell of disinfectant and the deeper odour from the commode.

There is suddenly nothing else to say. She hates this silence. She is ashamed of it and yet this room disgusts her, makes her feel nauseous.

Under her mother's eyes are dark bags of loose skin. He face and hands are a pale yellow in contrast to her dry, grey hair.

'I have a headache from all that talking,' Mary mentions.

Alice's look lingers, her mouth tightening before she says in almost a whisper, 'I wished Mary you still went to chapel.'

'Oh for goodness sake mother,' Mary answers strongly, 'Don't start all that again.'

'I'm not starting anything.'

Mary tries to restrain her irritation. The last thing she wants to do is upset her mother again. It is the reason she tries to avoid entering this room.

She looks at the fire in the corner crackling away.

'Mary, could….could you do me a favour?' her mother is asking.

Mary tries to slow down the inner nervousness she is feeling, that tight sensation in her throat and stomach.

'Could you go to the window….go and describe what you see. I want to know what it looks like.'

She does as she is asked, pulls back the curtains to look out on the window's late afternoon view. It is then a question of what should be described, pigeons flying about, smoke pouring out of every chimney, an old woman bent forward coming along the back lane.

'There is no one in the back lane,' she starts, 'Except for a dog trotting past and an old lady.'

'What else?'

'In the street lights you can see that the roofs are covered in frost and that the back yard looks treacherous. It's already dark and there's a mist coming off the canal. Is that enough,' she asks as she suddenly recloses the curtains.

'Winter,' Alice sighs.

'Yes, already.'

'Dark by half past three.'

'Today it is.'

'Thank you,' Alice says.

'I'm going for a lie down,' Mary mentions, 'And try and get rid of this headache. Sylvie shouldn't be long.'

'Things….things will work out Mary,' her mother tries.

Mary turns in the open door and answers, 'I'm not sure what that means anymore,' before going along the landing to where she kicks off her shoes and curls up on the bed trying to empty her mind of everything, every thought and feeling.

CHAPTER TWENTY THREE

Time is running thickly through her veins. She is so tired and yet cannot sleep. To be aware of time passing means only sadness and regret like the flow of a dark tide pushing her inexorably out to sea.

If only Mary was more settled. Alice sees her again describing what she saw from the bedroom window. Her words had been too rushed. She had wanted a little more warmth. It had left her irritated and disappointed.

The fire is crackling. Her body aches. The ends of her fingers feel slightly numb so that she is finding it hard when doing a jigsaw to place the pieces or to hold the handle of a cup or having so little sensation when she touches her face.

Sylvie had gone the previous week to see her friend Sally one afternoon when Mary had appeared at the door. She was still in her dressing gown. Her face looked pale and strained. Alice had known immediately that she wanted to say something.

'Don't you ever wonder what father is doing all the nights he is out late?'

Alice knew she had to rally her resources or refuse to answer the question. She chose to respond.

'There's nothing to wonder at Mary.'

'Isn't there?' she had persisted.

'And if there was do you think I'm in a position to do anything about it? That was a cruel thing to ask. Just because you have your own problems doesn't mean you…..you have to start on me.'

'I'm not starting anything.'

'Well why such a question?'

'Because I think father is acting badly.'

'And who are you to judge?'

'All men are just the same, aren't they mother?'

Alice hated this tone of voice. She could feel herself becoming agitated.

Mary had stoodat the end of the bed. When she saw her mother's strained expression she said, 'I didn't come to upset you mother.'

'Things are as they are,' Alice said with as much emphasis as she could manage.

Mary had her hands on the bed's ornate metal frame as she replied with, 'So things are just left.'

'Nothing's left and nothing is gained by talking this way, not for me, and if you were thinking more clearly Mary you'd understand that. This is more about you. You never tell me or your father anything about what's going on. You mope about the house all day and just expect us to leave you alone.'

'Yes mother, that's what I want.'

'But how you are affects the rest of us. You don't live in a vacuum.'

Outside came the call of the rag and bone man going on his horse and cart along the front street, the horse's hoofs muffled by a cushion of fresh snow.

'My nerves are bad, that's all,' Mary had eventually admitted, 'It takes me hours to get to sleep at night. I just don't feel right.'

'You should talk to the doctor.'

Mary frowned, her eyes narrowing slightly as she had answered, 'That's the last thing I want to do.'

'Doctors don't discuss their patients with anyone else. You know that.'

'Except when it comes to my sister's little chats every time he visits.'

'That's got nothing to do with me. That's him checking on how Sylvie is doing, whether she's coping.'

'Of course our little martyr is coping. That's how she sees herself. The worse you are the better it is for her.'

'How can you say such a thing?' Alice asks in a shocked and angry tone, 'You can be very cruel sometimes Mary.'

'But it's true mother.'

'No, it's nonsense Mary.'

Her daughter had lowered her head slightly as she untied and retied the soft belt of her dressing gown.

Alice could not believe what she has just heard and refused to say any more.

'Aren't you going to say anything?' Mary tries.

'I want....I want you to go.'

'But you're always complaining mother that I never come to see how you are and now I'm.......'

'I'd rather you didn't if you're going to making such remarks about your own sister.'

'It's what I think.'

'Just leave it Mary please.'

At that Mary had come round the bed, touched Alice's hand before going back to her own bedroom.

It had been a pathetic gesture, a few fingers in contact with the back of her right hand.

'Don't dwell on this,' she says to herself.

Its effect had to be pushed away. She had not the energy to think about it. Mary was in a dark place and Alice understood that when someone was in such a mood it would be expressed in any way it could.

She tries to slow her breaths. She feels sick and the pain in her chest and down her back seem worse.

Sylvie bought last summer a framed picture from a stall on the market thinking it might brighten up the room. It is quite a large painting and is hung on the opposite wall so Alice does not have to shift her position to see it.

A young woman is walking down a summer lane under an arch of bright green trees towards a low whitewashed cottage which has smoke coming out of its chimney. Alice slowly begins to calm down, begins to feel the warmth as she concentrates on the painting. Gradually she can see the insects buzzing and see them flickering in the low sunlight. The young woman is in a long white dress and straw hat, bending towards a spread of red and pink flowers on the embankment by the side of the narrow lane. Thankfully the woman will be in this position forever. So long as the painting survives she will be there on this summer's afternoon about to begin picking flowers to put in a vase for the cottage's kitchen table. Art stops in a moment all the passing minutes, hours and years. She always thought it was only culture that transcended everything impermanent.

Above the cottage are a few clouds in a light blue sky. Trees are bending low above her on either side of the lane with its rough, pale, yellow surface.

For a while Alice is the young woman in the picture. She can feel the warmth and the lowering sun on her face, can imagine picking one flower after another until she has enough for the jug on the kitchen table, a plain blue jug. The straw hat is prickling her head through her golden hair that trails in curls down over her ears. Around her are the sounds of birds and insects and the low moaning from a herd of cows in the distance.

She wants to stay here, wants to remain forever in that lovely summer's moment. But the sound of the rag and bone man returning along the front street breaks the spell and she was left with Mary's shocking and hurtful comment about her sister.

'The worse you are the better it is for her.'

'The worse you are the better it is for her.'

A dog starts barking outside as the town's church clocks start clanging out the hour and she can hear Sylvie coming up the stairs.

'What would you like for your tea mother? You can have soup and some left over beef.'

'You're very punctual today,' Alice answers trying to refocus on the present, 'I'd like…..I don't know what to…..'

'I've made some carrot soup.'

'Oh I love you Sylvie,' she suddenly finds herself saying.

Her daughter tries to smile, 'And I love you mother, but don't you get all maudlin on me.'

'I don't know where I'd be without you, where any of this family would be.'

'That's nice of you to say so,' Sylvie, quickly embarrassed, says and then changes the subject, 'What a carry on about this Halifax slasher who was frightening every woman in the North of England. It turns out all the victims were making it up. The slasher never existed. They've charged the women who made it all up, but according to the paper the police still don't know why they did it. Can you believe it? Mrs Tisley who lives above the fishmongers says she has a niece who lives in Halifax and told me everyone locked and bolted their doors when they got back from work. And to think it was those women lying their heads off. It's scandalous.'

Alice wants to respond but can only wait a few moment. She feels depressed and anxious. Somehow she has to rouse herself.

'People, when they are worried, do stupid things. It might be the threat of war. It might be. It sounds like a kind of hysteria.'

'The fear came here, the fear of this non existent slasher. Women were always talking about him in the shops and on the market, saying they didn't feel safe at night.'

'I'll have some soup if that's alright,' Alice manages.

'Do you want some bread and butter?'

'No....No.... just the soup.'

'Right you are,' Sylvie says sharply.

Alice holds out her hand for her to take, 'Thank you. I mean it Sylvie.'

'You're in a funny mood this afternoon. You're not upset are you?'

'I don't care if I am in a funny mood as you say.'

'Well I do.'

'If we didn't have feelings we....'

'Wouldn't be alive. You're always saying that.'

When Sylvie returns to the kitchen Alice tries to move position only to have her legs cramp up. Any movement is painful.

Arthur comes home home and an argument begins. She listens to raised voices but cannot make out what they are saying. It quickly becomes louder until she hears Mary's light footsteps coming rapidly up the stairs, going along the landing until her bedroom door is slammed shut.

'What was all that about?' Alice asks when Arthur finally comes up to see her.

He leans forward, kisses her on the forehead and sits himself down on the bedroom's only chair. His hair is shining in the light from the bedroom lamp, a light that emphasises his tired features and drawn expression.

'What were you and Mary arguing about?' Alice tries again.

'More to the point is how are you?'

'Arthur, what were you two talking about?'

'Her getting a job. I told her it was about time she starting looking and that she'd been moping about the house long enough. I'm sick of her traipsing about in her dressing gown at all hours of the day and night. We can't afford Mary not working. It's as simple as that.'

'You told her that?'

'I did. She knows. She understands her wages are essential. She's done nothing for weeks now and she won't tell either me or Sylvie why she left Dawsons except that she wanted a change which I find hard to believe. She's always been happy there and now all of a sudden she can't stand the place and would rather sit at home all day.'

'I don't understand what's wrong with her,' Alice says in a strained voice.

'I'm not even sure she does,' is Arthur's irritated response.

Alice pulls herself up against the pillows. He brings with him the usual smell of cigarettes and alcohol. He is in his blue three piece suit with a dark blue shirt and red patterned tie. He never takes off his shoes in the house, never puts on the slippers that Sylvie bought him for Christmas.

They are silent for a few moments. In the back lane voices are muffled. She has never any idea what her husband is thinking and would never ask him. The years have widened the distance between them. Now he is beyond her, out there in his own world. She has never been enough for him nor the children. She firmly believes that no one could ever totally satisfy him and all that this has done is make him more desperate.

She has not enough energy, not enough interest to explore Arthur's over complicated needs.

'What do you think she'll do?' she finally asks him.

He sighs, coughs, lays his hands on his knees as he leans slightly forward, 'Get a job I hope.'

She cannot tell him about Mary's awful comments about Sylvie needing her mother to be ill. She knows what his reaction would be. There would be a terrible row that would only make everything worse.

'So how has your day been? And what about the weather. I listened to the news. It's awful.'

'You should listen to it more,' he suggests, his face reddened and looking tired as he puts his right hand in his jacket pocket as though to check everything is there.

'I'll listen to it,' she struggles to say, 'To this evening's concert.'

After another pause he adds, 'Mary will sort herself out.'

'I hope so.'

'She'll soon get fed up with moping about the house and not having a weekly wage.'

'And you Arthur, are you going out tonight?' she asks tentatively while already knowing the answer.

He makes no answer to this, but instead says, 'You'll never guess who I met in the Black Bull this lunchtime, Frank Armstrong who I used to go to school with, the one who joined the army the moment he was old enough. I've not seen him in years. He was up seeing his mother, lives down in Shropshire and runs a grocery shop. After all this time I recognised him straightaway. Yes, Frank. We used to be good friends when we were younger. There was a wood up in the hills above Gargrave where we used to go thinking we were proper explorers. It was narrow wood on either side of a deep gulley. A stream ran through it. One day we were there and saw a ferret, the first time we'd seen one with its white bib, little shiny eyes and rusty coloured fur. From then on we called the wood Ferret Wood thinking we were the first people who'd discovered it. Yes, me and Frank Armstrong,' Arthur finishes before he gets off the chair and stands beside the bed looking down at Alice.

'I'll try and sleep,' she says wearily.

'Were you listening?'

'I'm tired now.'

'Alright Alice, I'll leave you then,' is his response before he kisses her again gently on the forehead.

She hardly feels his lips pressing against her skin.

Before he came up she was going to read but instead she turns off the bedside light, lying there on her back listening to the wind gaining in force while wondering about her husband, thinking that on some occasions everything seems how it used to be and then like this evening that grey veil lowers itself between them and nothing is the same.

'It's alright Alice,' she whispers to herself.

The fire is sending shadows across the ceiling.

'It's alright Alice.'

The window pane rattles as smoke is blown down the chimney. She can smell it just like she could smell Arthur's cigarettes and brandy. Outside the night is breathing heavily as she closes her eyes and drifts along a smoky trail towards a few minutes of nothingness.

CHAPTER TWENTY FOUR

Sylvie and Sally are in one of the High Street cafes busy with customers as outside cold rain falls.

'And what about those bombs going off in London?'

'The papers say it's the Irish.'

Sally pulls a face, 'As if the country hasn't enough to be getting on with.'

Sylvie tries to look through the steamed up window, wiping a patch clear and then turns to watch her friend carefully cut her cake into three pieces.

Sally picks up one of the pieces, lifts it towards her mouth before putting it back on the plate.

Her explanation is that she wants to relish every mouthful.

'You were always a fussy eater,' is Sylvie's remark, 'I remember at junior school you bringing your lunch in a biscuit tin. You were the only one who did that.'

That was my mother. She didn't trust what we were offered. Mind you, she was right. School food was awful.'

Sally is a short as Sylvie with the same frizzy hair and has wide inquisitive eyes. She too left school early to work for her father in the office of his printing firm.

She continues asking about a new young man seen at last Sunday's morning service.

'I always think tall men are good looking.'

'Good looking?'

'Well, handsome, dignified.'

'Poverty doesn't breed tall people,' Sylvie unexpectedly says in a serious voice, 'That's what my father would say to that.'

'Your Archie Andrews is....'

'He's not mine Sally.'

'But you know what I mean. He's ever so gangly. But you like him, I can tell the way you talk about him.'

'I feel sorry for him just as I feel sorry for the rest of his family. How his mother copes with all that brood I have no idea.'

'And is he learning anything?'

'I think he likes coming for the biscuits and lemonade, but everything else is a right struggle.'

'The last time I saw him he was running along the Keighley Road in his shorts and jumper with a football under one arm.'

'He goes everywhere with that ball.'

'Well rather you than me. You must have to be very patient,' Sally says before she finally decides to eat her first piece of cake.

Sylvie takes a mouthful of tea as two customers leave and three more enter.

'He's Mr Arkwright's son and his name is Paul,' she says then.

Sally frowns and then understands, asking, 'How do you know that?'

'My father knows his father. Paul is studying engineering at Leeds university.'

'Well I think he's rather dishy.'

'Sally, you think every man under the age of twenty five is dishy.'

'No I don't!'

Sylvie laughs, 'You should see your face, your cheeks have gone all red.'

'It's the heat in here, that's all.'

'Of course it is.'

'Stop sounding sarcastic.'

'I'm not being sarcastic.'

'Yes you are.'

They look at each other with happily challenging eyes until the mood is broken by Sally asking about Alice.

By now Sylvie is used to the question, but the longer her mother's illness has gone on the harder it is to find the right tone for her to answer without sounding irritated or just bored by having to repeat herself so often.

So for once she tries to be more open about the whole situation. She trusts Sally to keep everything to herself.

'She's getting worse,' she manages to admit, 'And it seems to be happening so quickly. Every day I notice little changes.'

'And what does the doctor say?'

'That there's little else they can do.'

Sally stretches to take a hold of Sylvie's hand, 'It sounds awful, awful for you and for Mary and your father.'

Sylvie forces a weak smile. For a couple of hours she wants to forget all about her mother's illness and yet it seems inescapable. It is a shadow to everything she does and thinks.

She lets go of Sally's hand as a waitress squeezes past. Now her mood has changed and anxiety taken over.

'Mr Elgin and doctor Donnolly are always suggesting that I have to think about myself more than I do.'

Sally's expression is uncertain as she answers, 'I suppose they mean you should be out of the house more, meeting your friends and eating lots of cake.'

'Oh yes!' she laughs, 'I'm sure that's what they mean. My trouble is the more bothered I am the more I want to eat.'

'You've always liked eating.'

'You're no different.'

'I never said I was.'

'Anyway, I'd rather not talk about my mother if that's alright with you.'

'Of course it is.'

'But when I say that, the only thing that comes to mind is what's going to happen in the world, in Europe and all Hitler's carry on.'

'Our cousin Harold who works in London says in his latest letter that all the talk down there is about gas masks, blackouts and rationing.'

'That's all we need,' is Sylvie's critical response, 'Can you imagine, rationing?'

'And everyone having to have thick curtains so no light shines from their house and all the street lights turned off and Harold says there'll be wardens going around to make sure everyone follows the rules and children having to take their gas masks with them to school. It just sounds terrible.'

'I don't know about your father but mine is convinced there will be a war. He get angry when he talks about no one learning any lessons from the previous war.'

'My father says the same.'

'And what about you? What do……'

'I've no idea Sylvie. I read the papers and listen to the radio news and it all sounds hopeless, and yet I want to think, want to believe that it can somehow be avoided.'

'And let Hitler have what he wants.'

'And what does he want?'

Sylvie takes another mouthful of tea as Sally has her second piece of cake.

'So which stall will you be on at the chapel bazaar?' is Sally trying to change such a miserable subject.

Sylvie glances around the busy café before she answers, 'Bits and pieces, what about you?'

Her friend smiles, 'The cake stall of course.'

'Trust you.'

'I hope the customers will.'

'Very funny.'

'I like our bazaars.'

'They raise a lot of money.'

'I hope it'll be busy.'

'So long as we don't have another snow storm. Last weekend was dreadful,' Sylvie says as she feels herself failing to resurrect her previous mood.

Sally greedily takes her last piece of cake before asking, 'And how is your Mary getting on. Has she got another job yet? It's strange going into Dawsons and she's not there.'

Sylvie uses her sleeve to wipe away some of the condensation on the window to look out at the rain bouncing off the pavement.

'She's talking about working in one of the big Bradford or Leeds stores.'

'She'll do well wherever she goes.'

Sylvie makes no response to this comment. Over the last weeks she has not been able to feel optimistic about anything to do with her sister.

'We're not getting on at the moment,' she decides to say.

'Just like me and my brothers. I love them both but they drive me mad sometimes. In the house they're so lazy and expect everything to be done for them. I tell them they're old enough now to join the army. That puts them both into a proper panic. To be fair I don't think Roger minds the idea so much but Alan I can tell is terrified when anything about war and the armed forces are mentioned. I can't imagine either of them being soldiers especially our Alan.'

'We're old enough as well.'

At that Sally suddenly looks serious, 'Thank our Lord that women won't have to fight.'

'But they'll be expected to do everything else. You just see. It'll be like mother describes about the last war, women in the factories, women working on the farms and all the while having to look after the children.'

CHAPTER TWENTY FIVE

Billy Smith is driving while Arthur sits in the back with Gordon like the three points of a triangle, the shape of his fear, its acute angles cutting into his guts.

'I want to smoke.'

'Fuck off Arthur,' Billy mutters.

'What's the harm in me having a smoke?'

Gordon turns and tries one of his thuggish looks straight from some Hollywood gangster film.

Arthur gives up and thinks instead of the evening he is supposed to be spending with Kitty. He feels sick, scared and angry at being forced to go with these two.

It Is January 1939 and a light rain is falling as they finally reach the outskirts of Bradford driving past a huge mill with its tall chimney belching out smoke. It is a miserable January evening. There are few people about. They pass two women pushing prams and a horse and cart full of bales of wool. Three men are standing smoking outside a corner shop, their coat collars pulled up against the rain.

Turning off the Manningham Road they enter an area of cobbled streets. On either side are warehouses with barred windows. Eventually they stop in front of the doors of one of these grim, high buildings.

Arthur follows Billy up wooden steps with Gordon behind. The office is on the top floor. It is a huge loft with the only light coming from a desk lamp at the far end.

'I hope you've brought the right customer boys,' comes a voice with a soft Southern accent.

Arthur's arms are released and without being told he starts walking towards the desk.

'Arthur Townsley. Arthur Townsley,' his name is repeated, 'Come and take a seat and tell me all about it. That's why you're here Arthur, to tell me all about it.'

Eventually out of the shadows appears a small, thin man in a smart suit and tie with short cut silver hair and pale, gaunt features.

Fear rises up like bile in Arthur's throat as he sits down opposite him. He knows he has to say something, has to try and gain some sort of position from which he can refuse to accept what is happening.

'This is bloody ridiculous,' he tries, 'Being…..'

'Yes, I agree, very melodramatic,' he is interrupted, 'But I really wanted to meet you face to face Arthur so we could have a proper conversation and sort out this problem. Because whatever happens Arthur there is a problem. At least admit that. If you're a proper gentleman I'm sure you'll agree. That's who I'm dealing with, isn't that right, a proper gentleman, one who understands the ways of the world, who understands how if you owe someone something then you pay them back? You pay them back Arthur and then everything is sorted neat and tidy. That's how we like it, don't we boys, neat and tidy?'

There is no sound from the other two lost in the shadows behind Arthur.

'I think that…..' Arthur starts only to be interrupted again.

'Mr Andrews. You call me Mr Andrews and I'm afraid nobody said you could speak. I don't remember telling you to speak so if I were you Arthur I'd just listen.'

Andrews is wearing a dark green tweed suit with a blue shirt and green tie, his grey hair brushed straight back from his thin forehead.

'I want to smoke.'

'You did it again Arthur.'

'I want to….'

'You're speaking when I…'

Arthur takes out his packet of full strength Capstan.

'No Arthur, not in here. There are strict fire regulations in these places so put the cigarette back and listen.'

'Alright, I'm listening,' Arthur replies trying to sound as confident as he can manage.

Andrews smirks, settles one hand on his desk and there is silence except the sound of heavier rain on the rooftop above them. Arthur feels the tension growing. He is more scared than ever. He knows Andrews' sudden silence is supposed to make him feel like that and he is succeeding.

'I run a business and you're one of my customers. I offer a service that is simplicity itself,' Andrews starts while rubbing the palm of his hand over the surface of the desk, 'Twenty percent interest that doubles each month on any arrears. I've invested in you Arthur and yet so far I'm not seeing any dividends, the ones I expected. In fact all I have from you Arthur is a big problem and I hate problems,' he continues in his soft, threatening voice before he suddenly asks, 'But don't imagine I run a small concern. I have over twenty employees out paying visits right now.' What do you think about that Mr Townsley?'

'I don't think anything,' Arthur forces himself to reply.

Andrews looks at him across the desk while still smoothing over its surface with his hand. It is a slow, hypnotic motion in wide circles until he stops, turns his hand into a fist and then relaxes it.

'We think but we don't think,' he says, 'And if we do think Arthur where do these thoughts come from? That's the million dollar question. I'm sure you have some idea, you being an educated, could I say a man of culture as well. Nothing like a bit of culture, a bit of old Michelangelo or Beethoven. Makes life worth living, doesn't it Arthur?'

'I want to know what….'

'No Arthur!' Andrews exclaims, 'I'm not at all interested in what you want. It's what I want that matters. That's what we're talking about here. It's what I want that matters, understand?'

'No.'

'Well you'd better speed up your mental processes and start understanding. Time is money Arthur. Always has been and always will be. Now…….'

He stops again, swivels his chair round so he has his back to Arthur. The rain is still falling heavily. Floorboards creak from where Andrew's two men are waiting at the far end of the office. Fear is acid burning in Arthur's stomach. He is terrified of what might happen to him. He has no idea how to react. All he knows is that he somehow has to get out of this place.

'You're not very interesting,' Andrews starts again still with his back to him, 'In fact Arthur I'd say you were a bit of a disappointment. I thought we might have had a friendly chat about the advantages of Capitalism over all other economic systems. What do you say Arthur? How about that for an in depth topic? Come on, I'm sure you have an opinion.'

'Why am I here?' Arthur asks boldly.

At that Andrews swivels his chair back round, his voice tighter as he replies, 'I would have thought that was obvious, as clear as a day in June. Go on, have a try. You tell me why you think you're here.'

Arthur forces himself to make eye contact, but for once decides to say nothing, trying his best not to be intimidated by this man.

'What a shame Arthur. Me and the boys wonder where all your hard earned money goes every month. We just can't work it out. Surely it can't be all on doctor's bills for your sick wife. Mind you, it could for your classy bit on the side, yes very classy is our Kitty. I would have thought a bit out of your league Arthur, a bit too posh for you. But you never know. Maybe when it comes to the fairer sex you're just a lucky man. At least it seems you might be lucky in something. The lady in question must have expensive tastes or yet again it could be you and your snappy suits or your regular nights out or maybe it's the car. It all adds up Arthur.'

It makes him sick, the amount this man seems to know about him. Suddenly he cannot focus. The whole situation seems unreal. It is as though he is acting a part in some stupidly clicheed film.

But Andrews has not finished, 'Let me see your wallet Arthur.'

For a moment this did not register.

'I want your wallet,' Andrews repeats.

Defiantly Arthur unbuttons his coat. He has his trilby resting on his knees as he takes out his wallet from his jacket's inside pocket and places it on the desk.

Andrews picks it up and counts the money it holds, 'Forty five pounds, not bad Arthur for a Tuesday evening. Is it for a night out or maybe a little present for the suffering wife or a classy negligee for the bit on the side? And who's this then?' he asks as he holds up a photograph of Mary and Sylvie when they were children.

'My daughters.'

'Of course, that'll be Mary the eldest and there's chubby little Sylvie.'

Arthur feels sick at how much he knows about his family and the rest of his private life. He senses that all this clever chat from Andrews is as much to impress Billy and Gordon as it is to intimidate him.

'And where was this delightful photograph taken?' Andrews asks about another photograph.

'Does it matter?'

'Yes, Arthur or I wouldn't be asking.'

'Scarborough, on the beach.'

'Did you take the picture? Were you even there?'

'My wife took the photo and yes I was there.'

'No need to sound so tetchy.'

'What do you expect?'

'Manners Arthur and a civil tongue.'

The large space of this warehouse loft has become a tight hole of darkness in which he is suffocating. Arthur feels strained and powerless. This man is in total control and knows it.'

Desperately he tries to find something to say which will show his contempt and disgust at what is happening here.

Suddenly he says, 'I want to borrow another five hundred.'

At least this has an effect as Andrews' eyes narrow and his thin features become even tighter.

'Or let's round it off to two thousand,' Arthur adds.

Andrews starts smoothing his hand over the surface of his desk again, but this time the motion is quicker and more agitated. When he stops he rests his elbow on the desk and points a finger at Arthur but makes no comment.

They sit there in a tense silence. Arthur is aware of the other two in the shadows behind him.

Finally Andrews lowers his hand saying sharply, 'This is not a game Arthur.'

'I never said it was.'

'You're trying to take the mickey.'

'No.'

'It certainly sounds it.'

'Of course, I'd expect a higher rate of interest.'

Andrews puts the photos back in his wallet, keeps the money except for a five pound note, and tosses the wallet back to him. Arthur's trilby falls off his knees when he reaches down to catch it.

'I see your reactions have not been dulled by the amount of alcohol you consume. Brandy is your tipple I believe,' is Andrews' sarcastic comment.

It is now that Arthur realises what is about to happen. He should have seen it coming all along. Something so obvious makes him feel even more vulnerable. Violence is on the edge of Andrews' every word. Its threat is so frightening and there is nothing Arthur can do except sit there and do what he is told like a pathetic schoolboy in front of the headmaster.

Finally Andrews continues with, 'This is what we're going to do so you'd better listen carefully. Are you paying attention Arthur or are you thinking of where you should be and what you should be doing this evening? Is that what's on your mind?'

'Seeing as Billy has your car keys,' Andrews continues in a more relaxed voice, 'You have them, don't you Billy?'

'Yes boss,' comes the loud answer from out of the shadows.

'For starters we'll take the car. Even you have the sense to use public transport after a few drinks with your lady friend. Driving home after a big session doesn't sound like a sensible idea and seeing as you think of yourself as being a sensible man then you'll catch the bus back to Skipton, all very discrete. Is Kitty discrete Arthur? I bet she is. How on earth did you manage to reel in a classy piece like that? But I forgot, you're a lucky man Arthur when it comes to the ladies and it's always handy to have a good handful of money to ensure that continues. Isn't that right Mr Townsley?'

'I need my car.'

'No you don't.'

'I said I need my car.'

'I'm afraid Arthur that's now out of the question. The car is ours as part of your repayment package, and from now on if you don't want Gordon paying close attention to your legs and arms you'll be smart enough to start on a hundred a month, and that's me being reasonable, very reasonable.'

'I'll never manage that amount,' Arthur tries.

'Yes you will.'

'Not on what....'

'Yes you will Arthur,' Andrews interrupts, 'And if there's a problem there's always Kitty and her rich parents who might be able to help. You see the way things are developing Arthur old Hitler is going to be demanding more and more so sensible people like me want to get out while they can. It's the big USA for me Arthur. That's where I'm bound before this whole thing kicks off and we're at war again, and as you know war can be a sorry business. You know all about that, don't you Arthur.'

Andrews stops, looks at his watch and adds, 'Anyway, the eight thirty five is about due so if I were you I'd try and catch it. Goodbye Arthur. I hope we don't have to have another of these get togethers. I find them very tedious, very tedious indeed. Gentlemen, will you escort Arthur here to the nearest bus stop?'

'I want to....'

'No Arthur, you're finished here,' Andrews tells him before he is aware of Billy and Gordon standing either side of him.

On the bus he empties the flask of brandy down his throat trying to melt some of the anger and revulsion he is feeling. Arriving in the rain swept Skipton's bus station instead of the Black Bull he walks down to one of the smaller pubs by the canal which he hardly ever frequents. He wants to be left alone. When he enters the half empty bar it is only the barman who gives him a quick glance of recognition as he orders a double brandy and a half of beer.

In a few minutes he is up at the bar to order another double brandy and a half. Returning to his seat he begins staring at the flames of the fire and the smoke twisting up the chimney. Then he lights a cigarette, tossing the match into the flames.

How the hell, he is thinking, did I end up involved with a man like Andrews? With him it was as much about power as money. But if it is anyone's fault it is his own. No one else is to blame.

Gradually the more he returns to the bar the more his frustration and resentment begin to melt. Nowadays it takes longer for the alcohol to have its effect. He begins to drift in front of the warm fire with muffled voices coming from the rest of the pub, drift into memories he is always trying to avoid. But on this night he is careless.

He is staring at the smoke going up the pub chimney remembering the mist curling away towards an unseen horizon. Hundreds of Chinese were in their traditional jackets clasped at the front and their flat, wide brimmed hats disappearing and appearing as the mist shifted about. They looked ready to be planting rice not levelling off a battlefield. He and his squad are sharing the same piece of ripped up ground as the Chinese work around them. There is the overpowering stench of rotting flesh mixed in with the odour from the sodden, heavy earth through which they have to dig and claw their way to pull up one piece of a body after another, search for name and number tags.

He drinks more brandy as out of the mist come the first tourists. Getting out of their cars is the absurdity of those wanting to see where their loved ones died when for all they know they might be squelching on top of who they are there for or about to step on an unexploded bomb. The ridiculous becomes normality. The war has been ended for such a short time and grief dominates over everything. He argues with these battleground voyeurs, tells them to bugger off, but they do not listen. How can they when grief consumes them as they look emptily around at the barbed wire and bomb craters, at his squad and the Chinese and sometimes the locals like scavenging crows picking into the ground searching for a juicy morsel.

'Come on you fucking shits! Get on with it! And you Townsley, keep your fucking mouth shut when there are visitors! Understand, you fucking piece of shit!'

The fire crackles. A piece of coal falls to the front. Someone is laughing. He looks up to see the men at the bar smoking, joking together as more memories slide out of the darkness.

'What did you expect Alice? What? Go on tell me! How did you think I'd be? That I'd just come back as though nothing has happened. Well, it has Alice. A lot has happened to me and all the rest, all the other poor buggers who have managed to survive. But what has survived? You tell me Alice, tell me what you think is left or who……who is left?'

He remembers but does not want to remember. He can see her stiff, miserable face. He can hear her.

'I don't expect anything Arthur. I'm not expecting things to be how they were before you left. How can I? We know what you….'

'No you don't!' he shouts when he does not want to shout.

Mary is in their bed listening to every word.

'Nobody knows what it was like. Why should they? They weren't there. You weren't there.'

'But I can try and imagine.'

'My God,' he had groaned, 'Listen to yourself, just listen.'

Some one is tapping him on the shoulder, 'Come on mate. We're closing up,' comes the voice of the barman from a smoke filled distance.

Outside the rain has stopped. Grey clouds are racing across the moon as Arthur concentrates on putting one step in front of the other along the canal path. It has become one of those nights when he feels defeated, when the past has brought out its ghosts. He is locked in a battle with himself. He has been threatened, lost his car and feels sick with everything he has just been through.

'Come on Arthur,' he mutters to himself as he walks towards the High Street.

'What do you want Arthur?' Alice had once asked him.

'Everything,' had been his reply.

CHAPTER TWENTY SIX

Is life just one long illness for which there is no cure?

Mary feels surrounded by sick people.

Aunt Rose is in her stark, cold stone sink kitchen. She will be making soup and thinly sliced ham sandwiches. She too suffers from her own illness, this longing for the past where she and her Edward once lived.

Mary is seated at the table shuffling the cards they have been using before placing them back in their tin for the next time. She is determined to cure her aunt and bring her into the present. No woman should sacrifice everything for the memory of a man however much she misses him.

It is the same with Frobisher. She cannot allow him to continue dominating her moods. Why should she feel such guilt and humiliation? It as so though the woman always has to accept the blame. She is sick of it, sick of allowing herself to be affected in this way. And yet it has to be a continual conscious effort to change how she feels. For weeks now she has been trying.

'Will you set the table Mary?' is the call from the kitchen.

The harsh, depressing days are worsening. Nothing is right. She is never satisfied, always on edge.

Frobisher will always be there like a constant threat. And yet she has to defeat his effect. There are dreams of his thing, his disgusting hard thing. There are memories of the pain between her legs and the blood trickling down the inside of her thighs as she struggled to make her way home, memories of her ripped nylons and the bruising on her arms where he had held her down.

'It's nearly ready,' Aunt Rose announces.

Quickly Mary sets the table for the two of them.

She knows to succeed she has to begin all over again to care for herself.

'There we are,' says Rose as she comes in with the tea tray.

Already her aunt has agreed to have the kitchen modernised, to have a new sink and cupboards.

They have their tea followed by a glass of sherry.

'Edward liked a cigarette after his tea,' Rose says after they have cleared the table and set themselves either side of the fire.

'You were married for such a short time,' Mary says.

Her aunt smiles, 'Not long enough. That's the trouble I suppose. We weren't together long enough to discover each other's faults. It was a perfect romance. It ended before…..Oh I don't know……before we really knew each other.'

As always she is in a dark coloured dress. When she goes out she wear a black coat and hat. The weekly seances have ended but Rose still attends the Spiritualist church.

'Edward is as close as the breath I breathe,' she had once said.

Mary is confronting the past for both of them.

'We can do this up together,' she says, 'So long as that's what you want.'

Rose glances at the fire and then looks at her niece with a doubtful but serious expression, 'I don't want to upset your mother or your father because I know what Arthur will say.'

'He can help, why not?'

'He can help, yes, with sorting this house, but he won't want you leaving yours.'

'It's not up to him,' Mary says strongly.

'Your father wants things his way, always has done. Our mother spoilt him so much. He got away with everything.'

At that Mary says no more for a few minutes. Her aunt needs time to consider things.

Mary feels more comfortable here than anywhere else. They are women of different generations but share a strong bond.

She could never have told the police about Frobisher. He would have denied everything and who would the police have believed? Certainly not her story of the virgin and the monster.

'But you're not changing your mind?' she has to ask.

Rose looks anxious, 'Of course not. I'm not Mary.'

'Because I want this to work just as much as you do.'

'And it will.'

'I know people will never understand, me leaving home only to move across town.'

'That doesn't matter,' Rose stops her.

Mary is surprised by her tone of voice.

'Sometimes I'm not sure what matters.'

'You feeling better. You getting a job. You Mary doing what you want to do.'

'You make it sound so simple.'

'I know it isn't. I know that, but we'll manage. We both have to start thinking about the future,' Rose adds, 'You're right about that and it's about time I started.'

'It doesn't mean you'll forget anything, especially Edward.'

'Oh don't worry, there's no chance of that.'

Rose sits upright with her hands holding tightly to the chair arms.

'It's Alice I'm thinking about,' she says then.

Mary feels herself suddenly losing any certainty.

'I won't…..I can't leave until……I just can't.'

'She's your mother and she needs you there.'

'Not that my being there helps.'

'Of course it does.'

'It's Sylvie who looks after her not me.'

'Alice needs you there.'

'I don't think so.'

'We'll be alright Mary. I want to think about the future but at times it seems….Oh I don't know.'

'I have to go,' Mary says suddenly.

Getting up she goes for her coat and hat in the hallway as Rose follows on, standing, there, forcing a smile.

'I'll see you on Monday then aunt Rose.'

'And you mind the pavements,' is Rose's warning.'

Friday night the High Street is busy. All Mary can think about as she walks quickly along the wet pavement is pictures in the paper of air balloons over London, sandbags outside government buildings and everyone with gas mask boxes strung over their shoulders. She looks at all the people coming from the cinema, coming out of the pubs and the fish and chip shops and there is no sense to any of it. What are they doing? Where are they going? It is meaningless. Life starts and life ends and everything in between is hopping from one little pleasure to another. That is all there is. Eating, drinking, getting married, all of it so hopeless, so pathetically sad. They have their children. If they are lucky they have their jobs and enough to live on and that is all there is. It is ordinary life repeated over and over again. There they are, people she recognises, scrambling about for a little enjoyment, a little pleasure. War is coming and all of it becomes more frantic, more desperate.

She wants things to be different. She wants to be different. She hates her insignificance. She hates being a consequence of someone else's actions.

A fine mesh of rain wets her face. She is aware of only this moment. There is nothing else except just now, just these steps towards home. They are taking her back into the world of illness, of that smell of disinfectant and medicine.

'I've been to see Aunt Rose,' she announces as she enters the kitchen.

Sylvie looks up from her book, 'You told me that's where you were going. How is she?'

'Is father out?'

'Yes, and his car is still in the garage, says it's worse than they first thought. He's having to walk to work.'

'Oh he won't like that.'

Sylvie goes into the larder, brings out cheese, butter and bread and makes herself a sandwich.

'Do you want one?'

'No, I'll make us some tea,' Mary answers.

'Mother's awake and listening to the news.'

'I can hear it.'

They sit at the table. Mary pours the tea and Sylvie finishes her sandwich.

'I might buy a new coat,' Sylvie tries, 'What do you think?'

Mary looks carefully at her before saying, 'I've written to Mr Norris for a reference.'

'Are you going to get another job? I know father wants you to get one.'

'Of course he does.'

'And are you?'

'Yes. I'm trying for John Lewis in Leeds and then we can both decide on your new coat. What do you say to that?'

'I'd like that.'

'Well that's settled then.'

'Does that mean having to get the train every day?'

'Yes.'

'It seems a long way to go to work.'

'I don't mind.'

Sylvie gets up and puts up the fireguard.

Mary says, 'It'll be alright Sylvie.'

Her sister turns and replies, 'I'm not sure if anything will be alright.'

'We can't do anything…..You can't do anything more than you do.'

'I think…..I think she's….I think she's getting worse.'

'Yes, I know.'

'I just don't want her to die.'

'Nobody does Sylvie,' says Mary as he gets up and stands there in front of her.

'It won't be alright, will it?'

Mary replies strongly, 'No, it won't be alright Sylvie.'

'I hate to think of it.'

'Then don't. You do enough.'

'I can't stop it, can I Mary?'

'No.'

'Well that's all that matters.'

'You matter Sylvie.'

'But she's going to die.'

'No one knows that for certain.'

'I know that.'

'No you don't.'

They stand there. Mary waits for her sister but Sylvie for once has nothing more to say.

'I'll sort the fire, you get to bed,' Mary tells her.

After Sylvie has gone upstairs Mary lights a cigarette warming herself in front of the last of the coals.

Later she stops on the landing. Music is now coming from her mother's room. She pops her head round the door to see Alice asleep, her mouth slightly open and her hands on top of the eiderdown.

She quietly turns off the radio and sits down on the chair against the wall trying to ignore the smell of the commode and her mother's slow grating breaths.

It feels as if she was walking over an abyss. Below there is nothing. Below is where the fear begins of her mother's death.

Alice's skin is a pale yellow. Her lips are swollen and her eyelids keep flickering as she sleeps.

Mary is for once totally absorbed. This is her mother. This is the person who once dominated her life. She was a governess, worked in the mill and the library. She brought up two children and somehow managed her wayward husband. She loves books, classical music and once enjoyed trips to the theatre. She is this person of so many parts. Like everyone she is a combination of infinite components. Like everyone she is a universe of thoughts, feelings, memories, ideas, plans. Lying there is the woman who gave her life. Lying there is the one she used to idealise, Alice with her elegant clothes, calm, easy manner and such grace, such obvious accomplishments that she made her so proud, made her feel special and different.

And now.......now is to look and feel such despair, such sadness. She is this whole world of life that is about to end. It will end. It will stop. She will stop. One second she will be there and the next she will be gone and it feels impossible, feels absurd.

Mary pushes herself against the back of the chair, gripping her knees, forcing herself to remain where she is. She wants to pick up her mother and hold her, wants her to go on, to breath, live now and forever.

Now and forever.

It is hopeless and desperate. Life fails. As it begins life is already ending. All anyone can do is find some sort of reason to live, children, food, love, sport, gambling, something that fills the hours and gives enough meaning to pretend that life will never end. It is the hardest game of existence, this pretence, this constant forgetting.

Mary has never felt so aware, so perceptively sharp, and yet all it adds up to is that her mother's illness is unforgiving, is irreversible. Human life is courageous and ridiculous at the same time.

'Goodnight mother,' she says calmly, softly.

But she does not move.

She repeats, 'Goodnight mother.'

She hears her voice as though it were an echo of what she is feeling.

Why be strong? She has to be strong.

What are her reasons?

Fear of emptiness, boredom, nothingness is the only reason.

But she knows she will keep going. That is the only thing she can do. If there is not that then she is lost and she refuses to be lost, refuses to be overwhelmed by her mother's condition and her own miserable situation that somehow she has to change.

Finally, she gets up, puts her mother's hands under the bedclothes, kisses her on her warm, sticky forehead, switches off the bedside light and leaves her.

Sylvie is sleeping. Mary undresses, puts on her nightie hurriedly, brushes her hair before she gets into bed. Rain is rattling against the window, a delicate washing of the glass as she lays there listening.

The town is close around her. It is January 1939. Already there are rumours of children being evacuated from major cities. Already there are those images of air balloons and searchlights.

How mad can she be looking for a job when war might be months, weeks away?

But there is nothing else she can do. She has to find a job. She will find a job. There is Aunt Rose and the possibilities of work that are keeping her going. And she has to keep going.

CHAPTER TWENTY SEVEN

Alice managed to pull herself up far enough for her to shift her legs sideways and eventually sit on the edge of the bed, her toes pressing into the bedside rug.

She breaths slowly while listening to the sound of the birds coming through the slightly open window. A breeze is wafting the lace curtains in and out. From her new position she can see more of the back lane and the opposite roofs shining in the morning sun.

Her world has expanded just a little. Her breathing becomes regular, less painful.

Overnight something has changed, less pain, less stiffness. She feels a different sort of day beginning, one that for once gives her a little more freedom, leaves a little more of herself.

She needs this. The doctor said there would be some good days. He did not have to tell her how precious they would be, how much a small degree of change could affect everything.

Momentarily she feels dizzy sitting there trying to keep her back as straight as possible as she grips hold of the edge of the bed. Her hair slides down either side of her face. She reaches and just manages to take hold of her glass from the bedside table to take a sip of water.

However difficult she wants more of life, more of each moment, to hear the birds, to breath in the warming air, to be able to move without Sylvie's constant attention even, to see her room from a different perspective.

'When the good days come don't overdo it Alice or there will be less of them in the future.'

Doctor Donnolly has a soft, concerned voice. She knows he really cares. He is doing everything he can to keep her alive and give her the possibilities of feeling like this.

She would like to stand but when she tries her arms are too weak to push her up off the bed.

But today it does not matter. She is satisfied and relieved even to get this far.

She has to decide what to do when she hears Sylvie coming up the stairs. Does she remain where she is or lie back down under the bedclothes and pretend nothing has changed?

Does it matter?

The air touches her legs, her feet. It feels like another layer of skin, warm, delicate and reassuring.

Someone is talking out in the back lane. She cannot tell what they are saying. It is a voice she does not recognise, a woman speaking rapidly with a tone of complaint in her voice. She can smell the smoke from Skipton's chimneys, hear a dog barking and the rumble of a lorry going along the Keighley Road. But it is the movement of the curtains that holds her attention wafting in and out being pushed by the breeze.

In her memory is a bright blue vision, sparkling light is bouncing off the sea as wave after wave crashes its spume up the beach. It is Bamburgh beach on a wild spring day and she is trudging along with her sister, the two of them holding hands for support with mother and father tagging on behind. They have their heads down screaming against the force of the exhilarating wind. Everything is in motion, is sound and colour, waves and flying sand. Their coats are flapping around their knees, their hair blown about in all directions.

She smiles as she remembers. She hears Sylvie clattering down in the kitchen with the radio playing. She is part of the life of the house. For once she is aware of everything around her, every sound, smell and movement.

She always believed in culture especially literature, the words she used to appreciate.

Does it really matter now?

She is content to savour these passing minutes and leave the rest behind her. It is enough to be allowed out of such a small prison cell into something a little larger.

Her illness is the prison from which she knows she will never totally escape, but all that counts are these days when there is less pain and her mind functions a little more accurately.

She hears Sylvie and makes the decision to stay where she is.

'Mother, what on earth are you doing?' she is asked in her daughter's shocked tone.

'Sitting up.'

'And how did you manage that?'

'I just did. I wanted to try to sit up and for once I managed it all by myself.'

'Goodness,' Sylvie laughs.

'Yes,' Alice smiles back.

'And are you alright sitting there?'

'I've not felt like this for weeks. The moment I woke up I knew something had changed, that there had been a shift and that I was a little better than yesterday.'

'Doctor Donnolly said this might happen.'

'Yes and thankfully he was right.'

'But you mustn't overdo it.'

'Don't worry Sylvie, I'm not about to ask you for a dance.'

'Now that would be a thing, the two of us dancing around the bedroom,' she says smiling.

She can see Sylvie is as glad as she is, sense her surprise turn quickly into relief.

'I'd like some flowers from the garden,' she says, 'What's growing at the moment?'

Sylvie purses her lips while considering such a question.

'Just a small vase of something on the mantelpiece. I'd like that,' Alice adds.

After a few minutes Sylvie returns with a vase of daffodils.

'These are the first of the year.'

'They look lovely. A bit of colour always helps, and I like it when tulips open out completely. Then they look like a different flower altogether. I'm glad you've managed to keep the garden going Sylvie. What with everything else you have to do I was worried it would be too much. I used to love being on my hands and knees digging and planting. Then I'd forget what I'd put in or where it had been planted so every spring and summer was a surprise, flowers appearing I had no idea were there.'

'I wasn't going to let all you've done to the garden just go to waste. We've the best front garden on the street. Most of them have a bit of a lawn, a few hedges and that's it. Whereas ours has different flowers growing right through the season. It'll be the bluebells next and then the roses and daisies. There's always something to look forward to.'

'Thank goodness we can depend on nature to keep up our spirits.'

'That sounds like a quote out of one of Mary's magazines mother.'

'Does it?' Alice asks happily.

'Anything nowadays that keeps people happy. Seeing you like this certainly helps mine.'

'I'm glad.'

'And is there anything else you would like?'

'Yes, there is, two slices of toast and jam and a mug of milky coffee. If that's alright?'

'Of course it is.'

When Sylvie is back downstairs Alice closes her eyes and slows her breathing before looking across the room and the shaft of sunlight cutting across the opposite wall. It forms a widening triangle of pale yellow light over the wallpaper like a widening path ending in the empty fireplace.

Sylvie returns with her late breakfast.

'Do you remember that winter when you went walking along the ice that was frozen solid over the canal? There was a whole gang of you.'

'I remember,' says Sylvie as she puts the mug of coffee on the bedside table and hands over the plate of toast and jam to her mother.

'And it was your father who saw you on his way back from work.'

'He wasn't angry. I expected him to be angry but he just told us all to get off the ice so we did.'

'You wouldn't get your father losing his temper in public.'

'Well he didn't, not until he got me home and then I was given a right lecture about the dangers of walking on ice.'

'That was a bad winter.'

'I remember us all spending evenings for weeks in front of the kitchen fire just trying to keep warm.'

'Or you were out sledging in the park.'

'That was the best, me and Shirley racing each other downhill.'

'It seems such a long time ago now,' Alice says.

'Not to me it doesn't.'

The same woman's voice breaks in as before from the back lane that Alice heard earlier.

'Who is that?' she wants to know.

'That's Mrs Davies and Mrs Tate having a right carry on about something. I heard them down in the kitchen.'

'What are they arguing about?'

'It's not an argument. It's Mrs Davies complaining about the price of meat at the butchers and Mrs Tate poor dear has to stand there and listen.'

'Brenda Davies?'

'The very same.'

'I remember. She's always got something to moan about.'

'It's a national pastime mother or so it says in the newspaper. We're a nation of moaners. We love to have something to complain about, the weather, the price of things, the Germans, anything and everything. It's what makes us happy.'

Alice notices the lace curtains being blown into the room and then sucked back again like a sail buffeted by the wind.

Sylvie goes to pull the window down a few inches.

'It must be hard not knowing how you're going to feel one day to the next.'

Alice carefully drinks some of the coffee and then says, 'I suppose it is. It's so unpredictable. I do nothing different one day to the next and then for no apparent reason I wake up like this morning feeling things are different, not a lot, but enough to appreciate the fact there's been a little improvement. My heart seems to have its moods like everything else. Anyway, sometimes it's better not to think about it too much and just appreciate when things have improved.'

'Do you want a face wash?'

'I will later Sylvie. Thanks for asking, but I'll do it myself today.'

'I should have asked earlier. It's past ten o clock already and I've stacks to do.'

'Well you'd better get on with it then,' Alice says warmly.

Sylvie stops at the door, 'It's good to see you like this mother. It helps me as much as it does you.'

'That's because we're a team. We depend on each other.'

'Of course we do.'

Alice finds herself smiling as Sylvie goes back down the stairs before she feels a fluttering in her chest.

'Now Alice,' she says to herself, 'Just a little longer please, a little longer like this.'

Why her?

Why is she the one to have a heart that is failing?

Why not Arthur, the man who suits himself and does exactly what he wants?

Why her and not him?

Where is the justice in any of it?

Why not Arthur? It would serve him right.

But God works in mysterious ways.

Then she stops thinking and allows herself to feel again the room around her, the air, the light, the noise of the radio downstairs. A hooter from one of the barges sounds out followed by a motorbike engine revving over the canal bridge and the sound of men working on a roof somewhere, their hammers and voices merging together. So many little things but they are enough. They create the day, create the small world around her.

CHAPTER TWENTY EIGHT

'Aunt Rose said you didn't want any tea.'

Sylvie is drying her hands on her pinny when she enters the sick room. That is what she now calls it

Her mother slowly shakes her head, 'I'm not hungry.'

For weeks Sylvie can manage the same determined, practical mood and then for no apparent reason her fortitude will crumble into an overwhelming confusion of feelings.

'Don't make things worse mother, worse for yourself,' she finds herself saying and then regrets it.

Alice makes no response as Sylvie comes closer to the bed to take her hand. It feels swollen and clammy.

It is too much, all the care, housework, worry. Her mother's illness dominates over her life and in moments like this she feels hopeless and frustrated.

'Things can't be worse, not really,' Alice replies in a low, strained voice.

'And that doesn't help,' Sylvie says back as she releases her mother's hand and brings up the chair.

Every accusation makes her feel worse, more guilty. She knows her patient is too weak and ill to resist whatever she says to her. But to see her mother's puffy, yellow features and exhausted eyes is to confront her own miserable failure. Her and the doctor have not been able to turn the tide and bring Alice back to anything like her old self.

She picks up her mother's glass and goes to the bathroom to replace it with fresh water.

'Here,' she says gently, 'You have to drink whatever happens,' putting he hand behind her mother's head to help her sit up a little and sip at the water.

When she rests back she sighs, 'I think it…..it would be best if I…….I didn't have any more visitors.'

'Why? I don't think…….'

'They leave me too tired Sylvie.'

'But you have to see other people.'

'No…. I don't want to see anyone but you, your sister and your father.'

'And the doctor.'

Alice lowers her eyes, looking at her swollen hands, 'Yes…and the doctor.'

'I don't want you going day after day without seeing any one else. Doctor Donnolly says it is important for you to….'

'Sylvie, please,' Alice says breathlessly.

'This room is too stuffy,' is all Sylvie can manage, 'Do you need the toilet because if you don't I'll empty this,' she adds, taking the bucket out of the commode and returning to the bathroom to flush it out.

When she comes back Alice has her eyes closed, her enlarged stomach rising and falling under the bedclothes.

'Aunt Rose has put too much coal on the fire,' Sylvie complains while returning the commode's bucket, her mind in a tangle of different responses.

How can she be angry? How can she want her mother to try harder when for over four years Alice has been struggling against an impossible condition?

'Mary will be over to Elliot street this evening,' she adds.

The rag and bone man is returning along the front street as children's voices shouting and laughing come from the back lane.

'They're out of school,' Sylvie comments.

'They're out of school,' is her mother echoing her words as Alice opens her eyes before adding, 'You would have made a grand teacher.'

The comment is too hurtful for Sylvie to respond. Every time she hears children playing out in the streets she feels that longing, that need to share in their lives, to try and help them in any way she can. All she has is poor Archie who will never learn to read and write.

'Well I've got another job, thank you, more important than anything,' is her attempt to change the mood between them.

But as the light fades slightly Alice's face turns ashen, her mouth rigidly set, 'Not....not for much longer Sylvie,' she mutters.

This is again too much. It is not fair. It is too destructive of all she wants to feel, tries to feel day after day.

'Oh stop it mother! Stop saying such things. You never used to come out with silly statements like that.'

'Silly,' Alice says back.

'Yes. What would doctor Donnolly say if he heard you come out with such things?'

'You promised me.'

Sylvie sits in the chair feeling the pressure growing.

'You promised me Sylvie.'

'Oh alright,' she answers.

'But it isn't, is it? You can't help yourself. I know.....I know what that feels like.'

'I don't want to talk about it.'

'Neither do I.'

'Well why bring it up?'

'It's you that mentioned the doctor, not me.'

'Oh for goodness sake mother!'

Nothing is said for a few tense moments. Sylvie has never allowed herself to be so irritated. She feels a rush of heat coming into her face and knows it is turning red as she tries to control herself.

'Please mother,' she starts, 'I know you're strong, but you have to keep like that, have to keep positive and believe that you will get better. That's all we want and every one who comes to see you wants the same thing. That's why they visit, not to tire you out but to try and lift your spirits, to remind you that life goes on and that you can become part of that life when you get better.'

Alice wets her lips with her tongue, her mouth forming then a strange smile that has Sylvie guessing as to what she will say next.

But nothing is said. Sylvie waits, watching that swollen stomach push up and down as Alice takes quick, shallow breaths.

'My back hurts. My chest hurts. My bed sores are worse. I'm swelling again and I can hardly swallow and I know you do everything you can, I know you do your best. You're a treasure Sylvie. I wouldn't be here now without all that you've done for me.'

'Mother that's enough,' she has to interrupt.

'That's the trouble with that life you talk about, nothing is enough. How can it be?'

'That's why we go to chapel, isn't it, to find answers.'

'Yes.'

'And we have.'

'I hope so.'

'We have to believe mother, have to be certain.'

'Yes.'

'You don't think….'

'It's just hard sometimes, very hard.'

'I understand that.'

'That's because you're too old for your years.'

'I'm coming up nineteen.'

'And been nursing your mother for nearly five of those years.'

'I don't care so long as you keep strong, keep believing.'

Alice's eyes narrowed with the effort of talking, 'I try Sylvie, all the time I try.'

Next morning, It being a Saturday when she comes down into the kitchen, her father is already up sat in front of the fire polishing his shoes on an old copy of the Craven Herald.

'You're up early,' she comments.

Arthur looks up from his work, his hair slicked back and his moustache neatly trimmed, 'But not that sister of yours.'

'Oh she won't be up until lunchtime knowing her.'

'She's still going over to Rose's all the time. What's going on there do you think?'

Sylvie resists telling him what she really thinks and instead answers with, 'I just think they get on well. They always have done. Mary has always thought highly of Aunt Rose.'

'I know that, but this traipsing over there every day to see her as if Rose hasn't always managed living on her own.'

'Maybe she wants the company.'

'But Mary, she should be out with her own friends, not visiting Rose all the time. Anyway,' Arthur sighs, 'There's fresh tea in the pot and I'll be out of your way in a minute.'

'So where to today?' Sylvie asks knowing what his answer will be.

'Leeds are playing Castleford. I'm trying a piece for the Post and Paul Arkwright is giving us a lift..'

'The car is....'

'Engine is finished, so the garage says,' he interrupts.'

'What will you do without a car? You're never without a car.'

'A good question Sylvie.'

'Can we afford another?'

'Not sure at the moment, will have to see how things go. It's not that I can't get a lift to wherever, it's just the inconvenience and having to ask. I don't like relying on other people.'

'You without a car,' Sylvie comments.

'I popped in to see how your mother is just now.'

'Was she awake?'

'A bit drowsy. I made her a cup of tea and helped her drink some of it, but she didn't want any toast.'

'And she didn't have any tea last night.'

'She needs to keep eating.'

'I know she does, but it's not easy when she just refuses, and she doesn't want any more visitors. She says they tire her out.'

'I suppose she' got a point,' Arthur says as he inspects his shoes.

Sylvie, disappointed with this response pours herself a cup of tea and starts making herself a jam sandwich sensing how easily dismissive of any change in Alice he can be. In her mind there is never enough concern coming from him, not enough worry. It is as though he runs on parallel lines from what is happening in the house and that has been the case even before her mother had her first heart attack. How can he be so balanced about it all? She resents his attitude. It frightens her.

'You don't have to agree,' he adds as he folds up the newspaper and puts it in with the rest ready to be made into firelighters.

'I just don't want her to become cut off.'

'There's her family.'

'I know.'

'We'll have to see how things go,' is another comment he often makes, 'I don't want you making yourself sick with worrying too much.'

'Of course I worry,' she says strongly.

Arthur stops in the doorway giving her a doubtful look, 'We just have to keep going.'

She thinks that all he means is that she has to keep going as he swans off to his next rugby game.

Later she goes out to the shops to find something for Sunday dinner. When she is in the town everything feels rushed by the pressure of returning to her mother as quickly as possible. When out of the house there is no respite.

She greets those who she knows which sometimes seems like half of Skipton crossing over the canal then to go to the butchers on Gargrave Road.

'And how's your mother?' Mr Baxter asks as he wraps her up a ham shank which she plans to boil for tomorrow's dinner.

'Just the same Mr Baxter but thanks for inquiring.'

'Good customer was your mother, always friendly, a nice lady, a very nice lady. Right, now is there anything else I can get you?'

A nice lady thinks Sylvie as she comes out of the shop which means in Skipton terms a bit above most of the town's folk. Anyone who used to look as smart as Alice, work in the library and go to as many cultural events as she could was placed in a different class to the workers of the town. She feels no pride in such a fact. It means nothing to her all this awareness of what class you were in.

But that changes the moment she sees the fight from the canal bridge, five men fisting and kicking out at each other on the road in front of the Queen's Arms pub. There is a crowd over the other side of the canal watching what is happening as more men pour out of the pub and join in. It is shocking, disgusting and worrying to see grown men on a Saturday lunchtime brawling in the street. It is as if the war has already started. Those with her standing on the bridge say nothing as they watch the fight unfold, not like the crowd across from the pub who are shouting and jeering at what is going on.

Sylvie forces herself to walk off the bridge. It makes her physically sick to see such a thing, people wanting to hurt each other, to kick and hit as though they want their opponents destroyed.

'What's wrong with you?' is Mary's first question as Sylvie comes into the kitchen, dropping her shopping bag onto the kitchen table before sitting down, her face all red and flustered.

'There was a fight outside the Queen's Arms,' she answers breathlessly before taking off her glasses to clean them.

Mary has the radio on and is standing by the fire with a cigarette in one hand and a magazine in the other.

'What were they fighting about?'

'I didn't stop to find out,' is Sylvie's reply.

'Men!' Mary scoffs, 'Absolutely typical. They're all still living in a jungle of their own making. They're as primitive as they ever were. They want a war. They want to fight.'

'Well, they've started already.'

'They're pathetic,' Mary says strongly, 'And there's father off to Leeds to see more men knocking lumps out of each other.'

'On a Saturday lunchtime,' Sylvie complains as she wipes the sweat from her forehead and starts unbuttoning her coat.

She is just making herself a cup of tea and calm down when she hears the familiar thump, thump fo Archie's football against the back yard wall.

'There's your friend,' Mary says looking up from her magazine.

'Thank God for Archie,' Sylvie sighs as she goes off to let him in.

'Come, I've come,' are Archie's first words.

He often slurs what he wants to say, his eyes bulging and his features constantly changing expression. But Sylvie is always relieved to see him. To her Archie has an eagerness and innocence that is unique. His world is so different to most peoples. His pride and joy is his football. Nothing else seems to matter.

'Do you want to come in?' she asks as he loiters at the back yard door.

'Fight Sylvie, men fighting,' he announces.

'Yes, I know Archie, I saw it.'

'Bad men Sylvie.'

'Of course they are.'

'Archie saw them.'

'I hoped you weren't one of that crowd shouting them on, encouraging them.'

Archie's tongue flopped out of his mouth as he thought about this. He had to keep flicking his head to keep the hair out of his eyes. He was dressed in his usual filthy jumper and grey shorts that went below his bruised knees.

'Where's your sister?' he next asks.

'In the kitchen.'

'Don't like her.'

'Don't say such a thing Archie.'

'She doesn't….doesn't like Archie.'

'And what makes you say that?'

'Come and play footie,' is his demand.

'Not just now Archie.'

'No one Sylvie will play with me.'

'I'm sure that's not true.'

'Nobody wants to play.'

'I will, some other time.'

At that Archie smiles, 'No you won't Sylvie. Just joking. Girls don't play footie. It's not allowed.'

'And who told you that?'

'My Mam.'

'I bet she never did Archie Andrews.'

'Fed up,' he complains then, holding his torn and scuffed football under one arm as he wipes his nose with the back of his other hand.

'So, you don't want to come in and have a drink of lemonade.'

'I'd like beer!' he says, raising his voice.

It was five thirty and the bedroom was freezing cold. Sylvia glanced at Mary's bed. In the darkness she could just make out the shape of her sister under the layers of blankets topped by a thick eiderdown. She found her glasses, slippers and dressing gown before going along the landing to check on her mother.

The bedside light was on and Alice was awake.

Sylvia asked in a hushed voice how her night had been.

'Not so good Sylvie,' Alice answered with a dry voice, 'I don't feel very well.'

Anxiously Sylvia asked whether she should go and get doctor Donnolly.

Alice shook her head, her face wincing as she did so, 'No….not just yet….not the doctor just now….I'll see how I am later.'

Sylvia went off to refill her water jug and then went down stairs, along the dark hallway into the large kitchen. She switched on the light, picked up the coal scuttle, unlocked the back door into the yard and hurriedly crossed to the coal shed. The February cold was bitter this morning as she fiddled with the latch. Inside the shed it was so dark she had to guess where she had left the shovel.

When the scuttle was full she trudged back into the kitchen to start on the fire, cleaning out the ashes, twisting pages from the Yorkshire Post into fire lighters and laying them on the still warm grid with a few sticks. She carefully took the tongs and placed individual pieces of coal on top of the twisted newspaper, swept the hearth, took the box of matches off the mantelpiece and got the fire started.

Next was filling the kettle to make her and Alice their first cup of tea of the day which would be followed by many others. By the sink she switched on the electric copper to prepare for the morning's washing. She had sorted the clothes the night before into four piles, woollens, cottons, colours and whites.

When the kettle was boiled she poured some of the hot water into the tea pot, rinsed it around before pouring it down the sink, taking down the tea caddie, putting three full tea spoons of tea into the pot followed by more hot water. She covered it with the tea cosy and let it mash. She then walked back along the hallway to unlock the front door, tightening her dressing gown around her. The whole house was cold. The winter seemed already to have lasted so long.

Every morning her worries about her mother were refreshed. She was getting worse and her moods were darker. Sylvia accepted that she was doing all she could each day to make Alice as comfortable as possible. The pressure was growing. It was like a thickening cloud pressing down on the house. All of its atmosphere was swirling around Alice and her terrible affliction.

'Here's some tea,' she said softly when reentering the bedroom.

Alice forced a weak smile.

'Did you get some sleep?' was Sylvia's usual question.

'Off and on.'

'I'll set the fire.'

'Yes,' Alice sighed.

Back in the kitchen she checked on the water boiling in the copper. That was one thing her father had done, made sure she had all the up to date appliances including the electric copper and an electric kettle and iron all paid for on hire purchase so Mary had told her.

After she had taken up a bucket of coal, paper and sticks she got Alice's fire going before she was back down in the kitchen to start on the washing. First she worked on the dirtiest clothes, kneading them like dough in cold water in the sink then rubbing each garment on a scrubbing board before putting them through the mangler into the now boiling water in the copper. It was hard work turning the three legged dolly to rotate the clothes, over and over twisting it round to keep the clothes in motion. With the fire starting to warm up the kitchen Sylvia soon started to sweat and because they steamed up so easily she worked without her glasses on.

Another turn of putting the washed clothes through the mangler into the sink and then hanging them on the pulley over the fire to dry meant the woollens and some of the cottons would be ready for ironing first.

It was then that Mary appeared, thinner, agitated as usual, moving quickly, dressed for work and asking Sylvia if there was any tea in the pot. She was followed within a few minutes by Arthur, his face scrubbed, his moustache glistening, in his dark blue three piece suit, hair slicked back, putting on his watch as he came in from the hallway.

'You've been well at it Sylvie lass,' was his first comment as he noticed the fresh washing, 'How long have you been up?'

She noticed how concerned and interested he had begun to sound. Ever since his car had been put in the garage he had been home earlier each evening and spent more time in the kitchen reading the paper and listening to the news on the radio. These were unexpected changes. Sylvia wondered whether it was because Alice's condition was worsening. Even Mary was making the effort to be more pleasant with her. But instead of these changes being welcomed they had done the opposite and made Sylvia more anxious.

'What a miserable morning,' said Mary as she went into the hallway to put on her coat.

'If you're not careful you'll miss your train!' Arthur called from the kitchen only to hear the front door slam.

'That girl is always in a rush,' he added while buttering himself a slice of bread.

Sylvia asked him whether he had been in to see mother.

'I have,' he answered before taking a bite of the bread, 'And she's says she's had a rough night.'

He switched on the radio, moved his chair back a little so it was not under the washing most of which was dripping onto sheets of newspaper that Sylvia had laid on the hearth and settled down to listening to the early morning news which was all about the situation in Spain and how Franco's Nationalists were moving on Barcelona.

'They'll never stop him now,' Arthur muttered critically.

'And what about all of the British men who have gone over there to fight?'

'Against him Sylvie, against Franco. Doesn't look good for any of them.'

'And they were so optimistic when they left.'

'Ready to defeat the Fascists, not any more,' was Arthur's final comment on the subject.

Sylvia stood near her father listening to what the news announcer was saying in his plum Southern accent that always grated on her. It sounded so false, so alien to how the folk in Skipton and the Dales spoke.

After popping up again to see how Alice was she went to get washed and dressed. She put on a skirt and pullover, tied her curly hair back with a scarf and put on her glasses prepared then for the rest of the day.

She waited for Arthur to come up the stairs on his way to see Alice again before he left for work.

When he had gone Sylvia made herself some breakfast, thick slices of bread and jam and a fresh pot of tea. Outside cold mist had filled the back yard blurring the out buildings and smearing over the kitchen window.

While looking out she imagined car headlights illuminating the mist and ghostly sheep up on the hills. February could be the bleakest month. Even though it was the shortest of the year it seemed to last forever when the weather was bad. On the radio were more posh voices, women talking about how to lower the weekly budget. It was as though the country was already preparing for rationing, something talked about more and more in the shops and on the market. That and these Anderson shelters that had been mentioned on the radio several times. Seeing as they had no back garden Sylvia wondered what they would do if Skipton was ever bombed and then asked herself why the Germans would ever want to attack a small town like Skipton before remembering that there were rumours that the Dewhurst factories would be solely weaving cloth for uniforms, parachutes, webbing and anything else that would help the military.

For a moment she went cold even thinking about it especially what they would do with her mother stuck there up in her bedroom. It was all beginning to seem inevitable. How safe would any of them be? What would happen to Arthur's job and Mary's? What would people be expected to do? Would they all have to take to the hills if the Germans invaded?

It was frightening not knowing anything. Like everyone else Sylvia was anxious especially about her mother. Then she realised that doctor Donnolly might have to join the armed forces, her doctor sent away to tend the wounded and the dying, her doctor in danger.

She had to pray that none of this would happen, pray that somehow this man Hitler could be stopped in his tracks and leave the world alone. All of it made her feel so much older. She was tired of so much anxiety, so many negative thoughts.

She remembered the fight she had witnessed outside the Queens Head pub down by the canal one summer's afternoon, two men fisting each other in the face before they had finished up on the ground wrestling, biting, punching, blood all over them before it was finally halted by a group of young farmers who had just come out of the pub. Was that how it would be, men's bodies smashing into each other? Her father had told her, when she had asked him one evening, that it would be a lot worse because no one would see the pilot dropping his bombs, the tank crews firing or the artillery men from miles behind the front line sending off their shells. It would be what he called an anonymous war. Most of the time the enemy would be unseen which made it all the more frightening and unpredictable.

After washing the breakfast things, putting the previous day's rubbish in the back yard bin, mopping the kitchen floor's lino and dusting the front room she went up to tell Alice that she was going to the shops for a few things for tea.

'What's it like outside?'

Her mother's voice was dry and forced.

'Misty, cold, just like yesterday,' Sylvia answered aware as always of the huge mound of her mother's stomach and her face so lined and pale as she looked across the room towards the window before Sylvia went over to open the curtains.

All that could be seen was the mist pressing against the glass, a grey, shifting mass of cold air covering the town.

'Your father says his car might be unrepairable,' Alice said then with difficulty.

Sylvia lifted the tea cup from the bedside table for her mother to take a drink.

'I know he's not happy.'

'He's never been without a car, not for nearly…….nearly ten years now. How is he……how is he going…..?

'Mother be settled,' Sylvia interrupted, 'I'm sure he'll work out something.'

'Not how things are Sylvie, not as things are.'

'And what does that mean?'

'What I hear on the radio and what you read to me from the paper. I want to know as much as I can about what's happening.'

'And you do mother. You know as much as anyone. I'm not trying to hide anything from you if that's what you're thinking.'

It was said lightly, an ironical reprimand as Alice took a sip of her tea and Sylvia started on cleaning out the fire.

Later out on the High Street the mist was so bad all the shops had their lights still on, gold and silver panels of light hovering over the pavement and out onto the road.

For a moment Sylvia with her string shopping bag stopped at the window of Fattorinis the jewellers. There were bracelets and necklaces, tiny ladies' watches, engagement and wedding rings. To her it was like Aladdin's Cave full of treasure, full of things she would never have and was determined to keep it that way. She wanted but forced herself not to want. The spiritual had to be more important than the material Mr Elgin had often preached. Loving and giving was more important than having.

But none of this stopped Sylvia from at least looking. There was no harm in seeing what the jewellers had on display.

A lot of the social world of the town was spread daily from shop to shop. The nearer the sense of war the more people had to talk, to gossip, to express themselves and share their fears and predictions. It was the same in every shop she entered. First would be the usual question about how her mother was doing followed by a whole list of now regular topics, Hitler, Franco, Anderson shelters, the poor performance of Chamberlin and our weak French allies when it came to any kind of diplomacy which meant standing up to the Germans, rationing, conscription, Dewhursts making cloth for uniforms, the weather, the last time the canal was frozen up. Sylvia found it a struggle to get through the morning shopping. Everyone greeted her and accepted her as though she was a regular housewife, Miss Townsley daughter of Arthur and Alice the mother who was very ill.

From the High Street she would regularly make her way to the street where doctor Donnolly lived, walking past the gate that opened onto the path that led up to the doctor's large detached house and then back again wondering if he was there or on his rounds or in his surgery, imagining him sat before a fire reading the paper, smoking his pipe, relaxed, breathing slowly, breathing as Sylvia breathed into the motion of her thoughts, her fantasies that were always with her.

The morning mist was beginning to gradually lift. Back in the house she sorted out the shopping, popped up to see Alice who was asleep before taking down the nearly dry washing and then beginning on the colours and whites. She banked up the fire, hung out the wet clothes and started on the ironing which was electric and saved her so much effort. Instead of having two heavy irons on the go, one by the fire getting heated up while she used the other, having to constantly change them she now had the luxury of an iron she plugged in and away she would go with the radio on, singing quietly away to any music into the rhythm of her work with the heat making her sweat again in contrast to the freezing cold outside.

When Alice was finally awake she helped her to the toilet before giving her a quick wash and helping her on with a fresh nightgown. Downstairs she started on the tea, sausages, potatoes and peas followed by a tin of peaches with Carnation milk.

Arthur was first to return and would wait for Mary whose train got into Skipton station at half past six so the three of them could sit down and have their tea together around the kitchen table. It had become a new routine now that Arthur was coming home straight from work. Sometimes he would go out later on but more and more he stayed at home reading or listening to music.

After first Mary and later Arthur had popped in to see Alice before going to bed Sylvia would be the last one up having locked the front door, put up the fire guard, taken down any washing that was dry, emptied out the tea pot, covered the butter and everything else that needed to be done before she could come to bed.

Sometimes Mary wanted to chat but usually by the time Sylvia was ready for bed she would be asleep. There was still a strained distance between them, something that however hard she tried Sylvia could not change. It was more accepted now. There were too many other things on her mind to be too bothered by her reticent, moody sister.

Now there was hardly a time when Sylvia did not wake at some time in the early morning in a panic about her mother, going quickly along the landing, quietly opening the door to check that Alice was still breathing, watching that huge mound beneath the bed clothes rise and fall like some huge wave of hidden flesh under which her mother was slowly being drowned.

When she returned to her own bed it took her a long time to settle herself back down and manage eventually to sleep. It meant by the time she had to get up again at half past five she would be still tired from the day before. There was an exhaustive accumulation, day after day piling one level of tiredness onto another until it became automatic what she had to do.

Sylvia knew she could not go on like this. In her heart she was rebelling while her mind tried to keep her disciplined and focused. Even though there were more and more doubts her faith was strong enough to still answer the growing conflict within her. Where was life just for her? Where was a future she could look forward to? Her mother's illness and the threat of war was all she had and it was not enough. The world was conspiring against her. How could she imagine anything beyond her constant need to see her doctor? Was that all there was some stupid crush on a married man with two children? But he was still close. She could hear him breathing. She could see him mounting their stairs in his flannels and tweed jacket. Would the Germans kill him? Would he survive and return one of Skipton's heroes? Men were marching in row after row down the High Street and in her imagination Sylvia was in the crowd watching as doctor Donnolly went past, stiff backed, frowning in concentration, eyes to the front while she was hoping that he would give her a glance, a smile, anything to recognise she was there.

CHAPTER TWENTY NINE

Arthur is on the Sunday morning train from Leeds, smoking, looking out of the rain smeared window while thinking about Kitty. They had met for dinner in the Dome hotel with its large, busy restaurant, indoor plants, large chandeliers and a trio playing background music to the hum of voices and the movement of waiters.

Kitty in an elegant black dress, sharply made up with bright red lipstick, hair freshly groomed talking about her trip down South to her parents in Somerset. For some reason he had felt tense and found it hard to concentrate, hard to relax into the evening. He could smell her classy perfume, watching the way she sipped her wine. Everything should have been as he wanted and yet it all felt at a distance. He became angry at himself for being such a fool. These were moments that had to be appreciated, savoured and not lost under this self made pressure.

Half way through their meal he had confessed that he no longer owned a car to which her response had been totally unexpected. She had been critical, obviously irritated that he had not told her about his debts.

'Why Arthur, why now? You must have been struggling ever since I met you,' she had said.

He had tried to smile, 'That's the trouble, everything's a struggle.'

'No self pity Arthur, it doesn't suit you.'

'Oh I got past that stage long ago. Any way I never told you because I was embarrassed and still am about the whole damn mess.'

'I can help.'

'That's what I'm afraid of.'

'And what is that supposed to mean?'

He had lit a cigarette, trying to pull himself together as she waited for his reply. So many people were talking around him. Waiters bent and swerved around the tables. Music sounded like water in the background.

'It means this is a situation I have to sort out myself.'

'Why Arthur, when I want to help?'

'I know you do,' he had said as lightly as he could.

Kitty, sitting straight backed had looked critically at him, her eyes sparkling with frustration, 'So let me, let me get you out of this man Andrews clutches. He sounds like a thug.'

'He is.'

'Well then.'

'It's not right that I….'

'Oh don't talk nonsense,' she had interrupted, 'I have the money and I….'

'No Kitty.'

'Why not?'

'I'll sort it.'

'With my help you'll manage to do that a lot quicker.'

For a while nothing else had been said on the matter. They had finished their meal and finished up at the bar before Kitty started again. The brandy he was drinking had settled him down enough to start taking more seriously what she was saying. She was offering to pay off his debts, something he had never expected. And yet the more accommodating Kitty sounded the more anxious he had become. It made him nervous. All evening her tone towards him had been softer, more accepting, more giving and he had found it hard to manage.

Now on the train he finds it hard to understand what had happened the night before. He had booked a room at the hotel. They had drunk more, before going to bed. She had been so eager, loving, wanting and he had done his best to respond. Afterwards they had talked until the early hours of the morning when he had finally accepted that the next time they met they would discuss how she could help him financially.

The rain dribbles in angled lines down the dirty train window. The rest of the passengers are lost in their own thoughts. No one is talking, a sure sign of this being a dreary Sunday morning, the worst time of the week for many who like him do not go to church.

Why is everything so difficult and fraught with conflict? Whatever he does or feels there is always an opposite version. It makes him physically sick sometimes this tension of opposites. It creates an unreality where he is on the other side of everything, trapped inside a glass house looking out longingly on who he knows he should be. He should have been the good husband, the good father instead of living this life of lies and greed.

At least when he gets off the train there is that burnt smell of smoke covering the station as an express from Carlisle comes to a halt on the other track. He loves the smell of ash filled steam that billows along the platforms. It is the smell of journeys, of metal power and man's inventiveness.

For a moment he remembers the woman pushing her pram across Settle's frozen white cricket pitch as a Jubilee class in its green livery was forcing out huge plumes of steam ready for the long drag up to Ribblehead and Blea Moor. Last summer he took the Golden Lion's proprietor George Tindale's son Harry to watch Yorkshire play Lancashire at Headingley as had he had promised he would. Harry had enjoyed himself and so had Arthur. It was only a few months ago and yet felt a world away.

He has lost so much since then. Nothing feels as it should. He walks out of the station, bending slightly against the constant cold drizzle thinking of Alice there in her bed while he walks home from a night with his mistress. Guilt is like a sound droning through his brain. The more ill she has become the worse he feels. Once he managed his two track life, but not anymore. Now he is confused, angry and hopelessly needing to escape from what is happening.

Without warning as he nears the end of his street he sees the ambulance, hears the shells, watches himself clamber out of the cab and with head down throw himself into the nearest ditch. Within seconds the ambulance is directly hit, pieces of it flying in all directions as well parts of the six men who he had been transporting to the nearest field hospital.

Quickly he blocks out any more images. To survive he has to force back every image of those nightmare years. Guilt is in the sound of that shell. Guilt is in the flames and pieces of flesh and metal blasted into the grey sky. Since then he has never been able to escape what he did. Since then there has only been the struggle to find some sort of balance, an attempt that he has repeatedly failed to do.

Next day after work he makes his way to his sister's house. Desultory flakes of snow are falling out of an ashen sky as he reaches Elliot Street. He walks up the steep pavement and knocks on her door.

He waits and knocks again.

'Arthur,' Rose says in a surprised tone as she finally opens the door to him.

'Can I come in?'

'You don't have to ask,' is her answer.

He follows her down the dingy hallway and takes of his wet trilby. To him the house always smells of gas and damp. He has given up trying to convince Rose that it needs modernising.

'Do you want a cup of tea?' she asks as they go into the parlour where Rose spends most of her time.

Arthur unbuttons his wet overcoat and lays it on the back of a chair.

'I won't be stopping,' he says a little harshly as he sits by the fire.

'Is something wrong?' Rose inquires as she takes her seat across the hearth from him.

'That's what I've come to find out.'

'I don't like your tone of voice Arthur.'

'I'm here to ask what's going on with our Mary and why she's never out of your house.'

'And why should that be a problem?'

'I'm not saying it is Rose. I'm just wanting to know why over the last months she comes here such a lot when before it used to be once a week if that. I know she's not been happy ever since she left Dawsons and that's been a mystery, why she left there in the first place when she seemed to be getting on so well.'

'That had nothing to do with me if that's what you're thinking,' Rose retorts in an irritated voice.

'Something happened and she's never been the same since. All she does is mope about the house, getting up when it suits her and making no attempt to find another job. That's not our Mary. She's never been like she is at the moment. She's always been so smart and clear about what she was doing with her life.'

'And she will be.'

'I'm not so sure.,' he says, studying her concerned expression, thinking how things have always been strained between them ever since they were children.

'How's Alice?' Rose asks then before getting up to poke the fire.

'Not so good, no, not good at all. She's saying she doesn't want any more visitors. Not just you Rose, but everybody including Mr Elgin.'

'Things must be bad.'

'And the carry on with Mary is not helping. I'm not sure Rose whether you understand that what you're doing is not helping either.'

Rose's face tightens the lines of skin under her eyes, 'I'm not doing anything.'

Her reply is said so strongly Arthur has to decide whether to continue and really upset her or back off and leave it for another day.

'She might not see much of her, but Alice needs Mary in the house. She needs to know she is there. You can understand that Rose.'

'Of course I can, but you're still implying I'm trying to coax Mary away when that's the last thing I want to do.'

'If you don't want it then why is she here so often?'

'Arthur, can we stop this?'

His answer is wrapped in anger. He wants to show her how strongly he feels as he watches her sit down again while he lights a cigarette.

'I want you to tell me what you think is wrong with her.'

'I don't know!' Rose exclaims in exasperation as the voices of children sound out as they run past the front window and down the hill.

'And would you want her to live with you? Is that what's going on here?'

'Mary's old enough to make up her own mind what she wants to do.'

'So you do?'

'If that is what she really wants.'

'My God Rose!' Arthur says raising his voice as he gets up and stands in front of the fire before turning to flick his half smoked cigarette into the flames, 'You have no idea what you're doing,' he continues.

'I think I have,' she retorts.

He tries to slow down his reaction. Instead of arguing with his sister he should be having this conversation with his daughter, and yet he knows trying to change anything Mary has her mind set on is a waste of time. She has always been too determined, too self centred. Alice has always said that Mary takes after her father, something he accepted a long time ago.

Rose sits stiffly in her chair, her hands clasped together on her lap.

'Have you finished Arthur?'

Her tone is bitter. It makes him realise he still understands so little about what she feels.

'You're lonely, is that it?'

'No, I like my own company, thank you.'

'Yes,' he sighs, 'You always have.'

'And what's that supposed to mean?'

He decides he has gone too far, picks up his coat as he says, 'It might not be long now before everything changes.'

'You mean for the Townsleys or the rest of the world?'

He buttons up his overcoat before answering, 'Both,' and then goes out into the hallway for his hat.

Rose finally follows him, her expression still uncertain, still angry, 'So I won't be seeing Alice?' she says in a flat voice as she opens the door for him.

He puts on his hat, turns to look at her and steps out onto the pavement as the snowflakes fall between them.

'Not for the time being.'

'Give her my love then.'

'I will,' he answers curtly before setting off down the hill while Rose stands at the doorway watching him.

He walks quickly. He is not satisfied. He did not go far enough and yet is not sure whether he went too far. It was all too abrupt. Rose defended herself which only made him more exasperated. In the end it is not her of whom he is critical but himself. He has made a fool of himself in his sister's eyes and his own.

Over the next days the tension grows. Nothing is right. There is only a mess of confusion and bitterness. He is losing control and does not know what to do about it except drink more, his usual answer to when things are going wrong.

It is at the Thursday discussion group which has been running over the winter that he drinks too much while feeling critical of everyone and everything at the same time.

The talk is as usual all about the political situation. It has become the sole topic since the group restarted in the previous autumn.

'We have done nothing, not a thing to help those poor buggers. Hitler and Mussolini pour in planes, men and weapons and all we do is stay well out of it,' Tony Johnston is saying in his broad Yorkshire accent.

They are seated around their large table in the room above the bar. Agnes has brought up the first round of sandwiches and there is a roaring fire sending shadows over the walls and the six men who are drinking, smoking and getting louder by the minute.

'And what about your chum Stalin,' counters Dave Thornton, one of the managers at Dewhursts, 'What's he been doing? How is he any different? You just see it as usual Tony from one side and not the other.'

'There is no other.'

'There always is.'

'If you're so damn concerned you should have joined the International Brigade and gone over yourself to fight.'

'If I didn't have a wife and three children and a gammy leg I would have done.'

John Metcalfe intervenes, 'You're too old Tony to be doing any fighting.'

'Speak for yourself.'

'I will then if you insist. It's all too late to be doing anything. Franco has won, which means we have another fascist dictator to join up with the rest.'

Sean Fuller leans across the table for another sandwich saying, 'We had to stay neutral. If we hadn't there would have been another World War.'

'Rubbish!' Tony exclaims.

Arthur finally contributes with, 'It's all rubbish Tony. One side is as bad as the other.'

'And there was me Arthur thinking that you were a Republican.'

'Who says I'm not?'

'Of course he is,' is Dave Thornton's next comment.

Arthur is flowing quickly into the heat of the argument on a river of brandy and beer, 'And what if I am? Would you rather see the bloody Nazis marching down the High Street because I wouldn't. This country has been farting about for too long, far too long. Chamberlain is like a wet fish. He's hopeless. He'd give away his right hand if he thought it would keep bloody Hitler quiet. It's done, done and dusted. I bet anything that in the next few days there'll be jackboots marching into

Czechlosovakia. That'll be the next country to go, and then what? Who's next? Is it Poland, Hungary, France? Go on Dave, have a guess.'

'There's no need to sound so angry Arthur. We all have our opinions,' Dave says angrily.

At that Paul Arkwright announces that it is only facts that matter.

'Facts become opinions,' John Metcalfe counters as he looks across the table at Arthur's surly expression, 'That's the trouble. Everyone has their own facts to back up their argument.'

'There's no argument,' Arthur continues before lighting another cigarette, 'This is about the bloody future of Europe.'

'We heard Arthur, we heard,' a red faced Paul mutters back before adding, 'Chamberlain is doing his best.'

'Well it's not good enough. It never has been.'

'So you could do a better job?'

'Anyone could do a better job than that weak willed bugger.'

'Come on lads, take it easy' is Sean Fuller's attempt to calm things down, 'We're not here to start throwing insults at each other.'

'Who Sean is insulting who?' Arthur wants to know.

The brandy opens his brain like a flower of discontent. He is becoming increasingly frustrated. He is not interested in what anyone else has to say. His mood refuses to accept any other argument but his own. His wife is dying. One of his daughters is lost. His mistress is being too generous and all he can manage is to feel guilty and resentful.

He takes a mouthful off beer and then adds, 'War, it's a bloody certainty.

'And there was me thinking 1940 was going.....' Sean Fuller starts only to be interrupted by Arthur.

'No Sean, not a bloody chance. There's no point thinking anything beyond where we are at the moment except to say there'll be no trip for you and your family to Blackpool next year.'

'Shame Arthur. There was me thinking we'd be back on the old Golden Mile.'

'Conscription is already on for the early twenty year olds,' Dave tries.

'It'll be you next Dave,' says John.

'Oh ay, that'll be right. I did my stint in the last war thank you.'

'We all did, one way or another,' is Paul's more pointed remark that Arthur immediately picks up on.

'And what is that suppose to mean, one way or another?'

'Nothing Arthur. Keep your shirt on. You're in a right frame of mind tonight.'

'Now let's not get personal,' is Tony's intervention.

For a moment nothing else is said. Arthur glances across the table's surface that is sheened by firelight. It feels as though his mood is the same, trying a smooth surface of reason while failing to manage how he usually is when the discussion becomes heated. Tonight he is past facts and reason. All he feels is a growing outrage about everything.

He finishes his brandy and follows it by a mouthful of beer. Momentarily he thinks of Kitty and her unexpected commitment to pay off his debts. At last he might be free of Andrews and his thugs. But instead of this being a relief it has only created more pressure, a conflict of guilt and uncertainty.

'I was there!' he suddenly exclaims, 'I was there in bloody France and Belgium, and Belgium,' he repeats looking from one to the other.

'We know you were,' John says.

'I was there,'

'Yes Arthur.'

'So enough of your bloody innuendos Arkwright.'

'Nothing meant Arthur.'

'You never say anything that hasn't got a point. Am I the point?'

'Don't sound so bloody daft,' Paul says as he bangs down his pint glass.

'We're all bloody daft, sat here talking and talking when we can do bugger all. We're as helpless as everyone else and all because of the usual twisted mentality that wants power. That's all it is, Hitler, Stalin, Mussolini, Franco, all little individuals working out their clever madness over the rest of the world. And who says history isn't made by one man, one after another after another?'

At that he pulls himself to his feet adding, 'I've had enough, tonight for once I've had enough.'

'Arthur, what are you doing?' his friend John asks as he stands up as well.

'Going home,' is the answer as Arthur collects his cigarettes and lighter, pushes his chair back and unsteadily turns for his coat and hat that are laid on a small table behind him.

'Goodnight,' he says loudly as he makes for the stairs.

The rest watch him but say nothing in return.

The cold March air hits him like a bucket of freezing water. He stops, takes time to button up his coat as he looks down the High Street that is filled with evening smoke from all the houses mixed in with a frosty mist hanging a few feet above the pavement.

It is the mist of the trenches. It is the smoke from burning villages and towns. It is the time for digging up more bits and pieces of the dead. The shovel is sucked into the thick, stinking mud. A skull stares with hollow eyes up at him as the rats dance across every patch of ground. These are the shadows that follow him night and day. These are the horrors that have tortured his soul, twisted it around into the opposite of who he once was.

'Goodnight,' a man passing by says brightly.

'Yes,' is all Arthur can manage.

There is no such thing as a good night, not now. Even with Kitty nothing is like it used to be.

More than anything he resents himself.

He is the constant liar. He is the one who cannot talk to his own daughters in any natural way. He is the one watching his wife die while another woman pays off his debts and is willing to wait.

'Fucking hell!' he forces out in a loud, desperate voice as he unsteadily turns the Woolworth's corner.

He stops, bends over and vomits out the night's food and drink that splatters over the pavement.

Still leaning forward he searches for his handkerchief, wipes his mouth and straightens up as the cold mist clings to his face and hands while he searches across the road for the ghosts of dead soldiers stood there watching him.

CHAPTER THIRTY

'They say war is certain now the Germans have taken over Czechoslovakia.'

Mary, flicking through the pages of her magazine, makes no response to her sister's comment. Instead she tosses the magazine onto the kitchen table, 'Why I buy this, I've no idea. It's so old fashioned.'

Sylvie is washing underwear in the sink.

Mary lights a cigarette.

Late spring sunshine is coming through the back window reflecting off a jug full of early roses.

'Has father said anything about his new car?' Mary eventually asks.

'Not a thing.'

'And he's wearing a new suit.'

'I know he got that made by the tailor he likes in Bradford.'

'Must have got some big kind of bonus from old Mr Slater then,' Mary says.

'He's so secretive about money.'

'He always has been. I bet mother has never had any idea of what he earns or what he spends. He certainly won't have told her.'

'He surely can't afford a new car,' Sylvie persists, 'I just can't see how that's possible. One minute the Standard was a right off and the next minute he turns up in a new one.'

'It could be all on higher purchase although I thought he didn't believe in HP.'

'Maybe his opinion has changed,' Sylvie says as she drops down the pulley and starts hanging the wet clothes.

'I'm going over to Aunt Rose's this afternoon,' Mary tells her.

'I should come with you sometime. I like aunt Rose. She's good company.'

'Yes,' is all Mary can manage.

Later in her neat spring coat and matching hat she walks quickly over to Elliot Street. There is a heavy smell of smoke from all the town's chimneys. It trails high into an otherwise blue sky like soft grey fingers dissolving upwards.

'Your father was here last week,' is the first thing Aunt Rose tells her after she has mashed the tea and put the pot on the table.

Mary thinks about this for a moment before saying, 'I bet I know why.'

Aunt Rose smiles,' Well go on then, why do you think?'

'He'll have wanted to know why I'm over here so often.'

'You know your father better than you think.'

'I'm not so sure about that.'

'Well, you obviously do. Yes, he came asking about you, implying I was trying my best to coax you to live here.'

'As though I'm not old enough to make my own decisions. That's typical of father. He can never accept anything that doesn't suit him.'

'He said you should stay at home with your mother being so ill and I think he's right about that Mary.'

'Yes,' Mary sighs, 'I know you do.'

'I just didn't like how he spoke to me,' Rose complains before pouring the tea.

'He's been very moody recently, bad moods.'

'It's this worry about another war. Everyone is anxious, but that doesn't excuse the way he came in here making his comments.'

'Even though he's got a new car he's angry most of the time nowadays.'

'He has Alice to bother about.'

'Like we all have.'

Rose hands her a cup of tea before sitting down near the fire, saying, 'Nothing is getting any easier except the weather thank goodness. This is the warmest day we've had since I don't know when, last autumn some time.'

Mary reflects for a moment on her father and how he is changing for the worse. Their house is full of tension and uncertainty. She hates its depressing atmosphere, the sense of her mother upstairs, how her illness dominates over everything.

But Aunt Rose gives her an alternative, a way out. More than anything she likes to hear Rose describe her and Edward's courting and their brief days of marriage. In one way it is such a sad story and yet sounds so perfectly innocent like another Hollywood version of how life could be.

'We were happy. For a few months we were happy,' Rose had said a few weeks ago. We'd go out walking, in the park or Castle woods or walk by the canal out to Gargrave. We were lucky that it was the summer, such a beautiful, long summer. I don't think we've had a summer like it since then.'

'A perfect summer,' Mary had commented.

'Edward was never a great talker and if he wanted to say something he'd always take his time thinking about how he wanted to say it. But that didn't matter to me. I could talk enough for the two of us. Love I suppose affects some people like that. You see I don't mind talking about it. Why should I? It was the happiest time of my life.'

Mary had listened and felt how different things were before the First World. Rose described a world unprepared for what followed, unprepared for the slaughter that had taken her young husband.

Rose sharing her memories brought them closer together. Mary often wondered whether it had been the same for her mother and father, whether they too had found a brief period of happiness before the war had begun.

'We were married at the chapel and now I can't remember why we chose Harrogate for our honeymoon except that Edward had been called up and we had three days together before he had to leave so I suppose we thought of somewhere close.'

'Three days before he left to fight,' Mary said.

'Three days before he went off to training down near Birmingham somewhere. I saw him off at the station and never set eyes on him again.'

Mary had watched her aunt's features for any sign of distress, but Rose had been looking into the fire, her eyes reflecting the small flames that were just managing to warm the room.

Then she continued in a tenuous voice with, 'Nothing happened if you know what I mean. Edward was so shy and I had no idea really. All my mother had told me was to prepare myself. I had no notion of what she meant. Of course I knew what was supposed to happen but not how it was supposed to happen. Now it's funny really, the two of us in that hotel room too nervous to manage anything. I don't regret it. I don't think back and bother myself with that side of things. I just remember the best part and that was the two of us just strolling around Harrogate as if we owned the place, Edward in his best suit and me in my new summer dress and hat.'

'You must have looked smart,' Mary said, still being careful in how she responded.

Rose had got up to put more coal and the fire. She had turned and added, 'I've never spoken about any of this to a living soul, no one Mary. But I'm glad there's someone who I can at last share with what I felt back then, the best time of my life and it helps. It changes things, changes things in a way I never expected would ever happen.'

Mary asks her what she means. Rose answers, 'It's makes me think more about now, makes me realise that there's still life to get on with. I have the past. It's not going to go away. I have my memories and instead of accepting that's all there is I have to realise that the last thing Edward would have wanted would be me turning into a bitter old maid with only memories to keep me going. That doesn't mean there won't be the odd séance I'll attend, and I'll still go regularly to the Spiritualist church. I still want to try and be as close to Edward as I can. But now....'

'Now,' Mary had interrupted, 'You've got me to worry about.'

'I'm not worried Mary. I just wish we knew what the next months were going to hold.'

For a moment Rose had leant forward, taken Mary's hand and smiled warmly as though this expression was enough to seal their feelings for each other, enough to show her niece how much she cared.

Now a few weeks later everything is different. Mary has had received a letter saying she had been successful in her application for a job at the John Lewis store in Leeds and together with Aunt Rose they have begun discussing what changes might be made to the house if Mary decides to come and live there.

'I'm sure father has plenty of contacts for any building work,' Mary says before pouring them both another cup of tea as they sit at the table with the evening light fading outside.

'Not that I'd ask him,' is Rose's response.

'Yes, you're probably right. It would just set him off again.'

'He's angry enough as it is. Nothing's ever been enough for your father. There's always been something wrong, something that he's always been fighting against.'

'Himself probably.'

'Yes, more than likely,' Rose agrees.

Later on her way back from Elliot Street Mary thinks about her new job and whether she will be able to manage, whether she can see herself back working in a shop after everything that has happened. On the way down the High Street she feels reassured by Rose and her plans. Her aunt is giving her an alternative to continuing to live at home.

She tenses when she sees a man walking towards her in the semi darkness, his coat collar up and his cap pulled down so it is hard to see who it is. The street lights are on but only spread a weak light over the pavement.

The man is about to go past when he stops as she purposefully continues on her way.

'Mary!' she hears behind her, 'Mary Townsley, it's me, Billy, Billy Rogers!'

The voice abruptly penetrates her memory. She ceases walking and turns to the shadowed figure who is coming towards her, passing under one of the street lights so she can see the smile on his face.

'You remember me?'

'Of course I do Billy,' she answers with a forced voice.

She tries to relax, tries to tell herself that nothing is about to happen in the middle of the High Street with a few vehicles going down the road and a noisy group of men going into the Black Bull. And yet she is still nervous. Billy she remembers used to work in the store room and was always joking and messing around. He was the only one who could make her laugh at his cheeky remarks and hopeless jokes.

He has a new moustache and looks different.

She asks whether he is still working at the shop.

'No, I'm working at Shipley in the burling and mending warehouse.'

She inquires what it is like.

'Better paid than Dawsons,' he answers and then asks, 'And what happened to you Mary. One minute you were there and the then you were gone. I remember seeing you there on the Saturday and then when I came in on the Monday they said you'd left and nobody knew why.'

She tells him she was looking for a change and is about to start at the Leeds branch of John Lewis, an explanation he seems to accept.

She can smell he has been drinking and notices how he keeps stepping unsteadily from side to side.

'But you're still living here?' he asks.

She answers that she is and will go by train to work every day.

Billy takes out a packet of cigarettes and offers her one before lighting his own after she has refused.

'It's only just past nine o clock, what do you say Mary, what about a quick drink for old times sake.'

She feels the tension beginning to stretch as she informs him that she has to get home.

'Oh come on Mary, just one, just one quick drink.'

She shakes her head and begins to turn away from him.

'Bloody hell,' he mutters, 'You don't half make it difficult.'

She repeats that she has to go home.

'So you say!' he shouts after she has started to walk away, 'You were always too stuck up Mary Townsley, too bloody full of yourself. Christ I'm only asking you to go for a drink!'

She ignores his comments and quickly turns the corner at the bottom of the street.

In the kitchen Arthur is having his supper while Sylvie is sat with him at the table him listening to the radio.

'What do you think Mary?' Arthur asks as she takes off her coat and hat.

'Think about what?'

It is Sylvie who answers, 'Father thinks we should use the sitting room on a Sunday like we used to.'

'I'm thinking of buying a new three piece suite.'

Mary smooths her hair down with the flat of her hand trying to forget about Billy Rogers.

'Wouldn't that be very expensive?'

Arthur puts down his sandwich looking critically at her.

'I just wondered whether we can afford it,' she persists.

'We?' Arthur queries, 'Who's we? I'll be the one paying for it.'

'Well, can you afford it?'

'None of your business young lady,' he forces back.

'No, I don't suppose it is,' she says sarcastically.

Sylvie interrupts with asking Mary, 'Have you told him about your new job?'

'What new job?'

'No I haven't,' she retorts before going over to the kitchen cupboard for a glass.

'What job?' Arthur asks in an exasperated voice.

Mary fills the glass, turns round and slowly takes a drink.

'For God's sake!' is her father becoming angry.

'Tell him Mary,' Sylvie tries to intervene.

'If you must know I've got a new job at the John Lewis shop in Leeds.'

'My hell, after all these weeks and finally…..finally…'

'Yes finally, I've got a job.'

'How will you get there?' Arthur tries.

'By train.'

'That'll mean not much left from your wage packet at the end of the week with the price of a train ticket nowadays,' is Arthur's surly comment which Mary ignores.

'You should have told him sooner,' Sylvie says later that night after they are all in bed, 'You're always arguing with him. I think you enjoy getting him worked up.'

'So where do you think he suddenly gets all the money from? How can he afford the car and then start talking about another three piece suite when there's nothing wrong with the one we've got? The only explanation is that he's borrowing and getting into debt.'

'Father would never do that.'

'Of course he would. He's like all men. He's no different. He expects to get what he wants. The only difference is that he sounds and appears smarter than most. He always has done.'

'Why do you say such things?' Sylvie asks, 'Why do you hate him so much?'

'I don't hate him.'

'You sound like you do.'

'Well I don't.'

They say nothing for a while before Sylvie admits, 'I pray for him like I pray for all of us.'

'It's mother you should be praying for never mind me or father. And yourself, don't forget yourself.'

'It's hopeless talking to you when you're like this.'

'Like what?'

'You think you'd be pleased having a new job.'

'I am pleased.'

'You don't sound it.'

'There's a lot more to be bothered about that me getting another job, and who says I'll like it? Father might be right, it might cost too much getting to Leeds and back every day. I'll have to see how it goes.'

'Can't you love him Mary?'

There is another silence. Sylvie sits up looking across in the darkness to Mary's dim form.

'He's just another man. There are questions he will not answer.'

'What is that supposed to mean?'

'I don't trust him, and people are talking about him. You can't live in a place like Skipton without folk gossiping. Our father has a reputation and it isn't a good one.'

'That's a terrible thing to....'

'It's what I feel,' Mary interrupts.

'But you can change how you feel, you can if you really want to.'

'I might not want to.'

'Anyone can alter their feelings if they want to badly enough.'

'Like you can with the doctor.'

'Yes I can.'

'Not that it looks like it to me.'

'Well you don't know.'

'No, I don't.'

When she is sure her sister is asleep she gets carefully out of bed and goes along the hallway into her mother's room.

Alice is breathing heavily. There is a vague light coming from outside through the closed curtains to allow Mary to see her mother's swollen face that is a strange yellow colour.

As she stands there she tries to breath through her mouth to avoid the smell from the commode.

Suddenly Alice murmurs, 'Sylvie, is that you?'

'It's me mother, Mary.'

'Mary?'

'Yes.'

'Mary is here?'

'Yes.'

'I never…..never expected…never…'

'Here,' Mary says as she reaches for the glass of water on the bedside table and helps her mother take a sip before Alice's head flops back onto the pillow.

'Dry…..' she mutters.

'I've got a new job mother,' Mary tries but there is no response as Alice closes her eyes followed by slow breaths.

'Did you hear?'

There is no response.

'I've got a new job.'

Alice's face screws up in pain for a second and then relaxes.

Mary stands there for a few minutes longer before returning to her room. She lies down waiting for sleep that seems to take hours to come, long, difficult hours.

CHAPTER THIRTY ONE

It is the light, the diffused light that warms the room, a yellow warmth. The window is open slightly. Alice can hear the birds. Sylvie tosses scraps of bread for them onto the roof of the coal shed every morning.

It is May 1939 and Alice feels more alert today. She has managed a little milky porridge for her breakfast and now is propped up against her three pillows. The taste of the porridge is still in her mouth. She can smell the remnants of Sylvie's fried bacon, that and the washing which she will have hung up out in the yard, white sheets blowing and flapping in the wind like sails of brilliant light surrounded by the dismal yard walls.

She feels the warmth, the light of spring, of change, of life.

'I'm only guessing and trying not to be cheeky at the same time,' Arthur was saying from a long ago past wrapped in spring sunshine.

And she was answering, what? What had she said back then on their walk through the Castle woods one Sunday afternoon.

'Are we courting?' had been one of his cheeky questions.

'And what makes you think that?'

Yes, she had asked, 'And what makes you think that?'

Arthur smiling, eyes flashing, hands outstretched to emphasise his words, 'Well, this is our third walk out. If we go on like this people will start talking.'

'I don't care.'

'That sounds brave Alice, brave words.'

'Which I mean.'

'I know you do.'

There are new buds sprouting tiny green leaves. Wild garlic has spread everywhere interspersed with small clumps of bluebells.

'If we're courting I should be holding your hand Alice.'

She feels excited. This is unexpected, not wanted but needed. She needs to feel like this back then in the past before the war after Paul, after her one and only love, after those brief romantic years that will never happen again, not with Arthur, certainly not with him.

Brash, clever Arthur trying to impress her on a woodland walk passing other couples and families on their own Sunday strolls on that bright spring afternoon.

The sunlight glides between the branches. Complicated shadows pass over them. Arthur's face keeps changing colour in this movement of natural light and shadow.

'You talk a lot.'

Arthur, pretending to look shocked, says back, 'It's because I'm nervous.'

'No, you're not.'

'And how would you know what I'm feeling?'

'Well what are you feeling?'

'That I want to hold your hand and kiss each of your fingers one after another.'

She laughs. She should not laugh. But he is amusing. He is clever, sharp, good looking, smartly dressed except for the flat cap he wears with its peak pulled too far down to shadow his eyes.

She wants him to take it off so she can see the whole of his face.

'I like the way you walk Alice,' he continues, 'You walk elegantly with such a straight back. It's unusual. Women in Skipton don't walk like you do.'

'What nonsense!'

Again his shocked expression, 'It's not nonsense. I never say anything that you could describe in such a way. You're very rude sometimes Alice.'

He stops. She knows he expects her to stop as well, but she does not. She continues along the mulchy path with no idea what he will do. Is it a challenge? Was that what she was doing all those years ago, a different Alice, a different Arthur?

A small battle is won when he runs up to her and takes her arm asking, 'And where do you think you're going?'

'For a walk in the woods. You can join me if you like,' she jokes.

He makes her want to joke, to flirt.

Arthur takes off his cap, placing it on her head.

'Now you look like a real worker.'

'I am a real worker.'

'Of course you are.'

'And you can have this thing back,' she had said, gingerly handing the cap over.

'Thing, what do you mean thing? This is to show everyone you are a member of the working class. Bowlers for the toffs, flat caps for the men who matter.'

'So, you're a socialist?'

'I am, and proud of it.'

'I'm not sure there's anything to be proud of,' she says sarcastically, enjoying this repartee.

Another couple come towards them. Sunlight ripples over the path's soggy surface. Where is Alice? Where is Arthur? They are ghosts of her imagination. Memories become stories that develop into false myths. Block out the bad. Leave only cherished moments for that person.

Did she love Arthur? She needed him. He gave her the chance to restructure her life, to give it a more secure shape, to help her believe there could be a future.

He is smiling, his cap balanced on the back of his head as they walk along. She can see the whole of his handsome face with his dark eyes and thick, black hair.

'I have to be proud about something,' he is saying as they cross the stream over a narrow wooden bridge.

'I wouldn't have thought that was a problem to you.'

'Listen to her!' he exclaims, 'Miss critical.'

'Just being perceptive.'

'Oh, is that what you're doing?'

'I think people are very capable assessing what someone else is like.'

'So, go on then, describe me, describe what I'm like.'

'You're overconfident, cheeky, think yourself educated and….'

'Alright,' he interrupts, laughing as he does so, 'That's enough. You've got me pinned to the board. And there was me thinking I was sophisticated and enigmatic.'

'There's you trying again to show how educated you are.'

'What, sophisticated or enigmatic?' asks Arthur playfully.

'Big words.'

'I can read you know.'

'I should hope you can.'

'And what do you like to read?'

'Any novel from the nineteenth century. After that I'm not that interested.'

'That's a bit of a sweeping statement Alice, isn't it?'

'I don't think it is.'

He reaches out to touch her hand, his fingers laid on her warm skin for a moment before she shifts away from him.

Sylvie is coming up the stairs. The memory has gone. She is suddenly, frighteningly in the present.

'I don't feel very well,' she tries in a croaky voice, 'And I've wet the bed. I'm sorry Sylvie.'

Her daughter is used to such mishaps.

There is a procedure to changing the sheet which is difficult and takes a long time, too long to endure when she is feeling so frail and hurting all over.

Somehow it is managed. Sylvie leaves Alice in the chair while she takes the soiled sheet downstairs to be washed.

She used to hate the embarrassment, her daughter seeing her unable to control her bladder. Now there is nothing that Sylvie has not experienced. She helps her over to the commode, changes her wet sheets, brushes her hair.

'I can smell myself,' she complains.

'I'll get you a fresh nightie,' is Sylvie's matter of fact response.

'I don't like smelling myself.'

'It's alright mother.'

'No, it isn't. It isn't alright.'

Sylvie sighs before going out to the airing cupboard on the landing for another nightie.

'Get the mirror,' Alice finds herself saying.

'And why would you want that?'

'The one that Mary uses in your bedroom,' she adds sharply.

Sylvie has interrupted the past. This makes her angry, suddenly desperate as she now orders Sylvie in a stifled voice to get the mirror.

'Please Sylvie, do as I ask.'

She waits, sat there as the full length mirror is wheeled in.

'Help me stand,' she commands.

'This is silly mother,' is all Sylvie can manage.

'I said help me up.'

With wobbling arms and shaking legs and Sylvie supporting her she gets to her feet. She feels giddy. It is her anger, her exasperation that is driving her to do this, to have Sylvie pull the nightie over her head so that she is naked.

'I want.....I want to look at myself. I want to.....I want to see....' she gasps before turning to look at her awfully thin legs, swollen stomach, sagging breasts, taught neck and bloated face.'

'Mother, sit down,' Sylvie says in a loud voice.

There is a hideously fat bird with no feathers. There is an old woman ready to die. There is this disgusting, shocking image of herself and all she can do is allow Sylvie to turn the mirror away and help her on with her nightie before she struggles with her over to the bed.

'That was silly mother.'

But Alice is too exhausted to respond. The pale yellow bird has already become a nightmare image. That puffed out face has become a hideous mask behind which she hides.

'I should have washed you,' Sylvie tells herself, 'Do you want me to wash you?'

She sounds upset. Alice is aware of her sounding bothered. Sylvie's voice trembles around the edges when she is not happy.

Alice has her eyes closed and is breathing rapidly.

Suddenly there is Archie out in the back lane shouting his head off for Sylvie to come and open the yard door.

Sylvie pulls the bedroom window further up to lean out and tell him to come back later.

Alice hears his complaining voice and then the thud, thud of his football hitting the back wall.

'What's that?' she mutters as though to herself.

'It's only Archie,' Sylvie explains as she draws down the window.

'Archie?'

'Archie Andrews.'

'Do....do I know him?'

'Yes you do mother.'

'I can't remember.'

'It doesn't matter.'

'Of course......of course it matters,' Alice says weakly, 'Everything matters.'

Sylvie wipes her eyes with her pinny before she responds with, 'I know it does. Archie definitely matters. He keeps me going does Archie.'

'Is he your beau?'

Sylvie laughs,' No he isn't and I haven't heard that word in a long time. Beau, it sounds like it comes from one of your Victorian novels.'

Alice has her eyes open.

'Do you want me to read to you?'

'No,' is all Alice can manage.

'I'll just move this,' Sylvie says before trundling the mirror back along the landing.

Alice hears it wheels. The light has changed. She feels exhausted. .

'I'm sorry,' she murmurs when Sylvie returns.

She takes Alice's hand, 'What are you.....?'

'Everything, I'm feeling everything,' she interrupts in almost a whisper.

'You can't help any of this mother.'

'No, I can't help, can I? Can't do anything.'

'You're doing your best.'

'I think I'll rest now.'

'Are you sure you don't want a quick wash?'

'Just leave it Sylvie. Just leave it,' she sighs.

The empty room begins to float in the changing light and Alice is floating with it. In her imagination the window is wide open and she can drift through it out into the fresh sunshine, can hear the birds, can smell all the chimneys of the town and hear its muddled noises.

But the palpitations begin, the breathlessness. Suddenly she is back in the dark cell of her illness. The pain is so bad it feels like red hot iron bars are being pressed down onto her chest. In a desperate reaction she thrusts out her arm knocking over the bedside lamp, her water glass and the radiogram that crashes to the floor.

CHAPTER THIRTY TWO

Dust particles float through the shadows. The shift into the shafts of light coming through the chapel windows like a swarm of tiny insects disturbed by Sylvie's polishing as she moves from pew to pew.

She works methodically, carefully, absorbed in the heavy silence. This is a place where she has worshipped ever since being an infant. Time is held here in the walls and the dark wood, in the deep red carpet and shining pulpit, in the high organ and the oval gallery. She feels this sense of significance, this hushed sense of meaning all around her.

Her concentration is broken by Mr Elgin arriving.

'Hello, I thought Sylvie it was Mrs Beamish turn this week,' he says, walking up the carpeted aisle towards her.

'It should have been, but she sent word she's not well so I'm here instead.'

'Well good for you. And how's your mother today?'

Always she is prepared for this question.

'Not so good, she had a bad turn last week that got us all worried.'

He clasps his hands in front of him and clears his throat, a mannerism of his she recognises when he is not sure what to say next.

'Doctor Donnolly has been twice this week,' she adds.

'She has the best care thanks to you and the doctor.'

'I hope so.'

'It's certain Sylvie. I know it is. Your mother could not have wished for anyone better to look after her.'

She feels herself blushing as he continues, 'That's not saying it hasn't been hard on you and your father and Mary.'

'It's not easy.'

'But your mother is strong in her faith. She's always had that.'

'Yes, yes she has.'

'And that must help, and you Sylvie, it must help you as well.'

'It does most of the time.'

'Of course there'll be times when that faith is challenged. Things can seem so bad you begin to doubt everything. That's natural. It's not a sin to have doubts. We all have doubts. I do too you know.'

Later it is Hazel Beamish from three doors down who comes rushing up to her as Sylvie is about to open her front gate.

'Sylvie! Sylvie, you've got to come. They've thrown Archie into the canal. He won't get out, says he wants you.'

'Where is he?'

'Across from the mill,' Hazel says breathlessly as they start along the street as quickly as possible.

'The water must be freezing,' Hazel manages as they cross over the canal bridge and start along the tow path.

They see the small crowd up ahead, hear the shouting and jeering.

Sylvie pushes her way through to see Archie standing in the middle of the canal with the filthy water halfway up his chest.

'Just clear off you lot!' Hazel shouts.

'Just having a laugh Missus,' one of the young men exclaims.

'I don't think so,' is Hazel's stern reply, 'Go on home, all of you and leave that lad alone or I'll be calling the police.'

'Archie,' Sylvie says, aware of the group moving away as a final piece of turf is tossed in Archie's direction.

'I'm cold.' Archie is shivering, tears streaming down his dirty face.

'Come on out Archie.'

'No.'

'Archie, I'm here and Hazel. You know Hazel.'

'They've gone now Archie,' Hazel tries, 'No one is going to hurt you.'

'Don't like em.'

'I don't blame you.'

'Come on Archie,' Sylvie tries again before she notices a few faces at some of the mill's windows watching them.

A huge billow of dark smoke belches out of the mill's tall chimney and then is caught by the breeze to swoop along the surface of the canal.

Archie starts coughing, wet hair plastered over his white face.

At that moment a barge appears coming round the bend, its tin pot chimney trailing more smoke into the cold, spring air.

'You have to move Archie and then we'll get you home.'

'No, don't want to go home.'

The engine of the barge sounds closer as Sylvie quickly unties the laces of her shoes and then unpins her hat, takes off her coat which she hands over to Hazel.

'What are you doing Sylvie?'

'He won't budge.'

'You can't go in there, it's filthy.'

'I have to.'

'Archie! For God's sake, get yourself out of there!' is Hazel's last loud attempt before she has to help Sylvie step down into the cold, oil stained water.

She can feel the mud churning under her feet as she pushes herself forward through the freezing water watched keenly by Archie who has begun to smile which widens into a grin as Sylvie approaches.

'Them bad uns,' he says as she gets within a few feet of him now being watched by two men on the barge that has come to a slow halt.

Another man on a bike stops. 'What's going on?' he inquires.

'Archie, you get hold of my hand,' Sylvie is saying in an urgent, but careful voice.

'Them bad uns,' he repeats, 'Shoved me in Sylvie, shoved me in.'

'Well they've gone now.'

'Wanted you, wanted you to come.'

'I'm here now.'

'Wanted you Sylvie.'

She reaches out and he takes his hand.

Slowly they start dragging their feet through the mud, the murky water churning around them.

'Come on Archie, we're nearly there, nearly there,' Sylvie coaxes him to keep moving.

By now another small group has gathered. The man with the bike rests it down and then reaches out for Archie's hand to help him out of the water as Hazel and another woman do the same for Sylvie, each gripping one of her hands and pulling her onto the tow path.

The barge sounds off its hooter as though in celebration.

'You alright?' the man with the bike asks Sylvie as she lifts her dress a little to ring out some of the water before she tells Hazel to wrap her coat around the shivering Archie.

'We're alright, thank you, aren't we Archie?'

'Cold,' is all he can manage.

'Nice swim?' one of the men on the barge asks as it chugs past.

'Not really,' is Sylvie's half amused response.

Dripping water and leaving wet footprints on the pavement she, with Hazel's coat now hung over her shoulders take Archie back to the house.

'Your clothes will smell awful,' Hazel says as the three of them reached the Townsley's front gate.

'We'll be fine Hazel. I'm glad you found me when you did or goodness knows how long he would have been in there.

In the house Archie stands shivering and dripping water in the middle of the kitchen as Sylvie stirs up the fire. In a hurry she looks out some of her father's old overalls from the cupboard under the stairs.

'Here, I'm going to get my wet clothes off and you Archie dry yourself on this,' she says while giving him a warm towel from the pulley, 'and then put these on.'

Archie pulls a face of complaint,' What are they?'

'Father's overalls. He hasn't worn them in years. They won't fit but that doesn't matter. Now just do as you're told Archie and I'll be down in a minute.'

She checks on her mother before going along to the bathroom.

Archie is still standing where he was, his hair glistening in the light coming though the kitchen window, Arthur's faded blue overalls hanging off his thin body.

'I feel stupid,' is the first thing he says when Sylvie comes back down.

'Never mind that, you get near the fire,' she tells him, 'And I'll make some tea.'

'You saved me Sylvie.'

'Archie, the water wasn't that deep.'

'Cold though.'

'Yes, and filthy.'

'They pushed me in.'

'Who were they?'

'Just lads.'

'Town lads. Did you know any of them?'

'Yes, town lads Sylvie.'

Archie sits forward and reaches out towards the now blazing flames while she makes the tea, hands him a mug before taking hers over to the kitchen table.

She looks at his thin back, his pale features and scruffed up hair.

'What are we going to do with you Archie? If it's not one thing it's another,' she sighs.

'You saved me Sylvie.'

'Alright, yes I did. Goodness knows what them gorping from the mill windows thought or those men on the barge. I'm just glad I ran into Hazel when I did or I don't know how long you'd have....'

'Lost my football!' Archie suddenly exclaims.

'Not so loud or you'll wake mother.'

'I've lost it?'

'Where did you last have it?'

'Don't know,' Archie answers, his face pulled down into an abject expression.

'We'll get you another one.'

'Don't want.....want my football.'

'Well you'll have to look for it.'

'Can you come Sylvie?'

'No Archie, I think you can do that by yourself.'

'Please Sylvie.'

She drinks her tea, bothered by his desperate look.

'Them gypsy lads, town lads, gypsies,' Archie starts saying, 'Took my football. Hate em. Hate em Sylvie.'

'Just leave it for now Archie. I'm sure your football will turn up. Now drink your tea and warm yourself up and then you'll have to be getting yourself home. I'm sure your mother will have heard all about you in the canal by now. The jungle drums will have been beating out loud.'

'Drums,' Archie repeats.

'Yes, those people who like telling other people what's happening or what they thinks happening. Do you understand?'

Archie stares at her with a frown creasing his white forehead, 'Don't Sylvie….don't understand.'

'It doesn't matter, now drink your tea.'

Finally she takes Archie home. Mrs Andrews has already heard what has happened and greets him with a concerned expression, 'Now what's been happening Archie? You look in aright state.'

'And he's lost his football,' Sylvie informs her.

'Oh that thing,' Mrs Andrews says in irritation, 'He's always losing it. I'll be glad when he can't find it and that'll teach him a lesson to look after his things. Are you listening Archie, you daft happorth?'

Later that evening Hazel knocks on the Townsley's front door. Arthur is out. Alice is trying to concentrate on a radio play while Mary, now it is warm enough in the evenings, is in the front room without a fire listening to her records on the new radiogram.

It is Sylvie who goes to the door, 'Hazel,' she says brightly, 'Come on in.'

'I don't want to bother you. I thought I'd just pop by and see if you're alright after that carry on this afternoon.'

'Yes, it was a carry on, a right carry on,' Sylvie agrees as they go along the hallway, past the loud dance music coming from the front room and into the kitchen.

'Mary's listening to her records so we'll leave her to it,' Sylvie explains, 'Do you want a cup of tea?'

'No, I won't stay long,' Hazel answers.

She is a woman in her early thirties who has two children and a husband who works for the council. Sylvie and her have always chatted when they meet in the street.

'Archie said it was some gypsy lads who pushed him in.'

Hazel sits at the table, 'Yes, I recognised a couple of them. They have their caravans on the site where that warehouse burnt down last year just off the Gargrave Road. One of them is called Tommy something. He's a right chancer. I often see him in Woolworths, trying to pinch something or other. I know he's been in trouble with the police.'

'I'm glad you were there.'

'Oh, I was on the bridge and saw Archie. They were throwing rubbish and clumps of turf at him off the canal bank. I shouted at them but it made no difference and then Archie started screaming for you, screaming his head off poor thing. I was just relieved I could find you as quickly as I did or goodness knows what they would have done.'

'Archie is terrified of them,' Sylvie says then.

'No wonder if they carry on like that.'

'It's not the first time they've bothered him.'

There is a pause before Hazel adds, 'I don't know what things are coming to. They must know Archie can't stand up for himself. He's a simple lad and they should leave him alone. He's too easy to target. We should really inform the police.'

'He's too easy a target.'

'At least he has you as a friend.'

'Oh, me and Archie get on like a house on fire,' is Sylvie's easy response.

'Anyway, I just came to see if you were alright.'

'Thanks Hazel. I appreciate you coming round.'

'Right, I'd better get back,' Hazel sighs before asking, 'And how's your mother keeping?'

'She's.....she's better than she was last week.'

'I heard she had a turn for the worse.'

Sylvie forces a weak smile, 'Yes, you could call it that.'

'I don't know how you do it.'

'Do what?'

'Look after your mother and all the rest of it.'

'It's not something to think about.'

'Well I admire what you manage. I don't think there's many young women who would do what you're doing.'

'I have no choice Hazel.'

'And if you had, would it be any different?'

Sylvie is unprepared for this. She turns the warm mug of tea around between both her hands thinking.

'I honestly don't know Hazel. I suppose I hope it would be no different, but I was only fourteen when all this started and you can never tell.'

'Of course you can't.'

'But I agree, it's not easy, necessary, essential, but not easy.'

'Well I think you're doing a grand job, and now I'd better get back.'

Sylvie sees her off down the garden path before closing the front door. Another record starts from the front room.

Hazel has left her thoughtful and bothered. She returns to the kitchen and stands looking out over the net curtains at the pale evening sky with the rooftops and chimneys shaped almost in black against it.

She does not want to feel resentful. But whatever else she feels it is the fear of her mother dying that rips through every other emotion.

When she fails herself she fails her mother. She is so scared. When she thinks about each passing day they are a torture and a challenge.

But she sighs, automatically rubs her hands down her dress before going to the foot of the stairs where she stops for a moment.

Dance music is coming from the front room. Sylvie imagines a London ballroom with hundreds of well dressed couples all moving together, the men in dark suits and the ladies in silver white dresses. The image leaves a bitter impression as she starts up the stairs, the music merging into voices from the radio drama coming from her mother's room creating a confusion of sounds and emotions.

'You alright mother?' she asks as comfortably as she can as she enters the bedroom.

CHAPTER THIRTY THREE

Before Arthur leaves the office he checks with Annie that they have gone through all the mail before checking tomorrow's delivery of sand and cement to Jim Saunders and then thanks Foster Armstrong at doing such a good job clearing up the yard.

'Mikey, you be on time tomorrow morning!' he shouts across the yard before getting into his car.

He drives out of the yard up the lane that finally joins the Gargrave Road. It is only over a mile to the Black Bull where he parks up on the cobbles. Usually this is where the car will stay overnight before he picks it up the next morning.

'And how's Arthur this evening?'

'Not bad Agnes, not bad,' he answers as he walks towards the bar, which has a few customers.

'New suit I see Arthur, very smart.'

'I've had it a while now,' he answers, straining to sound cheerful, but I'm glad you approve Agnes.'

Automatically she pours him a pint of bitter and a double brandy.

'And how many do you expect tonight?' Agnes asks as she takes his cash.

'Oh the usual I suppose.'

'Sandwiches at nine?'

'That'll be grand. Thanks Agnes,' he says before going over to a seat at a corner table near the unlit fire.

He puts his trilby on the table, unbuttons his jacket, rests back and takes a drink.

It takes a lot more than it used to before he feels the first warm flood of alcohol through his brain. Now he has to wait until he has drunk at least a few brandies. It has become an expensive business getting to that state between sobriety and inebriation. But he is used to it. The trick is to eat as little as possible through the day. Then on an empty stomach the alcohol heats everything up a lot quicker.

He takes a copy of the Yorkshire Post from his jacket pocket and starts to read with the sun still shining through the Black Bull's windows reflecting off all the tankards above the bar.

But he cannot concentrate. The effect of the dream has lingered all day, the Black Pennine approaching along a fog bound road. Its black windows allow only the faint shadow of each passenger to be seen. With dread he waits for it to stop. He knows it will stop as it always does. He waits for the doors to open and he is terrified, sick with fear, in a panic that makes him want to run away but he cannot. He has to mount the steps and join the rest of the dead who are sat there stiff and silent.

He finishes his brandy and then his pint before going over for a refill.

He sits back down and tries to clear his mind, hoping that watching the other customers will help him forget. But even though his mood has been strained all day he at least has managed to hide it from everyone at Slaters. He does not believe in taking any emotional baggage to work. He has had enough experience of men who are never the same one day to the next.

But now he is here in the bar he begins again to analyse what he is feeling about the effects of the Black Pennine dream, that recurring nightmare. Nothing is real anymore. He is imprisoned inside a world of his own making.

Instead of a sense of freedom because of Kitty's generosity he feels disgusted by his constant need for money. He never has enough even now with all his debts paid up, hardly enough for the budget that Sylvie depends on to keep the house going.

He drinks, feels the evening sun warming the bar, wondering how much Sylvie must hate him. And Mary, she has changed so much over the last months, quieter, tighter, always serious. Has he lost both his daughters? It often feels that way.

A group of council workers push through the door and stride over to the bar where Agnes is wiping some glasses. Arthur falls into deepening fear for Alice. He finds it impossible to accept that she is dying. His wife is dying and all he can do is drink.

'For God's sake,' he mutters before furiously opening his evening paper.

John Metcalf walks in, nods at Arthur before he comes over and asks him if he wants another drink.

'Daft question really,' he adds while taking off his hat and coat and laying them on one of the chairs next to Arthur's.

'And how is the medicine business?' Arthur asks after John returns walking carefully with the drinks set on a brass tray.

'Well,' he sighs as he sits down, 'I think it must be all this talk in the newspapers that's helping every chemist in the country. Everyone wants something for their nerves or headaches or pains here, there and everywhere.'

'We're all on edge.'

'Speak for yourself.'

'I am.'

'Good.'

They drink. Arthur lights a cigarette. The bar becomes noisier.

'It's the good weather that brings them out,' John comments, looking at the busy bar.

'The lull before the storm,' is Arthur's response.

'Could be, and there again it might be that just like me they've all had a hard day and need a pint to dissolve some of the worry.'

'Are you worried John?'

His friend smiles and winks at the same time before answering, 'Like I said, business is getting better by the day and all because of old Adolf mouthing off, telling everyone he's going to take over Europe and then the world.'

'And is he?'

John purses his lips to consider the question.

'Maybe we should save such a subject for this evening's debate.'

'I'm not going to be there,' Arthur announces.

'And why's that?'

'Just can't be bothered. It'll be the same old arguments from the same people and all of it is....'

'You can't give it up Arthur, not now, now after all these years, not when everything is getting so bad.'

'Bad?'

'I mean politically.'

'You mean you need me there to balance the argument.'

'You've never done that!' John exclaims with an edge to his tone.

There is a momentary silence leaving Arthur to think how it is always so different and harder when talking to men in general than it is to women.

'Anyway,' I never asked about Alice,' John resumes after they have both said hello to men they know in the now busy bar.

'A bit better this week. She had a bad turn a couple of weeks ago but since then she seems to have improved a little.'

'That's good Arthur. You must tell her I was asking of her.'

'I will John. She's not having any visitors. They tire her out.'

'I can imagine.'

Arthur wonders if he can. How can anyone imagine living in a house where someone is slowly slipping away from life?

The thought has him up and over to the bar for more drinks where he chats with some of the Black and Bull regulars.

Only once did he ever express some of his real self to another man and it ended in disaster when he realised that the other's interest could only go so far.

'Thanks Arthur,' John says as the next round is put on the table, 'I was just thinking,' he continues after a mouthful of beer, 'The first time you joined the debating society. I'd been going at you for weeks to come along and finally when you did there wasn't half a right barny between you and....what was his name....a history teacher...?'

'Robert Thwaite,' Arthur tells him, aware of the bar filling with cigarette smoke and the smell of beer, an atmosphere he relishes.

'That's him. He had that goatee beard and wore thin framed glasses.'

'And we argued about....'

'Wordsworth. My hell yes!' John exclaims, 'You two had such a blazing row about Wordsworth.'

'And whether where he lived should be taken into account when reading his poetry.'

'That was it Arthur, you remember.'

'Robert Thwaite believed there should be nothing but the poet's actual words on paper, and I said that it was impossible to appreciate what Wordsworth wrote if you didn't know anything about his life in the Lake District.'

'The rest of us just sat back and let you two get on with it.'

'I'll say this for him, he was right persistent. He wouldn't accept anything I said. A few years later I drove Alice and the girls up to see Rose cottage where Wordsworth had lived and it made even more sense to me that you had to know about that house in that area of England or you could never understand what Wordsworth was trying to express.'

'He left the group a few weeks after that. Don't know what happened to him.'

'Not like the rest of us. We've been at it ever since.'

'At it?'

'Arguing.'

'Nothing like a good argument.'

'Depends who you're arguing with.'

'It's been you and Dave at the last meetings.'

'Let's say Dave and I do not see eye to eye on anything really except that the Black Bull's bitter is the best in the town. And now John,' Arthur adds as he finishes his brandy followed by a mouthful of beer, 'I should have been home by now,' he adds as he stands up.

'It's a bit early Arthur.'

Arthur forces a smile as John looks up at him with a puzzled expression.

'And there was me thinking you were joking about not coming tonight,' he says then.

'No John, sadly not a joke. To be honest I've forgotten what that is. When did you ever hear a good joke lately that isn't about damned Hitler?'

'True enough. But what about us having to become air raid wardens or join the home guard or help the fire brigade. What sort of choice is that?'

'Someone has to do it. Anyway give my love to Shirley,' Arthur says of John's wife.

'I will.'

'And you try and keep calm when Sean starts on about the country not being ready.'

'Sean!' John laughs, 'He's the one who's not ready.'

'I'll be in here at the weekend probably. Maybe you'll be here.'

'I'll see you then.'

'Yes, hopefully you will,' are Arthur's last words before he picks up his trilby and pushes his way through the now crowded bar.

Outside the light is dimming. The air is full of the smell of coal fires still burning as he sets off down the High Street leaving his car parked outside the Bull.

As he turns the Woolworth's corner he sees Billy Smith and Gordon coming towards him. Even though it is a mild evening they are wearing black coats. They are both hatless with their hair brylcreemed straight back. Arthur is about to cross the road when a truck approaches and he has to wait.

'Trying to get away from us are you Arthur?' Billy shouts above the noise of the passing truck, 'That's not very friendly,' he adds in a quieter voice when it has gone.

'I've nothing to say to you,' Arthur says still trying to walk past them.

But Billy grabs his arm, 'Oh but I've got something to say to you.'

'No you haven't Billy,' Arthur insists as he pulls away only to walk into Gordon's outstretched hand pushing hard against his chest.

'Settle down Arthur,' Billy says.

'Just let me past.'

'I said fucking settle down.'

'And why should I? Why the hell should I listen to anything you have to say? I'm paid up Billy so just leave me alone.'

'Listen to him Gordon, after all we've done for him, after all we've done for you Arthur.'

'You've done nothing,' Arthur replies strongly.

'We have a lot of customers in Skipton so this is us just finishing up. I can smell that you've been out and about enjoying yourself. Isn't that right, spending more of what you haven't got?'

Over on the other pavement three women walk slowly past, their voices drifting across the road.

'Just remember,' Billy continues with his face a few inches from Arthur's, 'That Mr Andrews will know if you try borrowing from anyone else and he wouldn't like it. He fucking wouldn't like it at all so you just remember when you're next a bit short you come to us. You got that Arthur? Nice having a girlfriend with plenty of dosh though, isn't it? Classy lady you have there, nice car, nice legs, what else could you ask for? You must feel very grateful. Do you feel grateful Arthur? Mr Andrews has this little motto that once a client always a client. We'll be seeing you again you can bet on that except I'm not a betting man, am I Gordon?'

'No Billy, I can vouch for that,' is Gordon's ready response.

'A mug's game that is.'

Arthur pushes past them but Billy has not finished and he shouts after him, 'Yes you fuck off Arthur! But we'll be seeing you again! Don't you worry about that!'

Angrily Arthur walks quickly away. He hates everything about them, but especially what he has been through with sharks like Andrews and all the rest of the Bradford money lenders. They have the power. It is only Kitty who has helped him escape from that grubby, miserable world.

'Once a client always a client,' he hears Billy saying in his cynical tone of voice, cynical and confident as always.

When he reaches home he drops his trilby on the hat stand and goes straight upstairs.

Alice is propped up in bed reading. She gives a weary smile and rests the book down as he approaches to kiss her on the forehead.

'That's good to see,' he comments before he pulls the chair over to sit near her.

'What is?' Alice asks in a dry voice.

'Seeing you reading.'

'I'm always reading.'

'Not recently.'

'No, that's true.'

'Except for the last few days.'

She gives another weak smile, looking at him with her exhausted eyes and then asks, 'Why are you home so early? I thought it was the debating society tonight.'

'It is, but I didn't fancy it. I had a couple of pints with John. The Bull was busy.'

'Men drinking, and how many women were in the bar, not many I'm sure.'

'A few.'

She finds her bookmark and closes the book, leaning awkwardly sideways to put it on the bedside table.

'What sort of day have you had?' he asks.

She gives a slow shake of her head before answering, 'Nothing different. There can't be anything different, not anymore.'

'You never know Alice,' he says warmly.

'Oh but I do Arthur, I do. I know I'm never going to get better. I've known that all along. Nobody has to tell me how bad things are. I have a heart that might stop at any moment. There is a pain all the time in my chest that is warning me of what is to come. I know I'm lucky to have managed this long.'

'That's because of who you are.'

'No, Arthur, it's just luck or bad luck, whichever way you look at it.'

He senses the failure in her voice, that desperately sad tone that is now always there.

'Do you want anything?' he asks.

Her breathing is shallow and quick as she looks glances across the room and then focuses back on him with her dull, weary eyes.

'I never ask you that question, do I? I never inquire what you want Arthur?'

Suddenly he is wary. He has never seen her look so tired, and yet her voice has a ring of strength in it, something he has not heard from her in a long time.

'It's not important what I want. It's you who.....'

'But....it's always been important Arthur. You can't....you can't deny it,' she interrupts.

He makes no reply. The radio is on down in the kitchen. Voices sound out from the back lane and the breeze coming through the slightly opened window puffs out the lace curtains like a small, filigree sail.

'Anyway, I'm glad you're home early,' she adds.

But he cannot trust these moments. Everything is suddenly threatened. Even though she is dangerously ill there is still a spark of pride, of antagonism towards him.

'You make it sound unusual, when it isn't,' he tries and then immediately regrets what he has just said.

Alice just looks at him and makes no response.

'I'm sorry,' she sighs then.

'Sorry for what?'

'Being....being like this.....being like this for so long....so long now I've forgotten how things used to be, how I used to be. I can hardly remember. I suppose if I try hard enough I can see myself before all this started.'

'Well, I certainly can.'

'That's because the past is always close to you.'

'What does that mean?' he asks warily.

'It.......it doesn't matter,' she answers breathlessly before running her tongue over her dry, cracked lips.

'I'll get you a fresh glass of water,' he says before taking the empty glass along to refill it in the bathroom.

'Thank you,' she murmurs, taking a sip at the water.

'You can tell....tell the weather's changing.....the tap water is getting warmer.'

'It's been a better day,' he says hoping her tone has changed.

'All I feel is the light......feel the air...' Alice says, 'I like it when I can have the window open.'

He sits back down and takes her thin, rigidly veined hand.

'Sylvie told me that Mary......Mary is working late tonight.'

'It's a long day for her with all the travelling.'

'Better than moping about the place Arthur.'

'Yes, it is. She was in a strange state a few weeks back and it lasted long enough.'

'I'm not sure whether she knows what she wants to do.'

Arthur thinks of Rose and Mary's plans.

'No, I don't think she does,' he awkwardly agrees realising that Sylvie must have said nothing to her about what her sister was thinking of doing.

'She'll be alright…..Mary will be alright.'

'Of course.'

Alice pulls her hand away, her face suddenly stiffening, 'I don't need any apologies Arthur. It's a bit…..it's a bit late for that.'

Again he hears the critical tone. It scares him. He does not want things to end this way but accepts there is nothing he can do now to change Alice's opinion of him.

'I'm just sorry that I can't do more to make things…..'

'Stop it Arthur, 'she interrupts, 'It makes no difference. None of it does. But don't worry,' she sighs painfully, gripping hold of the bedclothes, 'I'm way past caring….. I mean it Arthur. I don't care about any of it…..the past….what you've done….who you've been with.'

'I've….'he starts only for Alice to start shaking her head.

'No Arthur,' she says grimly, 'Just leave it. Please…..just leave it now.'

She closes her eyes for a moment and then looks at him blankly.

'I'll ask again, do you need anything, want anything?' he tries.

Her eyes are full of cynical mistrust, of doubt and disgust as she again shakes her head before settling back against the pillow.

'Right,' is all there is left for him to say before he leaves the room, goes down the stairs, takes his trilby and goes back out, checking he has his wallet in his inside jacket pocket.

CHAPTER THIRTY FOUR

Mary remembers Sylvie dressed as a clown in the Sunday School part of the parade, boys and girls being carefully watched by their teachers and the policemen tending the crowd lining both sides of the High Street. And such a lot of people all in their summer best, the women and girls in pretty dresses and straw hats and the boys and men in their slacks, open necked shirts and light jackets, standing four deep, some forced under the awnings coming out over the pavements from all the shop fronts.

'I would have picked you,' Aunt Rose had said kindly when it was all over.

Rain angles across the stuffy compartment of the return train from Leeds. Each bead of rain is like another memory flickering across Mary's consciousness as she drifts along the boring journey home.

Leaving school and that summer desperate to be the Gala queen, dreaming and fantasising about the coming event. She had to be picked. It was her one chance. It was the only advantage to be still attending chapel. The most likely choice would come from one of the churches and chapels of the town.

But Marjorie Philips, the awful, buck teethed, slit eyed, stumpy Marjorie Philips had been chosen instead. Mary had wept. She had rushed up to her bedroom after she heard the news and like a silly fool had cried her heart out. She had been full of anger and jealousy sure that it was a conspiracy against her. Now the opposite applied, going to chapel was the reason she had not been chosen. She should have been attending the Church of England or even the Catholic church to stand a chance. Methodists, Wesleyans and Congregationalists had been doomed from the start and she should have realised it before getting her hopes up. Nonconformists would never be picked. She had hated the gala, the town but more than anything her self for being so stupid as to think she could have been the queen for a year, Mary Townsley with her crown and flowing gown paraded in front of everyone, the dream of a fourteen year old.

The town's brass band had played. The fire engines had trundled past with the firemen stood holding onto the sides and backs of each vehicle like Viking warriors in their plumed helmets. Junior school pupils had wandered along in their fancy dress followed by a small man wearing only a nappy and baby hat in a pram being bottled fed by another small man in trousers held up by braces across his naked chest.

The scouts had marched past in lines carrying their poles with small pennants fluttering in the summer breeze, a huge wooden wedding cake five tiers high, a horse pulling along a cart on which three girls sat in deck chairs pretending to sunbathe, a blackened man in trunks being scrubbed by an angry father. And then the only frightening part of the parade, those men on high stilts, men with moustaches and long white robes staring ahead like ghosts marching down the High Street. They had been awful and real and silent except for the noise of their stilts clacking along the tarmac, the band away in the distance and the crowd watching intently as the men up at least ten feet in the air bent forwards and backwards in their long stepped motion. They were there in her memory and they were still just as frightening as when she had first seen them.

And at the centre of it all was queen Marjorie Philips followed by her four maids in waiting, Mary being one of them, the final indignity, to have to walk in step behind the fat Marjorie holding onto her long silk train despising every step her entourage had to take.

Aunt Rose in her long black coat and small black hat had been in the crowd, had waved as Mary had gone past and then had looked to the side and bent a little as though talking to someone, just for a moment, an inconsequential gesture that had stuck there in Mary's memory, a silent shift of emphasis from her to this other person in the crowd. Like every moment it had passed so quickly, a tiny piece of time flicked over from one brief page to the next. Everything was sad and tragic.

The train pulls into Keighley station sending a rush of steam along the platform followed by umbrellas opened by those getting out and closed for those getting on board as the rain is driven across the busy station like a huge wet curtain flapping in the early evening breeze.

'Miserable weather,' says the young man who is taking off his sodden mackintosh and putting it up on the rack above their seats.

Mary ignores him and looks out of the window as the train moves off with more steam blown past.

When he sits down beside her he smells of the rain and fresh air suffused with coke from the engine pulling them forward.

'Sorry,' the young man persists, 'Just trying to communicate with a fellow human being.'

She turns to look at him, at his sandy coloured hair and thin moustache, his prominent cheeks bones and hazel eyes.

'And what if a fellow human does not wish to communicate?' she asks pointedly.

He smiles,' That's better.'

'Is it?'

'Yes, you're speaking.'

Mary turns away pretending to look out of the window.

Just then two more men slide open the door and come into the now full compartment.

'Thank God!' one of them exclaims.

'I didn't fancy standing all the way to Carlisle,' says the other before they put down their briefcases on the seats. They take off their macs and trilbies and finally sit down.

A mother, father and child plus an older man make up the rest of the passengers. Out in the corridor people push past each as the train gathers speed.

'How far you going?' the young man tries next in a quiet voice.

'Skipton,' Mary answers abruptly.

'I'm Hellifield. Not much of a place really. The only thing going for it is the railway. Without that it would be a ghost town. But I like Skipton,' he adds.

Nothing more is said as the two new passengers take over with their talk about Yorkshire's chances of another championship and whether they will manage Ascot this year.

'I might see you again,' the young man says as eventually the train begins to slow again, 'By the way my name is Roger, Roger Simpson.'

Mary gives him a stiff, empty smile before she stands to retrieve her coat from the rack, squeezes between a line of knees and then slides open the compartment door to find herself in the corridor crammed with other passengers.

She follows the crowd out of Skipton station, all of them bent slightly against the heavy rain.

Her father is home. It is his new routine now that mother's condition is worsening, as though he is making a last attempt at being a normal husband and father. Mary finds this so hypocritical, so blatantly obvious.

'Here she is,' says Arthur, polishing his shoes by the kitchen fire.

'Why do we need a fire?' she asks.

'I like one lit when the weather is as bad as it is.'

'I would have thought that was a waste. Where's Sylvie?'

'Upstairs washing her mother,' answers Arthur.

Mary returns to the hallway to take off her wet coat before checking herself in the small hatstand mirror which she does automatically every time she returns from work.

'There's tea in the oven for you,' her father says when she re enters the kitchen.

'I'm not hungry.'

'You should eat.'

'I might have it later on.'

'It'll be cold and your sister won't be happy. She doesn't like it if you don't eat what she's cooked.'

'My sister is never happy,' is her sharp retort.

'And you, what about you, are you happy?' Arthur asks while continuing with his polishing.

'I don't think it's important, all this carry on about happiness. How can anyone feel right about things when we're about to go to war?'

'Not yet, well I don't think just yet.'

'Who knows what might happen? Silly men making one stupid mistake after another. They should all be put on a boat and pushed out to sea, the lot of them.'

'And you think that would be the answer?'

'At this very moment I couldn't care less.'

'Has it been that bad a day?'

'No,' she retorts sharply, 'I've had a good day, as good as they come.'

Arthur sits back in the fireside chair and asks, 'And how are things in the big city?'

Mary is still standing close to the door, her face pale and tightly drawn as she answers, 'They're talking about gas masks for everyone, air balloons going up and children being evacuated to the countryside.'

'Has to be done I suppose.'

Just then Sylvie carrying an empty basin comes along the hallway and squeezes past her sister.

'There's tea in the oven,' she says while going over to the sink.

'I've told her,' Arthur chips in.

'I might have it later,' Mary says again.

Sylvie turns round and looks critically at her, 'It'll be cold.'

'And I told her that as well,' Arthur adds.

'I'll pop up and see mother,' Mary tells them as she turns and goes along to the foot of the stairs where she stops to listen to Sylvie saying something from the kitchen,

'I don't why I bother sometimes. What else does she expect?'

'Nothing and everything,' she hears her father answer.

'She's never grateful, I know that.'

'You just have to give her a bit of leeway Sylvie, a bit of a wide berth or she might snap your head off.'

Mary quickly mounts the stairs, takes a deep breath before entering Alice's bedroom.

She is laid listening to the radio, her face a pale yellow except for the grey bags under eyes. Her hair looks dry and streaked with silvery grey.

'Mary,' she sighs, 'You can turn the radio off if you like.'

When it has been switched off Mary stands there trying to breath through her mouth to avoid the different smells in the room.

'Have you had your tea?' Alice asks wearily.

'It's terrible weather, been raining all day,' Mary answers, 'And the train was jam packed.'

'I've been listening to it this afternoon, rattling against the window.'

Mary glances across at the unlit fire in the corner before leaning over to kiss her mother on the fore head. Her skin is warm and clammy. For a moment Mary takes in the smell of fresh soap mixed in with the deeper odour coming from Alice. Her illness has a distinct smell. It revolts Mary. Everything about her mother's condition is abhorrent, but especially the smells, disinfectant from the commode trying to mask what it used for, her mother's bodily odour adding a sour tinge to the atmosphere.

'And how has work been?' Alice inquires, turning her head slightly.

'There weren't that many in today. The weather was too foul.' Mary replies.

'You look very smart.'

'You have to working at John Lewis. It's what they expect.'

'But you like that. You have always liked looking your best.'

'Whatever that is.'

'You know Mary. You know what suits you.'

'I hope so.'

'I was the same,' Alice says, 'I liked to dress as well as I could. It made me feel better…..better about myself.'

'You always wore nice clothes.'

'I'm not sure about always, not about the house, but yes, when I went out I tried to look my best.'

'And you will again mother,' Mary states and then immediately regrets it, 'It's just a hope,' she quickly adds.

Mary has stayed long enough. She is beginning to feel nauseous and guilty at the same time for wanting to be out of the room as quickly as possible.

'I'm going to wash my face and change my clothes,' she tells Alice before giving her a breathless kiss and leaving the stifling room.

The next day the rain has stopped leaving a sky full of huge billowing white clouds. She misses her usual train so has to wait in the canteen on Leeds station for nearly an hour for the next one. On the return journey she again drifts along a vein of memory as she watches a trail of steam curling along past the window. It begins with the usual thoughts about her inability to cope with her mother's illness.

Unexpectedly these thoughts are followed by her remembering playing in Aunt Rose's back garden. The path to the privy was made up of slabs of stone. There were others covered in moss that were holding back the grassy mound that ran along the rest of the back gardens. She had only been five or six when she first noticed the names and dates on some of these slabs. When she played out there usually by herself there was always the smell of dank earth that she associated with the dark green moss, the standing slabs of stone and the names carved in large letters with chiselled dates that she soon learnt were headstones taken from some graveyard long ago.

Through her aunt's kitchen door she would step into a frightening world of moss and stone and a deep, earthy smell. It was that smell she registered whenever she was in her mother's bedroom. It terrified her. The house was beginning to be pervaded by that odour. She smelt it the moment she came through the front door. In desperation had come the idea of moving in with her aunt now that the privy had been knocked down and all those slabs of stone had been dug up and replaced by a back area covered with small pebbles.

It being a later train there is only one fellow passenger in her compartment, a large middle aged lady eating from a box of chocolates while reading a Penguin novel. It is when the train reaches Keighley station that the door of the compartment is slid open.

'So here you are,' comes a familiar voice, 'You're on a later train. Were you were trying to avoid me?'

Mary looks at the young man from yesterday dressed in a smart grey suit as he puts his briefcase in the rack and sits down beside her just as the train starts moving.

'I hope you haven't forgotten me already, Roger, Roger Simpson,' he says in an educated voice that has only a slight Yorkshire tone in it.

'No Mr Simpson, I hadn't forgotten,' Mary replies.

At that he smiles, 'That's a relief. I was hoping to see you, but I had to work late so thought I'd missed you, you being on the earlier train yesterday. Were you in the same boat as well, having to work late?'

She has to make another decision as to whether to continue this one sided conversation or just ignore him, which would be difficult with this Roger Simpson sitting beside her in an almost empty compartment. At least there is the woman eating her chocolates who thankfully creates some sort of security.

'If you must know,' she finally responds, 'I did some shopping after work.'

'Lucky you and lucky me, if you see what I mean.'

'Yes, Mr Simpson, I see what you mean.'

'Call me Roger and if you'd tell me your name I could…..'

'Mary Townsely.'

'Mary?'

'Yes.'

'Well nice to meet you Mary.'

Now it has gone this far it begins to feel better having someone to talk to than following that vein of memories which has been absorbing her thoughts.

'Can I ask where you work?'

At Roger's question the lady with the chocolates suddenly seems interested.

'The John Lewis store,' Mary answers looking directly at the other woman forcing her to return to her novel.

There is a pause. The train rattles over some points as more steam billows past the compartment window.

'You're supposed to ask me what I do?' Roger tries then.

Mary turns to him and gives him one of her sharp, determined looks but says nothing.

'Sorry, just a suggestion,' Roger continues.

In a moment she decides she likes his face, his eyes, his smart suit and his voice. But all that does not mitigate against the fact he is a man and therefore cannot be trusted.

'You'll be getting off soon.'

'Yes.'

'And I might never see you again especially if you keep changing your usual train.'

'So what do you suggest Roger?' she asks pointedly.

He seems suddenly uncertain before he smiles again, 'We should arrange to meet?'

'I don't think so.'

'And have tea or go for a drink, something like that.'

'And why on earth should I agree to that? You're a complete stranger.'

'Because you're a very attractive looking young lady.'

'And who says so?'

'I do and I think of myself as an expert in such matters.'

'Well good for you.'

'I'm only joking. In fact, right at this moment I feel nervous, embarrassed and a little desperate if you must know.'

By now the other passenger has stopped eating her chocolates and has closed her book.

'A cup of tea Mary. Where's the harm in that?'

'I said I don't think so.'

'I'd like to know why.'

'No reason.'

'There must be something.'

'Just leave it please.'

'I'm afraid that's impossible.'

She could not believe it. By the time the train reached Skipton he had persuaded her to meet him the following Saturday in a Leeds tearoom after she finished work.

Walking out of the quieter station she feels irritated, glad, self critical and somehow relieved. She still did not have to keep her promise to meet him.

CHAPTER THIRTY FIVE

'Angels are messengers, are God given thoughts, are the symbols of all that is holy,' Alice had once read and never forgotten.

'That's a proper looking angel,' Arthur had commented.

Gabriel standing in front of a kneeling Mary, the apparition towering over the supplicant woman, God's power over all that was humanly divine.

It had been such a beautiful angel with huge silver wings and white flowing robes.

'Perfect Italian Renaissance,' he had added as they had walked around in the silence of the Leeds gallery.

Her mouth is dry. She can feel the palpitations thudding in her chest. Even though she is used to them they still cause a panic which makes them worse.

'What would you like to look at Mrs Townsley?' the shop assistant had asked.

Yes, another memory, the first time she had gone into Dawsons after Mary had started work there, being served by her own daughter.

'What would you like to look at mother?'

The light is coming through the laced curtains. Summer is approaching. Soon Sylvie will come up to read to her. Now Alice only listens to the sound of her voice. The words she reads create too much confusion.

The pain stretches around her like a steel band gradually being tightened.

Does anyone ever know anyone else and does it really matter?

She feels weepy and lost.

Last night Paul Jameson kissed her, over and over again he kissed her whispering how much he missed her, needed her.

Outside the town is noisy, voices, dogs barking, a horse's hooves clattering along the front street mixed in with the grind of trucks on the Keighley Road.

Arthur took her to a concert in Bradford city hall. It had been a wild, stormy night, listening to Elgar and Vaughan Williams with thunder and lightning as a background to such beautiful English music.

Rest and sleep, that is all there is now.

'Oh please God,' she murmurs, 'Help me.'

A cat howls. A window is slammed shut. She can smell the smoke from all the chimneys.

Why does she remember Scarborough so clearly, why that holiday above all others?

Was it the perfect weather, the children just the right age to enjoy themselves? Or had it been Arthur for once relaxed with them instead of the usual jealousy he had of his daughters.

'There's you three and I'm left out of it,' had been his constant complaint.

It scared her, such emotional madness. He felt everything. It was like an illness. What he felt was so crazily distorted. He was mad with it. Everything to him was a threat even his own children.

'I come back. I come back and don't you think it's hard, damned hard? You have no idea. Why should you know? The last thing I want is to describe what I've been through. That would only make things worse for you and me. It can't be shared Alice so you can forget that. We can only try and manage, and I'm not saying it's going to be easy. I've learnt that much. We have a young child and that's enough. We start with Mary. I start with her and then see what happens. I used to think over there that when I got back that somehow everything would fit back into place, but after a few weeks I realised that nothing would be the same again, nothing like it used to be. So here I am and I'm sick in my guts, exhausted, not knowing what the hell I feel.'

An explanation or was it only Arthur warning her?

That tiny rented flat above the butchers smelling of stale meat and damp, the three of them in two rooms.

It only took a few weeks before the tension between them was obvious, the strain of attempting to resurrect what they pretended had existed before the war.

Sylvie says Skipton has its air raid wardens now and soon there will be a blackout for the whole town.

'Stop German bombers using us to navigate on their way to the docks at Liverpool.'

Sylvie's serious voice.

'Do you want me to read to you?' She comes and sits beside the bed with book in hand.

So she reads, Trollope again. Alice drifts along the words as though they were a river flowing slowly towards a warm sea.

Could she really remember anything Arthur had said back then, back in the depression, hundreds of men standing there on the High Street waiting to be hired for jobs that did not exist.

He had been lucky, straight back to Slaters full time, then foreman and eventually promoted to manager.

Lucky Arthur. Sylvie was another attempt to resurrect their marriage, two daughters, a good job and then the house, a car. It had happened as she had wanted and yet none of it was what she had wanted. Superficially it was all there, the happy family in their new home with even an indoor toilet and bath.

Then the change within a few months, new suits, haircut and moustache trimmed at the barbers every week, shaving every day, new shoes, ties, underwear. The slick, confident, angry Arthur, greedy and wanting it all.

And what had she required? Had she really wanted to play role of the wife in a game of happy families?

Alice, what? Alice what were you searching for? Answer me Alice. Answer me.

'Do you want me to continue?' is Sylvie asking.

Poor Sylvie, so many years nursing her through, on and on, week after week, month after month, time slowing down, drifting like that river approaching the warm sea.

They had paddled on Scarborough beach, Arthur with his trousers turned up, his white feet trailing through the frothing water.

Paul Jameson kissed her last night.

Where are you now?

Paul where are you?

Does it matter?

'Yes, please Sylvie, keep reading.'

'Trollope has no idea about women.'

'No,' she sighs.

'But he's a good writer. He has a good style, don't you think?'

Say yes while she thinks of Arthur's lies, thinks of Arthur's many indiscretions, such a Victorian word for all his affairs.

Alice thinks as Sylvie's reading voice makes a background noise.

She tried to trust him. Out so many nights a week, drinking with his friends, he said.

His articles in the Herald created another excuse to be at all the matches, home and away, it made no difference.

Arthur the man about town when all she had wanted was to share their lives together with their two daughters.

Mary and Sylvie becoming strangers to their father.

And Alice as well becoming a stranger to her husband.

The Black Pennine.

He had told her the story several times. It was the ultimate reason he said for his anger, depression, frustration, fear, such terrible fear he said because of that Black Pennine bus coming along the road for him.

Death, the final excuse.

Life starts as a failure and ends as a failure and in between we try to forget about it.

But he could not.

Or so he said.

He resented that she did not share the same fear, resented the fact that her faith kept her strong when all he could do was drink and everything else he got up to.

And where had the money come from for the suits and car and nights out?

Slaters paid well but not that well.

Arthur the contradiction with his socialist principles wanting to be rich, hating to be poor, needing to have everything he wanted.

'Mother, you're dribbling.'

Sylvie wipes Alice's mouth with a fresh handkerchief. It smells of peppermint.

She wipes her mouth so gently.

The window is still open letting in the warm evening air.

Summer is coming.

People will paddle along the edge of the frothing sea.

Alice can see them, figures far away like thin shadows in contrast to bright sunlight and voices echoing over the sandy distance. She is standing on the promenade holding onto her straw hat so the sea breeze does not blow it away.

'Thank you for reading,' she says.

Sylvie has her hands on her hips, her eyes shining through her glasses, some of her curls flopping over her forehead.

'I'm scared,' Alice suddenly admits.

'Please mother,' Sylvie says.

'Just a little.'

'There's nothing happening mother. Doctor Donnolly says you're having a better week.'

'Better,' she repeats.

Sylvie's face is full of worry.

'Please mother.'

'Just a little,' Alice says again, 'Because of the palpitations. I don't like them.'

'It'll be alright.'

'Have you finished reading?'

'Yes.'

'Thank you Sylvie, you're a treasure.'

'Oh I don't know about that.'

'Well I do.'

Later the room darkens. Sylvie comes up with a cup of hot milk before she shuts the curtains, kisses her on the forehead and wishes her good night. Mary follows for a few brief moments. Arthur is last to put in an appearance. After their last conversation he has been more wary, more careful in what he says.

The family have paid their nightly obligation to her, the necessary routine. Should she be thankful? There is so little left to be thankful for.

The bedside lamp remains on. Alice thinks back to the winter with the fire in the corner sending shadows flickering around the walls and over the ceiling. She would switch off the lamp just to be able to watch this dance of light and dark.

Like the kitchen fire on which she and the girls had toasted thick slices of white bread, Sylvie being helped by Mary, the three of them sat on the mat taking turns to use the toasting fork. Winter evenings without Arthur, just her and the girls, sometimes drawing, writing stories just for Sylvie, building tall towers with her coloured bricks, all in the glow and warmth of those long ago fires that seemed to burn more intensely, the memory creating its special image.

Or in the chapel choir standing up in the gallery looking down on Arthur and the girls, then over time Mary with Sylvie and finally Sylvie just by herself, the other two long since abandoning their faith.

The chapel had been a crucible of sound and feeling with a full congregation. She had felt happy and absorbed in those Sunday services.

'Education is a good thing only if it prepares you for a good death. We have to learn to accept our ending.'

She remembered the terrifying words of that visiting preacher. What a thing to say with all the Sunday school children listening to his every word. But Alice had never forgotten them. It was only recently in her darkest moods how prophetically true his words seemed to be. She heard them, heard his voice booming from the high pulpit. A good death is all we can achieve. Will she be able to follow his advice?

With an effort she leans over to switch off the bedside light. There is still a dull silver glow coming through the curtains. A cat screams from further down the back lane. A truck rattles along the main road, its engine chugging away into the distance. Men's laughter echoes through the stillness.

The pain tightens round her chest. Her back aches and her throat is so dry.

She rests down into the deepening silence, her breaths coming quickly, thinking that in front of those winter fires with Mary and Sylvie were her happiest times. They feel so close, so preciously close. But she will have to let go of them, release herself from all the memories and allow herself to seek out how she manages what is left. What is left? Dare she ask that question?

She will not sleep, not tonight, not until the dawn light appears.

CHAPTER THIRTY SIX

Margaret is waiting for her at the station. The platform is crowded as the train pulls in with smoke and steam blasting over everyone and wheels grinding to a stop. It seems everyone has the same idea. Some with suitcases are going for the week whereas the rest are having a day out.

'We'll never get on!' Margaret happily exclaims as they push their way into the corridor already packed with holiday makers looking for a seat.

Eventually having tried a few carriages they accept they will have to stand.

'How long does it take?' Sylvie asks as the train starts forward blowing out more steam. With all the windows open there is the smell of soot and coke as the 8.10 from Leeds to Morecambe moves out of the station.

'Nearly an hour and a half,' Margaret has to shout over the noise of everyone else.

Sylvia is wearing a flowered summer dress that Mary made up for her. She is carrying a soft bag and wearing sandals. Margaret's dress is a creamy yellow with red stripes.

'How did you manage to get away?' Margaret asks.

'Doctor Donnolly had a word with father, said I needed a break.'

'So you do.'

Just then two soldiers squeeze past them, one of them saying, 'I could see you in heaven darling.'

'Or hell,' says the other.

'What was that about?' Margaret asks as she watches the soldiers' retreating figures pushing through the crowded corridor.

'Soldiers,' is Sylvie's derisory response, 'They think they own the country already and they've done nothing because they have nothing to do. They're not fighting.'

Outside they watch the early summer landscape go by on this bright, blue sky morning. There are tractors ploughing up fields of grass with flocks of land gulls following behind.

Sylvie can feel the excitement and the expectancy filling the train.

'What have you brought?' she then asks, nodding at Margaret's handbag.

'Oh just makeup and my purse. What about you?'

'The same except I've brought us a snack if we get hungry on the way there.'

'Sylvie Townsley, never without food.'

'Of course not.'

'Now then ladies, can I just get past with this lad of mine? He's feeling a bit sick,' says a man holding onto the hand of a pale and sheepish looking young boy.

A woman slides open a compartment door and asks if someone could open another window, 'It's very stuffy in here,' she complains in a whiney voice.

Cows in deep grassed fields watch the train go by. Smoke from the engine trails past like a long grey scarf. There are voices and laughter and someone is already playing a mouthorgan.

The train rattles and shifts over a set of points, 'When were you last on a day trip like this?'

Sylvie pulls a thoughtful expression and finally answers, 'Not since school when a group of us went for a day out with our history teacher to Bolton Abbey.'

'God, that's years ago!'

'Yes, I know. That's why this is a real treat.'

'We're going to have a rare day Miss Townsley.'

'Of course we are Miss Lumsden.'

'Unforgettable!'

'Memorable!'

Doors are being opened long before the train comes to a stop in Morecambe station, people crowding out the moment the whole of the twelve carriages come to a halt with more steam being blown out like a sigh of the train's relief that the journey is finally over.

Out on the sea front there is a warm breeze full of salt smells. They can see the brown waves of the Bay and in the distance the high steep hills of the Lake District.

Letting the rest of the crowd disperse in all directions with umbrellas, bucket and spades, food baskets the two friends wait to decide what they are going to do.

Margaret takes out a packet of cigarettes and is shocked when Sylvie says she would like one.

'You never smoke! I've never seen you smoke!'

'Well I am today,' says Sylvie as she pins her hat more securely into her hair.

'You can take a puff or two of mine and see what you think so I don't waste a good cigarette.'

'Please yourself,' Sylvie responds before she takes a puff at the cigarette and then starts coughing and spluttering.

'There you go!' laughs Margaret, 'I knew that would happen.'

'How….how do you smoke those things?'

'It's easy you put it in your mouth and then….'

'Oh, alright clever clogs!'

'That's me, clever as a pair of clogs.'

'We sound like a pair of school girls.'

'Well if the last time you were on a day out was when you were at school then no wonder.'

Sylvie looks around as an open topped bus goes past full on both levels with children waving from the top deck and women holding onto their hats.

'What are we going to do first?'

'I've thought about this,' Margaret says before emitting a mouthful of smoke that is caught on the breeze and blown over the pavement, 'And what we should do is leave everything to chance. We toss a coin when we want to make a decision and don't tell me that us Congregationalists believe in fate and all that stuff and that there's no such thing as chance. Well today we're going to forget all that. It has to be a half crown.'

'We'll use one of yours then. I've only got a few and I'm not going to lose one rolling into the gutter and down some filthy grate.'

'Please yourself, so we toss to see if we're going to walk along the whole length of the promenade or go on one of those bus tours.'

'I think we….'

'No Miss Townsley, we toss, heads for the bus, tails for walking.'

Two hours later they are sat on one of the seats along the pier next to a family eating ice creams. People stroll up and down along the promenade beside the brown sea. The tide is in. In the distance they can hear a brass band playing.

'Is it a cornet or a wafer?' Margaret asks as two men walk by with long fishing rods avoiding a group of teenage boys running past. In front of them three mothers are pushing large prams. It is the same everywhere else. Morecambe is packed on this warm summer's day.

'Personally,' Margaret continues, 'I like when the wafer goes all soft and you suck right round it and then start round it again so it gets thinner and thinner. That's the best part.'

The major decision of the day is mussels or winkles, whether to wear a holiday straw hat and put their own in their handbags, candy floss or a stick of rock, to try the boating pool or give it a miss. The biggest decision is whether they should go into Woolworths, buy a towel and costume each and go for an unplanned swim in the resort's famous outdoor pool.

'Come on Sylvie. It'll be a laugh,' Margaret says as they stroll along the promenade amidst all the crowd going in both directions with all the shops and arcades across the road selling everything from children's coloured windmills to huge photographs of famous film stars as well as a fortune teller in her gypsy caravan.

For once Sylvie is fully concentrated on the way the half crown will fall as Margaret flicks it into the air and traps it on the back of her hand.

'We're going for a swim!' Margaret shouts at the top of her voice.

'Are you sure about this?'

'Now don't you start changing the rules Sylvie. We agreed to go with the toss.'

In a crowded Woolworths they buy brightly striped towels and one piece bathing costumes before heading across the road and along to the gleaming white façade of the open air lido, past the flags blowing in the breeze, the crowds in the ornamental gardens and the sight of pleasure boats cutting up the coast.

When they have found the changing rooms and put on their costumes, Sylvie is aware of the contrast between her shape and Margaret's. She knows everyone will think she is fat. She struggles to put the costume on and feels embarrassed when they finally emerge. The huge pool reflects the bright sun flickering lines of silver. There are life guards, high diving boards, seats busy with those watching, popular music sounding through loudspeakers and everywhere a huge assortment of different bodies in different coloured trunks or costumes. Beach balls are being batted about. Children are screaming while teenagers are splashing each other.

Sylvie tentatively approaches the water. Her father taught her to swim in Skipton's swimming baths, but this is something totally different. This is a crowded pool with everyone shouting, splashing, diving into the fresh sea water.

'Go on then!' Margaret is laughing, 'You first!'

'It's freezing,' Sylvie complains having dipped in one foot.

'Well no wonder, it's pumped straight from the Irish Sea.'

'But cleaned first.'

'I hope so.'

'Come on then!' Sylvie shouts before walking deeper and deeper until she begins to swim.

It is cold, the water in a confusion of waves caused by the amount of people all in the pool at the same time.

Both of them are soon laughing and splashing water over each other. Sylvie feels so alive and thrilled by the whole experience. Chance has turned out to be lucky. She is away from her mother and the house and Skipton, free for these few hours, for once enjoying herself.

After an hour they are both exhausted. The get dried and sit watching some of the high divers.

'My hair takes ages to dry,' Margaret complains as she gives it a good rub on the towel.

Just then two youths came up with slicked back hair and white bodies.

'What's your friend's name?' one of them asks Sylvie.

'Why don't you ask me directly young man?' Margaret butts in.

'Young man is it?'

'Young boy more like.'

'Suit yourself,' the other laughs.

'We will, thank you,' Margaret tells them emphatically.

'What a cheek,' she adds, 'They're only trying their luck.'

'We should have let them toss the half crown,' Sylvie jokes.

For tea it is fish and chips from one of the kiosks on the promenade.

The sun is lowering. The atmosphere is beginning to change.

They have been around the noisy fairground, walked past the Winter Gardens wishing they could stay on and see a show, past the posh Midland hotel and the Watchtower. Then they had stood watching the tide going out and the hills of the Lake District begin to turn golden in the lowering sunlight.

'Why do people love the seaside?' Margaret wonders aloud, her hair wetting the back of her dress.

Sylvie thinks she could do with a cup of tea to take away the fatty taste from the fish and chips.

'Because it's different. It's like nowhere else. It's magical The Victorians started it all and some doctors said sea air was good for your health they've been busy ever since.'

'Thanks for the history lesson Miss Townsley.'

'You're welcome Miss Lumsden, anytime.'

'I'd like to live by the sea. It must change all the time depending on the time of year and the time of day. Not that I'd want to stay here. I mean somewhere more deserted.'

'Up in Scotland.'

'Too cold.'

'But at least it's quiet or so they say.'

'Or so they say.'

Walking arm in arm they return towards the station amidst the crowd of holiday makers purchasing things at the stalls and kiosks, wearing daft hats, moustaches and huge fake noses, the children with their sticks of candy floss, tired faces and sand stuck to their legs. There are sweet smells, fish smells, fatty smells, body smells, sea smells and all the rest merging into the evening atmosphere.

The platform is even busier than they expected. It seems everyone is returning home on the same train. When the station master opens the barrier everyone surges forward. Sylvie and Margaret find the last two seats in a compartment in the fourth carriage that is quickly filling up.

They sit across from each other, knees squeezed together, handbags and baskets they have bought to hold their wet towels and costumes in their laps, hair finally dry and faces reddened from being in the sun. The corridor outside is crammed with passengers. Finally the whistle is blown and the 7.15 to Leeds is under way. The engine blows out a cloud of steam and slowly moves forward.

There are ten passengers in the compartment including a baby, two young children and their grandparents and mother and father with the final section of seat taken by a middle aged man in slacks and open necked shirt. In the corridor there is a lot of shouting and laughing. Someone starts playing a plastic trumpet as others squeeze by on their way to the toilets. Everyone looks flushed, tired but happy. The day by the sea has cleaned away the grime of the city and left them satisfied and feeling happy.

Sylvia smiles across at Margaret. The baby starts to cry. Its mother rocks it backwards and forwards while the two children keep getting off and on their seats. Behind them is a framed poster of a crowded Blackpool, its famous tower looming behind all the holiday makers. Outside the sun is beginning to set over the fields of Lancashire with their hedges and bright green grass. Trees flicker orange light and Sylvie looks out feeling happier than she has in years. She also feels a sadness that the day is over and she is returning home. Time has passed too quickly and yet the day has seemed so long. The coin had been tossed and decisions made and all of it has fitted into place, as though the whole day had been planned. There is no difference between chance and destiny. In the end it makes no difference.

The crowded train becomes quieter. The children fall asleep. Steam from the engine spreads over the fields beside the track.

When they stop at Hellifield, Margaret says, 'Nearly there Sylvie.'

'I wish we could do the same tomorrow and every other day,' is Sylvie's response.

'We all do chuck,' says the father of the baby and the two children, 'A day's not long enough.'

'We've had a grand time,' agrees the grandmother with red cheeks and tired, smiling eyes.

'Yes we have,' adds Sylvie as she thinks of her mother for the first time in hours and begins to feel a growing unease again.

CHAPTER THIRTY SEVEN

The Skipton batsman puts down his left knee, sticks out the other leg at the required angle, swivels the wrists to start the movement of his bat that hits the ball sideways low and hard to the boundary.

Arthur jots down a few notes comparing the stroke to the sweep of a scythe cutting through the corn. He sees the golden field and a line of men swinging side to side their silver blades glinting sunlight with each movement.

Then he rips the page out from his notebook and crunches it up in his hand. He hates clever words put in a vase like flowers for all to see and admire.

'Doing alright Arthur,' Tom Cowley, one of the committee members, comments as he walks past, a pint in either hand, 'Mind you, not as good as Sutcliffe's 165 at Old Trafford.'

'No,' is all Arthur wants to say.

Cowley gives him a puzzled look and then carries on round the boundary.

For once Arthur is well away from the locals. He is on the far side of the ground. Today he is not interested in the usual chat. He wants to be by himself and hopes he has made that obvious.

Lighting a cigarette, he watches the smoke drift and curve up into the branches of the trees hanging above him. He is shaded here from the strong sunlight that flickers through the bright green leaves. He takes off his straw hat to smooth back his hair and dabs the sweat off his forehead with a handkerchief.

A plane drones overhead followed by the sound of a train leaving the station. A group of boys are sat on top of the wall near the ground's main gate watching the match. Everything is as it should be except what Arthur is thinking about Kitty, hearing her voice and the bitterness and worry her words have created.

Her idea is that they should not see each other until things at home are settled which can mean only one thing.

His fear is of losing her, of never seeing her again, all his hopes smashed to bits. He hates the turmoil this has created, hates himself for being so weak and desperate.

'You know what that means, don't you?' he had asked her at their last evening together and then immediately regretted the question.

They both knew.

But he had been angry and worried.

'Why now?' had been another of his attempts to understand what Kitty was doing.

'Does it matter?' she had replied with a dull, empty tone.

She had already reached a decision to keep apart from him.

'For God's sake Kitty. This is stupid. It's unnecessary!' he had exclaimed.

But whatever he had said had made no difference. They were not to see each other again until there was a change at home as she had put it.

His thoughts are interrupted as the crowd claps another good shot from Skipton's number three batsman.

He is in suspension. Here he is watching a cricket match while his wife is dying. What sort of monster does that make him? But at home there is nothing he could do for Alice. She is too ill, too lost in herself or so he tries to tell himself.

Nothing could make a difference. Is he just to wait, and for how long?

What a shocking question. It disgusts him how even more cynical he has become.

'Come on you fucking bastard Townsley! Get on with it!'

Sergeant Barton would have shot him. He wanted to shoot him. There was no doubt about that. He was just waiting for his opportunity.

It was all there in his memory like a deep pool of poisoned water.

One pit they had dug had a slope so the skulls rolled to one end, yellow, green, white and blackened bone heads with their empty sockets and jutting teeth. Another was for the larger bones and beside that the piles of what else remained, badges, bits of uniform, cigarette cases, letters, photos, diaries, bits of rifles, machine guns, shell casings and anything else they found.

Taff never managed it, too sensitive, too innocent. They had discovered him floating in the grey, oily water of a nearby shell hole. Taff with his ginger hair and an attempt at a moustache crying all the time, moaning, being sick, unable to cut his mind away from it all.

The rest had gone home, but not the conscies. They were the mud and dead squad, the meat and soil factory.

How had anyone managed coming out of it all? How did some of them lucky enough to return adapt and just carry one?

'Good shot!' comes a shout followed by more clapping. Arthur looks up to watch the fielder collecting the ball from the boundary.

'The Germans should play cricket,' someone had said in the Black Bull one night, 'That would put some sense into them.'

But there is no sense thinks Arthur as he stubs out his cigarette, just talk of gas masks, air raid wardens, blackouts, munition factories, agreement with France about Poland, conscription for all 20 and 21 year olds, Anderson shelters, evacuation plans for city children, an alliance with Russia and on and on stepping straight into the next war with the Irish throwing in a few bombs just for good measure.

He gets up and walks around the far side of the field to avoid the pavilion and out of the main gates.

He walks stubbornly without any idea of where he is going only to find himself finally walking along the path that leads into Skipton's cemetery.

They are all here, the generations of Townsleys going back into previous centuries. He looks for them in the quietness broken only by the noise of another train passing through the station and the call of crows up in the trees above him.

He feels sluggish, unconcerned, stepping from one headstone to the next through the high grass between each grave.

He spits into his hands, leans down and rubs them on the tall grass, walks onto the main path and lights a cigarette as an old lady carrying a full shopping bag approaches.

'Nice day,' she says feebly.

He just nods and walks past.

'Come on you fucking coward Townsley, get on with it!'

He walks and at the same time hears the shells coming over the trenches towards the main mud churned road. He is trying desperately to keep the ambulance upright. There are six of them, three stacked on each side, badly injured, moaning, one screaming almost as loud as the incoming shells.

He returns onto the Keighley Road and makes his way down to the canal to a pub he hardly ever frequents.

Taff cried every night and every morning he started shaking. His body became a raft for the rats to float from one side of the crater to the next, the rats eating their way through Taff who stared up at a grey, endless sky.

He orders the usual and goes to sit in a quiet corner of the bar, takes off his hat, wipes his face with his handkerchief before lighting a cigarette.

'You're a fucking bastard Townsely. Now get down there with Jones and pull his fucking body out of that shit!'

Taff already bloated, turning slowly round, the other bodies floating beside him.

Arthur knew his spade would split bodies, cut off heads, feet, arms. So many were unseen under the thick layer of Belgium mud, stinking, sucking down everything it could as though it wanted to claim all of them, the living and the dead.

He drinks and tries to stop thinking, to stop remembering. It being past tea time the bar is busy, full of voices, smoke and the stench of beer.

'There's no answer Arthur lad, none at all,' he could hear the voice of Lance Corporal Tanner, a forty year old cockney giving out advice, 'You just have to find something that suits, doesn't matter what it is. You search until you might be lucky enough to find what works for you, what means enough to get you through each day. It can be anything. No one has the right answer cos there aren't any. There's just ways to find to muddle through, that's all and fuck anybody who says different. Oh there's so many buggers want to think they're right, that they're the only ones to find the truth and it's a lot of cobblers, absolute shite. Their way is no different to anyone else's no matter if its God, food, drink, women, books, music or whatever, doesn't matter a sod.'

And now all he can do is wait. He detests this state of suspension between Alice and a future with Kitty. He can do nothing for his wife and nothing for the woman he wants to spend the rest of his life with. At the moment Alice is dying and Kitty is keeping well away from him.

He orders more drinks, aware of how rough the pub's customers are compared with the Black Bull's in their working clothes, hobnailed boots, flat caps, shouting, spitting, swearing, smoking and smelling of sweat and something worse. Just at this moment these men sicken him. They have no style or dignity. They are doing what Tanner had said, just muddling through in a mindless sort of way.

When he comes out onto the canal side road the light is beginning to fade now the sun has gone down. He walks while still hearing the men's voices coming from the noisy pub. It is like an echo of other times, easier, happier.

He has never believed in happiness being the only goal. It is superficial compared with the deeper emotions.

'So what is there Arthur?' Alice had once asked, 'What else is there except to care for others and yourself?'

He had made no answer, knowing she would never understand and why should she, why should a woman like Alice agree with his ideas?

He approaches the house and has a sudden dread of going in. A group of young girls and boys rush past him rolling hoops, carrying sticks, one wearing a Red Indian chief's head dress.

He opens the gate and walks up the front path trying to calm down.

In the kitchen he pours brandy from his flask into the coffee he has made before sitting down beside the unlit fire.

The house clicks and squeaks around him like an old ship. The sky is darkening leaving him in deeper shadow as he tries to concentrate on what is happening out in the back lane.

It is Mary who finally appears.

'You're home early father,' is the first thing she says, 'I've come for a glass of water. I thought there was a glass in the bathroom but there isn't.'

'I'm not early,' is his response before he lights another cigarette.

Please yourself,' is her quick retort.

'I will.'

'I know you will.'

'And what is....?'

'Nothing. It was nothing, forget it.'

'I'm asking what that was supposed to mean?'

'And I said nothing,' she says more forcefully waiting for the tap water to cool.

He takes another mouthful of coffee, the brandy in it beginning at last to tip him over the edge.

'We've never managed, have we?' he asks as Mary is about to pass him.

She stops, takes a deep breath and says, 'Managed what father?'

'Getting on together.'

'That's because you're never here. How is anyone supposed to get on with somebody who is never here?'

'You watch what you're saying,' he responds in a suddenly angry tone.

'Why, it's the truth?'

'The truth!' he scoffs, 'There's no such thing. You think you'd know that by now.'

'I'm going to bed,' Mary mutters exasperatedly.

At that he gets to his feet, 'And you.....you and your moods.....for months now....just stop working at Dawsons without any explanation. You said nothing to me or your mother, but I bet Aunt Rose knew what you were doing. I bet she did.'

By now Mary has put her glass deliberately on the kitchen table and is stood looking at him with a cynical expression that drives him mad. Now there is a blind need to hurt her, to force her to listen to him.

She says nothing, just watches him start a cigarette, the light from the back street lamp shining through the window to give just enough illumination for them both to see each other's faces.

'I don't have to tell you everything,' she finally counters.

Arthur feels the alcohol induced heat in him, the blood rising.

'You're not bringing in enough money. Travelling to Leeds and back each day is stupid.'

'Oh now we're getting there, aren't we, getting to the usual subject.'

'You just listen to what I'm saying young lady.'

'Why should I?'

'Because I'm trying to talk some sense into you, sense, ever heard of the word?'

'It's always comes back to money.'

'What else is there? We have to live.'

'No, it's you who has to get on with living while the rest of us just exist and that suits you fine. It always has done. You must spend the money on something or someone.'

Arthur stares at her, 'Now what the hell are you saying?'

'I hear the rumours.'

'About what?'

'You can't live in a place like Skipton without gossip doing the rounds, gossip about you.'

'You're talking nonsense.'

'You mean you wish I was.'

'I mean you've no idea what you're talking about.'

'You and your....'

'Stop this Mary! Stop it now!' Arthur shouts at her.

'But it's alright father because as you say there's no such thing as the truth,' Mary says in a harsh tone of voice.

Arthur forces himself not to respond. There is a strained, dangerous silence as he takes a drag at his cigarette, standing unsteadily in front of the fire while Mary in her nightdress puts her hand on the kitchen table as though for support.

She suddenly changes the subject, 'So what did the doctor say to you yesterday about mother?'

He is unsure about this question. It is not what he expected.

'You spoke to him, didn't you?' Mary persists.

'Not good,' Arthur answers.

'She's dying, isn't she?'

'He never said that.'

'But it's what he means to say.'

'He never said that,' Arthur repeats in a muted tone of voice, 'He never said that.'

'And if you must know I work in Leeds because at the time it was the only job I could get.'

'I'm surprised you haven't thought of moving there.'

'Oh don't worry father, it's crossed my mind several times.'

'But you'd rather move in with my sister instead.'

'I might. So what? I can do what I like.'

'That's exactly the attitude! Exactly that!' he says strongly.

'Go on.....go on...say what you want to say father and then I can get back to bed.'

Arthur pulls a hard expression, his mouth twisting upwards slightly. He wants to berate her into some sort of submission but finds it hard to focus on what he wants to say as though the brandy has pushed him too far. He can feel himself becoming desperate, becoming increasingly upset.

'You'll leave,' he goes on in a quieter voice, 'And we'll never have a chance to manage anything.'

'I'm twenty four father. We've been together for all that time. I would have thought even you could understand that if it was ever going to happen it would have by now. I'm your daughter but it's never felt like that.'

'No,' Arthur sighs, 'And it's all my fault. You're right.'

'You're doing it again.'

'Doing what?'

'Taking it all on yourself as though it always has to be you who is right or to be blamed or whatever.'

'For God's sake Mary! I'm not saying that.'

'What are you saying then?'

He sits back down, flicks his cigarette into the empty fireplace and finishes his coffee as Mary picks up her glass and goes back upstairs.

Within a few minutes he is up again, out of the back door and over the yard to the shed where he gropes in the dark for the shovel. After finally finding it he goes back into the kitchen where he takes off his jacket and rolls up his sleeves.

Staggering slightly he opens the front door, steps onto the front path where he stops, the shovel in both hands held across his waist and looks up at a pale blue, cloudless sky. It makes him dizzy to stare up at this empty space. It feels like his brain is expanding to the vastness of all that is above him, above the town, the country, the world.

He carefully lifts a foot over the front garden's low wall followed just as gingerly by the other until he is standing on the rose beds that Sylvie planted the year before.

There is another low wall with railings on top at the foot of the garden. Across the road is another row of terraced houses.

But Arthur wants to dig. He has to dig. He wants to find Taff and all the others.

He grips the handle with his right hand and the shaft with his left and raises the shovel high above his head.

His body starts shaking as he moans and cries while lowering the spade slowly, letting it come and rest on the dark soil. Using it to lean on his back shakes with the effort of release, the effort of letting go in the pale early summer night wanting to bury himself with all the rest.

CHAPTER THIRTY EIGHT

'Have you told your father you're courting?'

'I'm not courting auntie Rose.'

'It sounds like it to me.'

'I've only met him on four or five occasions.'

'It only takes one.'

Mary wants to enjoy her aunt's sparky mood, enjoy their walk through Airedale park with all the other people strolling about on this bright Sunday morning. Instead there is the nervous worry around everything. She is tired of it, tired of always feeling strained and bothered.

'What does he do this Roger Simpson?' Rose asks as she nods to someone she knows.

'He works for an insurance company in Keighley.'

'Is that where he lives?'

'No, he lives in Hellifield. That's how I met him. We were on the same train one night and he came into my compartment and he just started talking.'

'And you talked back?'

'Eventually I did, yes. But it's not serious. It's nothing really,' Mary found herself saying as a group pf young boys come running down the path. Rose and Mary have to step aside as the boys dash past laughing and shouting to each other.

'Anyway, I wouldn't tell father anything at the moment,' Mary continues, 'We had a proper row last night.'

'What about?' Rose asks, sounding even more interested as she looks across at her.

'Oh, it's just him. He's been in a bad mood for I don't know how long.'

'It'll be worry about your mother. It's only natural he's feeling like that.'

'I wish that was true.'

'And why shouldn't it be?'

'No reason,' Mary answers vaguely not wanting at that moment to try and discuss her father's emotional state.

Their walk takes them to the top of the park where they turn and start descending back down between the bright leaved trees. Church bells are ringing while children run about like colourful insects.

For once there is no mention of Mary moving to live with her aunt. Rose seems distracted by the increasing threat of war. She finds it unbelievable that people could be so stupid as to start another one. It upsets her. It reminds her too much of the atmosphere before her Edward had to go off and fight.

'At least this time there'll be no cheering crowds or flags being waved. Well, I hope there aren't.'

Mary senses the seriousness of her remarks. There is now always tension in the air, a morbid sense of expectancy, of waiting for the worst to happen.

It is the same in Leeds. The following week John Lewis is quieter with a strangely subdued atmosphere. Everyone seems pressed back into themselves as though the present is only preparing for a dreadful future.

Roger Simpson comes to meet her from work on the following Wednesday. To begin with after they are seated in a small, busy restaurant near the station he talks about his fears of being conscripted.

She would rather talk about anything else. She is being stretched by herself and everyone else. Desperately she wants to escape thinking about her mother and now this compulsive rush to war.

At last Roger breaks off from such a hopeless subject by suggesting they hire bikes next Sunday and go for a ride.

'I like cycling, always have done. How about it Mary?'

'What?' he asks when she gives him a doubtful look, 'What's wrong with that?'

'Nothing,' she answers.

'Come on Mary, what is it? It's only a suggestion.'

She puts down her knife and fork, 'If you must know I can't ride a bike and I don't want to learn. To be honest I think people look stupid riding bikes.'

Roger momentarily looks baffled and then smiles, 'You're pulling my leg.'

'I certainly am not.'

'Crickey! You actually mean it!'

'So I suggest you think of something else,' she says in a tone that is more serious than she really wanted.

'Why don't you do the suggesting then?'

'Alright, I will.'

He takes a mouthful of food carefully watching her.

Around them the restaurant is full of subdued customers who seem more concerned about what they are eating than having any chit chat.

Mary glances around and then says quietly, 'Have you noticed we're the only ones talking?'

'I haven't and the reason I haven't is because I'm too absorbed in you Mary Townsley. Did I ever tell you that I think you're the most attractive woman I've ever known?'

'Known a lot, have you?'

'A fair few.'

'Nothing like boasting.'

'Friends, just friends.'

'Where you live?'

'I'm afraid Hellifield hasn't that much to offer when it comes to desirable young women, not like Skipton. If you're an example of what there is then I think I'm living in the wrong place.'

However much she tries to remain at a distance he is still amusing, sharp, good looking, well dressed and even it seems honest, the hardest aspect of his character in which to believe.

'Let's go for a walk if it's a nice day on Sunday,' she suggests.

'I wished I had a car, then we could go anywhere we liked.'

'And where would we go in your car?'

'Oh, I don't know, The Lakes, Blackpool, Harrogate, Fountains Abbey, Bolton Abbey, you name it and we could....'

She glances at his bright, enthusiastic features. It is the last thing she expected, this growing attachment. It is too threatening, too uncertain. And yet she likes being with him, enjoys his sense of humour, enjoys how knowledgeable he is and how generous he can be.

She knows anything other than a casual relationship is impossible. She does not want anything more serious. She will never want anything more serious. She is sure of that, and Roger Simpson is not going to change her mind. Stupidly it makes her feel sorry for him. He has no idea who she is and especially what she feels. She has told him a little about her mother's illness and how her father writes articles on rugby and cricket for the Craven Herald. Other than that he knows hardly anything about her and she wants to keep it that way.

'So a walk on Sunday?' Rogers inquires before he starts on his dessert.

'Skipton Woods would be nice.'

'I don't know them.'

'Then I shall introduce you,' Mary says lightly.

On the Sunday she meets him off the Pennine bus near the top of the High Street. He smiles and exaggeratedly squeezes her hand before they set off past the castle's high walls into Skipton wood.

'It's nice here,' is Roger's comment after they have walked for a few minutes beside a narrow stream.

'And popular,' Mary says as other couples walk by.

'I bet the lord of the manor went hunting here. It looks like that sort of place.'

'A long time ago maybe.'

'I can just imagine you as a damsel in distress stuck in some musty old castle.'

'I don't think so Roger. That doesn't sound like me.'

'Oh, alright,' he responds in an exaggeratedly disappointed voice.

He stops, quickly takes her hand and attempts to pull her towards him, pulls quite hard so her face is brought towards his as he prepares to kiss her.

In an instant Mary jerks back, slaps him hard across the face and then without thinking slaps him again even harder before she turns and walks quickly away.

He shouts after her, but she keeps on walking.

Breathlessly he catches up with her, 'Mary….Mary, for God's sake, what was that about?'

But she gives no answer, just ignores him and keeps walking as another couple approach them ensuring Roger says nothing more until they have passed by.

'What did I do?' he tries while trying to keep up with her.

Mary feels nothing except a bitter disgust.

'I'm sorry if I….'

'It doesn't matter,' she finally mutters.

'Of course it matters!'

'Don't shout at me.'

'I only wanted to kiss you. What the hell is wrong with that? I thought we were getting on fine. Was I wrong? Mary was I wrong? Answer me, please.'

A family comes towards them, the father pushing a high wheeled pram while the mother holds a toddler's hand.

'This is stupid Mary,' Roger says in a more restrained tone until the family have gone by.

She feels sick and scared. She has known all along what would happen and yet tried to pretend that somehow it could be avoided, that somehow Roger would be different.

Suddenly she stops and turns to him, her face white and stiff as she finally says, 'If you must know it's me who's been stupid, really stupid thinking that we could just go for a walk without wanting anything else, without you Roger wanting anything else. I know that must sound silly, naïve even, but I don't care. Why should I care? It's what I feel. It's what I want, what I hoped we could manage. I know you won't understand. Why should you? Why should you expect someone to react like I did?'

'You're right,' he says firmly, 'I didn't expect a slap across the face. I don't think I deserved that.'

'I'm not sorry if you're looking for an apology.'

'Christ Mary, you are in a state.'

'No I'm not,' she replies strongly before starting to walk again, 'I just think we should leave it. I like you Roger and that's all I want to say. There's nothing more I can say except I don't want to see you again so if you do see me on the 5.30pm train please do not…..'

'I wouldn't think of it,' he interrupts.

'Good,' is her last word before he stops and lets her walk out of the woods by herself.

She keeps on walking. Church bells are ringing and smoke is spiralling out of Dewhursts' tall chimneys that rise above the rest of the town.

It is past eight o clock when she finally reaches home, going straight upstairs to her bedroom where she takes off her summer jacket and sandals and then returns along the landing to see her mother.

Alice is asleep, her mouth slightly open letting out a low snore with every breath. Beneath her eyes the skin is puffed up like two small pillows. Her skin is yellow, her hands above the sheet heavily veined and her hair thin and silvery grey.

Mary stands as usual breathing through her mouth to avoid all the smells of illness. At least the commode has gone. Now Alice uses only bedpans. There is a densely suffocating atmosphere in the room. It pervades the rest of the house, filling each room with a terrible sense of decay and death. She has to move out. She cannot manage the fact that her mother is dying. She hates the unavoidable fact that everything is about to change forever. It is too upsetting, too ridiculous, too threatening, too absurd.

Now she cannot bare to touch the body lying there. Alice's mouth opens a little wider as a thin dribble of saliva drops from her bottom lip.

'Goodnight mother,' is all Mary can manage before she returns to the bedroom hoping that Sylvie down in the kitchen has not heard her.

She sits on her bed to start sewing, hoping that this will settle her down. But instead as she watches the action of the needle going in and out of the material she thinks of how everything is connected, everything from starting to work in Dawsons to Frobisher to Roger. Everything is a consequence of something else. There is no real freedom only this lottery of circumstance. One tiny event could change the whole course of any life at any time. The needle weaves its way along the hem of the dress as though it is stitching all Mary has gone through over the last year and beyond back to school, back to childhood and finally being born just before the start of a World War.

There was no decision to slap Roger. It was just an inevitable reaction. She did not decide sometime in the far past that she would hate change, would hate illness. Fatefully the only thing she could consider as a conscious choice was to mount those stairs that night up to Frobisher's office.

She finishes her sewing and instead of trying on the dress she hangs it up in the wardrobe just as Sylvie enters the room.

'I never knew you were home,' are her first words, 'You said you'd be back in time for me to go to chapel.'

'I'm sorry,' Mary replies with an edge to her voice.

'You said you'd be back.'

'Yes, but I wasn't. I'm sorry. What else do you want me to say?'

'There's no need for that tone.'

'Just don't go on Sylvie, I'm not in the mood.'

'You never are these days.'

'I just…..just…..oh it doesn't matter,' Mary sighs.

'What does? What does it matter to you? That's what I'd like to know,' Sylvie counters.

She is in the bright green suit she wears in the summer to go to chapel.

'If you must know, I have something to tell you.'

Sylvie stands on her side of the bed, her hair neatly brushed. She is wearing new glasses and a large butterfly brooch pinned to her jacket.

'I know what you're going to say.'

Mary's face tightens as she looks across the bed at her sister.

'What do you know?'

'I just do.'

'I don't see how.'

'You'll do what you want whatever anyone else has to say. You always have,' Sylvie says accusingly before she unpins her brooch and puts it down on her bedside table.

'I just want you to listen,' Mary tries already feeling that this is leading to some sort of crisis.

'Why should I when I know what you're going to say? I've known for weeks, months even. You've been going over to Aunt Roses more and more. It's obvious what's happening, well it is to me, and I know father thinks the same.'

'Why, what has he been saying?'

'Nothing.'

'Oh come on Sylvie. For God's sake this is important. It is Aunt Rose who wants me to move in with her.'

Sylvie starts unbuttoning her jacket she says, 'Well go on then. Do whatever you have to. Just forget about everyone else, especially mother.'

'That's not fair.'

'Forget that it's her kidneys now that are packing up as well as her heart. Why should you be bothered? You've got your own life to lead so you'll do exactly what you want.'

'I can't stand living here,' she tries, no longer concerned where this is all going to lead.

Sylvie takes her jacket over to the wardrobe.

'You said you'd be back in time for me to go to chapel,' she says again.

'For goodness sake Sylvie. I've already….'

'It's just another example,' Sylvie interrupts, 'of you doing what you want without a single thought about anyone else. I just hope Aunt Rose knows what she's letting herself into.'

'It is her idea, I've already told you that.'

'So you keep saying.'

'Why can't you for once….just once see it from my point of view?'

'Because I'm not you thank God.'

'I'm trying to make you understand Sylvie.'

'Well don't bother.'

There is a strained silence before Sylvie sits on her bed, leans over to take off her sandals, sits back up, her face looking flushed and tired, 'You've never wanted to do a thing for mother. You've never lifted a finger to help me or her. You've no idea how hard all this is. You waltz off to Leeds every day as though you haven't a care in the world.'

'Stop being so childish. This doesn't sound like you.'

'That's because you don't know me. How could you when you never show any real interest in me or anyone else. You've no idea what I've been through. I've had to…'

'Sacrifice everything, I know.'

'Yes, that, and you Mary, what have you done except suit yourself?'

'And I suppose that makes you a martyr to the cause. It's what you think you are.'

'I used to be scared of you, scared of you sounding so nasty.'

Mary starts fiddling with a loose thread, 'I don't want to scare anyone.'

'You've always been…..been….scary'

'Highly strung? Wouldn't that be a better description?' she asks sarcastically.

'Yes, that's you. I remember I was six and you were about to start at the High School. You were in a terrible state, crying and going on about how you'd never fit in and that all the other girls would hate you. It was awful, you and your nerves and always worried. You were always certain that things would go wrong.'

'And they have, haven't they?'

'Yes, they have.'

'And it's making me ill.'

'That's just an easy way out.'

Mary looks up abruptly, her mouth drawn tight, 'No!' she says in a louder voice, 'No, it damn well isn't.

'Don't you shout or you'll wake mother, yes mother. This is about her, not you and not me. I wished you felt that sometimes.'

'I do, of course I do.'

Sylvie scoffs at this, 'Ever since you left Dawsons you've never been the same. You work at John Lewis, but you never talk about it. I don't even know what you do there.'

'Just stop Sylvie, stop going on. All I wanted to……'

'I'm not interested.'

'Other than chapel and being a martyr to the cause what are you interested in?'

'More than you'll ever know.'

'Tell me, tell me Sylvie'

'No I won't.'

'I thought I'd just tell you that I'm going…..'

'Yes, I know,' Sylvie cuts in, 'I know.'

'I have to make my own decisions,' Mary adds and then thinks how that no longer sounds right.

'Well I think it's awful, absolutely awful that you think of leaving when mother is so ill, so terribly ill.'

'She's dying,' is Mary's sudden retort.

Sylvie's eyes behind her glasses immediately moisten. She shakes her head but cannot make a response.

'I didn't mean to sound so brutal.'

'Well you did.'

'I'm sorry.'

'It doesn't matter,' Sylvie mutters before she gets up and leaves the room.

Mary thinks about going after her but then sits back down. For a moment she sees herself being pulled towards Roger, his mouth forming into a kiss. What immediately follows such an image is disgust and anger before again she remembers the blood drying down the inside of her thighs and the pain throbbing between her legs. And then there was that long, slow, dreadful walk home of which she remembers little when all she wanted to do was lie down on the pavement and curl up into a tight a ball as possible.

She ties the thread she has been playing with round her middle finger. Her breaths gradually slow. Her mind slowly settles as she forces away any more memories.

She liked Roger. It would not happen again. It could not happen again.

Finally she gets up to go downstairs to try and make peace with her sister, hearing the sound of those low, quick snores coming from her mother's bedroom as she passes along the landing.

CHAPTER THIRTY NINE

'At all times their souls are even and calm, their hearts are steadfast and unmovable.'

There has been no more swelling since Alice was last drained. Instead she has become so terribly thin. She can feel her bony shoulders, elbows and knees, her ribcage and flattened breasts, a skeleton with just enough skin.

'All things that they have done are brought to their remembrance and set in array before them.'

Recently she has thought a lot about her childhood, the tall, skinny girl with the long flaxen hair. She sees herself standing beneath a horse chestnut tree sheltering from the rain, holding her mother's hand as they both wait patiently for the storm to pass.

She feels sorry for that child who was often lonely, living in a private world as all children do. She wants to love who she was and try and connect being the adult to who she once was, shy, quiet, watchful.

Alice lies there thinking of her young self, running down a hillside with some of her friends, watching huge purple clouds shift slowly across the sky, wondering where everyone was going and why when she went with her mother to the market, questions, visions, fears accumulating like those storm clouds building and building.

Is she just a combination of her mother and father or so much more that is different from either of them? Did so many ingredients make up her soul? Would God claim all of it?

Sometimes she is elated, excited for no reason, her heart pumping fast until she goes too far and the palpitations begin. Just as strong are the fears of what is to come that again sends her heart racing until it hurts.

'Strong emotions open the door to a sense of our own mortality,' the minister at Guisborough had preached more than once, the belief that everything was to prepare for a death without worry or fear.

He believed that education was to prepare everyone for a good death.

His words had frightened her. With her sister she had stood between her mother and father while the vicar had been up in his pulpit wearing his black cassock which made him look like a huge crow hovering above them.

'I know I have to eat,' she had said to Sylvie, 'I know that.'

They had been arguing. She had heard them last night, Mary and Sylvie with raised voices. It troubled her when they argued like that. She could not remember ever having such disagreements with her own sister. Maybe they had all been forgotten. What else of importance had been lost?

The Jamesons would go on Sunday hikes up into the hills above Grassington and Paul would tell his daughters all about what lay beneath where they walked. Alice would be absorbed in his every word. His description was of wonder and mystery, of unseen, silent worlds.

She loved Paul's voice. She can hear it still, soft, serious and yet tinged with humour that made everything sound intriguing and challenging.

The light is warming her face. Her mouth is dry and her bones feel as though they are being forced hard against the mattress. Every day the pain in her chest increases its pressure.

She often wanders around the house in her imagination from room to room trying to remember every detail. She closes her eyes to concentrate. First she sees the room in which she has been lying for the last five years. She smiles to herself. It is like the game where objects are placed on a tray and you have a short period of time, only seconds to focus on what is there before the objects are covered by a tea towel. You have to wait for another minute before you try and list everything that is on the tray.

The fireplace, the chair, the wardrobe, the lace curtains, the picture of the girl in the country lane, the bedside table on which is a lamp, her radio, usually a book. Now the commode has gone, thankfully replaced by a vase of roses on the mantelpiece that Sylvie picked from the garden, the only new addition to the room.

The landing has a dark green runner that continues down the middle of the stairs secured by brass rods on each step. On the left hand side of the landing is Arthur's room that has been divided into a bedroom and bathroom. There is his bed, a picture of sailing ships hanging on the wall above it, a mirror on his set of drawers, a large wardrobe where he has his suits, clean shirts, two winter coats, a mackintosh and all the rest of his daily attire. On the wall beside the window another painting of two fishermen stood on a harbour wall with a cluster of fishing boats beneath them. The bathroom has a sink, bath and toilet and has a wall cupboard fronted by a mirror that is full of Arthur's shaving things as well as extra bars of soap. Mary and Sylvie's bedroom is on the left, two beds with a small gap between them, another large wardrobe that they share, two tiny bedside tables, a large poster advertising a Blackpool show on the wall beside Mary's bed, her stack of magazines in one corner and on the mantelpiece above their boarded up fireplace are her bottles of perfume and makeup bags.

Now she is tired. The game nears its end as she goes straight to the kitchen. This is more difficult. She finds it upsetting to try and go through the room's contents, the larder, the back yard with the wash shed, coal shed and lean to where Sylvie kept her gardening tools and the door that leads out onto the back lane, wide enough for a horse and cart with the walls and backyards. This was where she had her happiest moments, winter nights in front of the fire with Mary and Sylvie, baking, drawing, she and Mary writing stories. It was when Arthur was out that they had their best times.

How could lies become the truth?

The light warms her face and through the partly open window she can hear the noisy town on this Monday morning. This is followed by memories of her father taking her to see the harvest coming in, the famer's carts stacked high with the bouncing, swaying, golden wheat.

'I want to be a farmer,' and growing up she had said, 'I want to work in a book shop,' and then later, 'I want to be a teacher.'

Now she can hear the pain, hear her body contracting even more, shrinking until she becomes only pain, the last residue of who she is.

'Poor Mary,' Alice says to herself. She lost God a long time ago and now she is leaving. Alice can understand why. Poor Mary has always hated illness. Any sign of bodily weakness and she thinks we are all going to die, just like Arthur.

Memories are often in black and white. Will heaven be the same or will there be colour and light, warm light like this morning?

"Safe in the way of life, above.

Death, earth, and hell we rise;

We find, when perfected in love,

Our long sought paradise."

When she closes her eyes she enters a world where everything seems closer, deeper, threatening as well as reassuring.

Her mind slides quickly towards the edge and in one gasp, one shocking moment she is about to fall off into the darkness.

'Save me Lord……save me,' she whispers to herself.

The curtains are wafting in and out on a warm breeze. She is sitting on the doorstep of her childhood house watching the washing she and her mother had just pegged up on the line, glistening white sheets and pillowcases dancing and flapping in a summer wind. The sheets curved and straightened and lifted and falling back over and over again. They were alive, this constant movement of light and sound. She had been totally absorbed in this childhood vision, a sense of total life dancing before her.

It is not sad to remember those moments. It is energising.

To feel deeply is to feel time passing, the source of all sadness.

Russians have so many words related to sadness, pity, longing. They are the experts in the tragic flow of time.

She remembers the play they went to see, the sound of the Russian train in the distance, the life Chekhov's characters were missing longing to be somewhere else.

Alice considers these thoughts. They are hers and she will share them with no one.

She listens to the afternoon concert. Sylvie carefully spoons the soup into her mouth.

Brahms is being played by a full orchestra from Broadcasting House. All she wants to do now is to listen to the radio especially the evening concerts, Haydn, Bach, Beethoven, Chopin.

'Just listen,' Arthur had instructed her, 'Don't think about anything. Don't try and interpretate what the composer is trying to say. He isn't trying to say anything. He just wants you to listen and go with the music.'

Clever clogs Arthur thinks Alice. For once he was right. He did not have to lie about the music.

'When men came back from the war they were the lucky ones, but none of them felt like that. In one way or another they were all broken.' A voice on the radio describing Arthur and thousands more.

Arthur returned cynical, greedy, his mind tunnelled to what he wanted.

'Did you enjoy the concert?' Sylvie asks as she props Alice forward so she can puff up her pillows.

But talking now is such an effort.

Sylvie slowly guides Alice back into her usual position.

'I'm not good today,' is all she can manage.

She is a puppet and her daughter pulls all the strings. Without her she could hardly move.

Thank God for Sylvie. Alice knows that without her she would have died years ago.

'Is Mary home?' she struggles to ask.

Sylvie takes a wet cloth to wipe her mother's face, 'This should freshen you up.'

'Mary?' Alice repeats her question, 'Is she back from work?'

'She is. She's having her tea.'

'When……when she's finished could you….could you ask her to pop up for a minute?'

She waits. She is nervous, hoping she will have the strength to say everything she wants. This is important.

'Sylvie said you wanted to see me,' Mary later says tentatively as she approaches the bed.

Alice swallows hard before asking her to sit down.

'Are you alright?' Mary inquires after she has pulled up the chair closer to the bed.

Alice waits for her to take her hand but Mary sits back in the chair waiting for her to say something.

It all suddenly feels too much. But for Alice it is essential. It has to be said.

'I wanted to say something Mary. I just hope I have the…..have the strength to manage it.'

'Leave it mother if you feel tired,' Mary says in a puzzled, hesitant voice.

'I am tired….but I'm always tired.'

'We can talk some other time if you like.'

'No Mary….I want…….I just want to say that I understand….that I want you to do what you need to do. You have a future and that to me is more important than anything…..anything Mary.'

'Mother, just leave this for now. Please.'

Alice can hear the desperation in her appeal. Mary has always been hard to talk to, more restrained and careful in how she responds.

'Your aunt Rose has always had a soft spot for you. She's looked out for you ever since you were born. I think since her marriage to Edward lasted such……such a terribly short time Rose has been like a second mother to you. She loves you Mary. You have been the child she never had. This is….is something you should cherish,' Alice struggles to say.

Her mouth is dry and she is afraid she is not going to be able to manage all that she wants to express.

'I need to know that you're doing….you're doing what you want to do.'

'Mother, just leave it for now,' Mary tries as she sits there stiffly aware of how difficult her mother is finding it to speak.

'I can't Mary.'

'I don't know what I'm going to do.'

Alice tries to take a deeper breath, her chest hurting with the effort, 'Yes you do Mary….and it's alright…..I want you to know it's alright.'

'That only makes it worse. Please, let's just leave it for now.'

'And another thing,' Alice persists. She has to persist or will regret it for the rest of the time she has left.

'I don't like hearing…..hearing you and Sylvie arguing. You're six years older than she is. She looks up to you. She always has so it's up to you more than her that you get on as best you can. It's……it's your……your responsibility Mary and I know whatever happens you'll still need each other.'

She stops and gulps in more air. She stops and feels dizzy with the effort as Mary stands up.

'I'm sorry mother.'

'There's no need for you to apologise. That's not what this is about.'

'Isn't it?'

'Of course not Mary. Why should you think that?'

'All that matters is that you get better.'

'And you know that's not possible.'

Mary's face looks so stiff and pale. It is like a mask with staring eyes.

'Please mother, can we stop this?'

'I've…I've already stopped.'

'You need to rest.'

'I needed to talk to you.'

What she has said about Rose is only half of what she feels.

Why is her daughter abandoning her and why now? Why could she not wait?

'You sleep mother,' Mary finally says before she leaves the room.

It is such an empty, dismal ending. Alice knows she will never speak to her again, not as mother to daughter. Life is now for her too short. Each moment is passing into the next and the next until soon there will be none left.

CHAPTER FORTY

'You have to prepare yourself for the worst Sylvie. I'm afraid that's all there is now.'

'I already have,' she tells the doctor, 'I try to be prepared. I've known for a long time that it had to come to this.'

'And I'm sorry, deeply sorry.'

She tries to smile but fails, just nods and then takes a mouthful of tea.

She can be more honest, more open now her feelings for the doctor are thankfully less than they used to be. There is nothing else she needs from him only the support he has always offered.

They are in the kitchen. Even though it is drizzling outside the back door is open for some fresh air.

'It's a miracle your mother has managed as long as she has and so much of that is down to you.'

She feels her cheeks reddening at his compliment, 'And you doctor,' she has to add.

'I just wished we could have done more.'

Sylvie listens to the rain. They have been in this situation so many times, years of it, and yet today everything is different. She feels empty, drained and scared of what is to come. And even doctor Donnolly looks tired and for once sounds uncertain.

'I talked to your father last week. I arranged for him to see me in the surgery after he had finished work.'

'He never said anything.'

'I had the same conversation with him as I'm having with you Sylvie. You know as much as he does. Whatever we've managed for your mother is no longer working. It could be only a matter of days now.'

She makes no response. His words are being washed away by the rain now coming down hard, rattling on the shed roofs.

She goes to close the back door.

'Miserable day,' the doctor comments.

'It couldn't be much worse,' is Sylvie describing everything she feels.

Later after he has gone she makes herself a large sandwich and sits at the kitchen table listening to the rain and for the first time feeling hesitant about going up to see her mother.

The house feels empty, echoing the sounds from outside. It is as if Alice has already gone.

She finishes the sandwich, gets the biscuit tin from the cupboard and quickly eats one after another and another.

She thinks of the street and all its people and wonders if she could ever live by herself like old Mr Fisher next door. The town is her security like a friend, fussy, smoky, noisy, busy.

Could she ever leave it? Will it come to that? Her future is suddenly rushing towards her like a fast train and she feels helpless, unprepared, lonely.

'Please mother,' she says quietly to the sleeping form of Alice as she stands there watching her every breath.

'You have to......you have to keep going. I want you to.......'

She goes over to the window and stands there watching the rain rattling down in the backyard and over all the rooftops.

There is such a heaviness weighing her down. She cannot do anything about this forlorn feeling.

She turns to look at her mother. Alice's face has sunk into its bony outline, a thin mask of skin covering her pale features.

Sylvie sits down by her bed and takes her mother's cold but clammy hand.

'We all love you mother. We love you,' she says in almost a whisper.

Arthur said he would be returning home straight after work to give her a chance to go and see Margaret.

She hears him come him in and waits before going back down.

'What awful damn weather,' he says as he comes into the kitchen, 'Feels like we should have a fire on.'

'I could light one if you want,' she says automatically.

Arthur undoes his waistcoat, loosens his tie and asks, 'How is she today?'

'She's been sleeping mostly. Doctor Donnolly came this morning.'

'And Mary, has she gone?' he asks in a hard tone of voice.

'She took a day off to move the rest of her things.'

Arthur's face tightens as he sits at the table set out for their tea, 'I've no idea how she can do this. You know her better than me Sylvie, what's she thinking about, why now, why now?'

'She said she couldn't stand it anymore, mother's illness.'

'For God's sake. Your sister is such a....such a coward.'

'She has always hated anyone being ill.'

'But she's been ill herself especially when she was younger. She should remember that. She was always complaining about one thing or another. You think by now she would have been used to......'

He stops, picks up a fork, puts it down again before taking up his knife which he holds for a few moments and then sets it back in its place on the neatly laid out table.

'No one is used to this,' Sylvie says.

'No,' you're right. I just wished Mary could have been a little stronger, that's all.'

'She was making herself ill you know.'

Arthur says nothing in reply.

'I'll get the tea. I've done some lamb with potatoes and cabbage,' Sylvie adds before going over to the cooker.

'And I blame Rose more than anyone. It must have been her idea in the first place. I can't believe even Mary would have thought up this one.'

'I don't know,' is all Sylvie wants to say as she sets down their plates.

'But she must have talked about it. You must have known what they were up to.'

'It's only recently that she said anything. I've been kept in the dark as much as you have.'

'Thanks for my dinner,' is his unexpected comment about the food, 'I'll eat this and then pop up and see if your mother is still asleep.'

'She will be. Doctor Donnolly said she'd sleep more and more.'

'It can't be easy for him. Alice was one of his first patients. I remember the first time he came. Even though he was trying his best not to look a little flustered. I felt sorry for him, but not anymore. He's done his best whatever that means. What's a doctor's best I wonder, keeping your mother going over all these years, you and him Sylvie.'

She is not hungry and quickly finishes most of her tea and then waits for him.

'There's tinned peaches and custard if you want,' she tells him when he finally wipes his plate with a piece of buttered bread.

'That was just the ticket Sylvie, and yes I will have some pudding.'

Arthur goes upstairs leaving Sylvie to put on her coat. She shuts the front door, shuts away some of this dreadful reality before heading towards the High Street.

But instead of going to see Margaret she turns to the canal, over the bridge from where she had seen Archie up to his waist in the filthy water. Like everything else it seems so long ago now. It can only been a few weeks and yet to her it feels years away. Time is slowing down, is being extended. Minutes have become hours and the hours have changed into days.

The late sun reflects yellow light on the canal's smooth oily surface. Two men ride by on their pushbikes. Across the canal is the huge side of the Dewhurst mill, its regular windows in line after line and the tall chimney belching out smoke.

Her mother is dying. It will not be long the doctor said, not long now, not long until she will be gone, and then what? Not to be thought about, that's what.

A barge chugs its way in the other direction. She feels so lonely and lost. She thinks of going to the chapel and then changes her mind. She wonders if Margaret will be at home but cannot face another interrogation about her mother's condition.

Life is all a terrible mess, confusing, unpredictable and has to end tragically. Everything is coming to some sort of climax and she has no idea how she will manage or what she will do afterwards. There will be an afterwards.

She cannot help feeling sorry for herself.

Mr Elgin has tried to convince her that only her faith will get her through, but how can she believe that when her mother is dying, how can she retain her faith when what she is faced with seems so absurd, so numbingly awful?

There is no answer. She just hopes her religion will help her. That is what she has promised her mother, that the faith they share she will always follow.

She turns round and heads home. Finally turning into the back lane she sees Archie kicking his ball against their wall. He is in his usual shorts, filthy shirt and old boots.

'Archie, what are you doing at this time of night?' she asks.

He grabs the ball as it comes back off the wall and turns to her, smiling, 'Was waiting for you Sylvie.'

'How did you know I was out?'

'Knew you were.'

'Yes, but how?'

'Knew Sylvie.'

She stops, noticing someone has tried to cut his hair leaving it almost bald behind his ears.

'Who's been cutting your hair?'

'Was waiting for you Sylvie,' he happily repeats.

'Yes, well, it's late Archie.'

'Not night though, not dark. Do you want to play footie with me?'

She has to smile, anything to stop herself from crying.

'You're always asking me to play football with you?'

'Asking now. Please, please.'

'Well I'd loved to but I have to go home Archie.'

'Got my ball.'

'Yes I can see that.'

'Lost it last week.'

'You're always losing it.'

'Mother found it in the bin.'

'Who put it there?'

'She says it must have been me but it wasn't, honest Sylvie it wasn't.'

'Alright, it doesn't matter Archie so long as you've got it now.'

He grins, what's left of his hair flopping over his eyes.

'You be in goals,' he says.

Just then a Mrs McDonald from further down the street passes asking Sylvie how her mother is.

'Who was that?' Archie wants to know after Mrs Donald has gone in her back door.

'Just a neighbour.'

'Neighbour?'

'Someone who lives nearby.'

'We have neighbours.'

'Yes you do.'

'They shout a lot.'

'That's not very good.'

'Archie covers his ears, don't like shouting. My father used to shout, was always shouting at me and my mother. Glad he's gone. Glad he went away.'

'Archie, I have to go,' Sylvie tries.

His frowns in disappointment, hugging the ball to his chest.

'The next few days I'm going to be busy, but we'll continue with your lessons soon.'

'Don't like them.'

'We can stop them if you like.'

'No!' he suddenly exclaims, 'Not stop them!'

'Alright, well we won't then.'

'Going now,' he says in a sulky voice, 'Seeing as you're not playing.'

'Not tonight Archie, I'm sorry.'

'See you Sylvie!' he shouts running off down the lane while managing to bounce the ball in front of him.

'Was that daft Archie?' Arthur asks when she joins him in the parlour where he is listening to one of his records on the radiogram.

'He's not daft father.'

'Well, what is he then?'

She can tell he has been drinking. He always has a bottle of brandy on the larder shelf and she has seen him topping up his hip flask on many occasions. His voice is different and his eyes are moist as he sits there with a cigarette in one hand and the Yorkshire Post in the other.

'I'm going to make some cocoa, do you want some?'

'I'm fine, thank you. No, that's wrong, I'm not fine at all,' he adds, 'Not tonight, not when one of my daughters has abandoned ship and your mother is up there, up there looking terrible. It's the worst I've seen her, the worst.'

She has never got used to his drinking. It has always frightened her.

'Sit down Sylvie, take off your coat and I'll make your cocoa.'.

She wishes she had stayed out in the back lane talking with Archie, thinking she would have probably got more sense out of him than her father when he is in this sort of mood.

'You stay here, I'll make it,' she says as forcefully as she can.

But Arthur is insistent, 'I can do it. I can manage to warm up some milk for God's sake.'

While he is in the kitchen she hurries upstairs to see her mother.

Alice has her eyes open but shows no response as Sylvie enters the bedroom.

'Do you want anything mother?' she asks quietly.

There is no reply just Alice looking down at her hands resting on the top sheet.

'Father is downstairs,' Sylvie tries.

'I'm alright,' Alice finally mutters.

'You sure?'

'I'm alright.'

But her voice is dull and empty. Sylvie waits until she closes her eyes and then goes back down the stairs and into the parlour.

A few moments later Arthur returns with her cocoa.

'Here you are, nice and hot.'

Carefully she takes the mug thanking him as he sits across from her.

The music is still playing quietly she supposes so it will not bother her mother.

'What's playing?' she asks him.

'She's dying,' is his brutal answer, 'She's leaving us Sylvie.'

This makes her angry and suddenly ready for him, ready for his half drunken mood and bitter tone.

He lights another cigarette before going back to the kitchen to refill his glass.

'Did you hear me?' he asks when he returns.

'I heard you father.'

'And what have you got to say about it?'

'Nothing, I've nothing to say.'

'Cat caught your tongue?'

'No, I just don't want to talk about mother.'

'You usually do.'

'Well not tonight.'

Arthur pauses, sips at his brandy and then asks, 'So what do you want to talk about? I'm ready for any topic you like so long it's not about this bloody war we're all getting ready for. Are you ready for it?'

'No.'

'Quite right.'

'There's enough going on as it is,' she says with a tone of bitterness in her voice.

For once she refuses to be scared of how he might react.

'What about your sister then?'

Sylvie forces herself to look at him, 'What about her?'

'What about her!' Arthur exclaims, 'I'll tell you what about her. She's given up on us, that's what. She's given up on your mother and that's inexcusable. How can she just pack up leave and then only across town to stay with my sister. It makes no sense to me, none at all. This is Rose's idea. She's been feeling lonely, feeling old and this is her answer, this is the scheme she's hatched up and Mary has stupidly gone along with it.'

Sylvie cannot respond. It is too much. He sounds too angry, too ready for an argument. There is no way of her managing him when he is like this.

'Say something,' he urges.

'I can't change your opinion father.'

'It's not a damn opinion. It's facts, that's what it is!'

'There's no need to shout. You'll wake mother.'

He stares at her as though trying to comprehend what she has just said.

'I want to wake your mother, don't you understand that? I want her as awake as possible. I never want to see those eyes closed again. Surely you can understand that?'

'I'm going to bed,' is all she can say.

'It's early.'

'Not for me it isn't.'

'It's always been the same, hasn't it Sylvie? You've never forgiven me for telling you that you had to leave school to look after your mother. You've been against me ever since.'

'I'm not against anybody.'

'Just me.'

'Not you either father.'

'And I find that hard to believe.'

'If you must know I did, I used to resent you and what you had asked me to do. But now I'm not bothered. I can't change what's happened.'

'And if you could?'

'Could what?'

'Change it all.'

'We're here now, here and there's no point looking back.'

'It might be better than the future. Have you ever thought of that?'

'Stop it father, please.'

'Stop what?'

'I'm going to bed.'

'Stop what?'

At that she gets from her seat and leaves the room, waiting in the hallway for him to call her back, but all she hears is the music being turned up, violins and chellos following her mournfully up the stairs.

CHAPTER FORTY ONE

Arthur leaves the Black Bull walks home, gets in his car parked outside the house and drives onto the Keighley Road. It is half past eight at night and still light. Within an hour he is driving up the rough track to Kitty's cottage.

Knocking loudly on the door he waits until finally Kitty appears.

'Arthur, what are you doing here?' she asks sharply, stood there in slacks and bare feet.

'I've phoned and phoned but no answer. Why is that Kitty? Why wouldn't you lift up the receiver and speak to me?'

'We had an agreement, remember.'

'And I've changed my mind.'

'Well I haven't.'

'Come on Kitty for God's sake. This is…..'

'Is Alice…..?'

'No she isn't.'

'There's nothing more to be said then. You promised Arthur.'

'I want to see you, I need you.'

'And I've told you this isn't going to work, not like this. And you've been drinking and driving the car.'

'I needed to see you, that's why.'

'You said you would never do that,' Kitty states angrily, still holding the door half closed.

Arthur steps back. The horses are winnowing from their stable. A wind is blowing across the moors.

'You look so lovely,' he mentions.

To this Kitty makes no response.

'You look…..look stunning Kitty. I've missed you, really missed you.'

'You promised me, and I don't like promises being broken,' she tells him harshly before closing the door.

He listens to her locking it before knocking again, harder this time.

When nothing happens, he walks a few feet away from the cottage and stands there as the wind buffets him. It is as though he is being pushed further down the track, stepping over the rough stones.

Finally he gets back in the car, turns it round and accelerates angrily away.

The sky is darkening by the time he reaches the main road. With little traffic at this time of night he drives as fast as the car will go. Now he is seeing two white lines in the middle of the road, sometimes three, curving and curling as he turns on the lights and shifts his position so his face is a little closer to the windscreen as though this will help him see better.

At one point he stops by the side of the road so he can take out his flask to gulp down another mouthful of brandy before he starts the car and with a screech of tyres set off again.

'Bloody hell Kitty,' he mutters to himself, gripping the steering wheel as tightly as possible.

He is in a fast tunnel. There is nothing either side but the darkness tinged by a deep blue light. Instinctively he slows a little when he remembers the young girl all those months ago appearing out of nowhere, suddenly stopping in the middle of the road with his headlights glaring at her. In a slow, slow second of time she starts to move as he begins to turn the wheel, the car jerking slightly as he manages to miss her back leg by inches. She was a ghost there and then not there. She was the nearest thing to a disaster. Only sheer luck avoided him killing her, the front bumper smashing into her legs and taking her under to be flattened by the back wheels.

Again he stops by the side of the road, gets out, goes round the front of the car so he can vomit on the grass banking, mouthful after mouthful of beer, brandy, steak and chips, coffee, tea and everything else he has taken on board throughout the day.

Back in the car he lights a cigarette, takes in a deep gulp of smoke and slowly blows it against the windscreen. It spreads like a fine mist through which he can see very little.

'Kitty, for God's sake woman,' he says then, 'What the hell is the point of it? What is the fucking point?'

By the time he gets home it is past ten o clock. As he opens the door he sees Mary coming down the stairs.

'What the hell are you doing here?' is his outraged question.

She hardly falters as she descends the rest of the stairs and stops in front of him.

'I came to see mother. Why does it matter to you?'

'You don't like being here in this house, remember?'

'If you must know I came for a couple of things, felt sorry for Sylvie so said I'd sit in and give her a break.'

'And where is she?'

'Out seeing Margaret if you must know.'

'Yes, I must damn well know.'

'You weren't here as usual,' Mary says challengingly, 'But that's no different, is it father?'

He can feel his muscles tensing and his face stretched tight with the effort of refraining from a full blown row.

'Damn you Mary and your impertinence, your bloody cheek just turning up as large as life, turning up here as though nothing had happened.'

'And what has happened father. You tell me.'

'I've a good mind to....'

'To what, slap me, hit me, kick me or what, maybe all three?'

'Shut up, just shut up.'

'I won't shut up. You can't tell me what to do anymore.'

'If you're in this house then I can.....'

'No father,' she interrupts him in a loud voice, 'You can do nothing, just like you usually do, nothing at all except go out with your pals or whoever every night. Skipton is small enough that no one can get away with anything without someone finding out. Whether you like it or not you have a reputation and what most people say about you is probably true. They're not stupid. They hear what's going on. They hear about you having a mistress who lives outside Keighley. You think you're so clever, but you aren't.'

'Get out!' he tells her, 'Just get out.'

'I was just going, remember?'

'I said get out!'

'And I said I was just about to but seeing as you've probably woke mother and upset her I'd better….'

'You're going nowhere young lady except out of the front door and the quicker the better.'

At that he tries to grab her arm only for Mary to push him against the wall where he unsteadily tries to right himself.

'You're a disgusting mess, that's what you are. The idea of leaving you here alone with mother makes me sick. Do you hear me?'

'Get out,' he mutters back.

'I'm going,' are her last words before she furiously slams the door after her.

He is in the kitchen when Sylvie returns a few minutes later.

'Mary was here,' is all she says while taking off her coat and unpinning her hat.

'Yes, I know.'

'I was out seeing Margaret.'

'And I have to go out again,' he suddenly he mentions. There is no explanation. He is down the hallway and out of the house leaving Sylvie open mouthed staring after him..

This time his driving is steadier as he goes up the empty High Street, turns left in front of the castle, over the bridge and then left again along the road to Gargrave.

The sky is a dull grey with clouds blocking out the moon. His headlights reflect off the trees beside the road before he passes through Gargrave onto Hellifield and then Long Preston, each place now in darkness.

Finally he reaches Settle, turns left at the town hall to park up under the railway bridge. From there it is only a few yards to the entrance gate for him to walk through into the cricket ground. For a few moments he looks over the dark stretch of grass with high trees in the corner and then over to the high shadowed white washed wall with the roofs of the council estate over the other side.

He sits in front of the pavilion and lights a cigarette, frowning as he starts to remember how the field sparkled with its covering of frozen snow when he was here in January of the previous year. A woman pushed her pram across it and she was attractive enough for him to offer his help.

It feels like another life ago. Since then everything has been spiralling downwards, Alice, the coming war, his own drinking, Kitty, his guilt about Sylvie.

An owl starts hooting from the trees in the corner of the field followed a few minutes later by the call of curlews heading back to the hills above the town sounding like plaintive spells being cast on this warm, overcast night. For the first time in a long time Arthur settles into the moment. It feels familiar.

He is finishing the last of the brandy from his flask when he hears it, a low rumbling in the distance. Excitement starts. Is this why he is here, just for this?

Quickly the sound grows louder. Now it is unmistakably wheels clicking fast over the rails. He stands to look up at the huge railway embankment. The train appears in a sudden burst of steam and noise, the mail train to London. For a second he sees it all, the glow from the cab of the Jubilee class with sparks flying out of its chimney as it thunders past pulling its dimly lit postal carriages. On board the letters will be being sorted. He imagines the sorters oblivious to the speed on the fast journey down south.

Just as quickly it has gone, along through the station and on towards the Long Preston cutting, its sound quickly merging into the silence. It is the most exhilarating experience. It always is. He loves to see the trains at full speed on the downward line especially this one cutting fast through the night. Soon its sister train will be struggling past on its way up the long drag to Carlisle blasting steam as the fireman loads on more coal to give it enough power to manage the steep gradient onto to the Ribblehead, through the Bleamoor tunnel and on to its highest point at Dent station.

Arthur sits back down and lights another cigarette. He would like to sleep. He would like to lie down, empty his mind and let this quiet, warm summer night wrap itself around him. This is one of his favourite places. Trains and cricket are for him a contrasting but perfect combination.

The owl calls again. There is a momentary sound of some vehicle passing through the town followed a few minutes later by the drone of an unseen aircraft above the cloud covering, a reminder of what is to come. Will he be conscripted? Is it possible that eventually they will need men of his age? What would happen to Kitty and him then? Is another war going to destroy so much like the first one did?

'That Oswald Mosley wants locking up.'

'And now we're trying to form an alliance with Russia.'

'Can't depend on the bloody French, I know that much.'

'And the Americans are going to stay out of it.'

Voices from the Black Bull, everyone worked up, bothered, anxious.

But he is tired and he needs to rest, needs to stop all the thoughts, the worries, the fears.

The field in front of him is a dark pond with vague shadows from the trees lying across it. There is mystery in everything especially here, especially at past one o clock in the morning. He wants to live forever but understands that is impossible. He wants to feel his life is a success when he knows it is the opposite. If only he could turn failure into something richer, happier, deeper. Everyone fails because they have to leave each other behind. We have to forget and he cannot. We have to accept there is no escape, but he is too cowardly to manage it.

He is tired of it all, too many thoughts, too many constant questions.

He wants to be absorbed into the night, this warm, still night.

It is half past two when he eventually arrives back in Skipton. Quietly he opens the front door and goes straight upstairs to see Alice's shadow lying there, a dim shape that lets out quick, stuttering breaths. She is still breathing. She is still there. Her presence dominates over everything.

Carefully he pulls the chair nearer to the bed, rests his elbows on the edge and leans forward as he clasps his hands together and rests them under his chin looking at her, concentrating on the fast rise and fall of each breath while thinking that he has to do something, that things cannot continue like this. It is up to him. He has to make things happen. He has to do something.

CHAPTER FORTY TWO

Mary is out of John Lewis exactly at six o clock. Instead of the railway station she walks to the Queens hotel, pushes open the swing doors and heads straight for the bar.

On the platform are the same people she sees everyday. Mary has seen Roger Simpson a few times getting onto the train at Keighley. He always looks straight ahead and not once has he past her compartment when looking for somewhere to sit. If he did she would ignore him just like she ignored the rest of the passengers with whom she shared a compartment. She either pretended to read a paper she bought from a Leeds station kiosk just for that purpose or would flick through one of her weekly magazines.

Each day follows the routine she needs. She can forget everything and concentrate on her work in John Lewis's, the journey to and from Elliot street and her time with aunt Rose. The house is being gradually modernised. Rose listens to her niece's advice and has started buying some new clothes. They go together on shopping trips when Mary has a day off. This sort of change is manageable. It allows her to remain in a numbed off state of mind where she thinks about things as little as possible. This is what she wants. This is how she wants things to be so that each day is just like any other, each day like placing one similar brick on top of another, not to build anything except the most boring tower possible.

'Look at you! Look at you!' aunt Rose exclaims when she meets Mary in the hallway, 'You're soaking wet young lady, absolutely soaking!'

'I forgot my umbrella,' is Mary's explanation.

'There's a first. You never usually forget anything.'

'Well I did today.'

Rose fusses over her and suggests Mary takes a bath while she prepares the tea.

The bathroom is new with everything shiny and clean. Mary undresses and slowly sinks into the hot water.

She likes this time to relax and immerse herself in bath salts that smell faintly of roses. But instead her thoughts begin an inventory of all that has happened to her and Rose over the last weeks. It has been remarkable. Not only has the house electricity, a new kitchen and bathroom, it smells and feels so different. No longer is there the odour of gas and damp, no longer the cold stone slabs in the kitchen or thick velvet curtains in Rose's parlour where she spends most of her day when she is not out visiting friends or doing the shopping.

The rain was pouring down but for once Mary did not care. She had forgotten to bring her umbrella and as she stood on the canal bridge she was getting soaked to the skin by warm, torrential summer rain. She was holding her small hat so the water plastered her hair to the sides of her face and ran into her open mouth. Her clothes were sodden, pressing against her while she watched the canal's surface breaking into millions of circular rain drops. She felt awful and exhilarated at the same time. It was so different to not care, to lose control, to forget about how she looked to everyone. The strain was too much. She had to be free of it even if it was only for a few silly minutes. She wanted to be silly and carefree. She wanted to stand there and get soaked to the skin.

Nobody was happy. At least she was not the only one. The looming war had pressed the general mood further and further down.

She had to close her eyes to stop the water stinging into them. The falling rain made a special sound of shifting leaves along the road, of small waves on the beach, of numberless fountains. She was under its waterfall and it was good to just stand there as people hurried past her and a barge approached, a carrier full of coal with smoke coming out of its tinpot chimney as it chugged through the filthy, rain splattered water. For a moment her imagination hooked a memory and saw herself with friends from Elliot street tossing stolen flowers down onto a passing barge until for a moment instead of coal the barge was loaded with flowers, blooms of all colours and she saw herself stand up on the low wall of the bridge and let herself fall into the soft scented bed of fresh blossoms.

She smiled to herself and thought about nothing in particular. Her mind quickly emptied, washed clear by the rain.

What did the war mean? What were its implications? Did living in Skipton mean people were safer here? But she worked in a major northern city. That was certainly not a safe place to be. Would John Lewis have to close?

Tears were mixing with the rain and her closed eyelids could not stop them. The tears felt different, warmer, more viscous. They were dribbling down her cheeks and off her chin. She was crying for her mother and herself. It was all so awful, so depressingly inevitable. It made her angry. Life could be obscene in the way it ended. She was glad she was at her aunt's. She knew now she would never go back home. Whatever happened that period of her life was finished.

She turned off the bridge and crossed the Gargrave Road and onto the hill of Elliot street. There was a river cascading down over the cobbles and out across the main road. Children in bare feet and shorts were playing in it, letting the water run up their legs, two of them sat down with the rain flowing around them as they laughed and splashed each other.

'Look at you! Look at you!' Auntie Lizzie exclaimed when Mary came into the hallway, 'You're soaking young lady, absolutely soaking!'

'I forgot my umbrella,' was Mary's explanation.

'I don't think umbrellas would have been any good at this downpour. It's raining cats and dogs out there. I've never seen it so bad. You get yourself upstairs, have a bath and I'll put the kettle on.'

The bath was certainly Edwardian if not Victorian with its shaped metal legs and ornate taps. It took ages to fill, which meant sitting in a few inches of water to begin with and then letting in more hot followed by more cold until at least Mary got it almost up to her bent knees.

More tears began. She started soaping herself, pushing the sponge against her face, pressing it against her eyes to try and stop herself crying.

Instead of her mother, instead of her own strained situation she thought about her aunt and how extraordinary had been the change since Mary had first mentioned living with her and certainly even more so now it had happened. Aunt Lizzie was a different person. She had lost weight which meant she was a lot more mobile than she had been. Her clothes were less dowdy. A woman she knew from Chalmers Street had come to do her hair. She was wearing one of the summer dresses Mary had brought from John Lewis and a pair of new sandals. And she had been so generous. Mary had been given two bedrooms, one in which she could hang her clothes and keep her other belongings. The other had been transformed, new bed and mattress, new bedclothes, new makeup table, framed pictures put up on the walls that Aunt Lizzie and Mary had bought together in an old antique shop near the Plaza cinema and a new rug put down, everything in the room of Mary's choosing.

Strangely the only thing she had not been anxious about was living with her aunt. Mary knew it would work. Her aunt was kind, understanding, patient, nothing like her brother Arthur, not like him at all. Except for finding it hard to find plumbers and electricians and painters who all seemed to either have already been conscripted or lacked the materials they needed, everything was going as Mary hoped. Her aunt accepted her ideas without a quibble. She was sure that eventually electricity would replace the gas that smelt so strong and that all the rooms of the house would be repainted, that there would be a new stair carpet and that the kitchen will have its stone sink replaced and lino on the floor.

In the bath she finally stopped crying. The rain had fallen so heavily. She had got wetter than she ever remembered. What a beautiful image, a barge going past full of flowers and she had slowly, ever so slowly fallen into all those scented soft petals of every colour. A war was coming. Everything but her aunt was a worry, an awful concern. What was going to happen? Her mother was going to die. Would her father sell the house? What would Sylvie do? Only last Saturday afternoon she had seen three men dressed in fascist black fighting with other men outside the Craven Heifer. They had been Mosley's men going off to a march in Leeds. Even Skipton had its fascists. What did they really think? What did anyone think about now that war seemed imminent, and her mother was dying. She would be well out of it, her once beautiful mother who turned into a monster. How was that possible. How could a woman who had been so stylish and clever turn into that thing that she had become? It was so awful, so incomprehensible.

Out of the bath she put on her dressing gown and went along the landing to her bedroom. She seated herself in front of her dressing table mirror and started brushing her hair thinking about the one aspect of her aunt that she found uncomfortable, the one thing that to Mary made no sense. Even beyond death her aunt had dedicated herself to one man, to Edward her short lived husband who she still idealised and never stopped talking about. After the séance on Thursday of the previous week which had not been successful, she had started to describe all she felt about him, how his presence was still in the house, still in each room. She felt him close to her, talked to him, knew that he was in a world that was only a wafer thin distance away from this world. The seances were a reassurance. Edward's spirit was within her and this was the reason why she had never changed anything after his death, why the house had remained a shrine to him.

It was another mystery, how a sensible woman like her aunt could be so morbidly focused on her long dead husband. To Mary it was a grim, miserable attachment. It was something unimaginable to her. She was certain now she would never marry, that she would live her life as a spinster, would be free of all the usual ambitions. Her family would be herself and her aunt. This was her new freedom, this certainty that a man would never have any influence over her life, that physically she would never again allow any man to touch her, love her, need her. It was a pledge she had made to herself, a promise that went deeper than anything else.

All her cinema fantasies had been destroyed. All her youthful dreams about gorgeous men in romantic settings had been ridiculed and rejected for the rubbish they obviously were. She would of course in the future talk to men, socialise with them but never let them any nearer. She would never trust a man. Like her father they were full of lies, full of their own arrogance and egos. In the end there was only one thing they wanted. That was all that mattered to them. Just the thought of it made her sick and nervously overwrought. She had to blank it out, push it away from her consciousness or she would make herself ill.

'There you are,' her aunt said as she came into the parlour, 'Is that better?'

'Much better,' Mary agreed now in slacks and a thin sweater.

'Do you want some tea?'

'I'd love a cup.'

'And then you can have your proper tea. There's ham and cold potatoes and...'

'I'm not hungry auntie,' Mary intervened as she sat at the other side of the empty fire with the rain still rattling against the parlour windows that looked out onto the Methodist chapel across the street.

'You should have something.'

'I might have a ham sandwich later.'

'And are you going to see how Alice is?'

'I'm not sure. I might.'

'You should Mary.'

'I know I should. I probably will.'

They talked about her day in Leeds and what her aunt had been listening to on the radio and had been reading in the Yorkshire Post that she had delivered every day.

Later Mary went across town to see how her mother was only to be told by Sylvie that the doctor had been again and that he had given her some morphine to ease the pain and that had helped her get to sleep.

It was then Mary had to force herself to go upstairs into her mother's room and stand there looking down on her yellow, bloated features. It was a nightmare. It was not possible, not this total distortion of all her mother had been.

She could only manage a few minutes before rushing downstairs, saying a sharp goodbye to Sylvie and leaving the house.

That night in her room she had some dance music on low on the radio, another thing her aunt had bought for her. The half full bottle of gin was on the dressing table while she was pretending to read a magazine letting the gin start having its necessary effect, that warm, quick melting of some of the nervous strain that plagued her waking hours and her attempt to find some sleep each night.

Even though she had been living with her aunt for some weeks now having a room to herself and a dressing room still felt strange.

She had to put the glass down she was holding. Her hand was shaking and she felt dizzy. The dance music echoed through her consciousness as though it was coming from far away. She felt terrible, felt so miserably depressed. Her mother was dying and a war was about to start and all because of the ego of some ugly stunted man with a paint brush moustache. She had seen Hitler strutting about on the Pathe news at the cinema years ago. He looked ridiculous and yet he was the reason her life and everyone else's was about to be shattered in pieces, about to change in ways no one could predict. It was absurd. It was the same with her mother, how can life disintegrate like it was, her life torturously ending in so much pain?

Her aunt was in her room. The rain had stopped and there was still a glimmer of light in the sky. A truck drove along the Gargrave road, its engine sounding loud in the night's silence. She could look out on the gloomy chapel across the steep hill. Hours before children had been splashing about and sliding down the cobbles. Hours before she had stood on the canal bridge letting herself get soaked to the skin. Time was back there. It did not exist in the gloomy, miserable present.

It felt as though she was shivering internally. Her whole body was twitchy and stretched to an unknown breaking point. She could not break. She had to remain in control or get drunk or sleep or just listen to the radio and think of cities far away, Paris, Rome, New York. How could anyone travel with a war about to start? Where was there to go? But she did not want to go anywhere. She wanted to stay in this room, in this night and let herself just exist without all the pressure of death and war, without all these depressing thoughts that caused such a terrible reaction inside her.

Suddenly she saw her mother so clearly. They were walking in the wood beside the stream that ran near Skipton Castle. Alice was telling her some of the Castle's history, about the Civil War and how it held out for the Royalists. Shade shifted into sunlight and back into shade again as they had walked together. She had listened so intently. She always listened to her mother who had so much to say that was interesting and informative even though sometimes she did not understand all of it. She had been so proud of her mother, proud of how smartly she dressed and how clever she was. She had always wanted to look like her, dress like her. She knew she would never be as well educated. She was never bothered about reading or finding out about things. In that way she was lazy and depended on her mother telling her things about the world and history and her own childhood in Guisborough.

How disappointed had her mother been when she had left school and started working the next week at Dawsons?

But she did not want to think about that period of her life.

Frobisher was there with his thing trying to prod his way forcefully into her. She remembered afterwards the trickle of blood down the inside of her thigh and how she had put everything, her pants, stockings, girdle, petticoat, shoes, skirt, blouse, jacket into the dustbin. She would have burnt the lot that night if there had been somewhere where she could have lit a fire.

She did not want to remember.

She took another drink of gin.

The music drifted around her.

Her mother would soon……..would soon be dead. Her life would end and it was impossible to imagine. Life was turned back on itself, back into the nothingness from which everything came. If human existence depended on that thing bruising its way into a woman then it was not worth it, not the way it ended so brutally, the madness of an end, a stop, a cessation of breath, of her mother's breath.

It had to be faced. There would be a funeral. Would she manage it? Would she manage seeing her father standing there by the graveside?

And poor Sylvie.

What would she do?

What would anyone do when the war started?

She poured out some more gin.

It was good to drink, good that she could allow herself the luxury of letting go a little.

The last of the light was reflected in the dull chapel windows across the street.

Her mother had God. Would that be enough?

Sylvie also believed in Jesus.

She was a martyr to the cause.

Where was heaven?

On a cinema screen in the sky?

There was no heaven.

There was nothing but what there was now.

Somehow the future whatever it held had to be faced and lived.

She was crying again.

And now she knew why.

CHAPTER FORTY THREE

A band was playing, their instruments gleaming in the bright sunshine. There were people sat on striped deck chairs listening to a military march.

Where was she? Was she there?

If there is darkness there has to be light somewhere, bright sunlight shining on trombones and trumpets, saxophones and French horns.

Children played in a paddling pool. Mary was watching Sylvie splashing about. She and Arthur were standing close by arm in arm on an empty path.

'What a nice day.'

'Yes.'

'Just right.'

'Yes.'

Please oh Lord give me strength I need to face…….to face…..

Am I conscious? Sometimes I can hear Arthur's voice in the background of my thoughts. He is speaking to me, but I am not interested in what he has to say.

The pressure. The pain. They are killing me.

But I drift in the light and infrequently the band plays, summer light.

Am I in my room or a different place entirely?

I sense Arthur sitting close, waiting, watching. Is he waiting for me to die? Is that what he is doing? I want to speak but cannot. So I panic again which starts even more palpitations, my heart pounding quickly through a dark space.

I am Alice Townsley, no, Alice Thompson. I am married with two daughters. I was born in Guisborough to quiet, careful, loving parents and left school to become….to become……

In love with a doctor, a quiet, careful, loving doctor, so handsome and I loved him so deeply, still do, my rueful, serious Paul. His skin was the colour of a summer field, light brown, warm, smelling faintly of lemons.

Where is he?

Where is my Paul?

Is he still alive? Is he still with Julia?

I was never jealous of Julia because she was always unwell. She was Paul's wife but that hardly mattered to me because my love was different, more secretive, from a distance.

How do you contain love? Is it ever possible?

I am Alice and the pain is everywhere. My body is all pain with no relief except when doctor Donnolly gives me something that helps for a little while.

The walls of my room are closing in on me.

I think of Captain Scott with Bowers and Wilson in their small tent, such a small space for the three of them.

They had such a short distance between them and the supplies that would have kept them alive.

What is my distance?

How many steps have I to take?

I am cold.

Is it winter?

Oh God I am so tired now.

Oh Lord, I want to sleep.

I am not ready.

I am scared.

I want to live, to live, to live, another hour, day, month, forever.

He was my hero, Captain Scott, my tragic hero.

I am with the three of them in their tiny tent, my breath released in a frozen cloud that mixes with theirs.

It is so cold.

Cold steps.

How many oh God, how many?

Is that what death is like?

My death?

A long frozen walk into silence.

I am Alice......Alice.

Mary still cares, I know she does.

I feel like a whale stranded on a lonely beach, an Antarctic beach.

I read his diaries. 'It seems a pity, but I don't think I can write any more,' were Scott's last words.

And cried.

I cried a lot back then, cried about everything and nothing.

Arthur danced so well. He was a good dancer.

Love was different with him.

I loved him in a different way to Paul. Did I love him? Lost, bitter, confused Arthur who survived the war but died so many deaths.

Frightened now.

Won't someone take the pain away?

However bad life is I know I want more of it.

Not to end.

Not to stop.

Please God.

Please God.

I am not ready.

Not ready.

It is so cold now.

So very cold.

'Oh God what an awful place this is.'

Awful and cold and colder, shivering in the darkness, the very cold darkness.

To drift.

Please don't let me drift.

CHAPTER FORTY FOUR

'You did all you could Sylvie. There was nothing you or anyone else could have done. I wish it could have been different, but you did everything you could have and more.'

She once thought she loved the doctor, not long ago.

'I expected it.....I expected it,' she tries, 'I thought I did, but when it happened I wasn't ready. I just wasn't ready.'

'That's understandable.'

'I'm sorry doctor Donnolly, but at the moment, I don't understand or even want to understand.'

'You helped your mother for over five years Sylvie, five years.'

The tears start again, and she just feels terrible, as awful as it is possible to feel. And yet in a shameful way there is relief. She is free of all the worry, the constant anxiety.

The doctor's surgery is a large room that smells of disinfectant and polish. He looks tired. Everyone is tired. War is approaching and it is exhausting to be so anxious all the time.

There is a pause. The doctor has stopped talking. Words like echoes fill the emptiness. She does not want this silence. It is like a void between them.

'What do you think your father will he do?' finally comes a question that she cannot answer except to say the subject is too painful to even contemplate.

'I'm thinking…..thinking of becoming a nurse,' she suddenly announces.

The doctor looks grave and bothered, 'No Sylvie, I don't think that's a good idea. I really don't. You've been nursing your mother for a long time and the last thing you should be thinking about is nursing. I suggest you think about doing something totally different.'

His voice is strident and forceful. She does not like it. She has never had him oppose her in this way.

'Because,' she starts hesitantly, feeling too warm in her jacket, 'Because I'd been nursing mother I thought that it would make sense to…..'

'No,' he interrupts which she does not expect, 'Personally I think you've done enough. You should think of…..of I don't know….something….'

'Not nursing?'

'No, not at all.'

All of a sudden everyone seems to know what they want except her. She is sat here in the doctor's surgery and has no idea what she is doing. The war is coming and where does that leave her?

'Just think about it,' the doctor is saying.

It was unimaginable that she once had such a crush on him. Now he looks old, tired and lacking in authority. She does not blame him. It is not his fault. He has done everything he could. But still they share the same disappointment, the same failure. They will always have that together.

Outside the surgery Sylvie stands on the pavement adjusting herself to the warmth and the light. Her body aches with every step she takes coming out onto the High Street. It makes no sense seeing all these people going up and down the pavement. What are they doing? What is the point? It is all meaningless. Even for the time being God makes no sense. In the confusion of grief and anger her belief is being challenged like never before.

Why doesn't everyone know her mother is dead? Why do they not realise that she is dead and buried down at the cemetery with all the other lost folk of Skipton. They have lost life, lost it as though it had once been found and then had been mislaid somehow.

Life is a gift to be given and then taken away.

She walks slowly, the church bell tolling for the Townsleys' little drama, someone passing away, losing one of the family, such a shame but inevitable, eventually inevitable.

She hates that inevitability. It is worse than anything she could have imagined. How do you imagine a state of grieving? It is not possible.

What is the point of all these people shopping, talking, going in the bank? What is the point of any of it? It is all a sham, a pretence. There has to be a message in all this. God has to show what purpose mother's death has served.

She cannot hurry. She wants to be home as quickly as possible, but her legs feel heavy, and her breathing is not right. The summer sun blazes into her face bringing on a headache. It is too bright, too dazzling. She has her head down slightly. Her glasses seem to absorb the sun's rays and make her feel even more uncomfortable. Skipton is a haze of people and buildings, voices echoing, traffic rumbling from a faraway distance.

At last in the coolness of the hallway she stops to catch her breath, steadying herself by leaning her hand against the wall. She is sweating and her head is throbbing. She unpins her hat, takes off her jacket and hangs it on one of the pegs behind the door.

It is then she notices father's suitcases at the foot of the stairs. Puzzled she goes and lifts one. It is heavy with his clothes. It makes no sense and then in a sudden cold spasm down her back she realises what it means.

She turns at the sound of the key before he opens the door.

'There you are Sylvie,' he says in a forced friendly tone.

She has no idea what to say. Momentarily she remembers some of the things Marys had implied about him without telling her the full story. Now it is too late. She is too distressed, too tired and aching all over. She wants to go upstairs, lie on the bed and try and rest.

'Been out?' he asks.

'I've been to see doctor Donnolly,' she manages, 'You still have to pay his final bill.'

'And what had he got to say?'

'He doesn't want me to be a nurse,' she answers as she walks off into the kitchen.

He follows and asks, 'Why not? What's wrong with becoming a nurse? You'd be good at it.'

'He thinks I've done enough nursing already.'

She stops and then asks, 'What are your suitcases doing at the foot of the stairs?'

'I'm moving out,' he says quickly, his eyes avoiding hers.

'Moving out? Moving where?'

'I've got a new job.'

Her mother has just been buried and now this. It is too much, far too much for her to manage. She can feel the confusion of panic and anger welling up.

'What new job?'

'Like I've been doing at Slaters, but I'll be working for the government instead. Procurement they call it which is a posh word for getting all the materials they need for the war effort. That'll be my job to do that.'

'You're leaving.'

'My department is based in Bradford so.....'

'So what father?'

'Sit down Sylvie.'

'I don't want to sit down.'

'I was going to tell you.'

'When?'

'Sometime.'

She turns away and looks down at the empty fireplace. She feels sick. At that moment she hates him. She is disgusted, totally disgusted. She wants to hit him, to slap him hard across the face.

'I have to do this Sylvie.'

'No, you don't.'

'It's a good job and I need to get out of Skipton.'

'No, you don't,' she says again forcefully.

'Just listen Sylvie while I try and explain.'

She turns, pushes past him, kicks over one of the suitcases on her way upstairs. She locks her bedroom door and sits on the edge of the bed, her fists tightly clenched.

After a few minutes he comes up and knocks on the door.

'Come on Sylvie, open the door.'

She cannot speak to him. She just wants him to go away. It is as though he is turning her grief inside out and leaving nothing but disgust and anger.

'Open the door Sylvie.'

His earnest sounding voice is just another sham, another pretence. None of this is right. None of it fits with anything else.

'I'll be back later in the week.'

She wants him to go away. She does not care what he wants to do. How could she? Mother was dead and now this. There is no family, no shared grief or commitment or anything that makes a difference right at the moment. Where was she in all this? Who cared about her needs? Who was looking out for her?

'Come on Sylvie. This is stupid, open the door and let's talk.'

Without her realising it these are the last words she will ever hear him say. He waits a few more minutes before going back down the stairs and eventually out the front door.

Sylvie takes off her glasses and puts them on the bedside table then turns on her side and puts her hands under her head. Suddenly she is by herself in a house. They have all gone.

She lays there without moving for a long time. The light in the bedroom is dimming when she finally moves to lie on her back and stare up at the ceiling and begin to cry and to continue crying until the room is in darkness and she is exhausted.

CHAPTER FORTY FIVE

The two bodies roll away from each other.

'Christ Kitty I needed that,' sighs Arthur before he sits up to light a cigarette.

The summer rain is being swept across the moors by a strong wind. It rattles against the bedroom window. They can hear the fir trees at the side of the cottage being blown from side to side.

His cigarette smoke spirals up towards the low ceiling. Kitty's body is warm beside his.

'Was it very grim, the funeral?' she asks.

He hears himself speak as though it is an echo of someone else, 'If you don't mind, I'd rather not talk about it just now.'

Then he adds, 'You've saved me Kitty. You know that don't you? And you're here, we're here.'

'Glad to be appreciated,' is Kitty's easy response.

'You certainly are. My God you are,' he urges as though to convince not just her but himself as well.

After a pause while he finishes his cigarette she asks, 'We don't need anything bigger than here, do we?'

'I love this cottage.'

'Well, that's alright then.'

'And I've come with two suitcases and that's it, all my worldly belongings. There's nothing else.'

He is holding a conversation as though from a far distance, as though none of this has anything really to do with him when he, on the other hand, knows all of these moments are crucial to his future. They have to be real or he will fail everything he has promised himself.

He offers to go and make some coffee which means padding out of the bedroom into the rest of the cottage with its kitchen area at the far end. It means, even though there is only a wall between him and Kitty. He feels suddenly alone.

The Turkish carpet is soft under his bare feet. The two sofas are covered in today's newspapers and different books they have been reading. The previous evening they spent listening to some jazz while reading out extracts from whatever they thought might be of interest. Kitty's empty bottle of wine is on the stone hearth of the fireplace and their used dinner plates are still on the floor.

He reaches the sink to fill the kettle when the dizziness starts. He grips the edge of one of the cupboards and tries to slow his breathing.

He stood beside the grave with Mary on one side and Sylvie on the other. The rest of the mourners, some who he did not recognise, gathered around them. There was the well dug pit of moist earth that turned a lighter, sandier colour the further down it was. There were tiny white roots dangling out of the glistening sides of the grave.

While he stood there with the minister droning out his appropriate words Arthur saw himself digging his own wife's grave. He was the expert. Before Alice could be lowered down into the pit he had to climb in to check that other body parts were not exposed and if they were to pull them out and place them up on the edge of the grave, skulls, rib bones, femurs and all the rest. He had to ensure no dead soldiers would be buried with her.

He stood there with Sylvie weeping and Mary looking stonily straight in front of her and he was walking over mounds of the dead and the missing. The whole area stank of that sweet, disgusting smell of decaying flesh which had always been with him, on his clothes, his skin, up his nose, down his throat. He was the grave digger, the searcher for body parts and mementoes left behind. Alice was waiting for him to finish before she was ready to be lowered. She was the corpse whose bits and pieces he would dig to discover. The earth had been prepared by an expert. This was his way to grieve. He would dig for her and then watch her coffin squeezed down into a perfectly fitting grave.

She was not in the coffin. That was beyond imagination. It had not been her funeral. That was beyond comprehension. They had all gone through the motions, but it had not been real. Sylvie cried and Mary stayed as mute as the sky, a blue sky with huge white clouds that shifted slowly above the smashed up plains of France or Belgium or anywhere else where the dead of battle were hiding.

He lights the gas ring and puts the kettle on. He steadies himself and steps away from the stove. It is then he became aware of his nakedness and starts searching behind one of the sofas for his pants and trousers. With difficulty he puts them on, the braces dangling down either side as he pads back onto the stone slabs.

Any more remorse and guilt and he would never be able to manage any of this and his new life would be destroyed before it even got started. How much time was there before it all began, all the bombing and killing, all the bodies? Would that be what they wanted him to do again? He was the expert. Would they require his services to go digging and searching for all the bits and pieces that made up a human body, just one body among thousands and thousands. God help the dead. God help Alice there in her tomb of white rooted soil. What did anything matter when it all ended like that, like Alice, his wife, his dead wife, deceased, gone into the earth?

Instinctively he turns to see Kitty in her dressing gown watching him from the bedroom doorway.

'The coffee's taking a long time,' she mentions.

'I can only find Camp.'

'Because that's all there is, nothing to do with real coffee.'

'I don't mind.'

'Are you alright Arthur?' she asked then in a serious voice.

'No, not really. I'm trying to be. I'm trying to be alright, but just finding things difficult right at this moment. But it'll pass. Of course it will.'

'Are you sure?'

He hears the rain as a background to their voices. Kitty's is clear and sharp whereas his sounds muted and indistinct. This is far worse than he had expected. It feels as if he is disappearing as himself and instead a totally false impression is being created and he is doing the creating.

He tries to force a weak smile and finds himself sitting on the sofa.

Kitty does not move.

'I'm sorry,' is all he can manage as he sits back, sighs and closes his eyes, an action that makes him feel even dizzier.

'You look awful,' she says.

'I'll be alright if you give us a few moments.'

'You look like you need more than a few. I hope this isn't how it's going to be from now on, you having funny turns all the time. Surely Arthur we can do better than that.'

He is not surprised at her lack of sympathy. How can she know what he has been through when he has told her so little?

'I'll make the coffee if you still want some,' Kitty says as she strides across the room.

He makes no response. He is being overwhelmed. This has to be real or he is done for. This is the only chance he has. Kitty is the only opportunity left. He is too old to go searching for alternatives.

Stupidly he thought it would be seamless, one life into another, one step then another away from all the past, so simple. How idiotic, how mindless to think it could ever be like that. And yet somehow it has to be. Kitty has waited long enough. He knows she will wait no longer.

'Come on you cowardly piece of fucking shit Townsley.'

The sergeant had been right. He was a coward. He could not even face his own daughters, talk to them, try and explain. But he knew that would only make things worse. There were no explanations that did not sound like embarrassing excuses. How could he tell Mary and Sylvie what he was doing and why?

Kitty is standing in front of him with his mug of coffee.

'Here. Maybe I should put some brandy in it.'

Her tone is thankfully lighter.

'Thanks Kitty,' is his response as he takes the mug and carefully places it on the rug by his bare feet.

Was this real now or was this only an echo of who he once thought he could be? Kitty was real. Thank God for her.

'Let's go out for a ride. The horses haven't had any proper exercise for the last few days.'

'We could,' he says in another attempt to resurface.

Kitty sits beside him and takes hold of his arm, 'Do you want to?'

He turns and puts his hand under her chin so he could lean over and kiss her.

'A ride across the moors.'

'When it stops raining.'

'Who cares about a little rain?'

'I do,' she laughs.

'Then we will wait. We will drink this awful stuff,' he said picking up his mug, 'Put on some Duke Ellington and I will have a bath and….'

'After our ride, surely?'

'Yes, right, after our ride.'

'Good,' Kitty sighs before she gets up and goes back into the bedroom.

'Yes,' he muttered to himself, 'Of course Arthur. Yes. Stop fucking thinking and start getting yourself sorted, getting yourself up to scratch, getting yourself ready and correct and responding. You can fucking do this Townsley. You can do this. If you don't what's it all been for Arthur? What has been the point of all the fucking stories and lies, all the this when it was that and that when it was this trying to be so fucking smart Arthur when where has it got you? Where the fuck are you Arthur? You're going to throw it all away, that's what you're going to do, like you always do, one to another to the next except this time you fucking know there won't be another. You're past it Arthur. You're a boozed up middle aged old man who can hardly manage what you always want the most. You can hardly manage that any more. Too much fucking drink and fucking about. That's what's wrong with you. She's in the ground old chap, dead and buried and soon if you carry on like this you'll be down there with her and with all the rest, all of them, all the bits and pieces, a jigsaw of bones and medals and tattered uniforms and diaries, letters, photographs. Have you got any Arthur? Where are your photos of the family, the Townsleys who have lived in Skipton for centuries. Not anymore Arthur. You're the last of the line old son. There'll be no male descendants. You even managed to fuck that up as well.'

'Arthur!' came Kitty's call.

'I'm coming. Yes, I'm coming. I'll be right there,' is his reply as the rain suddenly stops and the horses start neighing from their stables.

CHAPTER FORTY SIX

When her sister sits there drinking her tea Mary knows the subject that is on both their minds has to be dealt with.

'Has he gone?' is her difficult question.

Waltons cafe on the High Street is busy with shoppers taking a break. The front windows are tilted open to create some ventilation.

Sylvie's eyes are red rimmed and moist under her glasses. The plate of toast and jam she ordered has already been eaten.

'Yes,' she finally answers, 'He's gone, and I don't even know where he's gone. He left no address for his work or where he's staying, nothing. He said he'd be back.'

'He won't come back Sylvie,' Mary says, reaching over the table to take her sister's hand.

'I know he won't.'

'But it's no surprise.'

'How can you say that?' Sylvie miserably asks.

'Because I know him better than you. Good riddance I say. I'm glad we don't know where he is.'

As she is speaking she watches Sylvie's head lowering as though each word is a blow too many.

'You can't mean that.'

'Why defend him Sylvie? Why do that?'

'Because he's our father.'

'So what? What difference does that make in the end?'

Finally Sylvie sits up and looks around, her plump features sagging under so much grief.

'I'm sorry to sound so brutal,' Mary adds.

'She's only just been buried,' Sylvie gasps.

Mary sits stiffly back and says, 'I know. I know that.'

'The funeral was....'

'Awful.'

'Except Mr Elgin did his best.'

'I suppose so.'

'And going back to the house with all the mourners was hard. Thank goodness they didn't stay long. Thank goodness they had the sense to just go.'

When the waitress comes over Sylvie orders more toast. Mary sips her tea while scrutinising the lines under her sister's exhausted eyes.

'Mother never said anything to me,' Sylvie then says.

'About what?'

'About father.'

'She wouldn't have done.'

'Why? Why wouldn't she have done?'

'She wouldn't have wanted to upset you.'

'What, poor innocent Sylvie?' is said in a loud voice that has others in the café quickly glancing over at her.

'It doesn't matter,' Mary tries.

'Of course it does. I've been kept in ignorance of what he's been doing all this time. All you've ever done is hint at things, that's all.'

'Sylvie, we can't let him keep on affecting things. That's not right. That can't be right.'

There is another pause while the waitress brings over another plateful of buttered toast.

'What will you do?' Mary asks when she has gone.

'I'm thinking of joining the ATS. That's what I'm thinking of doing,' Sylvie says doubtfully, 'I talked to doctor Donnolly about becoming a nurse, but he didn't think that was a good idea, said I'd done enough of that already. I saw this poster in the library about joining the ATS and that's what I've decided to do.'

'You in the army,' Mary remarks, trying to hide her surprise.

'Yes, me in uniform.'

'God, this war has really taken over.'

'Of course it has Mary. What do you expect?'

'I just don't want it.'

'No one does.'

'It's sickening and frighteneing.'

'Yes it is sickening, but that's not going to stop the Germans.'

'No, I don't suppose it is,' Mary says in a dull tone of voice.

'And what about you, what are you going to do?'

'Carry on working at John Lewis if they stay open.'

'And are they going to?'

'Sounds like it, as least to begin with, then who knows what's going to happen?'

'On the radio they were talking about evacuating children out of London.'

'I know. I read it in the paper,' she says and then adds without thinking, 'You could always come and live at Aunt Rose's until you get things settled.'

Her sister gives her a rueful look.

'I can't Mary. Mr Elgin has got someone who he thinks will help with selling the furniture and then tomorrow I have to be at the recruitment office in Lancaster. Why there I've no idea.'

'You'll be leaving Skipton completely then,' Mary comments.

'I never thought I would, never wanted to until now,' is Sylvie's response.

To Mary she seems so young and yet in other ways so old and tired and lost.

This is all a lot harder than she expected. She wants more than this but has no idea what.

'We will write to each other,' she says then.

Sylvie tries a forced smile before answering, 'I've never written a proper letter since I was at school.'

'But we will write?' Mary persisted.

'Yes, yes we will.'

'And you'll let me know how you get on at Lancaster?'

'I want to do something different.'

'I know.'

'Not nursing. I know now that was a silly idea.'

'No, definitely not nursing. The doctor was right.'

Back on the High Street they hug each other.

'Give my love to Aunt Rose,' Sylvie says.

'I will, and you take care of yourself.'

'I'll write!' Sylvie adds before she walks off along the street.

Suddenly Mary calls her back.

'What is it?' Sylvie inquires in an uncertain voice.

'I....I just want you to look after yourself.'

'I will.'

'Promise you will,' Mary says strongly.

This leaves Sylvie looking puzzled and unsure, 'Yes Mary, I promise.'

'Good. That's alright then.'

'It will be,' says Sylvie before turning away again and setting off along the High Street leaving Mary standing there feeling hopelessly confused and upset at what should have been said but was not.

She does not want to go back to Aunt Rose's house. If it were possible she would never go back there. But nothing is how she wants it, nothing at all. All she can do is return to the café, order another cup of tea and start planning. Now it is always the same idea, to return next Thursday to the Queens hotel. She knows what she will wear and how much money she will have managed to have saved.

Maybe Caroline will still be there or maybe she will meet someone else just as interesting. It does not matter. All that is important is the image she wants to present and those conscious moments where she is in control for once. That is all she wants.

She lights another cigarette, plucks a piece of tobacco from the side of her mouth and watches a truckload of soldiers pass the café windows on its way down the High Street.

CHAPTER FORTY SEVEN

And where is Alice?

Molly Bridges, once known as Molly Jameson, has left her friends and was out on the terrace smoking a cigarette at the back of her home in Hastings watching a squadron of planes fly along the coast like grey birds in rigid formation.

Jane Eyre started it. Dorothea has just read the book for the third time, Elinor has only just started it and Sandra promises it is on her reading list. The talk has been of governesses.

And where is Alice? In Molly's memory. Her image is so clear she could be seated on the terrace right now, Alice in a pale, long summer dress and straw hat with the sun gilding her hair as she smiles and takes Molly's hand.

Was that in the Guisborough garden or the one in Skipton? It did not matter because it was all so long ago. These are fond memories of a tall, soft spoken young woman who put an extra dimension into Molly's and her sister' Esme's childhood, such a knowledgeable teacher, graceful, tall and elegant. Alice had made those months and years happy, rich in discoveries, always creating, imagining, drawing, painting, writing stories.

'So having a crafty cigarette?' Elinor mentions as she comes out onto the terrace, adding, 'What a lovely day and what a lovely view.'

'Except for the barbed wire on the beach and aeroplanes flying about.'

'Yes, I suppose.'

'And it'll only get worse. Anyway,' Molly sighs, 'I was thinking of a governess Esme and I once had, well governess, teacher, nurse, everything really.'

Elinor smiles, 'You and Esme with a governess, no wonder you like Jane Eyre, how very Victorian.'

'Yes it was,' Molly answers, still holding her cigarette, 'She was called Alice Thompson so we always called her Miss Thompson in front of out parents and Alice when there was no one else around. She was really good looking and I always suspected my father had a thing about her, what with my mother being ill most of the time. Yes, I think father rather fancied our dear Alice.'

'How shocking and even more Victorian!' Elinor exclaims.

'Alice was very good looking and very knowledgeable. She must have read tons of books when she was a child. She taught my sister and me so much.'

'You sound as though you were very fond of her.'

'We were. We never really understood what happened when we moved from Skipton and she didn't come with us. Father said it was because we were ready for school and wouldn't need a governess anymore, but we never believed him. Now I can't remember why we didn't believe him. It was all a bit fishy.'

'Maybe your father had an affair with lovely Alice and your mother found out.'

'You should be writing novels Elinor.'

'Do you think so?'

'No, because the Brontes have done it all already.'

She stubs out her cigarette and carefully wipes her lips with her fingers.

'I can see Alice so clearly,' she continues as bees droned in the nearby flowerbeds.

'You make her sound far too perfect,' Elinor suggests.

'In our eyes she was perfect, not that we always did what we were told, of course we didn't, we were young girls looking for some fun and adventure and yet so was Alice. She was as bad as we were.'

'Do you two want another drink?' Sandra asks as she comes out with Dorothea.

'I'll have another G and T,' Molly answers before Elinor says she will have the same as well and then informs Dorothea that they were talking about Molly's childhood governess.

'My God, those were the days when labour was cheap.'

'She wasn't labour,' Molly puts in.

'But you know what I mean,' says Dorothea who is the eldest of the foursome.

Suddenly in Molly's mind the scene shifts to one winter when they had been tobogganing and she had hurt her knee and Alice had taken off her scarf to mend it.

'You're a nurse. Alice you're a nurse,' she had repeated sat there in the snow with Esme somewhere behind them.

Alice had smiled under her woolly hat, 'Yes, I am Molly. When either of you need a nurse, well that's who I become. I can change roles whenever it becomes necessary.'

'Can you become a fairy queen?'

'Of course I can. Any wish you like and I will grant it.'

'No you can't,' Esme had intervened.

'Try me!' Alice had chided.

'Make my knee better.'

'It's already wrapped up in my magic scarf, which in a few minutes will make your knee feel a lot better.'

And it had done. After that both she and Esme had started to believe Alice was capable of anything, Alice with her red cheeks in winter and long, delicate fingers.

That evening Molly writes a letter to her sister, which takes over a week to arrive.

Esme sees the postman coming up the steep lane towards the cottage. She watches him cross the stone foot bridge under which the stream is rushing down from the mountains. She thinks of it as her stream. It is one of her favourite subjects to sketch and paint.

"Dear Esme," Molly's letters always formerly begin, 'I was with my lady's group, you know the one that drinks me out of house and home and then they all invite themselves to come the following week, that group, Elinor, Sandra and Dorothea. I don't know where Ingrid has got to, haven't seen her in ages. Anyway we got onto the subject of Jane Eyre and I started thinking about Alice. I......"

Esme stops reading, drops the letter onto the messy kitchen table, pours herself another whiskey and lights a cigarette before looking at one of the canvases she is working on. It is her way of creating. There always has to be two or three paintings on the go at the same time. Throughout the day she will move from one to the other before eventually concentrating on the one that is the most interesting.

But instead of the huge, monumental rocks that are on the first canvas she can only see Alice, unforgettable Alice. She had loved her so deeply that as she grew up she had turned Alice into her angel, who was always there looking out her, her guardian angel. Every night after they had left Skipton and moved down to Kent and then Brighton her angel had been at the foot of her bed listening to her adolescent prayers.

Their governess had been the most beautiful woman she had ever seen. Esme had tried and failed to paint her on several occasions. She refused to use photographs. Alice was in her memory. Her image was so clear that it somehow impeded any painting she tried. Now it does not matter. She does not need her sister to remind her of how stunning Alice had looked. She thinks about her at some point every day. It had been a childhood crush that had changed into something deeper, much deeper.

She picks up the letter but then tosses it down again and goes outside, glass of whiskey in one hand, cigarette in the other. By now she is crying. It is stupid and yet it is the right thing to do, the way to release some of the pressure she feels whenever she starts thinking about perfect Alice.

One day when they were supposed to be having their afternoon nap and Alice was having hers with them Esme remembered quietly getting off her bed and tip toeing over to Alice to bend down and kiss her carefully on the cheek which smelt of flowers and warm grass. She had kissed her again just at the side of her eye which had opened as Alice had smiled and said, 'That was nice Esme.'

The stream is sounding out louder after the last days of rain. Without thinking Esme empties her glass of whiskey into the stream before flicking her cigarette into the rushing water. After Skipton she missed Alice so badly. She had hated the school she and Molly had to attend. All she had wanted was their governess to be with them always. Nothing of her childhood love had to change and yet it did and for that she never forgave her father. It was his decisions they always had to follow. It was his judgement that they were old enough to no longer need a governess. She had argued, gone into tantrums, tried to run away from home on several occasions. She had taken the loss of Alice and the move from Skipton a lot harder than Molly. And now she was writing letters as though Esme needed reminding of their childhood governess.

They had heard she had got married to a Skipton man and was still there the last they had heard of her. Once Esme had got as far as Leeds on her quest to find her old governess but had realised all she was doing was searching for the past and that those precious childhood years only existed in her memory. Alice was alive and would live on until Esme's mind stopped working.

She walks beside the stream leaving her Welsh cottage behind as the sun sends shafts of silver light through the clouds illuminating the edges of the further mountains. Alice is walking beside her with her straight back and long strides, smiling, turning her head so Esme can see her whole profile, the one she had never managed to capture.

The need had been there for Alice and childhood to continue forever, Alice to be her constant companion, to walk beside her as she was doing right now.

'Alice, bloody beautiful Alice,' Esme murmurs to herself, 'Where the hell are you now? Are you still in Skipton? Did you have children? Is your life happy and fulfilled or is it like everyone else's, rather dull, repetitive, passing time from one weary day to the next, one lonely day to the next. Bloody hell,' she mutters, 'What a bloody state Esme Jameson to get into just because your sister writes a letter about......about......oh hell.....come on Esme.....get back down and start doing some bloody work and stop moping about. Start painting. You're with me whether you like or not.'

She walks quickly back down towards the cottage built of Welsh slate, closes the door behind her, pours herself another drink and starts singing the nursery rhyme Alice used to sing to her and Molly all those years ago.

CHAPTER FORTY EIGHT

The rag and bone man is going with his cart along the front street. Sylvie is in the parlour listening to the horse's hooves clip clopping along the road. She is in her light summer and is seated stiffly in one of the armchairs.

The house is silent in contrast to the sounds from the back lane and the front street, children playing, women gossiping, dogs barking, a truck following on from the rag and bone man, the town busier than ever now the war has started.

She is trying not to think but to absorb these last moments. Her small suitcase is waiting in the hallway just like her father's had been only a few weeks ago. He has gone. Mother has gone. Mary has gone. It is she who has been left to organise the sale of the furniture. At least her father had sorted out all the paperwork about the house and had dealt with the bank. At least he had done that much.

There is nothing left to do. It is over with, brutally, depressingly over with. She feels so lonely and scared of what the future might hold. She has no idea why she was sitting in the parlour.

She has called in at the neighbours to tell them what was happening, that the house was to be sold and that she was hoping to join the ATS.

The next step would be to leave the house, to lock the door, take the key to the auctioneers and then they could sell the furniture.

Finally she gets up, looks round the parlour and goes out into the hallway along to the kitchen. She has washed the lino floor and cleaned the chairs and table. It is strange to see the larder shelves empty. Out in the back yard everything has been left neat and tidy. She has even taken down the washing line.

Walking back along the hallway empty of pictures she passes her suitcase at the foot of the stairs and forced herself to go up them. Each creaking step is familiar, too familiar. She wonders at the amount of times she must have gone up and down these stairs, countless times, up and down with everything for mother.

She stops at the doorway of Alice's bedroom. There is only the iron shell of her bed. The mattress has been taken to the town dump with all her bedclothes. Sylvie's camp bed has been folded up and leant against the wall, the bed in which she slept that last night. The guilt would always be there, the guilt of waking up in the middle of the night, listening but not hearing her mother's rasping breaths.

The fireplace has been boarded up. Alice's favourite picture has been taken down and wrapped in newspaper with the others that have been left behind the parlour door. The window has no curtains now. The room still smells of urine and disinfectant and of Alice.

Sylvie passes her father's room and looks quickly in at the one she shared with Mary before going back along the landing, down the stairs for the last time where she picks up her suitcase, gets the key from the hatstand where one of father's umbrellas remains and opens the front door. Momentarily she pauses before locking it behind her and sets off down the garden path out onto the pavement.

Next to the chapel is the auctioneers where Sylvie drops off the key with a cardboard label and address on it. She said goodbye to her friend Margaret the night before so has nothing left to do except pop in the baker's for a pork pie and then go round to the bus station where the Pennine bus to Lancaster is already waiting.

There are a few passengers already aboard. She squeezes past the ticket collector who is chatting to the driver and takes a seat halfway along the bus setting her suitcase down on the floor at her feet.

When the bus finally sets off, she looked out at the passing High Street, the Castle and the end of Elliot street with its steep hill and Methodist chapel. It is then she sees Archie striding along the pavement bouncing a football in front of him. She lifts her hand to wave but he does not see her before the bus sets off along the Gargrave Road and the ticket collector comes up.

'Well look at you Missie, you look like you're going a long way,' he jokes after noticing the suitcase.

'A single to Lancaster please.'

'A single, is it? So not coming back, eh?'

'Just a single please.'

'Right you are then, a single to Lancaster for the dear young lady here,' he laughs before going further up the bus.

Sylvie settles back to watch the fields and limestone walls as they start to skirt the edge of the Dales through Gargrave, Hellifield, Long Preston, Settle and onto Bentham where the bus enters a tree lined section of road shaded and dark so for a few moments the Pennine bus turns almost black before emerging into the sun.

Printed in Great Britain
by Amazon